FAITHFUL HERETIC

Smyth & Helwys Publishing
6316 Peake Road
Macon, Georgia 31210-3960
1-800-747-3016

Library of Congress Cataloging-in-Publication Data

Names: Sloan, Kee, 1955- author
Title: Faithful heretic : a novel about Pelagius / Kee Sloan.
Identifiers: LCCN 2025015244 | ISBN 9781641735926 paperback
Subjects: LCSH: Pelagius--Fiction | LCGFT: Christian fiction | Biographical
fiction | Novels | Fiction
Classification: LCC PS3619.L6274 F35 2025 | DDC 813/.6--dc23/eng/20250528
LC record available at https://lccn.loc.gov/2025015244

FAITHFUL HERETIC

A NOVEL ABOUT PELAGIUS

KEE SLOAN

Also by *Kee Sloan*

God, The Devil, & Lemon Icebox Pie

The Jabbok Series
Jabbok
Beulah
Prodigal

Contents

When I began, Christianity came before the great mass of my unbelieving fellow-countrymen either in the highly emotional form offered by revivalists or in the unintelligible language of highly cultured clergymen. Most men were reached by neither. My task was therefore simply that of a translator—one turning Christian doctrine, or what he believed to be such, into the vernacular, into language that unscholarly people would attend to and could understand.

—C. S. Lewis, *God in the Dock*

"For those who wonder,
for those who look for the truth,
for those who try to keep an open mind and heart.
My love and gratitude to my family and friends
who patiently encourage me."

Author's Note

Hello, friends,

You might be wondering why I would write a book about the 5th century heretic Pelagius. I have to admit it's a fair question; the whole time I was writing it, I was wondering why you would want to read it. I'm no scholar of anything, and certainly not of Church History, and this is by no means an academic work. I've written this book to look at the Church from a different point of view, looking at a thin slice of where we've been as a way to understand how we came to where we are, and where we may be going.

There's quite a bit I don't remember from my time as a seminarian—it was a long time ago now—but I'm pretty sure I wrote a paper agreeing with somebody else's idea that it was the great heresies that formed the Church. Pelagianism in particular struck a chord in my mind, as I quietly realized that I was likely something of a Pelagian myself, especially in thinking that sin is a choice we make rather than a condition we are born with because we are all born as the result of our parents having sex.

After I retired, I started to read more about Pelagius, my favorite heretic. I was surprised that almost nothing is known about his early life, or the end of his life, and what little we do know about him and his work comes almost exclusively from what was written by people who opposed what he taught and spent a great deal of effort in their often uncharitable criticism.

I wondered why anybody would have given a second thought to the opinions of a British monk or layman at all, and how it happened that he caught the attention of popes and councils. The more I read, the more I wondered, and when I started concocting a reasonable story, it became flavored with dyslexia and Druids and began with a young Irish lad who wondered about the gods.

I hope this story catches your imagination, and makes you wonder. You can tell me what you think at keesbooks@gmail.com.

God's Peace,

Chapter I

But Who Are You, Though?

An old man was sitting on the ground, leaning his back against a rowan tree, one of a circle of trees. He was enjoying the sun on his face and listening to the song of the birds, when his contented peace was disturbed by the voice of a young man.

"*Salve, Pater. Nomen mihi est Oswell, et misit me Pater Iosephus a te discere.*"

Latin, the old man thought—one of the students at the monastery, surely. "Well, *salve* back to you, Oswell," he said in the language of the people of that place and time. "I'm glad for somebody to come visiting, but who are you though, is what I'd like to know."

"Yes, my name is Oswell, and I'm reading theology at the monastery." The young man sounded nervous, almost afraid. "Father Joseph sent me to you, hoping that I will be able to learn something from you."

"Aye, so you just said." The older man was surprised to realize he was enjoying the conversation. "But still and all: who are you, though?"

At this point the younger man decided he must be dealing with some sort of idiot, so he repeated, this time more slowly and loudly: "MY NAME IS OSWELL. I AM LOOKING FOR PELAGIUS THE HERETIC. FATHER JOSEPH SAID HE WOULD BE SITTING IN THIS RING OF TREES. I AM PREPARING TO BECOME A PRIEST IN THE HOLY CHURCH."

"And why in the world would you be wanting to do such a daft thing as that?" the older man replied, shielding his ears.

"Well, I … Are you Pelagius, the heretic?"

"Oh, aye—mayhaps I am," the old man replied. "I have been called that for year on year, but in truth Pelagius was never really my name. As for being a heretic—oh, aye, I have been called that as well; I've heard it myself a time or two. Who told you that anyway, I'm wondering."

The younger man was also surprised, that the old heretic did not seem to be the blasphemous ogre he'd been expecting. "Well, the brothers at the monastery and the priests all talk about it."

"Aye, but what those fellas know about it, though, you might be needing to take with a pinch of salt or two. How do you think they'd come to know such a thing?"

"Well, I suppose they heard it from the bishops and magisters."

"Ah. And you're thinking those grand people all know what they're talking about, do they?

"Well, don't they?"

"Oh, I don't know –mayhaps some of them do, I hope so. I've never met many of your bishops and magisters; but unless things have changed mightily, there's a good many bishops and magisters couldn't find their own arses without appointing a committee. It's been many and many a year since last I spoke to a bishop. I think it generally works out best that way—for me and for them—to keep some distance between us."

"But you talk to Father Joseph?"

"Oh, aye—Joseph's a good man. He knows his own heart."

"I don't think I understand."

"Ah," the old man smiled, looking up at the young man as he sat on the ground leaning against a sturdy rowan, "most folks don't. It's not something you need to fret about; I fear people make far too much of understanding, all things told. You're welcome to sit down if you're of a mind to."

The young man sat down and rested his back against an oak. "But I want to understand."

"Well, what is it that has you so muddled then?"

"Well, are you Pelagius the heretic?"

The older man chuckled a little. "Ah, well, now you're thinking I must be a bit daft, and mayhaps I am—I suppose that's a hard thing for a body to judge about himself. You're thinking you've asked a simple question, but I'm telling you it comes with a complicated answer. In truth I have been called Pelagius for many and many a year, but it was never my name. My friends and family call me by the name my mam gave me: Pell—just Pell. But your question is whether I am some style of heretic. Oh aye, I suppose I was once, mayhaps I still am. Other people determine those things, too."

The old man paused for a few seconds, reflecting. When he spoke again, he had fire in his eyes. "But that doesn't mean I was wrong, or without faith. A heretic, aye, that was what they decided in the end. Myself, I wonder if a bit of heresy might not be such a bad thing, but the men who were clutching their power didn't see it like that. So, I stepped out of it—just walked clear away. But hear me now: I never stopped believing what I believe—though I will say it's been a struggle from time to time."

He continued, "I remember it all. I still remember those people, those days and places. As a fact, there's not much I don't remember. You will have heard that remembering is a great gift, and in very truth it can be useful, but I can tell you it can be a right pain just as well. Looking back through the long trudge of years behind me, I can see now whence I came, how I became myself and how I came to be here, but way back then I could never have seen where I'd go, nor where I've got to now, nor who I have become.

"Now you're saying you want to understand. Aye, well—then I reckon you'll have to listen to my story. I should warn you that it might be quite a long story, and it twists around from time to time, even if I leave most of it out. And you're sure to be disappointed: I'm not nearly as bad—nor as good—as I've heard some people tell it. The heart of the matter, since I was just a lad, is that I was looking for the truth.

"If ever it seems best for me to stop talking, you can tell me and I will, but I can't unsay aught I already said that might upset or disappoint you. I do tend to get riled about a thing or two. Can you sit still and quiet to listen to an old man's story?"

"Yes, sir," Oswell agreed. "I'll try, at least."

"Well, all we can do is all we can do." He thought for a moment before saying, "Still, though, it's a worrisome thing to know where a story should start, in truth it is. I might want to start by telling you this one thing, but then I think you ought to know two or three other things before you could understand that first one, and each of those three might need four or five more to put them where they could make any sense at all. Ah, it's a worrisome thing to start a story, right worrisome indeed."

The older man paused to consider, and the younger man saw his chance. "Excuse me, sir?"

"Aye?"

"Are you not Pelagius, who argued with the Bishop of Hippo, who wrote scholarly papers in Latin and Greek to contend that people are not born with the stain of original sin because of the sin of Adam and Eve?"

"Oh, well, aye. Bishop Augustine and I disagreed, as a fact we did. But what you have heard may not always the full truth. And aye, scholarly papers were written, stacks and piles of them, though I can't say much good ever came of them. But I should be careful to say that it wasn't me that wrote those papers, better to say that they were written using my thoughts and words and stretching them some. As for original sin—I've heard the term now and again, but it will likely be better to wait until we get to that part of the story, if ever we do.

"Mayhaps it would be best to start away long ago, when I was a boy. I remember much of my childhood, at least the parts I saw, or what I knew at the time."

"Sir—excuse me again," the younger man broke in. "I promise I won't interrupt you too often, but can I ask you another question before you start your tale?"

"Well, I suppose you should if you're feeling the need. But for someone who's telling me he doesn't want to interrupt, you've already taken several good cracks at it." The older man looked at the student, laughing not unkindly, and said, "Ask your question then."

"Well, I just thought you'd be ... more scholarly."

The old man laughed again. "Ha! And well I should thank you for saying so, friend. Nay, I was never a scholar, nor did I want to be, nor try to be. My idea of it is that scholars usually just speak with other scholars, being so scholarly and all. They talk scholarly things using scholarly words that have naught to do with the rest of us. But I see I haven't scratched whatever's itching you—what is it?"

"Well, I thought we'd be speaking in Latin—although I have to admit I'm relieved we're not—or we'd be speaking at least … um, more properly … with more … refined grammar or something."

"Ah, you want to know why I talk the way I do. Mayhaps this may be one of those lessons our friend Joseph has sent you to learn." The older man looked at the student more closely and said, "You do want to learn, don't you, Oswell?"

When the student answered with some enthusiasm, "Yes, sir," the older man continued with a faraway voice, as from a well-worn memory: "It's a grand thing to learn—a grand thing indeed. We should never let slip a chance to learn something.'

"This isn't a hard thing to understand, but it sure seems like a great many clergy don't seem able to catch on to it: talk to the people you're talking to, using words they know. So, I'm speaking the language of this land, this stew of languages the Saxons and the Angles people speak here in Angleland. It's a devilish hard language to learn, but this is how the people around here talk. We can speak in Latin, but it's been many a year since it was comfortable in my mouth. And it's such a precise, calculated language there's not much room for what you're feeling—all head and no heart. Too much Latin makes my head pound.

"So, let's talk the way we talk, not like scholars trying to impress people about how they're smarter than the rest of us—just talk to the people you're talking to. Don't talk like the scholars or magisters, and don't talk like me. Just talk from your heart to their hearts—not from your head to their heads. Nobody gives a bee's wing how educated you are—they want to know that you love God, and that you love them.

"Aye, well. I was saying that I remember my childhood. I suppose I remember more clearly than most people do. It's never been something I felt a need to brag on, in fact there are some things I'd as soon forget. But there it is—my great blessing, my great curse: I remember. And I learned to wonder, too, mayhaps another blessing and curse. I wondered about things rather than just letting them be as they are. I suppose that's what must have started all this, and that was all because of my sister Áine."

With this, the old man began his story.

Chapter II

A Wee Bright Flame Flickering Much Too Briefly

"We grew up in a wee fishing village called Port Láirge in southeast Éire, where the River Suir joins up with the River Barrow to form the Celtic Sea. Áine and I were raised up by my poor hard-working mother and her poor hard-hearted father. Mam was named Sadb, which she told me meant 'sweet,' and sweet she was. My father was … oh, but there's a question never fully answered, at least not to me. He was a Roman soldier, I was told, who was stationed there for a time, long enough to sire my sister and me, but then he was gone, and he never came back.

"It was my sister Áine that started me wondering—not just thinking about doing my chores or checking the fishing nets or trying to stay out of Papa's way but wondering about the hows and whys of things: the nature of the world, and about the gods. It was because Áine was born ruined, as my grandfather said it to me and anyone else who would listen to his bitter, hateful rants. She walked with a limp, because her left leg never fully formed—it was shorter than her other leg, and thin enough so you wondered how she could walk the first step. Her left arm wasn't of any use at all: all puny and drawn up almost to her shoulder—Papa said the gods had afflicted her because our mother had 'played the whore with her Roman soldier.'

"My grandfather Eóghan didn't approve of Roman soldiers, or aught else Roman, I think; he didn't approve of much at all, as far as I could see.

"My grandfather's brother was as loving and caring as his younger brother was mean and spiteful. My grandfather Eóghan was a carpenter; his brother Eóchaidh was a mystery. My mother would whisper—when there was no one around to hear it—that she'd heard that Eóchaidh was a Druid. But he didn't often come around—certainly not often enough—and never stayed long when he did."

The young man Oswell had been trying to stay quiet, but now he gathered the courage to interrupt again. "But sir—surely that could not have been true—there haven't been any Druids for hundreds of years! The Romans cleansed the land of them, for once and all."

"*Cleansed the land?*" The old man was indignant. "Did you hear that in some style of lecture? Ah, but you have to be careful who you listen to and wonder how it profits them to say what they're telling you."

"You think the magisters would lie to us?"

The old man was quiet for long enough so that the student was starting to become uncomfortable, and then he said, "Oswell, why do you think you're here?"

"Well, I—what?"

"Why do you think Father Joseph would be sending you to talk to a heretic?"

"I … don't know. In truth, I wondered that myself."

"Good! It's well you should." The older man smiled, and it warmed Oswell's heart to see it. "Aye, it's a grand thing to wonder. Well and so: here's another truth mayhaps you need to learn. There are lies, saying something which is just not true—and then there's saying a thing in such a way as helps whoever's saying it, which might be half true, or might just leave out the parts as wouldn't help the one telling it. And then there's passing along a lie you were taught when you were coming up, that you just haven't thought you needed to look at again."

Oswell didn't know what to make of that, and he said, "But the Druids made human sacrifices!"

"So I have heard as well. I have known two Druids, and as I'm telling the very truth, they were both honorable men, in their own ways, good men—two of the best I ever knew.

"Now, hear me say this," the old man continued. "It's one of the ugly truths we all must face if we're to grow up and see the world as it is, instead of how we want it to be. Every group of people does terrible things—the problem with any group of people is that they're just people, no matter what else they might claim to be. I expect some Druids did terrible things, I don't know about that. There's no shortage of mayhems and outrages wherever you look, and our good Lord knows the Church has committed more than its share as well. What I'm saying is that you must look at who a story like that hurts, and who it helps. Who would want to shame the Druids, and why, is what you need to ask."

Oswell had no answer he wanted to share, so the older man continued. "As I understand it, for centuries the Druids held a place of prominence and respect, far and wide. They were right learned men and women—shining with the light of open-minded curiosity, telling stories and singing their wisdom collected through the centuries. They were educated, but they wrote nothing down, believing that a thought written down became trapped in the writing forever. They still tell the stories and sing the songs from the memory of their people to pass their wisdom along."

"Still? But …"

"Nay, Oswell, the Druids are not yet disappeared from the green earth. The Romans will tell you that they were all killed on Anglesey of the Cymru, and that's—ah, like much you might have heard from the Romans—true and not true. True that the Roman soldiers killed many and many Druids on the Isle of Mona—men, women, and children—but not true that they were *all* killed. The Romans destroyed their gathering places and chopped down their sacred groves, but there were many survivors. Some went across the sea, to Éire, where I am from.

"Nay, if they'd all been killed," the old man said, shaking his head, "the Romans would have been done with them for once and all, and not needed to go on telling false stories about their evil teachings, about how they were consorting with the Devil, about how they practiced human sacrifice and such. Lies, exaggerations and twisted stories told about those who hold a different way of looking at the world, a different way to look into the mysteries of the unknowable God and the muddling physical world around us, lies to tear them down, to make them seem wicked and depraved. So, some Romans—aye, and some in the Church—treat people who hold a different way of thinking.

Again, he sat quiet for a long while. In time the old man said, "Heretic? Oh aye—I have been called a heretic, but you can't credit everything you hear. I wasn't marching in step—that was the trouble. I was holding up what seemed to be a different way of understanding about the Lord God and blesséd Jésu, and some in the Church couldn't tolerate a different way of looking at things. But mayhaps we'd be better off if we had more heretics. Do you understand?"

"Well, no sir, I don't think I do," said Oswell. "Wouldn't it have been easier to … I don't know … to agree with the bishops and all, or just keep your silence?"

"Easier? Aye, it would have been much easier, of a truth it would. But it was truth I was looking for, and truth is not always easy. But now I'm far ahead of the story I'm meaning to tell you here," said the old man, rubbing his chin.

"My sister Áine—I was meaning to start my story with my sister Áine—was crippled, not terribly but noticeably, and I wanted to know why. Papa said she was cursed by the gods, but I couldn't abide that idea. I couldn't understand why Papa would have aught to do with gods so cruel as would punish a little girl for what her mother did. I wanted to know why the gods would allow it. How could they be so uncaring, so harsh? I reasoned that either the gods were powerful enough to prevent her troubles and they did not, which made them heartless or malicious, or they weren't so powerful at all, which made them unworthy of my regard. So, I decided there and then that I was finished with the gods, all of them.

"She was a sweet girl, our Áine, as good a soul as any you'd ever hope to meet. Her arm and her leg were shriveled, but her heart was sweet and loving and kind. She was a wee bright flame flickering much too briefly in a world that seemed darker without her. Our mother loved her fiercely and protected us both as best she could.

My grandfather Eóghan, I was telling you, blamed Mam for Áine's condition, and he wasn't a man to keep a thought to himself, especially if it gave him opportunity to give voice to his hatred for the Romans, or the Britons, or the Saxons, or the Christians, or the Jews—or anybody that wasn't like how they were supposed to be, which the way it was when he was a boy."

"The Jews?" wondered Oswell. "Did he hate them because they killed Jesus?"

"*What?* Where in thunder did you hear such a boneheaded thing as that?"

"Well, ah … some of the other students said it."

"Ah, well. Mayhaps you'll need to stop listening to those boyos, as they seem to just repeat whatever they hear without even wondering if there's any truth to it or not. As for my grandfather's hatred of the Jews, I never found out why. He wouldn't have cared about them killing Jésu if he'd thought they had; he had no care for Jésu one way or the other. I don't think there were any Jews in the village, as far as I ever knew. I suppose he'd had some dealings with a Jew before I came along. But he hated them, worse than most, almost as much as the Romans, which was considerable.

"Papa was never what you'd have called open-minded, not by a stretch. I wouldn't say he was tolerant of anybody's religion—I don't think he gave a chicken's cluck about any of that. That was the way of it, in my village growing up: we thought the more gods you could friendly up to, the better off you'd likely be.

"He called on the old gods for help, for protection, for fair weather, for aught he couldn't control. He called on the Túatha Dé Danann: Dagda and the Morrigan, Danu and Manannán and the horned god Cernunnos and all. He didn't expect them to answer, and they didn't—but he still called on them. I asked him about it one morning, when the sun was warm and the breeze was soft, and he slapped the back of my head and told me to be not asking about things I couldn't understand. I thought to tell him it was because I didn't understand that I was asking, but I decided not to, thinking my day might go better without another slap to my head just then.

"For Papa, I think the gods were a mix of fiction and fact, superstition and hope and fear. But they weren't ever real: I don't think they were real to Papa.

"Now, Áine had never been strong, and when she died of a fever the wise woman of the village couldn't cool, she'd lived just nine winters, and myself only eight. Papa railed against his gods, shook his fist at the sky and cursed them in a mighty drunken rage. It wasn't the first time I'd seen him drunk, but it was the drunkest I'd ever seen him. He screamed at the sun all that day, and at the moon and the stars all that night—'Damn you all!' he shrieked, 'You should have taken me instead, you gutless bastards!' It terrified me—what if they *were* up there, what if they were listening? What if the Cailleach took heed of him and struck him down dead with a bolt of lightning? But she never did.

"Papa left it to my mother to prepare Áine's body for burial, and when she told him that she wanted the priest of Mithras to say prayers over her grave, he made no protest. Nor did he come to her burying—he went to the Bull instead, the Lazy Bull, the local tavern—to numb himself, I suppose, against his pain and guilt. Old Oisin who owned the Bull had to bring him home and put him on his sleeping pallet. I think Papa drank enough to let himself believe that Áine's death was a judgment of his gods, not only on my Mam, but on me as well. I don't know how he joined all that together in his mind, but I do know that he was a hard man before Áine's death, and he was even harder after.

"My mother put her faith in Mithras, the god of the Roman soldiers—in part, I expect, because she couldn't make herself believe in her father's distant gods, but more because she hoped if she held true to the god of her children's father, if she were loyal to his god, my father might return. It was a forlorn, senseless thought, but she could no more let it go than you could make your feet let go of your legs just by saying so. She'd never had much hope, and she wasn't willing to let even this desperate one go.

"When Áine was dead and gone forever, we buried part of my heart with her. It wasn't 'til I found my beloved that dead part of my heart could be coaxed back to life, like blowing on a wee ember until it catches fire again. Ah, but she comes later in the story.

"Áine's death was right hard on me, sure enough, but it nearly killed my poor Mam. She cried for months after that, uncontrollably at first, and then when she thought no one was looking until—well, until she died. Papa was as patient as he could be, I suppose, for as long as he could be patient, which wasn't much, and not for long. After that, he said his daughter was just 'putting on the airs,' he called it—pretending that she was still grief-struck to get sympathy from the people in the village, or as a way of getting out of doing any work.

"Even though it didn't seem like it should, life continued after Áine died. After a few wearisome days, Papa sobered up and went back to his shop, making boards and beams and a few tables and benches. Mam cried and cried, and cooked and cleaned, and took other people's clothing to wash and mend, and I did my chores and tried to stay out of the way.

"Now, in our little village there were two brothers, twins they were: Darragh and Deaglán. Their father was Diarmuid, the smith of the village, a gruff old bear of a man I was right scared of, and probably for good reason. The twins were two years older than myself, and had already started working with their da, pumping the bellows and fetching wood and water and such. They were right strong boys, both of them, and I had learned early on to stay out of their way if I could. It wasn't until I'd grown a little, 'til I was nearly as tall as themselves, that they ever took any notice of me. This is the way of bullies, those who take pride in being the biggest and strongest, the toughest and meanest—they aren't likely to welcome another body who was also big and strong.

"Darragh was the mean one, really, who enjoyed the cruelty to younger and smaller boys; Deaglán mostly just went along with it. Years later I wondered if mayhaps he was as scared of his brother as I was.

"One morning, three or four weeks after our sweet Áine had died, I had gone down to the River Suir to check the nets. It was a fair catch that morning, enough for dinner that night and the next, and I was happy to put the fish into my creel and start making my way back up the path to our house, thinking that mayhaps Mam would be so pleased with me she might forget to cry for a moment. I didn't notice Darragh and Deaglán until I'd almost bumped into them.

"They had planted themselves there in the path, so I asked them as polite as I knew how to pardon me past them. But they just stood there, staring at me like cows in a field. Then Darragh said, 'Ho, and what will you do if we won't pardon you, boyo? Go home and tell your father? Oh, but no—you don't have a father, do you?' I told them I wasn't looking for any trouble, that I just wanted to go up the path and give the fish to my mother. Darragh said, 'Your mother? Your mother the whore? She's not somebody who deserves these fish, is she—her who had consort with a Roman soldier, and birthed you and your ill-made sister?' He looked at his brother and asked, 'You think this fella's mam deserves such a fine catch as this?' Deaglán just shook his head, slowly.

"So, my temper took hold of me, and I snapped, 'You think a smelly oaf such as yourself deserves my fish? You're naught in this world but a swaggering guinnea-cock. You'll spend your entire life in this little bit of a village, stuck here forever, your life never aught more than that.' Ah, it was ever my temper and my tongue that landed me in trouble.

"Then Darragh stepped up so close to me I could smell the porridge he had for breakfast, and sneered, 'Oh, so you're going places and doing things, I expect—thinking you'll make a name for yourself, I'm sure. What will you do to make your mark on the world, Son of Nobody? Be a mighty warrior? Fah! You couldn't kill a Saxon if he came up and handed you his sword! You're just a weakling bastard, always at the mercy of the strong, like me and Deaglán! Aye, Deaglán?'

"This time Deaglán nodded, just as slowly. Then Darragh leaned even closer and whispered, 'Nay, I'm thinking we'll be taking these fish for *our* dinner tonight, boyo—they're too good for people like your whore mother and her drunk da and the Son of Nobody. Ha— it's no wonder the gods took your crippled sister!'

"Well I knew he was looking to start a fight, and well I knew I had no chance of winning any kind of fight with these two boyos. And he knew as well as I that I couldn't close my ears and heart to what he was saying about Áine and my Mam, no more than I could have sprouted wings and flown home."

Chapter III

A Grand Thing to Learn

Oswell had not known what to expect in a conversation with a heretic, but he had not expected this. He said, "So what happened?"

"Well," continued the older man, "I threw an awkward punch, missed Darragh's leering face by about a foot, and then I near got the life kicked out of me. This too I remember, all too clearly—I remember them punching me in the face and in the belly and then kicking at me after I fell down and raised up my arms and legs and curled up to cover my face and my balls. I remember thinking it would never end, and that I was about to die, never to see my poor Mam again. I remember I was determined not to cry or scream for help, and that I stayed quiet. After a while—I don't know how long—I think I passed out. I suppose they just wearied of it; when I came to myself, the sun was sinking down into the west. The fish and the basket were gone, I was aching all over and my nose was bleeding free.

"So, I dragged myself home and my Mam looked after my cuts and bruises as best she could. Then Papa came in and asked me what the hell happened to me. I told him and he muttered, 'You need to learn how to fight back, boy. You should've kicked them in the ballsacks and run back home. And where's my fish? And where's my hamper, is what I'm wanting to know. They took it, did they? And you're too much of a little girl to go and get it back from them?'

"Never mind that I'd never had anybody to teach me how to fight, that he'd never lifted a finger for doing that or aught else that would have helped me become a man—in simple truth fighting was one of many things I didn't know how to do."

Oswell was captivated by the story. Excitedly, he asked, "Did you ever get them back, the bullies—did you ever pay them back?"

"Well," said the heretic, "I just stayed out of their way for a long time after that. If I saw either of the smith's boys, I just turned my feet around and walked another way. Then my great-uncle Eóchaidh came along, stopping for a time in between one place and another, as he did sometimes, when it suited him."

"Your uncle the Druid?"

"Well aye, the same uncle my Mam told me was a Druid. He had been there less than an hour before his brother told him all about me taking a beating from Darragh and Deaglán. He looked at me and asked, 'Is that the way of it?' and I told him it was. Then he took a deep breath and told me to come out into the yard with him. He picked up a stone, not much larger than a duck's egg, and tossed it to me. I thought about dodging it, but I just reached up and caught it instead, and he nodded to himself."

Mystified, Oswell asked, "What was that about?"

The old man laughed again. "He wanted to know whether I was right-handed or left-handed. I caught the stone with my left, so he said, 'That's good—you're better with your sinister hand. Most of us are better with our right.' Then he fetched his horse's feedbag and filled it with oats, and hung it from a tree limb, and turned me so that I was sideways, with my right arm closest to the bag. Then he showed me how to make a fist and turn my wrist when I punch, and said, 'Now punch the bag, punch it hard, with your right hand.' Then he told me to come into the house and get him after I'd punched it one hundred times."

"Did you? Did you punch it one hundred times?"

"Oh, aye—a hundred times, and maybe another hundred after that. I was too ashamed to tell him that I didn't know how to count to a hundred, so I just kept punching that damn bag of oats until my knuckles were bleeding, and after some time he came out to see if I was still punching. I think he was expecting I'd have already quit, but I was still there, punching away.

"Then I had to tell him that I couldn't count—I'd never had reason to count much more than the fingers on my two hands—and he leaned down and gathered me up in a hug, chuckling a little. Then he got a bit of cloth from his saddlebag and wiped away most of the blood and wrapped my right hand up in that bloody cloth, and said, 'So, now you can learn two things at the same time!' He pierced me with a curious look and asked, 'You do want to learn, don't you, Pell?'

"I answered, 'Oh, aye!' and he nodded and said, 'It's a grand thing to learn, Pell—a grand thing indeed. We should never let slip a chance to learn something.' I've remembered that moment many and many a time since then: 'We should never let slip a chance to learn something.'"

"That's what you just told me!" Oswell exclaimed.

"Did you think I'm just making all of this up out of the air? Almost everything we say comes from somebody else, so I tell you again: we need to be careful who we listen to, and how we listen."

Oswell asked, "But why did he call you Pell?"

"Pell is my name, what my Mam named me."

The student wanted things to make sense. "But I thought you were Pelagius!"

"Oh, I was," the old man said, "or at least that's what they called me, those as never really knew me."

"Who started calling you Pelagius, and why did …"

Pell smiled and said, "Ah, well—we'll have to get to that part of the story when it comes. Just at the moment we're talking about my great-uncle Eóchaidh teaching me how to fight."

Pell continued his story. "Then my uncle told me I need to hit the feedbag one hundred times again, with my bleeding right hand, and this time we'll count the punches. 'One, two, three, four,' he counted the punches, and told me to count with him—one, two, three, and on up to one hundred. After we got to a hundred, he told me to stop and get some water from the well, and after I gave him some and drank some myself, he told me now I was to punch the feedbag with my left hand. I turned the other way, so that my left hand was closer to the feedbag, but he turned me back around and said, 'Oh, nay, Pell. This is your advantage, understand—you punching with your left will throw the other boyo off his balance, see?'

"Ah, well, as a fact I didn't know what he was talking about, but I didn't tell him that—I just punched the bag again, this time with my left hand, turning at my waist, throwing my shoulder into it. It felt better, easier than punching with my right—it felt right. We counted the punches to one hundred, and I didn't want to stop, but Eóchaidh said I should, and that we would do it some more the next day. And we did—the next day and the day after that and the days that followed. He showed me how to step into the punch, and before long he was teaching me how to block or dodge the punches the other fella would be throwing my way.

"So now when I went into the village, I wasn't trying to sidestep the smith's sons—now I was hoping they'd come for me. When they did—because of course they did—I got in a few punches, right and left, and I reckon I would have bested Darragh had it been just him and me, but when Deaglán stepped in, I wasn't ready for the both of them together. Aye, well—I dragged myself back home, and my Mam cleaned me up, and my grandfather sneered at me and told me I'd never to amount to much of a fighter. But Eóchaidh took me outside and asked me to tell him what happened, blow for blow.

"So I told him, 'I'd gone to the market, to fetch some salt and praties for our stew tonight, and the twins saw me and came over talking to each other like they owned the town and that I'm no more than some manner of mongrel, beneath their notice. This time I didn't skulk away, I stood my ground and turned sideways like you taught me, and it worked! I hit Darragh smack in the nose and knocked him clean down!'

"My great-uncle nodded and said, 'Well and good. But then …'

"I said, 'Aye, but then Deaglán came up behind me, and while I was gloating just a little bit over Darragh lying there in the dirt, he grabbed me up, so I couldn't move my arms. Then Darragh stood up and came at me with red vengeance in his eyes. The man who sells the praties and all came out and ran them off before Darragh could get much hurt done, muttering under his breath that some-body ought to do something about those boys.'

"Then my great-uncle Eóchaidh said, 'Pell, you have to stand up against the bully, do you understand? You have to stand up and look him in the eye and show him you're not afraid. Your fear is the bully's food and drink; you have to stand up, you can't run away. Remember that,' he said, 'remember that.'

"And of course I have. It's one of those things that shaped the rest of my life.

"Then my great-uncle said, 'Don't ever fight unless you have to, but if you have to fight, fight to win. If you're facing two bullies, pick the one you think is meanest or the better fighter, and punch him as hard as you can right in his belly.' He showed me, moving right slow, stepping into the punch and almost pushing me down when his fist continued slowly through me. 'Punch through his belly, like you're punching at something on the other side of him. That will knock all the air out of him. Then turn as quick as ever you can to face the other fella. If he doesn't run away like a scalded hound, punch him in the belly just like you did the first one. They won't hit you if they can't breathe.'

"Well, we practiced that for a long time, and then we counted the punches into the feedbag—one hundred with my right, and another hundred with my left.

"The next day I had to go into the village, to carry a bench Papa had mended for ol' Miss Caoimhe, and the smith's sons saw me as I was making my way home. Just as before, Darragh stepped into my way, and Deaglán sneaked around behind me. Darragh started to say something, but I didn't even wait to hear it—I just punched him through his belly, hard as I could. And just as my uncle told me, he was bent over double trying to catch his breath. I turned around quick as a chicken, and faced Deaglán, who looked at me for just a heartbeat or two before he started running like he had a *bodach* chasing him!

"And then, a curious thing—as I stood there watching Darragh gasp for breath, I felt like I was bigger and stronger than him or his brother, and most of the other boys in the village. Fighting feels different when you win. And I—I understood a little bit, why the twins did it. Not the cruelty, but the feeling of power in it. For about a week I strutted around the village like a banty rooster in the barn-yard, all puffed up with myself. I was thinking the other boys in the village were frightened of me, and that made me prideful. Arrogant, I was."

Oswell asked, "So, what happened?"

"Happened?"

"Yes—what happened to make you stop being arrogant?"

"Who's to say I ever did? Oh, there were other fights, many and many more, not with punches to the belly, but with words: letters and papers and opinions and councils and such. And there was a sword—ah, but that comes much later in the story. I realized that even when I won a fight, I always lost something, every time. That's the way of it: once you are in a fight, all you can do is try to lessen how much you lose."

"Did your great-uncle teach you that?"

"Well, no—I had to learn that on my own. A priest taught me that I needed to put my pride away and give up on being a bully, a proud priest and my grandfather.

"But Eóchaidh did teach me something more than just fighting. He taught me how to play the *cláirseach*—a little harp, you'd call it. Mam said he took it up when he was learning to be a Druid. Papa said he had time for such things because he never worked, and that might be so as well. But whatever the reason, he had a small harp, and it was magical to me. The first time he brought it to our kitchen table I knew that I wanted to learn how to play it just as well as he did.

"He would sit at our table, with me there peeling some praties, and when he played a little tune, it was like I'd heard it before, and after he sang the song that went with it, I knew it by heart."

"Did he write it down for you?"

"Write it? Have you not been listening? The Druids write naught down but carry their wisdom in stories and songs. Nay, he sang it, and I remembered it: 'The Power of One.' Do you know it?"

"No," Oswell replied thoughtfully. "I've never heard that one. Will you sing it for me?"

"I might, if it comes into the story. But understand this: it was wisdom he taught me, along with the chords and the words that go with them, and I would spend hours and days as happy as a pup in a puddle with that *cláirseach* in my hands, even enduring the scowls and muttering that it provoked from my grandfather.

"Mayhaps it was me playing the harp and singing Druid songs that was part of the reason that I started my apprenticeship with my grandfather so early. The tradition in our village was for a boy to start working with his father or grandfather on the day he turned fourteen, but I wasn't yet even thirteen when first I went to work in Papa's workshop. Mayhaps it was because I was large for my age, or because Papa was getting on in years and needed the help, but I think it was in some part because he and Mam were afraid I'd go off with Eóchaidh and become a Druid. And in truth I had been wondering about that myself; mayhaps it would have been better—for myself and many others—if I had.

"But however that might be, I picked up the basics of playing the harp like a trout learning to swim and started learning some of the songs he knew. It was the first time I realized that I learned things more easily than others—Eóchaidh said he was amazed at how quickly I took it to hand. He told my Mam that I learned the songs without even trying. Before that I thought everybody was that way, remembering the way I did.

"Then two things happened, and my life was forever changed. The first was that my great-uncle Eóchaidh left. I think he and Papa must have had an argument or something, I never knew the truth of it. One night he told me to be sure my dreams were stronger than my fears—he told me that every night when Mam made me put down the harp and go to my pallet—and the next morning he was just gone. I asked Mam where he'd gone, but she just shook her head, and something warned me I ought to not ask Papa about it; he was ill-tempered that morning at breakfast.

"I missed my great-uncle, and the salve his being there spread over the house, but I really missed his harp, and thought I would never get the chance to play another one."

"And did you?" wondered Oswell. "Did you ever play another harp?"

"Oh, aye," Pell continued. "Another harp came along, one that belonged to another Druid, that same fella planted these trees here, years and years gone now."

Pell pointed at an old satchel beside him, saying, "This is his harp here, waiting for the sun to sink down to the rim of the world when I'll play it again. I play a wee bit every night, and again when the sun peeks back over the edge of the morning, to offer thanks for him and all those I've loved who're gone out of my sight now. I believe playing a tune or two helps soothe the janglies out of my nerves."

"Who was this other Druid? Will you play his harp for me? Will you teach me how to play it, too?"

"Ah," Pell gasped, shaking his head, "that's too many for me all at once. Just now I'm telling you the story you wanted to hear. If it comes to it, I'll play a tune, and mayhaps teach you to pluck out a chord or two. As for who this Druid was, well—he comes later in the story. But not too much later: I met him when I was still just a scared little boy.

"I tried with all I could muster to do my work the way Papa wanted me to do it, working until my blisters bled, but it seemed like it was never enough. I learned to fetch and carry, to sand with the grain, to drill holes for the pegs and glue, how to mix the stains and tighten the clamps—but he only had eyes for what I'd done wrong, and it seemed there was always something. Still, it was good, honest work, and he taught me how to work the wood: chisel and saw, plane and auger awl. Papa said it was how I would make my living, and I accepted it as my life.

"But then along came the other thing that changed my life—the Christians came to Port Láirge."

Chapter IV

Better than a Pig Could Ever Hope to Be

"How many Christians were there?" asked Oswell. "Was there fighting? Did they have to kill many people there to get them to convert?"

"Ah, well," Pell exclaimed, "that would have made this story more exciting, and no mistake! Nay, there were just the two of them, and neither of them was killed. One was set to sea in a little boat, though. Nay, it was just the pair of them as came to our village: Father Cyneric and Brother Mellán. Brother Mellán soon became my truest friend, and I'll be telling you much about him, but first I have to tell you about Father Cyneric, that arrogant bastard of a priest who was my first wobbly introduction to our blessèd faith.

"He was tall and thin, was Father Cyneric, like one of those long-leggedy cranes at the edge of the sea scooping up the little fish there. He was cleanshaven, and his hair was dark but cut so short it was hard to tell; much later, Mellán told me it was cut in the Roman style. His eyes seemed to poke out of his face somehow, which was part of why I thought he looked like a bird. The first time ever I saw him, and the last time ever I saw him, and every other time I saw him in between, his face looked like he'd smelled something somebody else would be needing to clean off his boots. He didn't speak *Gaeilge*, the language of my people, and it seemed he wasn't trying to learn it, not a single word of it. His first language was some form of the muddle of this language of the Angles and the Saxons, but the bishop who'd ordained him insisted he learn Latin, and if you were wanting to talk to him, that's what you'd have to speak—he claimed it was the language of the Church.

"Not a soul in Port Láirge knew a word of Latin or the language of Angleland, but Father Cyneric would speak only Latin, saying he didn't want to dirty his tongue with any other language than that of the Church. That's why Mellán was there.

"Brother Mellán had grown up in Éire, but up north in the region of Baile Átha Cliath. His grandfather bred some kind of sheep that made for a right fine wool. He took young Mellán and his father and an uncle across the sea to Angleland, to teach them the family trade. Well, misfortune and calamity struck when they were ambushed by brigands, and Mellán's father and grandfather were killed for a small bag of silver and a wagon full of wool they'd been hauling to a monastery. Young Mellán and his uncle were found by the brothers there, and taken into the monastery, just eight years was Mellán, and he was raised up by the monks there for eight more.

"When the bishop thought it right to send a priest to Éire, he sent Cyneric for reasons of his own, but he knew that he would need to send an interpreter with him. He sent young Mellán, who'd grown up speaking a form of Gaeilge from up in northern Éire, and who had learned the boggling tongue of the Angles and the Saxons growing up among the Britons, as well as learning a fair bit of Latin, being raised up in the Church as he was. He'd just then become a brother monk, had Mellán, and he was eager to help spread the faith.

"When Cyneric and Mellán came to Port Láirge, there were some as were right glad to welcome them; they tried to welcome them both. I heard people in the village talking about this new faith, this new god Jésu who died—we had plenty of gods, after all, and they seemed to all get along well enough, they said. Anybody with any sense knew they ought to do what they could to be on the good side of as many of the gods as possible. But we'd never heard of a god who'd died before, so there were some as were curious.

"Now, about a week after they came, Brother Mellán went all around to tell the people that the true god had come to us, and that they were having a worship in two nights' time, under the Tree of Wisdom in the village square. Papa heard old Oisin talking about it in the Bull, and said he was going—'What harm could come?' he said. So, I decided I would go and hear what it was all about."

"And that's when you became a Christian?" Oswell asked.

"Nay. Oh, nay, that came later, after much else came first. Cyneric waited until the moon was rising, until most of the village had gathered, and then he orated at us with words he knew we couldn't possibly understand, pausing every time and again for poor Mellán to translate it into his style of our language."

"What did Father Cyneric say?"

"Well, in truth it took us a good bit of time to understand Mellán—his accent was that flavored and colored by his upbringing up north. So, we didn't catch a lot of what Cyneric said, but I believe it must have gone something along this path: 'We come to you in the Name of our blesséd Lord and Savior Jésu, the very Son of the One Holy God, the only true God, to bring the Good News, the Gospel of Jésu. We come to tell you that you must repent of your heathen and sinful ways, and surrender yourself to Jésu, or you will be damned to the everlasting fires of Hell forever.'"

The student was appalled. "That's … that's what he said?"

"Aye. Well, something close to that, anyway. But this was the way of it: Cyneric would speak out something, and then Mellán would translate it into a form our language, and then it would be repeated, with various conjectures and improvements, by people in the front of the crowd passing it to their friends and neighbors behind them, who'd pass it along to the people behind them. Every pass took it a step or two away from whatever it was that Father Cyneric had said, so that by the time it got back to where I was standing, it didn't make much sense at all. Whatever he was trying to say didn't find much harbor with us—our other gods seemed less demanding.

"Now it didn't seem strange to me just then, as I didn't know aught else, but the more Father Cyneric was talking and Brother Mellán was putting his words into ours, I just started to understand some words the priest was saying in Latin. I suppose I just thought everybody was doing the same, but everybody else was just listening to Mellán.

"The more Cyneric and Mellán talked, the more people decided they'd heard all they needed to hear, and started going back to their homes, or into the Lazy Bull. And the more people left, the louder Cyneric orated so they could still hear him as they were leaving, to the point where he was just yelling at us, which went over like a great stone dropped in a little boat. Soon everyone was gone, leaving Cyneric even more certain of what he had already concluded, that we were all barbarians who refused to hear the message of Jésu. As I stood there and watched, I saw Mellán walk off a few paces so the priest couldn't see him, crying out his embarrassment and frustration, his tears dropping down onto his monk's habit.

"So, the days crept on, and so did Cyneric, with plans to build a church for holy Jésu there, just outside of our village. He bought two hectares of land from Fiontan the pig farmer, land that Fiontan couldn't use, and not a good site for the building of aught where you didn't like the smell of pigs, but it was the only land close to the village, and Fiontan had a way with selling things, being well raised in the art of making a pig sound better than a pig could ever hope to be.

"Still, none of that had much to do with my life, until the day Father Cyneric and Brother Mellán came to Papa's workshop to talk about what they were needing to build a church. Beams and boards, aye—and joists and trusses and a hundred other things. Papa told me to come listen, because he knew I would remember."

"Why didn't he write it down?" Oswell asked.

"Well, nay," Pell shook his head. "The world was different then. Papa had never learned to write, or read, and had never needed to. But this church-building, this would be the biggest deal he'd ever made. He saw it would give him, if not wealth and fortune, at least a comfortable reserve set aside against his old age.

"So Cyneric would say what he needed: 'Ten boards four cubits long, two inches by six inches,' and then Mellán would tell me. I heard the Latin, and then the Gaeilge—and I just started putting one thing next to the other, and by and by I was starting to learn some Latin. I wasn't really trying to, but I was curious to hear people talking in another language, and I thought it might be well to know some of it. I remember—it wasn't something I had to work on, I just … remember.

"The priest rattled off his order, and Mellán told Papa, and then Cyneric and Papa agreed on a price, which even I knew was much higher than it ought to be, more silver than anyone in our village had ever seen or even thought of. Then Father Cyneric told Mellán he needed to write it all out for us, and I didn't understand that part, so I asked Mellán what Cyneric just said. When he told me, I said he didn't need to write anything, and that it wouldn't do any good, as neither of us could read it anyway."

"Wait—you couldn't read, either?" Oswell asked.

"Nay, of course not, is that not what I've been telling you? There were no schools then, except for the Druids, who were far away and protected in secret. All this reading and writing had naught to do with my life in Port Láirge. Nay, I didn't know how to read or write."

"When did you learn? Did Mellán teach you?"

Now the old man looked uncomfortable, but he said, "Ah, well— he tried. Here's the truth of it. Many and many a time I have tried to read, but the words and letters all swim around like eels in a bucket. Nay, that's just something I was never able to do."

All Oswell could think to say was "You still … you don't know how to read?"

"Is that not what I'm just telling you?"

"But you wrote those papers, all those theological arguments!"

"Oh, well—aye," said Pell, not happy with this unwanted scrutiny. It had long been something of a sore point for him. "They were my words, but other people wrote them out for me. I can remember; I learn quite easy. But reading and writing were always something for other people to do. It isn't something I'm ashamed of, nor proud of—that's just the way of it: writing and reading were always for other people.

"Now: Mellán was muddled about the writing and the reading, but I promised him I'd remember. When he told Cyneric, I could see he was skeptical, and he told Mellán to tell me to repeat the order, which I did, to the last board. I said it to Mellán, and he said it to Cyneric, who still thought it must be some style of trick.

"Then the priest told Mellán he'd have to come back and check on us every other day or so, just to be sure. So he did, and when he came around, I wanted to talk to him, trying to learn a little more Latin here and there. And at the same time, Mellán wanted to learn to speak Gaeilge as it was spoken on the southern coast of Éire. It was Mellán who first told me that I had a gift for languages; he told me it had taken him years to learn what I've learned in just a month or two, just from listening to him and that haughty priest.

"We worked hard, Papa and me, from before the sun was peeping over the sea 'til after she settled down beyond the hills to the west. We gathered up logs from mills around the county and cut and shaped and planed them just as the priest had ordered them.

"One morning the priest came in to say that they would be needing more boards—boards for a floor they wanted! Eóghan the carpenter stood up and explained that we don't have floors made of wood in this part of the world, that we all put our feet on the solid ground, inside our homes and out. But Cyneric said through Mellán that 'The altar of blesséd Jésu will not rest on the soil of this filthy land.' So, the priest said he will be needing one hundred smooth-cut pine boards, five cubits long, one inch thick and six inches wide.

"When Mellán told us that, Eóghan just laughed at him and told him it couldn't be done—we couldn't saw a board that thin. They haggled back and forth until they agreed that we'd make the boards an inch and a half thick and eight inches wide. Then I asked Mellán what an altar is, just being curious as I am. Well, Cyneric wanted to know what I asked, and then I heard him telling Mellán what to say.

"Cyneric said, 'Tell the wood boy that the altar is the Table of our Lord's Last Supper with His disciples, on the night in which he was betrayed. It is a reminder of our Lord's sacrifice for the redeeming of the world, as He offered Himself as *expiato* for our sins.'

"Mellán relayed all this to me, and when I asked him what *expiato* is, he looked frightened. He just shook his head and gave me to understand that I shouldn't ask. Cyneric didn't see the look Mellán gave me but asked me how many of the boards we'd finished and how many we had left to prepare; I told him how many we were to make and showed him the stack of boards we'd already done. Mellán went over to count the boards we had finished, and then they left.

"The next day, Mellán returned and came straight over to me. He whispered, 'I'm sorry, my friend, that I couldn't answer your question. I didn't want Father Cyneric to know that I don't know what *expiato* is; it's a word I've heard over and over in the monastery, and I should know it, do you understand? He becomes … cross when I don't know something he thinks I should know.'

"So we started some little nattering, just chatting about one thing and another. I was drilling out the holes at the end of boards for the pegs to fit in later, and when Papa looked over, he saw me hard at work. Brother Mellán told me he had some time because Father Cyneric was saying he has a fearsome headache, and that the monk should not disturb him until lunchtime. Then he looked at me all wily and shrewd and said, 'Probably because he was out all hours down at the tavern, wooing the fair Saoirse.'

"'But Saoirse is married,' I said, 'and I think her husband Aodhan is some manner of cousin to myself.' Then he said, 'I don't think that matters to Father Cyneric—he thinks because neither of them is baptized, they can't really be married, either. I asked him, 'But surely that can't be right, can it?'

"Then, wouldn't you know, Brother Mellán took a deep long breath and started talking. He talked a long time, like he was free as a trout that's slipped through the net. He told me his story, some of which I've already told you, about being ambushed when he and some of his kin were delivering wool to the monastery and being brought up there among the monks. I was surprised to realize that he was only three years older than myself, and him already a monk and all.

"I asked him about monking, and he told me it was a fair life. He said monks were just like other people, and that he knew a good many priests and bishops, and they were just the same as anybody—some being better than others and all.

"So I slyly asked, 'And Father Cyneric, now—is he better than some?' Mellán just shook his head slow and answered, 'Nay, I don't think so—I don't think I've ever met a priest—or any other style of man—who I'd say Father Cyneric is better than.' He looked over at me then, and stopped talking, like he was wishing he hadn't said that, like he'd said something to be ashamed of, trying to judge which way my wind might be blowing. So, my heart warmed for him and I said, 'Nor I, friend. I fear your work here will fail, because he's such a …' But then I had to stop."

Oswell crinkled up his brow and asked, "To see which way his wind might be blowing?"

"Aye. So, Brother Mellán just looked at me, and I knew that I'd be the next of us to say aught, so I thought, go on then: just say what you're wanting to say."

"Did you say it?"

"Oh, aye—I said it."

"What did you say?"

"Well, it wasn't proper, though, what I said."

"It wasn't proper?"

"Oh, nay: it was something as was rude."

"Something rude such as?"

"Something rude such as weren't proper and shouldn't have been said by a young man about his elders."

"But such as what, though, just to be more specific?"

"Such as things as aren't proper and shouldn't have been said and shouldn't to be repeated to a boyo like you." Pell turned away, as to indicate that the matter was finished.

Chapter V

Brothers Forever

The young man was concerned that he had offended the older man, but the smile in his eyes reassured him that he had not, as he turned back toward Oswell to continue his story.

"But I called him something, a profane disrespectful insult, and Mellán laughed at it—the first time ever I heard him laugh—so I said something more along those same lines, something else rude and improper, and then he said the boys in the monastery kitchen used to call him … something rude and offensive, as well as disrespectful and hilarious, and then I had another, and he had another, and I had another until we were laughing so hard we were crying, and presently my grandfather wanted to know what was so funny of a sudden about drilling holes, and I couldn't answer because the laughing had such a hold on me. Papa just shook his head at my foolishness and went back to his work.

"But then Mellán did something curious—curious and wonderful, it was. He took up the wee knife I'd been using to finish the holes in the boards, and scratched himself, just there, on the palm of his right hand, so that a little drop of blood pooled up, and he held it out to me. I didn't know what he was about, and I told him so, and he said I should scratch myself just so, and then we'd clasp our hands together. Well, I was chary about it, thinking it must be something to do with following Jésu, or some style of English custom, or even Roman mayhaps. But he said, 'Nay, Pell—this is something just between you and me. You bring the blood to the palm of your good right hand and take up my hand so that our blood mixes, and then we'll be brothers forever.'

"And I was that moved that I did it: a wee little scratch just there—well, it looks like the years have taken it away now, but I did it, and we clapped our hands together, and Mellán and I have been brothers from that moment to this.

"After that, Mellán gave Father Cyneric to understand that he would be more helpful to the building of Jésu's church if he went off to Eóghan's workshop, to oversee the production of the building materials. Just around then, Father Cyneric was spending much of his time in his prayers, or so he told Mellán. But as a fact, it turns out he was spending a good bit of time in the tavern, wooing my cousin's wife Saoirse. Oh, and she was a pretty, well-formed young woman, without question. So, he was chasing, and she was enticing, and that took up a good bit of his time, so Brother Mellán had some time to come to Papa's workshop. He helped me out some as he could, but mostly he talked to me in Latin, helping me learn it as I was helping him learn to speak Gaeilge the way we said things.

"So it went for weeks, and it was a happy time for me. Papa was too busy with his work to trouble me much, and I could tell he was pleased enough with the work I was doing, though he never breathed a word of it to me.

"One morning, just being curious as I am and all, I asked Mellán to tell me about his god Jésu, and he told me that Jésu was not the god but the son of the god, and also the god himself, and also part of the Trinity, which he named as the Father, the Son, and the Holy Ghost of the god. I told him that didn't make any sense at all, and that the idea of having a ghost for a god was worrisome, but the more he tried to explain it the more muddled I became. Then he used a word that Father Cyneric had used that night under the Tree of Wisdom when he was shouting at us: gospel.

"So, I asked him about it, and I could see the delight in him when he told me, 'Gospel means *good news*, Pell—the good news of the love of God through His Son Jésu the Christus.' Well, then I asked him about that word, Christus, and he told me that Christus was a Latin word meaning messiah, another word I didn't know in any language, and that messiah was the one the Jews had been waiting on for a thousand years to come and save them. So, I was thinking the good news is a Roman name for a Jewish savior, and why should any of that matter to me? Brother Mellán kept on talking, but I stopped listening, and after a time he shook his head and left me to my unenlightened work.

"Then one night as the winter was soon upon us, Father Cyneric came with Brother Mellán to Papa's workshop, saying he wanted to check our progress. I showed him the boards and beams, and he seemed pleased enough—he looked, but couldn't find aught to fault.

"Now, as it happened, Papa had already nipped down to the Bull two or three times that afternoon—he said the ale helped keep the cold out of his bones. So, he was already a bit loose with his tongue, and he wanted Mellán to ask the priest when he was to be paid—he'd spent all his silver and borrowed more to buy the wood we'd been turning into building materials, and we'd never had overmuch to start with. Father Cyneric told Mellán to tell him he'd have to finish making all the boards and such before he'd be paid, and Papa said he needed to be paid for some of his work so he could finish it.

"Father Cyneric, as you might expect knowing just a little about him, puffed up and took offense, and started talking about taking his trade elsewhere. Now Papa was thinking his plan to become rich was melting away into certain disaster, and I saw the panic gathering in his eyes. So, I whispered to him, 'Papa, there's not another carpenter anywhere around for mile on mile—there's nowhere else for this pig-headed fool to go. If he backs out of your deal, you'll have a workshop full of boards ready to sell, and he'll have naught and no way to get aught more.' And Papa looked at me like I'd just gotten there somehow, and smiled and said, 'You tell him that—you tell him exactly what you just said.' Then he walked away, a bit wobbly, back to his saws."

"Oh, no," moaned Oswell. "Did you say that to the priest?"

"Ah, well—here's the way of it," Pell continued. "I didn't want Father Cyneric to know I could understand some Latin, so I nodded to Mellán to help me translate, and then I looked the priest in his eyes and said in my best Gaeilge, 'Honored Father, it would be most helpful to my grandfather if you could give us the silver we need to buy the wood for your boards. In very truth, holy Father, we will not be able to continue without your generous assistance.'"

Oswell asked, "How did you know how to talk all formal like that?"

"In truth, I do not know," answered Pell. "It just came to me. I was just thinking that was the way I was supposed to talk to such an important person."

"And did he give you the silver?"

The old man shook his head. "Not a tenth of what he owed us, but enough for us to buy some salt and a few praties and a little pork, and to pay some of what Papa owed the woodcutters. The priest handed me a small purse of silver like it was his very lifeblood he was parting with, and my grandfather grumbled, but he was pleased enough.

"And then, as they were gathering themselves to leave, on an impulse I asked Mellán to ask Father Cyneric about the altar, thinking if it were a table, it might be something we could make for them. Father Cyneric listened to Brother Mellán asking my question and snapped in Latin, 'And what does this dirty *infidelis* wood boy know about altars?' not knowing that I could understand most of what he said. I didn't know *infidelis*, but the rest I knew. Before Mellán had to say aught to me, I said, 'Tell him if it's to be made of wood, we can make it.'

"Now I heard the priest tell Brother Mellán to bring Eóghan and ask if he could make an altar. Papa came back, but he was feeling like he'd gained some style of advantage over the priest now, and when Mellán asked him, he said, 'And what the hell is an altar, I'd like to know.'

"So Mellán told him it was to be a table used in their worship to remember the sacrifice of the Lord Jésu, who gave his life for us, and Papa sneered, 'Sounds like some style of daft make-believe foolery to me, to be sure.'

"Father Cyneric didn't understand Papa's words, but there was no mistaking his tone. He was quite serious about an altar, was Father Cyneric, and now he'd had enough of us. He pronounced something I didn't understand, but I think it was something like a curse. We didn't understand it, of course, and Mellán didn't translate it—or need to—as the priest's meaning was right clear. Father Cyneric turned and walked out, and Mellán held his hands out, palms up, showing his helplessness.

"But now Papa was enraged that the priest would say whatever he'd just said and then just leave with the last words in his mouth—in truth it didn't take much for Papa to become enraged when he'd had a pint or two. He roared, 'Come back in here, you Roman bastard!'

"The priest turned to face him all calm and smug, and said, 'You are not worthy to make an altar for Jésu.' And then he waited for Mellán to translate it, which he did. Then Papa picked up a hammer and came after him with ice and fire in his eyes."

"Did he kill him?" Oswell asked.

"Well, nay—nay," Pell shook his head. "Many a time I've wondered how different things might have gone if my grandfather had caught up with that puffed-up priest. But nay, as it happened, I reached out to try to stop him, and he got his foot caught under a board, and stubbled his toe. Then he looked at me with murder in his eyes, and I knew he was sure to blame me, even though I was trying to keep him from doing something terrible, and it was himself who'd dropped that board there. Well, I knew all the anger he'd been gathering up against Cyneric would soon be coming at me. So, in very truth I ran out of there like the building was afire, hoping to avoid or at least delay the beating Papa was swearing I would be getting soon.

"And what should happen but that I ran smack into Father Cyneric, who was busy scolding Brother Mellán about one thing or another. When I ran right into the back of him and almost knocked him over, I saw his anger shift to me as well, and I saw clearly that Father Cyneric was just another bully. I was still hearing my grandfather bellowing his threats against me, and I knew that Papa was a bully just the same as Cyneric. And that, young sir, is when I gave up any arrogant desire of being a bully—I just couldn't abide the idea of being like either one of those bastards.

"Even so, it didn't help me to know it, as they were both bullies still the same, and both of them angry. Well, I knew that I couldn't fight Father Cyneric, or that it wouldn't be worth all the trouble I'd be in if I did, just as well I knew that I would never be able to strike a blow on my poor Mam's father.

"So, I looked for something not utterly stupid to say, and what came out was, 'Sir, if it's a table you need, I can make it for you.' Mellán told him what I said, and now the priest looked down on me and said something to Mellán, who translated it: 'Not a table only, but an altar—a grand table, for a ritual.' Full of myself now and trying to calm the choppy waters I found myself trying to swim, I repeated my earlier boast, a little changed: 'If it's to be made of wood, I can make it.'

"The priest looked at me and sneered. He said something to Mellán, who translated, 'But your grandfather would not like that.' I said, 'He won't need know what I'm doing then.' Now Mellán looked at me like I've misplaced my mind, but the priest looked at me shrewd as a weasel, and told Mellán to say, 'If you can make an altar to my satisfaction, with a front panel with scenes from the life of our Lord, I will pay you handsomely. But hear me: if I don't like it, I'll not pay you, not even a copper coin.'

"So, I agreed, and Father Cyneric stalked away. Mellán wanted to stay and talk about all that had just happened, but the priest called for him like he was a dog, and Mellán had to go. But he came back the next day to tell me his ideas about making an altar, after admiring the shiner my grandfather had graced me with the night before."

Oswell whispered, "Your grandfather hit you?"

"Oh, aye," Pell acknowledged. "That night and many another night as well. He was holding a great measure of rage, Eóghan was, or mayhaps the rage had taken hold of him. Either way, I was an easy target, ready to hand. I couldn't fight back; he was my mother's father.

"But I'm meaning to tell you about the building of this altar. Mellán told me how long, how high and how deep the table itself ought to be, and that was no problem. We had plenty of pine scraps lying around the workshop I could use for hobbling together a table; that was just saws and sanders, pegs and glue, mortise joints, things I knew and understood. But the front panel was to have scenes from the life of Jésu, and the only way I could imagine it was for those scenes to be carved. That meant chisels and whittling knives; it meant using walnut, much harder wood but darker and prettier, and more costly as well. Still, there were odds bits and pieces of walnut just waiting to be used, and I could fit little pieces and glue them together as no seams need show.

"Now the problem was that I didn't know the first or last thing about this Jésu, other than what I was thinking Father Cyneric had said, which wasn't inviting, and the muddle I'd made of what Mellán had been trying to tell me. I was chary about asking Mellán again, for fear that he would try to convert me or some style of thing as that. But there was no other way about it, so I said, 'Brother Mellán,' reminding him that we were brothers, which would require some of his patience and understanding, 'I'm afraid I'm needing to ask you about this Jésu fella again.'"

Chapter VI

A Different Manner of God

Pell shifted his back against the rowan he was leaning against, warming to his tale. "So now Mellán set about telling me the story of Jésu, and I had a beehive full of questions. But no sooner than he was starting than I stop him, as I'm wanting him to tell it to me in Latin, thinking if Latin was the language of the Church, it must be the language Jésu himself spoke, and that I should be hearing the story in his own tongue."

Oswell asked cautiously, "Are you telling me that Jesus spoke Latin?"

"Nay, of course not. I was thinking Jésu spoke Latin, but Mellán quickly taught me He spoke Hebrew, or more rightly, Aramaic, a dialect of Hebrew—something like enough to Hebrew so if you could understand one, you could understand the other. Most languages are forever shifting—all except Latin, as far as I understand it. Hebrew and Aramaic were akin to one another, like Mellán's Gaeilge and mine—mostly the same, but different enough to be trip you up if you don't watch where you're stepping.

"Still, Mellán told me the story of Jésu in Latin, which made it take much longer as I was learning to work out the verbs and all those declensions—oh, aye, a powerfully convoluted language is Latin. Not nearly so hard to learn as Greek, though."

"You speak Greek, too?" Oswell asked.

"Well, I picked some up here and there. I met a young fella who taught me some of it, and then a pair of bishops who didn't speak much Latin. That was ever the best way for me to learn, when I needed to talk with people in their own language.

"But I'm trying to tell you the story of Jésu as Mellán told it to me. They would read it to the monks in the monastery, as it was written by a fella named Lucas, a physician Mellán said. Later I heard the story in different ways, and it got more complicated, but this I'm telling you is how Mellán first told me the story, trying to tell it about as simply as he could.

"He said, 'More than three centuries ago, when Augustus was Emperor of Rome, the very Spirit of God visited a young woman named Maria, in faraway Nazareth. This Spirit told her she was carrying a child, even though she was yet a virgin—and this child was to be God's own Son.'

"Well, she was greatly distressed at the idea of it, as you might imagine, for though she was betrothed to a man, they had not been so familiar with one another as that, and she was fretful about what he would say, and what her family would say. But she was faithful, was Maria, and she accepted that this was the way of it. Her husband-to-be, whose name was Joseph, must have accepted it as well, because when the emperor commanded that all people must return to the home places of their ancestors, he took Maria with him to wee Bethlehem, where his people were from. They must have been late getting there, as there were no rooms left for them to rent, but the innkeeper, seeing that Maria was about to burst, told them they could stay in the little cave where his beasts would come to get out of the weather."

"And that's where she had her baby," said Oswell, wanting to let him know that he knew the story.

"There she delivered the babe, using a feed trough for his crib. Some of the shepherds around there saw angels coming down from the heavens singing praises to God and telling them where to find the babe, and they went and made a right fuss over the child. Then a week or so later Maria and Joseph carted him up to the Temple in Jerusalem, just a league or two away, to observe a Jewish ritual. There, two people saw the babe clearly for who he was, even though the woman was old, and the man was blind, they saw the babe clearly for who he was, and they told it out that this babe was sure to change the world."

"Old Simeon told Mary the child would be a sword that pierced her heart," added Oswell, hoping to impress the older man with his knowledge of the story, and as a way of letting him know he didn't need to tell it again. "And the woman's name was … um …"

"Anna," said Pell, "the daughter of Phanuel, of the tribe of Asher."

Oswell nodded, and thought to himself it would do him no harm to hear the sacred story from a very different, if possibly heretical, point of view.

"Then they went back home to Nazareth," Pell continued, "and we don't know aught else for a long time after that. Mellán told me Lucas wrote that Maria's husband Joseph was a carpenter, which if I'm to be honest pleased me right well, as it's something I understood, and I liked the idea that mayhaps Jésu was apprenticed to a carpenter, as I was.

"Then, when he was about thirty, Jésu began to gather up his followers. The Spirit of God, that very selfsame Spirit who'd told Jésu's mother Maria that she would carry the child of God, led Jésu out into the wilderness to be tempted by the devil Satan. Well, this part took a long time to explain—and I still wonder about it—but this Satan was an angel, and the adversary of God, and he tempted Jésu to abandon his purpose, set aside his convictions and beliefs, and seek out a more lavish, comfortable life.

"Well, sure as the morning, Jésu shoved the devil away and began to preach and teach, and a crowd gathered around him. He healed some people as nobody else had been able to heal. People who were blind, or lepers, people with palsy—he brought a wee dead girl back to life! He fed thousands of people with just a bit of fish and bread, and there were other miracles and signs, but Mellán said all of that wasn't what he did that turned the world on its head, but what he said.

"'What did he say that was so remarkable as all that?' I wondered, and Mellán answered, 'He talked about love—not just for the people you like, but for every child of God, even your enemies, those who hate you, those who do or say what you think they shouldn't.' Mellán told me Jésu said, 'Blessed are the poor, the hungry and those who mourn.' Jésu said it all rests on whether we are willing to love God with all we are and all we have and love each other as much as we love ourselves.

"Now mind you: Mellán was pouring all these words about a god of love and mercy into a bucket formed to hold all the gods I'd grown up hearing about—savage, cruel gods, worshipped because they were mighty in battle, or admired because they were more clever than us. This Jésu was a new way of looking at the gods, and I tell you I was right chary about it. But at the same time, the idea of a loving god took a grip on my thinking.

"What Jésu said was grand and freeing to some, but it was shocking and scandalous to others. Some people who thought what he said was true followed him, but others who didn't conferred together and decided they needed for Jésu to die. To die because he was talking about love and compassion in a world that prizes hatred and celebrates greed—ah, me—things haven't changed much, have they?

"Now, well Jésu knew that he had threatened two bureaucracies—the Romans and the Jewish leaders. He was inviting a change, not in the government or the powers that be, but in the hearts of the people. Those who'd been enjoying the power the system gave them wanted to keep things as they were, since it was set up to keep them in their lavish, comfortable lives. They had accepted the lies the devil had used to tempt Jésu before.

"So the leaders of the Jews contrived with the Roman officials to take Jésu and have him killed. The night he was arrested by the Roman soldiers, Jésu gathered up some of those who'd been following him, those as were most familiar with his teachings. He brought them together to celebrate the Jewish festival of the Passover, a ritual meal to remember how the God of the Jews had freed them from slavery away in Egypt hundreds of years even before that. Part of that meal was to eat unleavened bread, as a way to remember that their ancestors had to leave their homes in a rush—the bread had no time to rise.

"But Jésu took that flat bread and held it up so they could all see it, and said, 'Take this and eat it: this is my body I'm giving for you,' talking about his death, which he knew would come soon. But his followers, these disciples didn't know what he was talking about, so they just ate the bread. They ate their meal and sang the songs that go in the Passover meal—oh, aye, these Jews turn out to be right musical people, part of what I love about them, if I'm to be honest.

"And there was wine—good strong red wine they drank as part of this ritual meal, something more for me to love. There were three or four cups of wine to drink as part of telling the story of God saving the people of Israel, and when they came to the last one, the cup of promise, I was told, Jésu held up his cup and said, 'Take this cup and share it among yourselves: this is my blood which I'm giving for you, for your sins and for the sins of the whole world.'

"This I've been telling you about is the Last Supper the way I first heard about it, and it was as I expect you know a powerful understanding about God saving his people with the sacrifice of Jésu. The priests who came later called it a sacrament, something we see or taste or feel that carries the very love and grace of God, something more than itself. Ah, but that right there is a rabbit hole we ought to save for another day, that's doctrine, is that, and doctrine is where much of the trouble with religion begins.

"At the Last Supper, one of his disciples, a fella named Judas, left to tell the Jewish leaders where they were staying that night, in a nearby garden, and they sent for the Roman soldiers. Mayhaps it was this Satan Mellán told me about that led him to do it, or it may have been common jealousy or greed or some other reason, but either path, Judas brought the soldiers to the garden, and they grabbed Jésu up and arrested him.

"The next day they hauled him to the Jewish king, who said it wasn't him as should judge Jésu but the Roman authorities, himself not wanting to take the blame. Pilate, the Roman governor, wanted naught to do with it. Even though the Romans had an army there to keep the peace, they were greatly outnumbered by a population they ought to be curiously passionate about their faith. But he was pressured—politics and all—and he agreed to it. Jésu was beaten and taunted and nailed to a wooden beam fixed to another beam standing up on a hill, making a cross of it.

"'And what happened then?' I asked Mellán. 'Did the great god come and rescue his son? Did he call down the power of lightning and thunder on those Roman bastards?'

"'Nay,' Mellán answered. 'He died, is what happened. Jésu died.'

"'Well, what manner of a god is that?' I wanted to know. I was just flummoxed at the thought of it: what style of a god just lets his son die, nailed to a pole on a hill? So I asked Mellán, and he said, 'I guess the same god who lets his son be born in a food trough for farm animals. A different manner of god, Pell, from the gods you grew up with—a god of love and mercy, not power and vengeance.'

"After a time, Mellán continued, 'But here now—if that had been the end of the story, in very truth this Jésu fella would surely be long since forgotten. And why isn't that the end?—because two or three days later Jésu came crashing out of the tomb and talked to his friends. Well, they had some difficulty believing it was really him, as I expect I would have as well, and Jésu asked, "Have you any fish?" Ha! And they gave him a wee bit of fish and Jésu ate it, just as they knew a ghost or some such could not have done.'

"This, Brother Mellán told me, is the Gospel—and now we're back to this again, I was thinking—this is the good news, Mellán said: that Jésu's father God loves every person ever born more than we understand, and to help us know this is the truth of it, he allowed his own son to die on a cross and be raised up to live again. Brother Mellán said Jésu showed us the way to live in love and showed us that we don't need to be afraid even of death, as we can follow Jésu through our own dying into the life that comes after. I told Mellán it would be a great help to me if that were true, and that I might be able to credit it myself, if I could see a dead man eat a piece of fish.

"But his friends did believe that it really was him, raised from the dead with signs and wonders, and they passed the story along to others, who passed it along to others, who passed it along to Mellán, who passed it along to me."

Oswell nodded his approval of the old man's rendition of the Gospel story, and added, "And so all men must be baptized, in the Name of the Father, and the Son, and the Holy Ghost." He looked at the heretic expecting some form of approval but was disappointed.

"Or what?" said Pell, suddenly agitated. "What happens if a body doesn't *want* to be baptized? Or if they're growing up in a good Jewish family, or some other style of religion?"

"Well," Oswell stammered, taken aback by Pell's sudden vehemence, "the bishop said those people will surely spend eternity up to their necks in a lake of fire that burns forever!"

"Well, that doesn't sound like good news to me. That sounds like something a bishop would say, but it doesn't sound like the God of love and mercy Jésu was talking about, does it? So, young sir, I want you to do something for me. I have a message for this bishop, tell him it's from the heretic Pelagius. Will you do that for me?"

"Yes sir, if I can. What's the message?" asked Oswell, curious what the old man would say.

"Tell the bishop he can … that his teaching is … ah, well—nay, never mind that, never give it another thought."

"Improper?" asked Oswell.

"Aye, improper and rude, and stirring up another fight I do not need and would not win. And it's not that boyo's fault; that was just the style of rubbish the bishops and theologians had jobbed down their throats when they were just young students like you."

"You want me to tell him that?" asked Oswell, now horrified again.

"Nay … nay. It will do neither of you any good and might bring you some harm. It just chafes me that the message of Jésu is being twisted around into another legion of the Roman army, everybody marching all in step, everybody saying the same things, with no room for a body to think a thought somebody else didn't tell him to think. Well, God love us, it's naught to do with me now, is it, me being just a heretic and all."

Chapter VII

Under the Tree of Wisdom

Pell cleared his throat and continued his story. "Well, I was telling you about building this altar, and the carved front-piece. I wanted Mellán to tell me the story of Jésu so I could know which scenes ought to be put on the front of this holy table, and I found there were many and many that we would need to choose from. I told Mellán I wanted to carve a scene of faithful Maria holding her wee baby with Joseph the carpenter and the shepherds looking on peaceful and calm, but he said Father Cyneric wouldn't like it, because he would think it made too much about Maria. Apparently, there was some arguing about the place of Maria among the followers of Jésu, and how much influence she ought to be having, because she was a woman, and women ought to be kept in their place, as Mellán told me Father Cyneric said it. Aye well, that made me want to carve that image even more, but Mellán said if I wanted Father Cyneric to use the front-piece and pay me for the work, I'd best leave it out.

"Finally, we settled on five panels, each with its own image: the baptism of Jésu in the River Jordan, Jésu sitting at table with his disciples at the Last Supper, the Crucifixion of Jésu on a Roman cross in the middle panel, the Resurrection with the stone rolled away from the empty tomb, and Jésu flying away into the clouds, what Mellán called the *Ascensio*, on the last one.

"Next, Mellán snuck out a small store of parchment they'd brought from Angleland, and we sharped up a piece of charcoal to draw out the panels. Oh, there were a lot of conversation about how they were to be, and how they should look and such. I'd draw something and then Mellán would tell me that this isn't right, or that was too big, or it should be over there on the other side of the whole damn thing and I'd have to scrape the marks off and start all over again. We did this for more than a week, laughing some of the time but getting mad or hurt other times, and wasting one whole day throwing sulks at each other.

"Finally, we drew out these five skeetches, Mellán called them, to where we were both satisfied, and I started the long slow process of carving the images."

"Sketches?" Oswell asked, not understanding.

"Nay, I think he said they were skeetches. Skeetches—is that right? Is it sketches? God love us, I've been using the wrong word all these years and nobody ever told me! Ha! Sketches, then.

"I have wondered, as the years melted away, why it seemed important to me that I carve this front-piece, and I think there were several reasons all woven together. One was for the money, of course, but that wasn't the main reason. Another reason was as a way to understand Mellán's god, by understanding the story of Jésu. Part of it was the challenge of it, to prove to myself that I could do it. But mostly I think it was a gift for Mellán, something he and I could do, something to please Father Cyneric. Well, so: whatever the reason, I worked on it every moment I could spare, and stayed up late, long after Papa had gone to his pallet, or to the tavern, more like. I kept it hid from Papa, as I didn't want him knowing about it until it was done. I suppose there was some little hope of making him proud of me as well, but in truth, I knew better, even then.

"I botched things up a few times, nearly cut my own thumb off twice, but by and by I understood what I was trying to do and the tools I was using to do it, and then it was better. I saved the Crucifixion panel for last, because I knew it would be in the middle and that most people would look at it first, and I was thinking I'd be better at carving by the fifth panel than I'd been at the first. Also, I carved it last because the idea of nailing a man to a beam was right disturbing to me and carving it into wood made it seem more real than I wanted it to be. But after a few weeks, I had it all done, so that I was pleased with it, or at least I couldn't find aught more I could do to make it any better.

"It was late one afternoon when I showed it to Mellán. He hadn't seen it stained and finished, just pieces and bits clamped together. At first, I thought he was trying to spare me a disappointment, so lavish he was in the praising of it. I was starting to feel some sulks coming for me, but he said, 'Nay, my brother. I swear on my faith this is a masterpiece, clearly inspired by God's own Spirit. Come with me, and we'll show it to Father Cyneric—he'll love it, I'm sure of it.'"

Pell sighed. "Well, he was wrong about that. I wrapped the front-piece up in some polishing cloths and we marched ourselves through the village to the room where Mellán and the priest had been staying, but Cyneric wasn't there. I suggested that the Father might be at the Lazy Bull, and Mellán agreed but said he'd not be going to check on him there. So, we waited for a while outside the room, sitting on a bench, and finally along came Father Cyneric, who obviously had gotten a few pints down him. He looked at the two of us like we were mud on his boots, and Mellán said, 'Father, Pell has finished the front-piece for the altar.' I was quick to nod as friendly as I could, and I said to Mellán, 'Tell him you helped!'

"But before Mellán could speak out another word, the priest sneered at us, and I understood when he said, 'And where is it?' even though his Latin was laced with a fair bit of tipsy. I waited for Mellán to nod to me before I unwrapped it and showed it to him. I was so proud; it looked much better than I'd ever imagined it could. But Father Cyneric took just one look at it, not more than three heart-beats, before he slurred, 'Nay, that won't do. It's just rubbish—take it away. I'll pay you naught, not even a copper coin!'

"Well of course I was disappointed and hurt, and as some silent moments passed me by, soon I was feeling the anger rising up in me. But I struggled to keep my calm, and I said in Gaeilge, 'Honored Father, mayhaps you might want to take a closer look—see: the panels are carved in precious walnut and depict five of the scenes of the life of blesséd Jésu.' But the haughty priest would have none of it. Mellán hadn't even told him what I was saying before he was screaming at me to get out and to take the front piece with me, or he'd use it for kindling!"

"What did you do?" wondered Oswell.

"I left."

"Did you take the front-piece with you?"

"Oh, aye," answered Pell with a little smile. "I took it away from there, and we took it with us when we left, and carried it along with us for many and many a league. Mayhaps I have it still; it may be the best thing ever I did for blesséd Jésu and his church. Not meaning to brag, but in truth it was a pretty piece of work."

He paused, content in his memories, before continuing. "I took up the front-piece and left as quick as a mackerel, not knowing what I was to do next. I stood outside, and as I waited for Mellán, I looked down on it, seeing for the first time past the walnut and glue it was made of, not looking at the work of my hands, weeks of carving and sanding and staining, but seeing the story of this man, this Jésu the god's son.

"I wondered then, looking at my front-piece in the moon's soft light, whether it truly happened the way Mellán had told me, and what it would have looked like if it did. What a peculiar thing, for a god to die, and then—and here is the strange and wonderful idea—for him to come back to life, not to save himself but to save us, so that we could know that death doesn't take the whole person, just the body. And I saw, standing there, that if all that were true, if Jésu really had died and come back from the tomb, if this story were true, it would mean that Áine, my sweet sister Áine, was still alive somehow, and that I would yet see her again. Years before, I'd given up on the gods, rejecting the cold uncaring gods of my grandfather and my mother, but this Jésu, if it were true, this would be a god I could believe in, a god whose main care was that we love. This was a god I wanted to believe in … if it were true.

"So, presently here came Mellán, all flustered and twitchy. He had the look of a man who wanted to say something but didn't know what to say or how to say it. I held out my hand and told him to take it, palm to palm, and he did. I said, 'Well, brother, I suppose he had some different idea for what he was wanting, mayhaps.'

"But Mellán said, 'Nay, my brother. The problem was never the front-piece. It turned out better than anybody thought it would, even yourself. Nay, the problem is—' and now he leaned in to whisper the terrible truth—'that Father Cyneric doesn't have the money to pay you.'

"'What?' I said, 'How do you know that?'

"'Well,' said Mellán, 'old Oisin at the Lazy Bull came to see Father this afternoon and told him Cyneric hasn't paid his bill for weeks. He said he owes him a fair fortune in wine and ale, and that Saoirse isn't happy with him, either—it seems he promised her things he hasn't been able to give her. Aye, sure as the world, he's spent all our money, or most of it, on ale and Saoirse down at the Lazy Bull.'

"Well, that was a right slap in the face, in truth it was. Before I even had time to settle out what it all might mean, I asked, 'Then how is he to pay my grandfather for all his work?'

Mellán said, 'Aye, but there's the very thing: I don't know. I think he was hoping to raise some money among the people of the village after he'd won them over for Jésu, but I can't say it looks like there's much of a chance of that now. If I'm to be honest, the people of the village don't seem as if they want aught to do with Father Cyneric, or myself, for that matter.

"'What does this have to do with you, then?' I wondered.

"He answered, 'Oh, they all think I'm like him, Pell—that I think and feel just as he does—every uncaring, arrogant self-serving word he's ever said to the people of the village has come out of my mouth!'

"We stood there lost together, and I asked him, 'What are you to do, brother?'

"He replied, 'In very truth I do not know. I can't go back across the sea to the monastery alone with such a sad tale to tell, and I haven't been able to convince Father Cyneric to forsake Port Láirge, or Saoirse, for that matter. He doesn't listen to me; he's put himself so far above me—above everyone—that he can't hear anything I say. I don't know, and there's the very truth of it.'

After a pause, Pell continued, "Well, I felt the sadness of it gnawing at me, but all I could do was to go home, so home I went. I hid the front-piece under my sleeping pallet. Mayhaps I should have told my grandfather that the priest didn't have the silver to pay him, but I didn't, because I was afraid, and that's just the gloomy truth of it. I knew that Papa was sure to be outraged, and he wasn't the style of man who would likely keep that anger all inside himself: I feared he would hit me, and that he would go and kill that damn priest. So, I didn't tell him, and we just kept working on those boards and beams meant for a church hall I knew full well was never going to be built.

"A week or so passed, not much more than that, and the day came that Father Cyneric's sins caught him up, like a salmon in a trap. That night, that most horrible night, Papa came back from the Lazy Bull, where old Oisin had been saying there was to be a meeting of the village council later, under the Tree of Wisdom, and all the village would be there. As a rule, Papa would never think about going to see such a thing, but this one was to do with Father Cyneric, so he said he thought he'd go see what was in the wind. He told me to close up the shop, that we were finished with our work for that day, and off he went.

"By the time I closed the shutters and doors and banked the fire and tidied up a little and trotted down to the village square, there must have been two hundred men there, and almost as many women, with a flock of children running around playing chase—it was a festive air, in very truth. I'd never seen so many people all in one place before.

"I looked around and found Papa, sitting right beside his friend Oisin, each of them holding a jar of ale and enjoying the merriment. I looked to see if I could spot Mellán, but him I didn't see, until some of the strong men of the village brought him out with Father Cyneric and sat them down in front of us. Father Cyneric was just as proud as ever, but my friend Mellán looked scared, like he was about to cry. I tried to catch his eye, to let him know I was there, but he just looked down at his feet, and he didn't look up.

"Now the crowd was starting to get nervy, waiting with scant patience for the meeting to start. Presently out came the elders, two old men and a fragile-looking old woman. The woman was my grandfather's aunt; she was named Danu after the mother of the Tuatha Dé Danann, the goddess of the land itself. When I was young, I thought she was the goddess—she looked like I thought a goddess should look.

"Tadgh, the man who did most of the talking for the council, was a fisherman, tall and strong, crowned by a full head of black hair with the beginnings of gray at his temples. He had a rich, strong voice, and when he cried, 'Friends! Kinsmen! Kindly keep your silence so this council may begin!' everybody became still and quiet, except for a few of the children.

"Tadgh held up his right hand and proclaimed, 'We come together as a village to consider the matter of Father Cyneric and Brother Mellán, who came here to spread the religion of their god Jésu. It is fair, I think, to say that they have had little success among us. A venture attempted and failed is no crime, but now we are given to understand that Father Cyneric has taken money entrusted to him by members of our village to make a church building, and spent it all at the Lazy Bull, all the while attempting to meddle in other people's married harmony. Our custom is to give the accused a chance to answer the charges; Cyneric, what will you say?'

"I looked to Mellán, thinking he would be speaking out the priest's answer, but it was Cyneric who stood to speak, shaking his head to sit Mellán down. Too late, it seemed, Cyneric had realized that he needed to speak Gaeilge to speak to the people of the village. Now he was damned and doomed by his own words and arrogance. He shouted, in his broken Gaeilge, 'No! Not true! I'm done naught wrong! My money I'm spent! I'm thought Saoirse not'—he looked to Mellán for help, and the good monk muttered a word so Cyneric could continue—'not wife. I'm done naught wrong!'

"He sat back down, and a restless wave of disappointed doubt surged through the people of the village; could it be that the charges were false, that the priest didn't know Saoirse was married, and the money spent at the Bull was his own? The attention of the crowd seemed to be scattering, until Tadgh raised his hand and everybody was quiet again, except for some children chasing each other. Then Tadgh called out in his sturdy voice, 'I now call on Niamh, the wife of Cathal the potter.'"

Chapter VIII

Wailing and Squalling and Yowling

Pell continued, "Now I looked at Father Cyneric and saw panic in his eyes—this was something he had not expected. The people were murmuring and speculating, until Tadgh raised his hand again, and up Niamh came up timidly as a mouse and stood beside him. Before she could say a word, Father Cyneric stood again and shouted, 'No! She a woman! A woman not speak! A woman not speak on me!'

"Just then, someone in the crowd threw a stick at Father Cyneric. It didn't hit him, but it didn't miss by much, and it shut him up for a bit—he knew there were plenty of sticks and a fair few throwable stones within easy reach of people who were becoming more and more hostile.

"Now Niamh looked out over the people there, her friends and family, and made her confession. She was embarrassed and afraid, and she didn't speak loudly or distinctly, so it was hard to hear her, but we all leaned in, every one of us quiet as a flounder. She told us that Father Cyneric had seduced her with promises of a gentler life, of going back to Angleland, mayhaps even to Rome. He'd told her he was going to be a bishop someday, and that they would be treated like a king and a queen. She was crying so hard that it was difficult to understand, but she told us that Cyneric was the reason that Cathal had left her, and that she was so, so sorry.

"Aye, well, it nearly broke the hearts of every person there, so plainly we all saw that Father Cyneric ruined her life with his pretty words and empty promises. And then, she said, he just discarded her like a worn-out shoe when he met Saoirse, so young and so pretty.

"Now it seemed to me even the children and the crickets in the trees were hushed as Cathal the potter came forward, as he walked straight up to Father Cyneric. I was thinking this would be the end of the pompous priest, but Cathal just looked at him hard, until Father Cyneric dropped his arrogant eyes, and Cathal turned and stepped toward his wife. He stopped about six or seven paces away from her, and after a tense pause, he held his arms open and she ran into his embrace. I joined with every other person from the village in cheering them together.

"Then Tadgh called out, 'Is there anyone else here who has aught to say about Father Cyneric that your elders should be hearing tonight?' We all looked around to see who might have something to say, but nobody stepped forward. I looked at Brother Mellán to see if I should tell the council that Father Cyneric would not be paying my grandfather for the work we've been doing, but Mellán was still studying his feet as if they were different than the ones he'd woken up with that morning. I didn't want Papa to know that I knew about Father Cyneric's financial problems, so I didn't say aught. And besides all that, I was young, and this was a gathering of elders, under the Tree of Wisdom.

"So, Tadgh told us the elders would step away to confer for a moment, and that they would soon return with their decision. The crowd relaxed, and a comfortable buzz of normal commotion surrounded us. Just then I saw Papa trying to catch my notice, and he motioned me to come to him. He said, 'Pell, take these jars and fill them with ale from the Lazy Bull; my friend Oisin here is saying he wants to buy me a drink!' Old Oisin, who was in a mood to celebrate, nodded his approval, and off I went.

"I made my way through the crowd to the Bull, which was quite empty; I filled the jars with ale, taking only one little sip from my grandfather's jar, and then I was making my way back through the crowd again, when I was shoved forward from behind. I dropped one jar on the ground and spilled most of the other, and when I leaned down to pick up the jar I dropped, thinking I'd have to go back to the Bull and fill it again, I was pushed again! I turned around and saw that it was none other than Darragh the smith's son, and his brother Deaglán. It seems they'd been helping themselves to the ale when there was nobody there to be looking after it; Darragh looked like he was standing on the deck of a boat pitching in heavy seas, and Deaglán like he was trying to keep his brother from falling overboard.

"Darragh belched out, 'Well now, you fatherless whoreson. What will you be doing, with all these people around us? What will you do, Son of Nobody?' So, I set down the jars and turned to my left, so that my right hand was closest to him, just like my uncle Eóchaidh had taught me, and the younger boys saw that a fight was brewing, and they started chanting, 'Fight! Fight! Fight!' the way young boyos always do.

"I thought Deaglán would be sneaking around behind me, but he was holding his drunk brother up, and I saw there was no fight in him. He looked like he was embarrassed by his brother, like he didn't want any part in any of this. So, in very truth I was stepping away, when I heard the voice of Danu the elder, and it was to me that her words were directed.

"Now, Danu the elder didn't speak much, but when she did, the whole village was bound to listen. 'Pell,' is all she said, but her voice was like the ringing of a bell, strong and clear. Every person there was looking straight at me—I could feel the touch of their eyes on me. Danu said, 'Well you know there is to be no fighting under the Tree of Wisdom.' I answered, 'Aye, ma'am—but' and she said, 'No fighting for any reason, no matter the provocation' and I said, 'Aye, ma'am—but' and she said, 'This is our way, Pell' and I said 'Aye, ma'am.'

"Then, chastened as I was, I was thinking that would be the end of it, but Cyneric was hoping that mayhaps I could be a way out of the mess he'd made of himself. He was desperate—like a drowning man, he was reaching out to grab onto whatever he can find. He called out, 'Wood boy! I'm been … good to you, good to old man! Boards for church, you make—I'm been good to you, fair, yes.'

"Well, I didn't know what I should do or say, and then Danu the elder said, 'So, Pell, since you have everyone's eyes on you, what will you say? Will you say aught to support Father Cyneric?'

"In that same moment I remembered my great-uncle saying, 'Pell, you have to stand up against the bully, do you understand?' So, I decided that was what I had to do. That voice of speaking formally came to me again, like the time I asked Father Cyneric if he could pay us a little so we could continue making his boards and beams.

"I raised myself up as tall as I could and said, 'Honored elders and people of Port Láirge, well I know I have no right to speak here—in very truth I am just a boy, and I know my place. But the lady Danu has invited me to speak, and who am I to decline her invitation?' That got a little chuckle from some in the crowd, and I was boldened to continue.

"I said, 'Father Cyneric has said that he had dealings with my grandfather, Eóghan the carpenter, and that is true. He also said he was good to us and fair, and that, I am sorry to say, is not. We have worked for weeks to make boards and beams for the church he said he was going to build, but he has paid us precious little, only a small bag of silver, and that after I nearly had to beg him for it. What money my grandfather had was spent on buying the timber to make the building materials, and now I'm hearing he has wasted away most of the money he came with and more given him by our friends and neighbors for the building of a church. Now I'm wondering if he has silver enough to pay Papa for even half of the work he's done!

"Well, at this, my grandfather came roaring up off the bench he'd been holding down all this time, charging at the priest like a shark closing in on a wounded seal. It took three or four men to hold him back, his rage was so great, but at a word from his aunt Danu, he settled right down. The elder Tadgh raised his hand, and the crowd settled down a bit, and he nodded once and said, 'Cyneric, what will you say to this?' Aye, so then Cyneric got up and looked like I had injured him with my slander. Slippery as a frog, he said, 'Wood boy not says true. I'm been good to him, good to old man, fair.' He looked so sincere, as if he were the victim here, that the crowd was again murmuring doubtfully. I looked at Cyneric's face and when he looked at me and I thought I saw him smirk a little.

"The idea that he might soon be walking away from the council with no harm coming to himself at all, that he would escape the consequences I thought he deserved, angered me so much I drew myself up again and raised my hand. This time it was Tadgh who saw me and asked me if I had aught more to say. I said, 'Aye, sir, thank you. You should also know that Father Cyneric was needing an altar to be built, like a table with an ornate front-piece, to be used in their Christian worship. I asked him if I could make it for him, and he said that I could, but that if it wasn't any good, he wouldn't pay me a single coin for it. Well, for four or five weeks I worked on that altar, carving the front-piece until I thought it was very good. But when I took it to show it to Father Cyneric, he didn't even look at it, and told me it was just rubbish, and that he would use it for kindling!'

"Again, the murmuring of the people shifted, again Tadgh asked Cyneric if he would like to say something, and again the wily priest stood up and spoke: 'Nay, wood boy not says true. Altar not good, I'm paid him naught! I'm done naught wrong!'

"Now Tadgh was looking at me kindly, and he said, 'Pell, if your work wasn't good enough, that's not this man's fault. He told you he wouldn't pay if it wasn't good enough, did he not?' I nodded and said, 'Yes, sir.' Tadgh continued, 'Now we are ready to speak our judgment. Cyneric, please …'

"But just right then I heard another voice, a voice I loved. 'Your pardon, honored elders—may I speak?' It was Mellán, my brother and friend; I was proud to note that his Gaeilge was much improved. Tadgh nodded, and even though he was clearly terrified, Mellán continued: 'Pell's front-piece is good enough—it is as good as aught ever I've seen, and better than most. In truth it is a very masterpiece. Father Cyneric didn't pay Pell because he has misused all the money he'd been given to build Jésu's church here.'

"Up jumped the conceited priest again, shrieking, 'No! Monk boy not says true! Altar not good, I'm paid him naught! Naught!' I'm done naught wrong!'

"The elders put their heads close and talked quietly together. Then Danu rose to her feet and said, 'Now it seems we need ask if this front-piece can be brought here, unless mayhaps it has already been used for kindling.'

"I told her that I could run and fetch it and be back as quick as a heartbeat, and when she nodded, off I went. It was a small village, and it didn't take much time at all to run to my house, get the front-piece and bring it back. When I returned to the Tree of Wisdom, Tadgh was telling the people, and Cyneric, that the judgment of the council would be final, and that no amount of arguing about it later would change the outcome.

"So, I brought the front-piece up to the elders, unwrapped it and handed it to them, and then I held my breath for what seemed like a long, long time as the whole village watched as silent as midnight. Then Tadgh looked up and spoke to the people, 'Aye, he was right.'

"I was devastated. How could I have thought that somebody like me could make such a thing—and now the bully Cyneric would soon be walking away, sneering at me and the whole village. Those thoughts took less than a heartbeat, and then Tadgh continued, 'He was right, the monk was right—this is beautiful work. Pell should be paid for this work, should be paid, what should he be paid? I say, twenty pieces of silver.' And Danu said, 'Nay, twenty-five, at least.'

"Then the crowd was cheering again—for me!—and people were clapping me on the back and I was laughing and crying and so full of joy I didn't know want to do. But before I had time to take it all in, Danu raised her hand, and the crowd fell silent once more.

"She said, 'In the matter of Cyneric the Christian priest, we are decided that he is to pay Oisin what is owed to the Lazy Bull, that he is to pay the carpenter Eóghan for what is owed for the work he has done, and that he is to pay Pell twenty-five pieces of silver for this beautiful front-piece. He will also repay both Aodhan and Cathal, whose wives he has attempted to steal, in a manner to be agreed with them. Hear the judgment of your elders, and go your way in peace!'

"Now the people stood as the elders left, and then they started to scatter, talking one with another in groups of two and three. I looked for Papa, thinking mayhaps I had made him proud, but I didn't see him, him or Oisin. I thought the council was over, as there was no way to dispute or make any sort of appeal, but now the arrogant priest stood up and held up his right hand, as if he was an elder of the village. Nobody there would have given him such respect, but we all stopped to hear him, just for the curiosity of it.

"He pointed at the elders and bleated, 'People of village, hear me! This mans and old woman not … says not true. I'm done naught wrong! I'm not paid nobody naught!'

"Then, before Father Cyneric could even sit back down, Tadgh stood and said, quite sternly, 'Nay, priest. The council is decided, and you will pay what you owe.'

"Then Cyneric set his sail on a different tack. He said, 'Nay, I'm paid naught. I'm not have money, I'm can't paid, nobody, naught. I'm not have money.'

"The elders brought their heads together again, and after some discussion, Tadgh stood again, and said, 'Well do we understand having little or no money. So, we are decided that the people you owe are to give you time to raise the money to pay your debts. As we have just celebrated Imbolc, the birth of the new year, you have the entire year, until the next Imbolc, to earn the money you owe.'

"Cyneric leaned over Mellán to try to get his words right, and turned to the elders and said, 'How I'm earn money? I'm *sacerdos*'—here he turned to poor Mellán for the right word in Gaeilge—'I'm priest, I'm not earn money. I'm not paid naught, nobody! I'm done naught wrong!'

"Fiontan the pig farmer proclaimed that he could work for him, and I was thinking it would be just about right, but nobody paid him any mind. The elders just looked at him sternly, and Father Cyneric saw that his appeal was doomed to fail. So he changed tacks again. 'Nay. Not rule me. I'm Roman, I'm Briton, not this village. Not rule me, *episcopus* rule me. I'm not paid nobody naught! I'm done naught wrong!'

"He sat back down, and we shifted our attention back to the three elders, talking together under the Tree of Wisdom. The silence of the moment was almost oppressive—nobody had ever heard of anybody challenging the decision of the elders, never. It was so quiet I was afraid to take a deep breath for fear the people around me would hear it.

"Presently Tadgh called Mellán to him and they had a few words—later Mellán told me it was to find out what *episcopus* meant. Then Tadgh stood up and raised his right hand, just for the form of it, I suppose—he didn't need to be calling us to order. He said, 'The elders have discussed the priest's objections, and we find that he is right—we have no authority over him as a Roman, as a Briton, and as a priest of the Christian god. So we will send him back to Angleland!' The crowd roared our approval, and Tadgh bellowed out, 'The tide is pulling out just now, take him and put him in a boat and start him on his journey!'

"Father Cyneric tried to run away, and when they caught him, he resisted with all the strength he had, which was next to naught when four or five of the young men of the village came to haul him to the docks. He was wailing and squalling and yowling with all his might, until they wrapped him up in an old sail. I followed along, just because it was something you don't see very often, and I watched as they dumped him into an old rowing skiff and pushed it out into the ebbing tide.

"Now, to be honest with you, I thought this was too much, that the priest would die out there on the sea. So, I called out to Declan, another cousin and one of the young men who'd hauled him into the boat, 'We don't want to kill the old fool, do we?' Declan just laughed and said, 'Ah, nay—though mayhaps he might deserve it. Nay, the Wee Maiden there will go out and fetch him up in a little while, never fear.' The Wee Maiden was the little boat we used to welcome and guide heavier boats in to the dock."

Oswell was impressed with the justice of it and said so. Then he said, "So is that the end of the story of Father Cyneric?"

"Well, nay," the old man shook his head. "I wish it were, but it's not. But here my story took a dark, disastrous turn, and what happened to Father Cyneric was soon the least of my bothers."

All Gone So Terribly Wrong

Taking a deep breath, Pell continued his story. "After the meeting of the council, and after I saw Father Cyneric put out to sea, it felt like everybody in the village was coming up and clapping me on the back and congratulating me. I looked for Papa, and for Mellán, but I didn't see either one of them, so I went home to tell Mam the grand news."

"She didn't come to the council meeting?" Oswell asked.

"Oh, nay—she would never. She didn't—she wasn't ... accepted by the people in the village, because she'd taken up with a Roman soldier. Our neighbors thought that was a betrayal, and then after Áine died, well—nay, Mam didn't leave the house much at all. That was just the way of it.

"So, I took up the front-piece and trotted along home. It had been snowing lightly earlier, but now it was a heavy snow falling, and all the village was cloaked in white silence. As I came up to our little house, I heard Mam and Papa having a big noisy argument. I stopped outside the door, just to hear what it was they were squabbling about, and I was gutted to realize it was about me they were fighting.

"I heard my grandfather shout, 'He didn't tell me he was building a damn altóir and using my best damn cured walnut to boot!' I could tell Eóghan was more than a little drunk, and spoiling for a fight. Mam and I both knew it was best to give him a wide berth when he was like that, but on that terrible night, Mam stood up to him. She stood up for me.

"She said, 'But it is beautiful, the Council said it is, did they not?' "I heard something crashing inside the house, Papa knocking something over, mayhaps throwing something. He roared, 'What do they know about it, woman? And what do *you* know about it, for that matter? It was my walnut and my tools he was using, and what little talent I have rammed into his thick skull!'

"Then my mother said, 'But it was Pell who did the work, was it not?'

"Just then I opened the door, thinking it was time for me to stand up to the bully, so I saw when he slapped her face with the back of his hand, knocking her down. Then he just stood there, trying to understand what he'd just done, and I came and put myself between them. I was crying and shouting, 'Stop it, Papa—stop it!'

"He looked at me with madness in his eyes and yelled, 'You Roman bastard! Get out of my way! Get out of my house!' Then Mam struggled to her feet and said, 'Well, then—we'll go. We aren't welcome here, so we'll go!' But Papa just laughed at her and bellowed, 'Where will you go, you daft besom? No man would have you, sure as my eyes.'

"So, Mam stood up and wiped a little blood from the corner of her mouth where he'd slapped her, and said, 'Then I won't have no man, that's all. Me and Pell will make our own way, so right we will.' But Papa wasn't the manner of man that could ever back down, even when he knew he was wrong. He said, 'Aye, you're just blowing the air around with talk like that. You can't leave here, you'd never last a week, you and the little Roman bastard.'

"Now I turned with my right side toward my grandfather, the way his brother had taught me, and raised up my hands like I was ready to throw a punch. I said, 'You need to step away, old man. You'll not be treating my Mam in such a way as that!'

"'Or what?' he said. 'What will you do, Son of Nobody?' His words—those words—froze me, froze me solid, pushed all the air out of my body. And old Eóghan saw his advantage and stepped closer to me, so I could smell the stink of ale on his breath, and he laughed at me. He murmured, 'That's about right: you're just the Son of Nobody, aren't you? That's what they say about you—just a fatherless little nobody, aren't you?'"

The heretic paused here, pushing away the pain he was surprised to find still had so much power over him, even after all the years and miles between that moment and this. The younger man, with a younger man's impatience, whispered, "Then what happened?"

"Well," the old man continued, "then I pulled back my left hand to punch him in the belly, but I hesitated, just for a moment—this was my Mam's father after all—and in that moment, he drew back and hit me, hit me hard. His fist took me on my left jaw and knocked me clean down. I think I might have gone into the darkness for a little bit, and when I came back, I looked up to see my Mam waving a wooden candlestick around, brandishing it like a sword. Papa was trying to get it away from her, and she was holding on to it like it was the only thing in the world that could save her. Then before I could get my legs and feet to cooperate enough to stand myself up, he shoved her away from him and she fell. I heard her head hit the stone of our hearth, I heard the crack of her neck, and I knew right then that my mother was no longer in this world."

The old man paused, lost in his remembrance. "I live with that moment every day, that terrible moment when I knew she was dead. It comes to me in my dreams sometimes, that terrible moment that haunts me still. My sweet Mam, and her hard-hearted Papa, their lives ruined. As for me, I was just left wishing I'd said or done something to stop it, or mayhaps it was something I should not have done or said. Ah, it was a horrible, dreadful thing.

"I crawled over to her lying there and pleaded with her to stay with me. I was crying so I could hardly see and trying to get her to sit up and kissing her poor cheeks, but ... she was gone. I was dimly aware of Papa crying, telling me it was an accident, that he never meant for it to happen, but I didn't listen, I didn't care what he had to say. I took her up in my arms, rocking her like a baby, just abandoning myself to my grief. After a time, I looked up to see that Papa was no longer there.

"I knew where he'd gone, he was down at the Bull, sure as snows in the winter, and there was some part of me that wanted to go and hit him, to hurt him as much as I could before he or some of his drinking buddies could take me down. But then there was another part of me that wanted naught more to do with him, never again. If I'm to be honest with you, I didn't know what I wanted to do, except that I wanted to get out of that damn house, now that all the love was gone out of it.

"So, I took up my heavy cloak and packed up some small-clothes and my spare tunic and heaviest stockings in a bag, made sure I had my good knife and a flint and striker, and I slipped out into the night. I was about out of the door when I remembered the front-piece, so I went back to get that as well, because it was the only thing I owned of any value, and to keep Papa from having it, or destroying it. I heard the door closing behind me, but I didn't look back. I walked away without knowing where I was going, just walking away from there.

"I stood there at the edge of the tree line, watching the snow as it covered up my boots, and then I thought mayhaps it would be best to just let the cold take me. Many a time I'd heard of a body getting caught out in the snow, and people said it wasn't such a bad way to die, that the cold just slowed you down 'til you fell asleep, and your breathing stopped.

"Then I thought if the story Mellán told me about Jésu was true, I'd see my Mam and Áine again, and that would be no bad thing. And then—and this is what saved me from an icy death—I thought I ought to tell my brother Mellán a fare well. It would hurt him, I thought, if I were to die without telling him. So, before my mind made itself up, my feet were already taking me to the place where Mellán had been staying with that fool of a priest.

"When I got there, I knocked on the door and waited a bit, and then I knocked again. After another bit, the door opened just enough to let a whisper through, and Mellán said, 'Who is it?'

"I answer, 'It's me—Pell. Will you let me in?'

"He opened the door and I went in to see that he was just sitting there alone in the dark, and that he was in a bad way. Then I forgot all about letting the cold take me away, and I asked him what he was going to do now.

"He moaned, 'Oh, but I don't know, do I? It was never supposed to be like this, Pell—I was just sent to translate for the priest. We were supposed to sing out the good news of the love of God in his blesséd son Jésu, but it's all gone so terribly wrong now. What can I do? Where can I go? Oh, Pell, I'm just lost, I … I don't know what to do.'

"Then were sitting there, both of us lost and rudderless like a sailing boat with no wind in our sails, and there was a knock at the door. He didn't answer it, and presently a voice from outside whispered, 'Mellán! It's me, Rory!' It was another cousin, ten or twelve years older than me, a fisherman in the village. I nodded to Mellán, and he let him in. Rory was surprised to see me there, but his message was too urgent to fret with that.

"Rory said, 'Mellán, you have to pack up and leave. There's some at the Bull—the smith's boys Darragh and Deaglán and a few others—who're saying we ought to have put you in that rowing skiff with your master. They're saying they want naught more to do with you or your Jésu, and they're drinking in some courage to come and fetch you up and put you out to sea. You have to leave, Mellán, you have to leave now!'

"And then, clear as the stars on a moonless night, I saw our path ahead. I thanked Rory, who faded away into the night, and then I said, 'Listen, Mellán. You need to leave, and so do I. My Mam is dead, killed at the hand of my grandfather, whose mind is … broken. I need to leave Port Láirge, to go away from here forever. Mayhaps I'll be leaving Éire, and mayhaps take a boat across to Angleland, and see what fortune awaits me there.' I looked over at Mellán, but he made no response, so I kept talking. 'I'm thinking it would be safer and better for both of us to go together than for each of us to be going alone.'

"Well, now I'd said more than he could hear all at once. He said, 'Your Mam's dead?' I said, 'Aye, and it was her own father that killed her. And now—hear me, Brother Mellán—now I have to go. And you have to go, do you understand? So we'll go together. Pack up some things, and let's go, before Darragh and Deaglán and those boys get here.' He sat there whelmed by all of it, and I took his shoulders in my hands and said it again, 'Mellán—let's go!'

"So, he stood up, still lost in all of it, and I asked him if he had a bag to carry things. He opened the chest under the window and got out an old cloth bag, and I told him to get some of his small-clothes and stockings and such. No sooner had we put those things in the bag but we heard the sounds of noisy drunk men approaching, talking about what they were going to do to the young monk, and I whispered, 'Mellán—is there a back door out of here?' He just shook his head and I murmured, 'Then it's out the window for us, now!'

"I opened the window and almost had to push poor Mellán through it; I came just after him and thought to close it behind us so they wouldn't know we'd just come through it. Not having any particular plan as to which way we ought to go, my feet just took us along the path toward the River Suir where I went to check the fish-traps. There was a little shed there that I knew was used to give shelter to those as needed some warm on cold days, so there was always some firewood and things to mend the traps and such, and I thought it would be good to get us out of the snow.

"Mellán didn't ask where we were going; he just followed me until we came to the shed. It was mighty cold, and dark as the inside of a cow, but he followed me inside. Soon I was fumbling around trying to get a fire lit, but I was too clumsy and cold and impatient, and Mellán came along and took the flint and striker from my hand, shred up a little of the bark of one of the logs in the shed and struck up a fire, swift as a sneeze. We were almost overcome by the smoke inside that little shed until he propped open a flap of leather up at the top of the roof to let some of it out. Some little bit of snow came in, but it was better than all that smoke.

"The shed warmed up quickly and the smoke cleared, and right soon we were as comfortable as we could be. I was very tired after the twists and turns of the day, and I was just about to drowse off when I heard Mellán singing, real soft, thinking I wouldn't hear him. The song was in Latin, and in truth I couldn't catch much of it, but it sounded like he was singing a song about a pasture. It was a lingering tune, and Mellán has a beautiful voice. I was still trying to listen to him when I fell hard asleep.

"The next morning, I woke up hoping all that I just told you was just a bad dream, that my Mam would be getting ready for the morning meal, but then I looked around and saw where I was, and I knew it was all true. I didn't see Mellán. The fire had dwindled down to embers, so I put some small pieces of wood on it until it livened back up, and then I stepped outside. I saw Mellán, who was trying to figure out how to get to one of the fish-traps without taking a cold bath in the river.

"So, I sang out, 'Ho, brother Mellán! What are you about so early this morning?' as cheerfully as I could. But Mellán was grumpy, and said, 'I can see the fish in the trap, but I can't get to it, and I'm about to starve!' Well, there was a rope to pull the trap out of the water that my friend hadn't seen, and when I pulled it up, we've got three pretty trout and a gurnard. I threw the gurnard and the smallest of the trout back into the river and set about cleaning the other two that were to break our fast. I found an old skillet in the shed, some oil and a rag to wipe out the rust and took the fish inside to cook them over our little fire. We had no salt or spice, but we were both hungry, and that helped the fish to be delicious.

"There was an old leather water bag in the shed, and I admit I was surprised it held water, but I rinsed it out and filled it with fresh clean water from the river, so we had all the water we could drink and all the fish we could eat.

"After a time, and before the peaceful took us over completely, I said, 'Mellán, we have to go.'

"Mellán answered, 'Where? Where can we go?'

"I didn't have any plans, but I wanted to sound like I knew what I was talking about, so I said, 'To Angleland, back to your monk house.'

"Mellán looked at me all sad and tired, looking much older than his years, and said, 'Ah, Pell my brother—it's an awful long journey back to Erith, all the way down past Londinium, it is. And to get to Angleland, you know we'll be needing to cross over the sea. That means we'll be needing to arrange for passage on a boat, and that means we'll be needing silver, which is just what we don't have.'

"He looked so forlorn I just wanted to happy him up some, and I said, 'Have a wee bit of faith, brother monk. Your Jésu hasn't abandoned you, and you needn't go abandon him.'

"Mellán smiled a little at that, and said, 'Aye, you're right, brother skeptic. We'll trust in our Lord, who'll guide our feet along right pathways.'

"I didn't know about any of that, but I didn't say so. Instead, I said, 'Somebody will be coming to check these traps, and it would be better if we were gone before he arrives.' He was lost in his own thoughts now, so I asked, 'So—which way is it to Erith?'

"To be honest," Pell continued, "I didn't really know where we were most of the time we were travelling, to Angleland and all the way to Jerusalem and back. I could usually tell you which way was east in the morning, or west in the afternoon, or north after the stars came out, but which way we were to go was a complete mystery; I just never had the knack of it. But Mellán knew, so I followed after him.

"We started heading more or less up the coast, with it in to mind to come to Baile Átha Cliath where Mellán's people were from. A fisherman ferried us across the river to Baile Hac, just of his goodness, and we set out across the country. He told us Dún Canann was where we ought to be going and pointed us in the right direction.

"But here now: I knew about catching fish and preparing them to eat, but neither of us knew the first thing about hunting, nor even which plants in the fields and woods were good for eating. In very truth I was fearful that we might starve that first night of travel, until we saw the light of a farmhouse out in the middle of naught at all. The farmer was leery of us but told us we could sleep in the barn with his cattle, for which we were grateful, and by and by his wife brought out a loaf of barley bread still warm from the oven and a bit of hard cheese, which was the saving of us.

"The next day we walked on to Dún Canann, and there by the very grace of God we met a man who touched our lives from that day to this: Twedwr."

Chapter X

I Am as You See Me

Pell paused, as his story began to shift. "I've mentioned Twedwr to you already, but now it's time to start his part of the story. He planted these trees we're leaning up against. He turned out to be a good friend to us, but it didn't look like it would take that path when first we met him.

"We'd never have noticed him at all but for the three young men who'd surrounded him. We saw what looked like an old drunk sitting against the outside wall of a tavern, and these boyos were taunting him and trying to take something away from him, something in an old leather satchel, something he was holding onto like his very life depended on it. When I saw one of the three fellas was about to throw a stone at him, I heard Mellán telling me we don't know what this was about, and that we shouldn't get involved, but I was already moving into the middle of their little circle and telling them to step away.

"Aye well, I've never been much for minding my own business when I see a bully ill-treating somebody who's smaller or weaker, or who's clearly outnumbered. Now the three boyos turned their eyes on me, while the old man was struggling to stand up. I could see he wasn't likely to be much help if it came to a fight, so I was grateful when *Mellán* stepped between them to stand beside me. Of course, I knew he wouldn't be much good in a fight, either, but he was doing his best to look menacing, and the three boyos of a sudden didn't like the balance of things—their easy prey had become more difficult.

"So, they threw some insults and threats at us, but they came no closer, and after a time, they went their way, fading into the gloom as the sun was almost below the horizon. The old man watched them leave and then sank down to where he'd been when we first saw him, propped against the tavern. He sank down slow, like a water-skin with a leak. I looked over at Mellán, who shrugged, and I said to the old man, 'Ho, friend—are you well?' He didn't seem to have heard me, so I said again, louder this time, 'Ho, friend—are you still alive and with us now?'

"His ruddy hair had got some gray in it, and his beard was going white, but as I looked at him, I saw he wasn't as old as I'd thought. I reckon mayhaps it was the dirt and neglect that made him look older. Then, as I looked a little closer, it came to me that here was a man who's completely given up on himself.

"When he looked up at me, it was from the bottom of a deep well, that same deep well I'd seen in Papa's boggy eyes after a long night full of ale. So, I was thinking I've already had my fill of dealing with drunkards, and I was turning to leave him to wallow in the misery he's made for himself, but Mellán just stood where he was, and said, 'Listen, friend. We're reaching out to you, to see if we could be of some help to you. If you think there's aught in you worth saving, we'll try, but if not, we'll just be on our way and bother you no more.'

"The old man made no response, didn't twitch a muscle, and when Mellán nodded to me, we started to walk away. Then behind me I heard a soggy voice saying, 'Thank you.'

"Well, it wasn't much, but it was enough, and both Mellán and I turned around. The man looked up and rubbed some of the dirt around on his face and pushed some of the hair out of his eyes. Then of a sudden he grinned like a little boy caught stealing a spoon of his mam's sugar, and said, 'Aye well, I might have had a wee bit too much last night.' I like a man who can admit when he's acted a fool, so I held out my hand to him. He took it, and I helped him to his feet and said, 'My name is Pell.'

"He looked at me and said, 'Aye, Pell, well met.' Then he looked at Mellán and said, 'And what's your name, friend?' Mellán told him his name, and now the man smiled, and wanted to know where we were from, and where we were going.

"So Mellán started, 'Well, I was born …' but I interrupted him before he got the wind fully in his sail, saying, 'You have a name just as we do, friend. Who are you now, where are you from, and what are you about?'

"He answered, 'Well, there's a flock of questions to answer all at the once. My name is Twedwr, I'm from here in Dún Canann, this wee town you see all around you. As for what I'm about, that's as much a mystery to me as it is to yourselves. I am as you see me, and you see me as I am.'

"Mellán asked, 'Why were those fellas all circled around you so? And what were they were trying to steal away from you?'

"The man rubbed at his face again, and said, 'Ah, well—those busters were just some of the local toughs. They go hunting and snooping around the streets and alleys to find them as are sleeping off the night before, and they rob them of their money, or shoes, or whatever they can take.' So I asked, 'And what was it they were trying to take from you?'

"Then the man did something I thought was a bit strange at the time—he looked at us like he was measuring us, judging us, like he was wondering whether he could trust us. Then I suppose he decided he could, and he reached down and picked up the satchel and took up ..."

"That harp!" Oswell exclaimed. "This is the other Druid you knew!"

"Aye—now you're listening quicker than I'm talking," Pell nodded. "Well, he picked up that harp up out of its leather satchel and showed it to us like it was his greatest treasure, which of course it was. It was much grander than ever my uncle Eóchaidh's little *cláirseach* was, and I was itching to see how it would feel to my fingers and sound in my ears. He saw it in my face, and asked, 'Do you play the harp then, Pell?'

"Well, Mellán didn't know aught about my uncle's harp or about me playing it, so he was looking at me with considerable curiosity when I answered, 'Aye—a bit, mayhaps.'

"The man whispered, 'And where would you be learning such a thing as that?'

"When I told him that my great-uncle had a little *cláirseach* and all, the man leaned in close and whispered, 'Hush! Hush now. And who's … never mind, never mind that now.' Then he stood back up, and said, 'I think I've an idea that might please you—in gratitude for your saving me and my harp from those ruffians, mayhaps I can buy the two of you a little bit of supper, how do you think of that?'

"Well, it was plain we didn't have any other plans and were in no position to refuse the offer of a free meal. And it was just as plain to me that I wanted a closer look at that beautiful harp, so we accepted his invitation.

"The sign over the tavern door showed a grand view of a great bird looking back over his back at us with his arse prominently displayed: the Bustard's Butt it was called. The woman behind the bar seemed glad to see Twedwr and called him by name, and he told her he'd be wanting three plates tonight—one for himself and one for each of his two friends. Just a short while after Mellán and I found a table and sat ourselves down, Twedwr came along, his face washed and his hair pushed back and tied with a piece of cord, which made him look more presentable.

"In a short time, along came the woman from the bar, with three bowls of stew and three jars of ale. We had to wait for Mellán to preach us a blessing, but it wasn't too much. We'd walked awful far that day, and if I'm to be honest with you, I was as glad of the ale as I was of the stew—fish and turnips it was, served with rich dark bread a day or two old, but soft enough after you sopped it in the broth. After we'd eaten and put back most of the ale, I asked, 'Will you let me see your harp again, Twedwr?'

"He looked across the table at me and said, 'Aye, and gladly.' He pulled the harp out of the satchel and put it on the table between us, but he kept his hand on it. I noticed some of his fingers were bent wrong as he said, 'The magic of the music has her hand on you, then.' I nodded, and he continued, 'Were you saying you've got an uncle who has a harp then?' I was wondering what he was about now, so I answered, 'Nay—I didn't say that,' just to watch his face. But I didn't read any sort of mischief in his eyes, just a heavy disappointment, so I said, 'It was a *cláirseach*, and it was my great-uncle who had it.'

"Now of a sudden, the man was intense. He asked, 'What was his name, this uncle of yours?' I said, 'Eóchaidh,' and he wondered,

'Not Eóchaidh ap Eóghan, is he?' Now I had to stop and consider
for a bit—my grandfather was named after his father Eóghan, and
Eóchaidh was his brother, so—aye, that would make him Eóchaidh
ap Eóghan, Eóchaidh the son of Eóghan. All that took a heartbeat or
two, and I said, 'Aye.'

"Now Twedwr sat back, taking his hand from his harp and
saying, 'Eóchaidh ap Eóghan. I've often wondered what might have
happened to him. Is he well, this uncle of yours?'

"'Aye,' I answered, 'or so he was last I heard aught from or about
him, which was—oh, two winters gone now. His brother is my
grandfather, Eóghan the carpenter in Port Láirge.'

"'Ah,' he said, 'Eóchaidh was never one to stay too long under
one roof, I suppose.' Mellán and I looked at one another just to share
our ignorance a bit, and I asked, 'And how is it that you know my
great-uncle Eóchaidh then?'

"Twedwr looked at us again, to reckon how much he could trust
us, I suppose, and then he said, quite softly, 'He was a teacher of
mine, when I was learning the Old Ways, the ways of the Druids.'

"I asked him, 'Are you a Druid?'

"Twedwr answered, 'Aye, but not much of one.' He waited for a
response, but we didn't know what to say, and we didn't say it until
he went on, 'Eóchaidh left our settlement a year or so before I did—I
heard that he got into a fight and killed a Roman soldier who'd left
a poor woman—some kin of his, mayhaps—with two more mouths
to feed, and never sent her a single coin to help. The Druids can't
abide killing, so he had to be banished. He was a good man, though,
Eóchaidh was, a good man, and a good friend.'

"Then I said, 'Mayhaps that woman who had two children by a
Roman soldier was my Mam. She had a hard way of it. I never met
my father.'

"Twedwr said, 'Ah, I'm sorry, lad. It was hard on you as well, I
can read it in your face.' Then, to snatch us out of the gloom, Mellán
asked me, 'Can you play the harp? Did your great-uncle Eóchaidh
teach you to play aught on it?'

"Twedwr pushed it over to my side of the table now, and my
curiosity brought me to pick it up, saying 'Aye, well—we'll see.' It

was considerably bigger and heavier than Eóchaidh's *cláirseach*, and there were more strings—twenty-one, when his had only fourteen. The strings were different, too: later I found out they were made of gut, while the *cláirseach* strings were horsehair. When I strummed it a little, it sang out clear and fine, but I knew as soon as I heard it four or five of the strings were out of harmony, like they were too loose or too tight. I wondered how the Druid could have let his harp get so badly out of tune.

"I fumbled around with it for a time or two and found the strings that needed a little touch. Before too long, I was feeling easy enough with it to play the first notes of the first song ever I learned: 'The Power of One.' I wasn't meaning to sing it, you understand, but I was no sooner through the first measures of it that Twedwr started to sing it with his fine strong voice, and then I just joined in."

Oswell said, "Excuse me, sir. . . . "

"Aye? What is it that's vexing you?"

"Well, I think it might help the story if you'd sing this song, if you don't mind."

"Oh, well—aye then, if you think it might help the story."

Chapter XI

The Power of One

Pell leaned over and reached into the old leather satchel and pulled out a beautiful harp. He held it out for the younger man to admire and then leaned back against his rowan tree and tuned the harp for a minute or two and cleared his throat. Then he started playing a simple tune, warming his fingers up a bit before he started singing.

> "The Divine Mother, the Star in the Twilight,
> > sings to me in the voice of an Owl:
> 'O my child, my beloved, wayward child—what will you ask?'
> 'Fairest of Heaven,' sing I, 'teach me a song!
> > 'Sing me a song of the Power of One,
> > > until my heart knows it complete.'
> 'One!' hoots the Owl,
> > 'the Power of One is united, whole and full,
> > the Highest Holy, the Unseen Giver,
> > > the Spring of Life.'"

The old man stopped then, and said, "Aye, and after that first verse, the other people in that tavern started taking some notice. There wasn't much by way of entertainment then or there, so two or three of the people there moved a little closer, just to hear the music."

Oswell nodded, and asked, "Did you continue with the song?" Pell nodded back, and sang on:

> "The Divine Mother, the Star in the Twilight,
> > sings to me in the voice of a Wolf:
> 'O my child, my beloved wayward child—what will you ask?'
> 'Fairest of Heaven,' sing I, 'teach me a song!

'Sing me a song of the Power of Two,
    until my heart knows it complete.'
'Two!' howls the Wolf,
    'The Power of Two is the bright lively Day
    and the dark hushed Night—
    the Sun and Moon dancing across the sky,
    and One is the Highest Holy, the Spring of Life.'

"The Divine Mother, the Star in the Twilight,
    sings to me in the voice of a Badger:
'O my child, my beloved wayward child—what will you ask?'
'Fairest of Heaven,' sing I, 'teach me a song!
    'Sing me a song of the Power of Three,
    until my heart knows it complete.'
'Three!' barks the Badger,
    'The Power of Three is the Virtue of Word,
    the Beauty of Song, and the Harmony of Harp.
    Two are the Sun and Moon dancing across the sky,
        and One is the Highest Holy, the Spring of Life.'"

Pell looked at the younger man and spoke. "And now there were people coming into the tavern, hearing the music from out on the street and such. And the woman behind the bar was as busy as she's ever been, and the owner of the tavern bustled in to stand beside me, trying to look like he's got something to do with it. And aye, before you ask it, the song continued:

"The Divine Mother, the Star in the Twilight,
    sings to me in the tiny voice of a Firefly:
'O my child, my beloved wayward child—what will you ask?'
'Fairest of Heaven,' sing I, 'teach me a song!
    'Sing me a song of the Power of Four,
    until my heart knows it complete.'
'Four!' flashes the Firefly,
    'The Power of Four is the Courses of Breeze and Wind,
        whence they come, and whither they go.
Three is the Beauty of Song,

Two are the Sun and Moon dancing across the sky,
    and One is the Highest Holy, the Spring of Life.'

"The Divine Mother, the Star in the Twilight,
    sings to me in the voice of a Rat:
'O my child, my beloved wayward child—what will you ask?'
'Fairest of Heaven,' sing I, 'teach me a song!
    'Sing me a song of the Power of Five,
        until my heart knows it complete.'
'Five!' chitters the Rat,
    'The Power of Five is how we know the world:
        Sight, smell, hearing, touch and taste.
    Four are the Courses of Breeze and Wind,
    Three is the Beauty of Song,
    Two are the Sun and Moon dancing across the sky,
        and One is the Highest Holy, the Spring of Life.'"

Pell continued, "Somewhere around verse five or six, the people in the tavern were starting to understand how the song was going, and some of them started joining in. You seem a clever fella, Oswell, and you'll surely be smart enough to sing along with me when you can now:

"The Divine Mother, the Star in the Twilight,
    sings to me in the voice of a Cicada:
'O my child, my beloved wayward child—what will you ask?'
'Fairest of Heaven,' sing I, 'teach me a song!
    'Sing me a song of the Power of Six,
        until my heart knows it complete.'
'Six!' buzzes the Cicada,
    'The Power of Six is the six Sacred Bards
        who guard and sing the First Songs.
    Five are the ways we know the world,
    Four are the Courses of Breeze and Wind,
    Three is the Beauty of Song,
    Two are the Sun and Moon dancing across the sky,
        and One is the Highest Holy, the Spring of Life.'

"The Divine Mother, the Star in the Twilight,
        sings to me in the voice of a Wild Cat:
'O my child, my beloved wayward child—what will you ask?'
'Fairest of Heaven,' sing I, 'teach me a song!
        'Sing me a song of the Power of Seven,
                until my heart knows it complete.'
'Seven!' mews the Wild Cat,
        'The Power of Seven is the seven planets
                that shine unblinking among my sister Stars.
        Six are they who guard and sing the First Songs.
        Five are the ways we know the world,
        Four are the Courses of Breeze and Wind,
        Three is the Beauty of Song,
        Two are the Sun and Moon dancing across the sky,
                and One is the Highest Holy, the Spring of Life.'

"The Divine Mother, the Star in the Twilight,
        sings to me in the voice of a Nightjar:
'O my child, my beloved wayward child—what will you ask?'
'Fairest of Heaven,' sing I, 'teach me a song!
        'Sing me a song of the Power of Eight,
                until my heart knows it complete.'
'Eight!' chirps the Nightjar,
        'The Power of Eight is the eight healing plants
                to be learned by those who tend the wellbeing of others,
        Seven are the unblinking planets among my sister Stars,
        Six are they who guard and sing the First Songs,
        Five are the ways we know the world,
        Four are the Courses of Breeze and Wind,
        Three is the Beauty of Song,
        Two are the Sun and Moon dancing across the sky,
                and One is the Highest Holy, the Spring of Life.'

"The Divine Mother, the Star in the Twilight,
        sings to me in the voice of a Hedgehog:
'O my child, my beloved wayward child—what will you ask?'
'Fairest of Heaven,' sing I, 'teach me a song!
        'Sing me a song of the Power of Nine,
                until my heart knows it complete.'

'Nine!' snuffles the Hedgehog,
    'The Power of Nine is thrice Three—
        Nine are the Sacred Trees in their Circled Grove.
        who shelter and gather us in wisdom.
    Eight are the plants to restore and heal,
    Seven are the unblinking planets among my sister Stars,
    Six are they who guard and sing the First Songs.
    Five are the ways we know the world,
    Four are the Courses of Breeze and Wind,
    Three is the Beauty of Song,
    Two are the Sun and Moon dancing across the sky,
        and One is the Highest Holy, the Spring of Life.'

"The Divine Mother, the Star in the Twilight,
    sings to me in the voice of a Mouse:
'O my child, my beloved wayward child—what will you ask?'
'Fairest of Heaven,' sing I, 'teach me a song!
    'Sing me a song of the Power of Ten,
        until my heart knows it complete.'
'Ten!' squeaks the Mouse,
    'The Power of Ten is both Hands Shaping the World –
        root and stone and sea
    Nine are the Sacred Trees in their Circled Grove.
    Eight are the plants to restore and heal,
    Seven are the unblinking planets among my sister Stars,
    Six are they who guard and sing the First Songs.
    Five are the ways we know the world,
    Four are the Courses of Breeze and Wind,
    Three is the Beauty of Song,
    Two are the Sun and Moon dancing across the sky,
        and One is the Highest Holy, the Spring of Life.'

"The Divine Mother, the Star in the Twilight,
    sings to me in the voice of a Fox:
'O my child, my beloved wayward child—what will you ask?'
'Fairest of Heaven,' sing I, 'teach me a song!
    'Sing me a song of the Power of Eleven,
        until my heart knows it complete.'
'Eleven!' yips the Fox,

'The Power of Eleven is the ways of a Woman with a Man,
    mysterious and strong.
Ten is the Shaping of the World
Nine are the Sacred Trees in their Circled Grove,
Eight are the plants to restore and heal,
Seven are the unblinking planets among my sister Stars,
Six are they who guard and sing the First Songs.
Five are the ways we know the world,
Four are the Courses of Breeze and Wind,
Three is the Beauty of Song,
Two are the Sun and Moon dancing across the sky,
    and One is the Highest Holy, the Spring of Life.'

"The Divine Mother, the Star in the Twilight,
    sings to me in the Nightingale's voice:
'O my child, my beloved wayward child—what will you ask?'
'Fairest of Heaven,' sing I, 'teach me a song!
    'Sing me a song of the Power of Twelve,
        until my heart knows it complete.'
'Twelve!' whirs the Nightingale,
    'The Power of Twelve is the coming of Winter,
        Twelve are the Needs of a Family in Snow
Eleven are the ways of a woman with a man,
    mysterious and strong
Ten is the Shaping of the World,
Nine are the Sacred Trees in their Circled Grove,
Eight are the plants to restore and heal,
Seven are the unblinking planets among my sister Stars,
Six are they who guard and sing the First Songs,
Five are the ways we know the world,
Four are the Courses of Breeze and Wind,
Three is the Beauty of Song,
Two are the Sun and Moon dancing across the sky,
    and One is the Highest Holy, the Spring of Life.'"

The old man's song stopped and he said, "Now I stopped playing, thinking that was the end of the song, and the people there in the tavern were all clapping and stamping their feet on the ground, but

Twedwr looked at me curiously, and sang out real slow, adding a verse I didn't know:

"The Divine Mother, the Star in the Twilight,
    sings to me in her own voice:
'O my child, my beloved wayward child—what will you ask?'
'Fairest of Heaven,' sing I, 'teach me a song!
    Sing me a song of the Power of the Uncounted,
        until my heart knows it full.'
'The Uncounted!' she sings in her own true voice,
'The Power of the Uncounted is the Truth we cannot Know—
    the Infinite stars in the Heavens,
    the limitless ambitions of greedy men,
        and the Mind of the Highest Holy, whole and full,
        Who is and ever was—One!'"

Pell continued, "Some of the people started clapping and stamping again, but still Twedwr wasn't done. He nodded at me meaningfully, and sang, soft and slow, but getting louder and faster as he went so I had to play fast to keep up with him:

"Twelve are the Needs of a Family in Snow
Eleven are the ways of a woman with a man,
    mysterious and strong
    Ten is the Shaping of the World,
    Nine are the Sacred Trees in their Circled Grove,
Eight are the plants to restore and heal,
Seven are the unblinking planets among my sister Stars,
Six are they who guard and sing the First Songs,
Five are the ways we know the world,
Four are the Courses of Breeze and Wind,
Three is the Beauty of Song,
Two are the Sun and Moon dancing across the sky,
    and One is the Mind of the Highest Holy, whole and full,
        Who is and ever was—One!"

Finishing his song, Pell continued, "Now the people waited a few heartbeats before they started clapping, just to be sure he was really finished. He picked up his cup and drained the rest of his ale, and the people were clapping and stamping so the whole place felt like it was shaking. It was a heady drink, like that night under the Tree of Wisdom when the whole village was cheering for me and my front-piece.

"The owner of the tavern leaned down over me and whispered, 'Play us another one, lad.' I looked over to Twedwr and said, 'This man says he wants us to play another, but I don't know what you know. Do you know 'A Pony in Spring'?'

"Twedwr shook his head and asked if I knew 'The Lay of King Llew', and I told him I didn't. Now the people were getting impatient, and the tavern owner could see his windfall melting away.

"He said, 'Play us another tune, and I'll give you your room for the night.'

"So I told Twedwr what the tavern-man said, and he said, 'I've got an idea brewing around here, I think—aye, that ought to work— just play the same chords as "The Power of One," none of the fancy fretting around but just the chords, and play it about twice as lively as you played it just then. I've got another song that'll fit with that same tune, or close enough. It's shorter, and simpler, but I'm sure you can make it work.'

"So, I played the opening chords a bit livelier, and the people were all keeping quiet as codfish, and then Twedwr sang 'The Beltane Fire.'"

"Will you sing it for me?" Oswell implored.

"Oh, aye," Pell agreed. "Well, that first night, we botched it up a few times, until harp and voice found the same pace—but it goes like this:

"The Beltane fire now is set, aye—stack it high!
Now call together the Beltane dancers
Lads and lasses over hill and glen, as we
Come to bring the summer days,
    aye, we come to bring the summer days.

"Ah, it's Summer herself we dance to call
The milder days of blooms and blossoms

Warmer days ahead, my friends, as we
Come to bring the summer days,
    aye, we come to bring the summer days.

"Now the lads, now the lasses
Jump high! to harp and drum, flute and lyre
Now the lasses, now the lads, as we
Come to bring the summer days,
    aye, we come to bring the summer days.

"Look for the flowers, listen for the birdsong
Wait for the thunderful clouds to roll away
We'll light the Beltane fire and jump it, as we
Come to bring the summer days,
    aye, we come to bring the summer days.

"Now the rams, now the ewes
Soon the fire to grow the herd
Now the ewes, now the lambs, as we
Come to bring the summer days,
    aye, we come to bring the summer days."

Pell continued, "The tavern-man was pleased, and of course he wanted us to play another. Twedwr and I talked about it, but we couldn't find another song we both knew just then—in very truth I didn't know many at all—and Twedwr whispered 'Let's just sing "The Power of One" again,' so we did, this time with everybody singing along as best they could, and it all went over a treat, so we sang 'The Beltane Fire' again, this time with me and Mellán singing a little bit of harmony.

"Now the tavern-man—Riordan his name was—said, 'If you'll play another tune, a different tune, I'll forget that you owe me for your supper and bring you another jar of ale for free.' Well, I couldn't think of another song we both know, and Twedwr was thinking hard but it didn't look like he was finding aught he thought I'd know, when Mellán told me, 'If you can play that last wee bit of "The Power of One," but play it proper and slow and all, I know a song that might fit.' So, we worked out which bit of the song he wanted me to play, and he sang us a song.

"Now, Mellán has a beautiful voice, not rowdy, but haunting, and clearly coming from his heart. And I mean to tell you, when he sang that night, and many another night after, of a fact there was surely some style of magic loosed on all those who heard it."

The old man nodded before the younger man could ask him if he'd sing the song Mellán sang, tightened a string and cleared his throat, and playing the harp softly, sang in a gentle tenor voice:

"Dominus regit me, et nihil mihi deerit:
  in loco pascuae ibi me collocavit.
Super aquam refectionis educavit me,
  animam meam convertit.
Deduxit me super semitas justitiae,
  propter nomen suum.
Nam, etsi ambulavero in medio umbrae mortis,
  non timebo mala, quoniam tu mecum es.
  Virga tua, et baculus tuus, ipsa me consolata sunt.
Parasti in conspectu meo mensam,
  adversus eos qui tribulant me;
  impinguasti in oleo caput meum;
  et calix meus inebrians quam praeclarus est!
Et misericordia tua subsequetur me omnibus
  diebus vitae meae;
  et ut inhabitem in domo Domini,
  in longitudinem dierum."

Oswell gasped and shouted excitedly, "That's Psalm Twenty-Three!"

The old man smiled and put the harp back into its satchel. "The people in the tavern didn't know that, though, did they? Nobody there knew whether to laugh or cry, to cheer or keep their silence. It was clear that they were all right touched by it, they all felt the magic of the singing; they just didn't know what they ought to do about it.

"Well, to be honest with you, I was just as dumbstruck. Mellán sang with the voice of the sea and the moon in the sky and the leaves in autumn, tender and soft and beautifully pure. It was the tavern owner who clapped his hands first, and then the place went up like a haystack afire.

"Then the young lass who'd been making eyes at me—oh, I didn't tell you there was a young lass making eyes at me, but there she was all the same—that same lass asked Mellán, 'What did that song say?' And Mellán was about to tell her when Twedwr stood up on his feet and looked at Mellán saying, 'I'll tell them, shall I, lad?'

Then he turned to the people and said, 'Hear now the tale of "The Fair Maiden's Regret."' And he went on to spin out a yarn about a beautiful princess seducing a young dragon to steal his fire, and then feeling the guilts and remorses that she tricked such a beautiful and noble beast."

Oswell said, "What? Why did he do that?"

Pell laughed and said, "That's just what we wanted to know, and later, when we asked Twedwr, he said that the people around there were resentful of Romans. Some of them suspected Mellán had been singing in Latin, and he thought it would be best if we herded them in a different direction. And he loved telling stories, did Twedwr.

"After that, Riordan the tavern owner said to all the people there, 'Thank you, friends! Come back on the morrow, and we'll see if we can persuade our friends here to delight us again.' There was some grumbling, but ol' Riordan whispered to Twedwr, 'We're all out of ale! On the morrow, we'll have ale aplenty, so we can expect a full house, if you'll come back!'

"I started to tell them we wouldn't be staying, that we were on our way to Baile Átha Cliath and then to Angleland and all, but Twedwr put his hand on my arm. 'Hush now,' he said to me all quiet, and then to Riordan he said, 'I'm wondering if you could give me just a wee moment with my young friends here?'

"After the tavern-man scurried away, Twedwr looked at us and said, 'Let's us just think about what's going on here, and talk about it a bit. The two of you are travelling, as plain as mud. But are you in such a powerful hurry to get wherever it is you're going?' Mellán and I looked at one another, knowing we were in no hurry, but what we didn't know was what Twedwr had in his mind.

"I answered, 'Well, nay—I don't think there's any great rush,' and Twedwr said, 'Well, then. This fella Riordan is telling us that he'd like for us to come back and sing again on the morrow. He's willing to give us a room, and with a bit of push and pull, we ought to be able to gather up a coin or two for you to take with you on your journey.'

"Now I was fearing there must be some style of trickery lurking in the shadows, but Mellán leaned over to me and whispered, 'It would be no bad thing to have a wee bit of silver to jangle in our purses, would you not agree? Mayhaps we could just stay here for another night or two, mayhaps learn another song or two, stay out of the cold rain and snow, and collect a few coins on top of it all. What will you say to that?'

"I whispered back that we'd be foolish to not take up such a chance if it were all as it seemed, but that we would be needing to keep our eyes looking for someone trying to swindle us. He replied, 'And what is it we have that they'd be swindling us out of?'

"So, I looked over at Twedwr and told him we could stay for one or two nights, and he went to find the tavern-man to work out a deal. After he was gone, I said, 'That song you sang in Latin, that was the song you sang in the little fishing shed, the night my Mam … the night we left home. It was some style of prayer, wasn't it?'

"'Aye,' said he. 'That was "The Shepherd's Psalm," one of the psalms I learned in the monastery, my favorite one. I hope you don't mind that I sang it here.'

"'Nay,' I said, 'it was a gift, a very gift you gave me, gave us all. If I had any faith in any gods, that's how I'd like to believe they might be. Was that a song about your Jésu? Is he the shepherd that guides his people to the green pastures?'

"Mellán had to puzzle over that for a moment, and then he said, 'In truth I don't know about that. The fathers talk about Jésu as the Good Shepherd, but that song is one of the psalms, and they were all written long and long before Jésu was ever born.' My face must have showed some disappointment or muddling about all that, so he continued, 'The psalms were written by one of Jésu's ancestors, though—King David.'

"'Where was he king of?' I asked, and he answered, 'David was the king of Israel, long and considerably long ago. It was because Joseph was descended from King David that he and Maria the mother of our Lord Jésu went down to Bethlehem, where Jésu was born.

"Well, I didn't know what to make of all that, but I wasn't much trying, as right around then here came Twedwr grinning like a simpleton. He said, 'Aye, well now. Our friend Riordan's already counting all the silver he'll be making on the morrow, when he says the whole town of Dún Canann will be here to hear us sing and play the harp, and to drink his ale. He wants to give us a room upstairs—his best room, he says—and our meals for free. He says he'll pass around a bowl for the people to drop in a coin or two for us on the morrow. So, I'm thinking mayhaps we could help him out a bit. How do you think of that?'

"Well, we hadn't found any plans since the last time he asked us, you understand, and so we told him. And then he looked a bit sheepish, and said, 'But there is just one wee small thing, though.' He waited, and I nodded, and he continued, 'Friend Riordan says we'll be needing to have two or three more songs to sing, is all.'

"I looked over at Mellán, who shrugged, and Twedwr said, 'Mayhaps four,' and we looked at him direct, and he mumbled, 'Five at the most.' 'Five new songs!' yelped Mellán, and Twedwr said, 'No more than six, surely that will be enough.'

"I said, 'Well, now. Twedwr—did you tell the tavern-man we would learn some new songs?'

"'Aye,' answered Twedwr.

"'How many new songs?' Mellán asked.

"'Aye, well, it was a matter of getting us a free room in this fine establishment, and …'

"'How many new songs?' was me repeating Mellán's question.

"Twedwr murmured, 'Five,' and I looked over to Mellán, who shrugged again, before Twedwr added, 'Or six.'

"'Five or six new songs!' whispered Mellán. 'I don't know … Pell, can you do that?' I looked at him blankly, and he went on, 'Aye, well, Twedwr here knows the songs he knows, and there are likely dozens more of them. I know some more psalms and the tunes they ought to go with. You're the one to play the harp, so you're the one who'll be learning them.'

"So, I just smiled and gave a little nod. I've always been one to learn things quickly."

Chapter XII

Twedwr's Tale

"If the room Riordan gave us was his best, it didn't say anything good about the rest of them. But there was a pallet for each of us, and fresh water in the washing bowl, and a clean chamber pot for the necessaries.

"The next morning, I was up while the sun was still thinking about rising, creeping down the stairs with Twedwr's harp in its satchel. I sat there playing it hushed, just getting my fingers lined up right, so I didn't have to think so much about where the strings were, and after a time, here came Mellán, all full of yawns and stretches. He listened to the harp for a while, and then he sang me another psalm in Latin, this one about being joyful, as we are the sheep of his hand, it said. There were lots of sheep and shepherds in those times, so it seems. He sang it to me again and I sang it along with him, until I had the tune, and then I piddled around with it until I felt like the harp had gotten ahold of it too, and we sang it again.

"Then we started working on a tune my Mam used to sing to me, 'A Pony in Spring.' I sang it through once or twice, then he mumbled it along with me two or three times more, and by the time we'd gone through it three or four times, he could hold the melody through the chorus, which freed me to sing the harmony. The words to the chorus aren't hard:

'Oh, let me be a pony in spring,
    when all the world is fair and new,
ah, let us prance up our heels again and sing,
    as when the sweet breezes of youth blew,
    as when the sweet breezes blew.'"

Pell paused for a moment, and then he said, "It's a gentle song, but sad, all filled with the regrets of an old man looking back at what a mess he's made of his life, wishing he could be young again, longing for the coming of spring."

"Do you wish you could be young again?"

"What? Nay!" The old man thought about it for a few seconds, and then said, "Nay, nay. I wish my knees were younger. I wish I could eat whatever I wanted without my belly telling me I shouldn't have eaten that. I wish the people I've loved were still here with me. And I'm fully mindful of some of the mistakes I made, and I wish I could have done some of that differently. But nay, I'm content to be who I am now, living the life I've been given." He thought for another moment and said, "Nay, lad—let the pony in spring prance up his heels. I'll sit here in this circle of trees and sing my songs and tell my stories gratefully."

Pell nodded his agreement with what he'd just said and continued. "Well and so, after the sun was well up, Twedwr got up and came down. It was clear he hadn't had much by way of rest, and Mellán said to him, 'You have the smell of a man who was up drinking most of the night.'

"Twedwr looked at us with bleary eyes and said, 'Aye, well, after I got you all tucked in and all, I thought mayhaps I'd just pop down to see if Riordan was needing any help, and he offered me a jar of ale and we started talking and then we had another and then mayhaps one or two more—I try not to count—and after some time had passed, I woke up with my face all smushed up on the back of my arm on the bar. Then I went up to the room and laid myself down for a little slumber.'

"Mellán was cross, and he meant for Twedwr to know about it. Mayhaps it was because he had spent too much time with Father Cyneric when he was drinking, but Mellán seemed to have little tolerance or patience when it came to drink. Oh, he'd sip an ale with his supper, but he wanted naught to do with a man who'd let himself drink too much. I heard him say it a hundred times, I reckon: 'A little is enough, and too much is too much.'

"He said, 'Here now. Pell and I have already learned two new songs, while you were sleeping away your ale. If we're to be working together, Twedwr, we'll all be needing to pull the same weight, do you understand?' Well, Twedwr wasn't happy about being scolded, and especially not by such a young man as Mellán, and he started to make a retort or some such, but I'll never know what he was going to say, because he didn't say it. Instead, he looked Mellán right in his eyes and said, 'Aye. I understand, and I'm woeful sorry.'

"Well and so, now I was feeling bad for ol' Twedwr, and thinking mayhaps it was time for us to be talking about something else. I held out his harp to him and said, 'I thank you kindly, friend Twedwr. It's a beautiful harp, and I'm grateful to you for letting me play it. But it's time for me to to be giving it back to you now. Surely you can play it better than I can.'

"But instead of making things any better for Twedwr, I was just making them worse. He looked at me as hopeless as a dog left out in the snow, and said, 'Nay, Pell, I can't—partly because you have a natural skill at it; I never played so well as you did last night. And partly because—well and it's a sorry tale to tell so early of a morning.' Mellán told him it was nearly noonday, and I said we'd be glad to hear his story, so he told it.

"'I was born here,' Twedwr said, 'as I told you yesterday, but this isn't my home. It's been many and many a year since last I lived here.

"'One fine spring evening just after my fourth winter, two strangers came a-walking down the main street, tall men with bright blue robes and grand tall hats, I was told. They came right to the door of this same tavern and busted through those doors like they belonged here. They told the men in here they'd come to fetch a young boy of this village, who was to come with them back to their sacred grove. They said the stars had showed them it was a boy of this town that was to come with them and be trained and schooled as a Druid. Then they just sat themselves down and waited for somebody to come and make them an answer.

"'My father's brother Ryan was in the tavern that night, and he said out loud for everybody to hear, "Well, are you offering gold, or silver, or some such?"

"'Well, these men were both tall, as I said, but the taller one stood up and said, "Nay, we're not here to buy a boy. We're here to give a boy an opportunity, a chance to become part of the soul of Éire." In that very moment, my uncle said he knew of a certain these two men had come for me.

"'For you! That's terrible!' said Mellán. But Twedwr shook his head and replied, 'I was the fifth of six children, the last of four boys, and my Mam had just recently passed delivering my sister Cara—just worn out, I reckon. So, it was no bad thing for my father, who was struggling to make his way as a fisherman, to have one less son underfoot. There are only so many boys you can take with you on the boat. Well, my Da bundled me up and told me to go with the tall men. To be honest, I don't really remember much about that.

"'I was raised up in a community of Druids, leagues and leagues from here,' continued Twedwr. 'And I did well among them, doing the chores I was given to do, learning long lists of animals and plants and stars, learning the stories, and—best of all—learning the songs of the Druids' wisdom. That's how I knew you'd learned that song from a Druid, Pell—"The Power of One" is one of the first songs a Druid singer's given to learn.

"'Much of the life of a Druid is secret, so I'm thinking there's not much I'll tell you about any of that. There have been seeds planted in the minds of many people that the Druids are evil somehow, which goes against my knowing of them and which I don't understand. Still, you have to be chary when you're talking about Druids. I'm promised to keep the secrets of the order, and that I will do.

"'One fall day after I'd been with the Druids ten or twelve years, my father's brother Ryan sent a message to me that he'd like to see me, just to be sure I was healthy and well. I sent word back that I could meet him in the alehouse in the nearby village, and what day and all. So, we met, and it was not an easy conversation, both of us more awkward than you ought to be around your kin. I told him he could go back to my father and tell him what he saw that I was doing fine and prospering right well with the Druids.

"'He told me he had a comfortable sum of money put away, thinking he would need it if ever he was to get married, but he never had. Aye, and then he asked me if I needed aught. I told him I had everything I needed, but he pressed me on it, so it seemed like he was wanting to give me something. Mayhaps he was feeling guilty about having sent me away to live with the Druids. He went on and on about it until I told him I would love to have a harp, as I especially loved the songs of Druidry.

"'The next fall, a package came for me at the alehouse, and I went and picked it up. It was all packed up in wool blankets and tied up with cord, and it took me a while to get to it, but there she was, the most beautiful harp I've ever seen. And there was a small leather bag, with ten gold solidi, more money than I knew existed in the world, to be truthful.'"

Oswell asked, "So why did he leave the Druids?"

"Aye," replied Pell, "That's the very thing Mellán wanted to know, and so he asked. Twedwr made a terribly sad face when he answered, 'Ah, well, there was a young woman. Her name was Eithne, and she was fair to look upon. She worked there in that alehouse where I met my uncle—that's when I noticed her, and she noticed me, and it seemed to me there might have been a wee spark of magic between us. I knew even then I had no power to resist that girl.

"'Aye,' said Twedwr, 'I thought she was a bit sweet on me, and the blessed Mother knows I was sweet on her, and every time I'd just happen to drop in to see her, she was sure to tell me that I had to buy something, this being a place of business and all. I would drop in to see her and buy a pint, and then so I could stay and do my flirting and all, I'd have to buy another, and then another, and so it went until I was hopelessly in love with a girl who was just trying to sell her father's ale, and I was a drunk to boot, and that's just the unhappy truth of it.

"'Some time later, I'd be itchy and feeling uneasy about myself if I didn't have a pint or two or three of an evening, and I didn't have the silver to pay for such foolery as that, and soon I owed the tavern more and more, until I decided I'd have to rob some travelers on the road to pay my bill.'

"'What?' I said, alarmed and distressed that our new friend was some manner of highwayman. 'You robbed somebody?'

"'Well, nay,' said Twedwr. 'One night I tried to rob an older couple in a wagon, but the man saw I wasn't much good at it, so he just hobbled up and punched me smack in the nose, and off they rode, bumping along in their rickety old wagon, leaving me with naught but a bloody nose.'

"Then I asked, 'What about the gold your uncle gave you?'

"'Aye, I've often wondered about that myself. As desperate as I was, I think I must have known in my water and bones I couldn't use that money for such a mess as I'd made of myself—I just couldn't.'

"'What did you do then?' asked Mellán. 'Aye, well,' answered Twedwr, 'I left the Druid settlement, thinking I'd soon come back, and went to work for Eithne's father down at the tavern. I was thinking, hoping I reckon would be more honest, that I could pay what I owed him, and she would fall in love with me and we would marry.

"'There I was at the tavern every day, hauling casks of ale, wiping the tables, cooking the stews and pies, learning to make ale, and what did I see but my beloved treating all the gentlemen customers just as she'd treated me, like she was sweet on every one of them, just as she'd been sweet on me when I was a customer. Now that I was a lowly worker, sleeping in the barn and sweeping the floors and such, Eithne scarcely noticed me at all. And when I asked her about it, she laughed at me and said, "I was just selling the ale, sweetheart." Ah, well—my heart nearly broke.'

"'What did you do then,' I asked, and Twedwr said, 'Ah, well, my choices were few—I could stay there in that tavern, or I could go back to the Druids, or I could find my way back here, to the town where I was born.'

"'Aye, so that's what you did,' I assumed.

"But Twedwr said, 'Well, what I did, being the complete fool that I am, was to go back to the brewing house and help myself to as much ale as I could stand, and then I drank a jar or two more, just to spite myself. Then the dark came for me, and mayhaps I'd still be sleeping it away but for Eithne's father, who carted me up close to where he thought the Druid settlement must be, leaned me up against a tree and threw a bucket of water on me.'

"'What did you do then?' asked Mellán, and Twedwr answered, 'I woke up.' I said, 'Aye well, of course you did. But after that, though—what happened then?'

"'When I'm telling you I woke up, I mean I woke up from being stupid drunk, and also that I woke up from all the lies I'd been telling myself. I was never going to marry Eithne; she was never interested in me. I decided there and then I'd never take another drink of ale, nor beer, nor wine, nor aught else that would poison my body and my mind so powerfully as that.

"'So I picked myself up and bathed myself in a little creek there, and walked back to the Druid settlement. One of my friends, Fionn, there saw me and took me aside, saying 'Twedwr! You're coming back?' But I said, 'Nay, Fionn, as happy as I am to see you, I'll not be coming back.'" Well and well I knew I had stepped outside the rules of the community, and there could be no coming back now.

"'The Chief Druid heard I was there, and he came out to greet me. He said, "Ah, Twedwr, it nearly breaks my heart to say what I have to say." And I said, "Full well I know it, Séaghdha, so you'll not need to say it at all. I'm just come to gather my things, and then after that I'll be leaving. I want to tell you that I know I've been a fool, and that there wasn't a thing in the world you could have done to save me from it. I am sorry for the hurt I've brought you and this community, and I hope you'll be willing to forgive me, and send me on my way with your blessing."

"'My friend Fionn started to make a protest, but wise Séaghdha put his hand on the back of my head and pulled me to his chest, holding me tight. Then he said, "Go your way, my son, and take some of our hearts with you. Go you now into the world with the protection of our divine Mother around, before and behind you, at every step, at every breath, at every sleeping, at every waking. Let it be so for all your long life, wherever you go." I whispered, "Let it be so. Thank you, Séaghdha."'

"'And then?' Mellán prompted him. 'And then,' Twedwr said, 'I went to the little bothán where I'd lived most of my life, got my few possessions, including my beautiful harp, and I left.'

"'And you came back here,' I concluded.

"'Well,' Twedwr said, 'aye—I am here, and here I am.'

"Now I looked at him like I could see him better, more clearly than I had the night before, and I knew I'd like to help him if I could. It seemed like he needed to tell the rest of the story, so I said, 'Will you tell me why you won't play your harp now?'

"He seemed smaller then, like a fig that's withered up in the summer heat, when he said, 'Aye. Well, between there and here there were many and many a mile to walk, and in truth it took me some years. Not just because it was a long walk, but because I didn't want to come straight home. I was ashamed of myself, and there's the very truth of it. I couldn't go back to the Druid community, but I was leery about coming home. I felt like I'd failed, do you understand?'

"We both nodded, and he picked up his tale. 'So, I took my time, taking some small jobs in one place and another, helping a fisherman for a couple of seasons, making ale for a tavern or two along the way. I was adrift, like a boat that's lost its anchor. I knew there might be robbers along the way, just waiting for a fool like me to come walking along with ten Roman gold coins. So, I took that gold and put it safe away, where nobody could find it.

"'I slowly made my way, and when it was time for me to go, I came in this direction, walking in the daylight and finding safe places to sleep at night, coming back here to Dún Canann. Sometimes I met people who thought I was a Druid, and they gave me a little something to eat, but there came a day, not even half the way here when I was needing to buy some food, mayhaps get a room at a tavern to sleep.

"'So, I looked for a merchant who would buy one of my gold coins. I found one who tried to cheat me and offered me less than half what I knew it was worth. I put the coin I'd showed him in the purse on my belt, and as I walked away, here came two great large toughs who told me I needed to pay them for their master's time. I told them I hadn't taken much of his time, and that I didn't have any money, but they said they knew I did, and they knew exactly where to find the coin I'd put in my purse.

"'I wondered if I was feeling my last heartbeats pounding in my chest like a hammer, and I stood up as tall as I could and said, "You boyos need to know that I am a Druid, and that I can call down the wrath of the Divine Mother on you, you and your families." I tried to look all scary and mystical, but I reckon it didn't work, as the next thing that happened was they snatched the purse off my belt and pushed me down so I fell flat on my arse.

"'I stood back up quickly as I could, and lifted up my right hand into the air, looking as magical as ever I could, and I told them I could turn the both of them into fish. They ignored me, so I started hollering: "*Baheeba! Baheeba gashundai!*" I don't know where any of that came from, but it sounded magical somehow, and I was thinking mayhaps they would think they were some magical Druid words and bring me my gold back. But what they did was naught like that. They came back and looked me all up and down, and then they saw that I had a leather satchel, and they wanted to know what I had in there. I told them it was a Druid harp, and sure as the moon at night I was scared they were going to steal that from me as well. But they told me to play something for them, to play something on the harp.

"'So, I took my harp out of its satchel and started playing "The Power of One," not knowing it was the last song I'd ever play. Well, these brutes weren't much for music, as they just nodded and walked away.

"'That would have been the end of it but for my red-headed temper. I watched them walk away with one of my uncle's gold coins, and I picked up a stone from the road, and I threw it just as hard as I could and hit one of those boyo right on his arse.'

"'Then what happened?' I asked Twedwr, desperate to know.

"'Ah, well,' Twedwr continued, 'then the fella whose arse I'd hit with a rock came over and took my harp. I struggled, but he was much bigger and stronger. I thought he was going to take it, or destroy it, but what he did was to hand it to his friend, and then quick as a kestrel he reached out and caught my right hand in a grip as strong as death. Then he looked down at me and grinned like a wolf, and as he broke two of the fingers of my right hand, he said, "Too bad you'll never play that pretty harp again, Druid."'

"We sat there, soaking up some of the sadness of the moment, neither Mellán nor I knowing what could be said. When Twedwr spoke again, it was from the bottom of a well of deep gloom: 'I told them I was a Druid, but they were not impressed, nor afraid of me, not for a moment. Time was when a Druid could get a little measure of respect, but the Romans made us all outlaws, sent all of us into hiding.'"

"Oh, that's terrible!" exclaimed Oswell.

Pell nodded solemnly, and said, "Aye, it's a dreadful sad tale. Twedwr picked up his right hand and showed us that his pointing finger and the one next to it were bent one way and another. 'Can you bend them?' I asked, and he just shook his head.

"'A little,' Twedwr said in return. 'I can do most everything that needs doing, but that bastard was right—I'll never play the harp again.'

"Well, we sat there quiet as bricks for a time, until Mellán said, 'But then you came home, as here you are. What did you find when you came back here? Did you find your father, and your sisters and brothers? Were they glad to see you?'

"Then we read the tragedy in Twedwr's eyes, even before he could say it out. 'Nay, when I came here, back to Dún Canann, I found that my father died of consumption two winters gone, and that two of my brothers had been lost at sea. The other brother wasn't happy to see me, thinking I'd come to claim some share of my father's land or money, not that any of that amounts to much. My uncle Ryan who gave me the harp, has left town, and nobody knew aught about where he might be.

"'Now I'm telling you as true as I know how, that I had not had a drop of ale or any other drink for many and many a day as I was coming home, but … to find such a bitter welcome as that, I just wanted to lose myself in ale and wash away all my misfortune. And so you found me there, sleeping away my sad.'"

Chapter XIII

Draining a Tavern Dry

"Now the tears were coming freely to my eyes," Pell continued, "and I heard a sniffle or two coming from where Mellán was sitting, as we walked in Twedwr's desolation with him.

"Then he perked up and said, 'So it was a grand thing to hear the harp sing again last night, my friends, a grand thing indeed.' I looked over to Mellán, who was wiping his eyes with the back of his hand, and Twedwr said, 'Now, tell me about these songs as you've been learning this morning.'

"So, we sang him 'The Joyful Psalm' and 'A Pony in Spring' and he said they were both fine additions to our stock. Then he taught us an old Celtic song called 'The Lay of King Lew,' a hero story that goes on for a long while. It's a song for one person to sing, which was fine with me, as all I needed to learn was the chords.

"After we worked that one out, he wanted to teach us another song about another hero, this one about the Túatha Dé Danann, god-like people who came from another world to settle in Éire, and how they defeated the Fir Bolgs, another magical group of people who'd also come to settle here. The Tuatha Dé Danann were led by Nuada, who killed the leader of the Fir Bolgs in the last battle. It was a gory tale, and it was Mellán who said what I was thinking, that it was too violent and too bloody for a night at the Bustard's Butt.

"Well, then Twedwr asked if we knew a song called 'The Butterfly's Blessing.' I told him I didn't, and he said it's a simple, silly little song, and sweet and innocent and nobody gets killed. The way he talked about it made me think mayhaps he was sulking about us not wanting to sing 'The Tuatha Dé Danann and the Fir Bolgs' but Mellán said, 'Well, let's hear it.'

"So, he sang it, and a peculiar thing happened. Mellán thought we needed to lively it up some, so he added some words to fill in the holes. And then Twedwr got the idea and added some more, so that this simple, silly song became the one we started with wherever we went, and the one the people seemed to like the most, as they could easily sing along."

Oswell was intrigued. "Will you sing it for me?"

Pell smiled and said, "Aye, with a glad heart I will. It's been many and many a year since I even thought of it, but it might still shine a light into this gloomy tale."

The old man reached down into the satchel and brought out the harp, tuned a few strings, and picked out a lively tune. Then he looked at the young man and said, "Ah, one night I think Twedwr sang the last verse first and then repeated it at the end—I'm not sure why, but it seemed to work, so that's the way we sang it after that."

And then Pell sang:

"If you see me fluttering by, a blessing to you!
If you smell the flower I'm settling on, a blessing to you!
If you're fishing a pole I light upon, a blessing to you!
If you smile at the Mother and thank her for your day,
      a blessing, a blessing, a blessing on you and your kin!"

Pell stopped and said, "That's your part in it—'a blessing to you!' Then he continued, assuming his young friend would sing his part, which he did:

"When I was just a wee little egg
      (a blessing to you!)
I thought I'd never amount to aught at all
      (a blessing to you!)
Still I was safe and warm and hid
      (a blessing to you!)
But then—the sun hatched me out
      and I wasn't an egg no more!
            Oh—the sun hatched me out
            and I wasn't an egg no more!

"Then I was a wiggleful worm (a blessing to you!)
Crawling and climbing and gnawing all day
        (a blessing to you!)
Still, I was safe and full of leaves
        (a blessing to you!)
But then—the cocoonery came and I was lost away!
Oh—the cocoonery came and I was lost away!!

"Now I was locked in my cocoonery jail
        (a blessing to you!)
And I had naught to do all night and all day
        (a blessing to you!)
Still, I was safe and dry and nobody saw me
        (a blessing to you!)
But then—the flowers called me and I had to get out!
        Oh—the flowers called and I had to get out!

"So I bit and I chewed and I pushed my way out
        (a blessing to you!)
I stretched out my wings and I sang out a song
        (a blessing to you!)
Now I'm fluttering by you, a butterfly you see me
        (a blessing to you!)
And so—now I'm grateful for all of my life!
        Oh—now I'm grateful for all of my life!

"So—if you see me fluttering by, a blessing to you!
If you smell the flower I'm settling on, a blessing to you!
If you're fishing a pole I light upon, a blessing to you!
If you smile at the Mother and thank her for your day,
        a blessing, a blessing, a blessing on you and your kin!
        Oh—a blessing, a blessing, a blessing on you and your kin!"

Oswell clapped and said, "I like that one!"

The old man smiled as he returned the harp to its satchel and said, "Aye, it's been a favorite for many and many a year.

"We'd learned three new songs, which we practiced and sang until Mellán was ready to pull out his hair. Now we had just seven songs to sing, the three we'd sung the night before—'The Power of One,' 'The Beltane Fire' and 'The Shepherd's Psalm,' and the four we'd just learned—'The Joyful Psalm,' 'A Pony in Spring,' 'The Lay of King Llew' and 'The Butterfly's Blessing.' So Twedwr asked Mellán if there were any more psalms around for us to sing, and he taught us 'What is Man' in Latin, about his god taking notice of us even though we're no more than specks of dust, and Twedwr said that was very like a song he'd learned as a young Druid, called 'What the Moon Sees,' so he taught us that one as well.

"We sang them all two or three times more, and we were working in some little harmonies as we went along, and by the time the people of Dún Canann were coming through the doors, we had nine songs ready to sing.

"Well, we still had some lumps to soothe out, figuring out who was to sing what, and when to keep your quiet, but there was a magic in the music from that very first night. Aye, it was as we sang it, 'The Power of Three is the Virtue of Word, the Beauty of Song, and the Harmony of Harp.'

"We found ourselves settling into what became a pattern: we'd sing two or three songs and then Twedwr would spin us a tale. He must've had a thousand stories; the whole time I was listening I hardly ever heard the same one twice. But when I did, you can be sure he told it even better than he had the time before, as he told me 'The best stories just get better.' And then we'd sing two or three more songs, and Twedwr would spin out another tale, and on we'd go.

"That night, the tavern was packed full, just as Riordan hoped it would be. We sang our songs and Twedwr told us a story or two, and then the tavern-keeper passed around a wood bowl for people to drop in a few coins. He didn't quite say it, but he suggested that we'd be done with the singing if there weren't some coins to sway us— when the bowl came back around, it wasn't full, but it wasn't empty. So, I struck up the harp again, and we sang our songs again, this time with some of the people singing along or just tapping their feet.

"After Mellán sang the 'What is Man' psalm, I put down the harp and told them what it said. 'Hear now the words of the song Brother

Mellán just sang us, the words of King David, the ancestor of Jésu the god who died and lived again:

> "O Lord, our King, how grand is your name in all the earth!
> Even from the mouths of babes and infants,
> Your glory exceeds the heavens.
> You have made a fortress against your foes,
>   to silence the enemy and the avenger.
> When I gaze up at your heavens, the work of your fingers,
> the moon and the stars that you set on their paths;
> what is a man that you are mindful of him,
>   mortal folks that you would care for us?
> But you have made us a little lower than yourself,
>   and crowned us with glory and honor.
> You have given us charge over the works of your hands;
> you have put all things under our feet,
>   all sheep and oxen, the beasts of the field,
>   the birds of the air, even the fish of the sea,
>   whatever swims along the sea currents.
> O Lord, our King, how grand is your name in all the earth!"

Pell continued, "I couldn't have told you why I did that, I couldn't tell you still today, except that the words of that song touched me deeply, and touch me still. I suppose I just wanted the people in that tavern to understand what was being said, so the song could touch them, too.

"Then Riordan passed the wood bowl again, and we sang all our songs again, and Twedwr told us some more tales, and aye, the lass who'd made eyes at me the night before made them more fetchingly the second night. I saw her, and she was lovely, but it was all I could do to play the harp and sing a little, so I just tried to keep my notice on that.

"After a while, Riordan the tavern-man stood up to tell the people, 'Ah, my friends—I'm regretful to tell you, but you've run me out of ale!' There was considerable groaning at the news but mixed in with some distinct pride at the notion of draining a tavern dry.

Riordan quieted them down to say, 'Won't you come back on the morrow, and we'll have ale aplenty, and more songs and tales!'

"Then the people all left, though some stayed around for a short time to tell one of us to have a good night or something similar. I noticed the young lass who'd been flirting with her eyes was staying about, and Twedwr nudged me with his elbow, nodding in her direction and saying, 'You've got an admirer there, boyo—she's a fine sweet pear just asking to be plucked.'"

This caught the imagination of Oswell, who said, "So ... what happened there? Did you kiss her?"

"Nay. I was wary about fooling with somebody as would be interested in somebody like me, but I think the real reason was that I was just not ready. I didn't know aught about lasses, or love, or about life at all, if I'm to be honest. I was afraid I might fall into those eyes and never find my way back out."

"So, what did you do?" Oswell asked.

"I went up to our room and didn't come back down until the next day was dawning. That next morning, I sat and played Twedwr's harp for a time, but Mellán or Twedwr weren't up yet, and I got a bit restless, having spent the whole day before inside the Bustard's Butt. So, I slipped out quiet as a haddock and took a little walk around the town. Now that I've travelled a bit, I would say that it wasn't a town of much significance, but back then it was the largest town ever I'd seen. I expect my eyes were as big and round as goose eggs—it was a right wonder. That morning, for the first time, I realized that the world was much grander than my imagination—curious and complicated well past what I had ever known.

"Dún Canann was a harbor town, and there were ships and boats, not only from Éire and Angleland, but from Gaul and Hispania and as far away as Germania. All manner of goods and people were being loaded and unloaded from watercraft as colorful and different as the men who worked them—galleys and sailing ships and rowed triremes, some of them large and some small, but most between. The men working there on the docks were just as various: some were even more light-skinned than you, while others were as dark as a pochard's head, some bearing slave collars and others adorned with gold in their ear hoops or circling around their arms; men with long golden hair and others with curly black hair close-cropped. Aye and there were women there as well—some of them obviously owned, but others just as clearly the owners.

"It seemed to me I was the only one who wasn't busy going or coming or doing one thing or another or shouting at somebody else to come or go or do, so I sat down out of the way, just to watch. The noise of it all was gloriously loud, and I heard mayhaps three or four languages I'd never heard before.

"As I sat there, words for a song came into my head, not one of the songs I'd been singing with Mellán and Twedwr, nor any song I'd ever heard before, but a new song. So, as I sat there watching and listening, I made up this new song in my head.

"After some little time, and long after my belly had started complaining, I walked back to the tavern, where Mellán was relieved to see me.

"He jumped up and exclaimed, 'I thought you might have been taken!'

"I laughed and asked him, 'And who in the whole grand world would want to take such a big lump as me?'

"Then I told him I'd been making up a new song, and he said he's never heard of anybody ever making up a song that was new. He said, 'I suppose I thought all the songs were old.'

"I replied, 'Aye, but surely somebody had to make up even the oldest songs; there was a day when even the songs of old King David were new.' He looked at me like I was thinking too much of myself and I said, 'Ah, nay—this won't likely be as good as any of his, but I like it well enough.' So, he smiled and said, 'Well, let's hear it then.'

"I said, 'But this is a song in search of a tune.' So, I told him the words, and we had to talk some about the verse talking about the gods which was bothersome to him, but then he got the measure of it, and we changed a word or two for the timing of it, and presently he made a tune for it, and we joined the music and the words together. After a while, Twedwr came dragging down the stairs looking just as bleary as he had the morning before, and we told him we were making a new song. So, he asked us to sing it for him, and that's the very thing we did."

Oswell asked, "Will you sing it for me now?"

"Aye, gladly," said Pell. "It's the first song I ever wrote. But note now, it was written in Gaeilge, and it's been sung in Latin and in the language of Angleland, so all the rhyming and meter has all gone wobbly now. But still, I like what it says." The old man picked up the harp, and after making sure that all the strings were tuned just right, he played and sang a song he called "All of Us Looking for Truth."

"There's more to this world beyond what we see,
    each one of us look and sound different.
But it's the same moon and stars shining down on us all,
    and all of us looking for truth,
      all of us looking for truth.

Now the words aren't the same in Angleland and Éire,
    more different still in Germania.
But all over the world mothers are loving their babes,
    and all of us looking for truth,
      all of us looking for truth.

Where goes the sun when it's done with the day?
Why does the moon wax and wane?
What makes a king take his army to war?
And when will the rich have enough?
    It's all of us looking for truth.

Some people believe, while others don't
    and many's the names of the gods.
Well, I'm hoping there's something, but mayhaps there's not:
    it's all of us looking for Truth,
      all of us looking for Truth.

There is more to this world beyond what we see,
    each one of us look and sound different
The same moon and stars shine down on us all,

and all of us looking for truth,
    all of us looking for truth."

The old man put the harp back in its satchel and saw that his young friend didn't know what to make of his song, so he went on with his story. "That night we sang all the songs we knew, and then Mellán told the people that he and I had made a new song, which we sang, after which there was thunderous clapping."

Oswell said nothing, so the old man suggested, "It's a song as requires a broader view of things, I think." The young man continued to say nothing, and Pell went on. "Then Riordan passed the bowl while Twedwr told a story, and we sang some more, and there was another story, and more songs, until Riordan told us he's out of ale again, and the people left."

"What about the girl?"

"What girl?"

"The girl who was making eyes at you!"

"Ah well, she wasn't there that night, or I didn't see her. And I never saw her again, except in my dreams, for many and many a night after that.

"The next morning Mellán and I had a little talk and agreed it was time for us to be on our way. He had his heart set on going up to Baile Átha Cliath where his people were from, to see about his mother and the rest of his kin, and told me it would be just a short little boat trip from there over there to Angleland. As for me, I had nowhere to go and I was in no rush to get there, so I told him to lead the way, and I would follow.

"'But should we be telling our friend Twedwr that we're going?' he wanted to know. Twedwr was asleep, and it didn't feel right for us to just up and sneak away from him. So, I said we could wait for him to come down, but after we waited a while and he still hadn't waked up, we decided to go and wake him ourselves before the day got too far away from us.

"Back up the stairs we went, and after some little shaking, Twedwr opened one eye and told us to leave him alone. I said, 'Aye, and that's what we're here to tell you: we're leaving. Thank you for letting me play your harp, and fare you well.'

"Mellán told him, 'We took the coins and made three even piles—they're all the same, but you can take your pick which one should be yours.' Now Twedwr sat up on his pallet and said, 'Well now, I'll be glad of a moment, if you've got one to spare. I have a thought about that—if you'd be willing to hear it.'

"But before Twedwr could give us his thought, Mellán said, 'Nay, friend. We can't stay another night, or we'll just be in the same spot as this on the morrow. We're grateful to you, and glad to have a few coins to take on our way, but now it's time for us to go.'

"Then Twedwr rubbed his face with his hands, and when he looked up at us, he said, 'Nay—that's not what I was thinking to say. I was going to ask … if I could come with you.'"

Chapter XIV

Hoping to Come Back Home

"Well, my heart jumped up a little in my chest, partly because I had some fondness for Twedwr and was glad of the idea of him coming with us, but also if I'm to be honest with you, partly because I'd be able to keep playing his wonderful harp. But Mellán was not so pleased, and he wasn't of a mind to keep it a secret.

"He said, 'Nay, Twedwr. You'll not be coming with us. It's right far out of your way and all.'

"'Out of my way?' said Twedwr. 'And where am I going, I'd like to know, for it to be out of my way of? For months and years I was on my way here, hoping to come back home. But as it happens, you two fellas are the only thing I found here I'd like to keep. These last three nights—well, they've been the best nights of my whole entire life: the singing, the stories, people clapping and putting their money in the bowl and all—it was like something out of a dream for me. But that's not the best of it, though. The best of it was feeling like I, like I belonged, I suppose. I belonged to a group I chose, and wasn't chosen for me.'

"He hung his head down then, like all this talking had drained him, and then he said, just on the edge of my being able to hear it, 'And if you two leave me, what use am I at all?'

"So, I looked over at Mellán, who shook his head to tell me nay. I scrunched up my eyebrows at him to ask him why, and he held up an invisible jar of ale and downed it in one go. He even wiped his lips dry with the back of his hand. I nodded at the door out of the room and said, 'Twedwr, Mellán and I need to have a little chat.'

"We left the room and before I could say whatever I thought I was going to say, Mellán said, 'Nay, Pell! I'm not going off into the big scary world with a drunk old Druid. I say let him stay here, until he drinks up all the ale in Dún Canann!'

"'But Mellán,' I said, 'I'm just thinking if Twedwr was to come with us, mayhaps we could find another tavern or two along the way—and instead of sleeping in some farmer's barn, or on the cold ground, we could get ourselves a warm room and free meals. How do you think of that?'

"'So,' answered Mellán, 'would you rather sleep on the cold, cold ground with a friend you can trust, or in a room over a tavern with an old drunk?'

"Well, I took a time to think, and then I said, 'Brother Mellán?' He knew I was up to some sort of foolery when I said that, so he was chary when he said, 'Aye, Brother Pell?'

"I said, 'Tell me that story that your blesséd Jésu told, the one about the younger son who took his inheritance and went off to spend it like some style of fool, and then when he came back home his father went out to greet him. What did the father say to him?'

"Well, Mellán had the makings of a sulk coming at him, and he mumbled, 'I don't remember.' I said, 'But, sure you do! The father told his slaves to bring his son his best robe, and to put new sandals on his feet, do you remember? He told them to kill a fat calf so they could make a grand celebration, because it was his son who came home, his son who was lost was now found again. Now, that's a pretty story, and I'm just wondering if mayhaps Twedwr has been lost a time or two, but now he's trying to come home, trying to be found again.'

"Mellán looked at me like he saw me for I'm the rascal I am, and said, 'You never forget aught, do you?' I gave my head a little shake and said, 'Nary the first thing.' Now Mellán had a think, and said, 'Well, he can come with us, and I admit I'll be glad of it, but I'm going to need him to make us a promise.' I nodded, and he continued, 'For our sake and for his, Twedwr will have to put the drinking away.'

"Well now, for most of my life I'd lived with a man who drank too much too often, but I'd never understood the strong need of it. So, I told Mellán that it wouldn't likely be any manner of difficulty at all, but Mellán answered, 'Nay, Pell, it will be terribly difficult, for all of us. Still, if Twedwr is willing to try, and if he wants to put it down, I'm willing to help.'

"We went back into the room and I told Twedwr we'd be glad for him to come, but we needed him to promise that he wouldn't be drinking when he's with us. I reminded him that he'd quit before, after he'd left the Druid settlement, and told him I knew he could do it again, and he'd have us to help.

"Well, that wasn't an easy moment for Twedwr, but after a short little time, he stood up on his feet and lifted his right hand with his palm facing out toward us, putting his left hand on top of his head. Then he made this vow, 'By oak, ash and apple, by hazel, rowan and yew, by elder, birch and willow, give I thee my solemn word, that I will try with all my strength, and that I will look to my good friends for help.'

"And so touched by this was Mellán, that he took his knife and made a little cut on the palm of his hand, just as he had with me, so that a wee drop of blood came beading out, and then handed the knife to me. Well, I cut myself again, on the same spot as I had before, so there was a little drop of my blood as well. Then I held out the knife to Twedwr, who looked at it all chary and asked, 'If I cut myself, does that mean I have to be a Christian?' And Mellán told him nay, but if he did this, then we'd all be brothers in blood until we die, and mayhaps past even that.' And then Twedwr took that knife gladly and cut his own palm and we each one of us took the palms of the other two.

"It was all right touching for all of us, and especially for Twedwr, who sat down on his pallet and wept a while, holding his head in his hands, just sobbing. Mellán and I left him there, to give him some time, and because nobody wants to just stand around watching a grown man cry.

"After a time, Twedwr came down the stairs and we told Riordan we were leaving. He asked where we'd be going, and Mellán told him we're going to Baile Átha Cliath, up the coast. Riordan said never been that far astray, and told us he thought we'd be crossing the sea there at Dún Canann if we were going to Angleland.

"'Aye,' said Mellán. 'We're going to Angleland, but first we're going to Baile Átha Cliath.' Riordan's face showed some muddle, and Mellán added, 'That's where I grew up, and I've not seen my family since I was just a lad. Before we go over to Angleland, I want to see what's become of them.'

"Riordan told us how much he'd enjoyed our being there, and that he hoped we'd be coming back. Then we could see he'd remembered something, and he told us to stay just where we were, that he had something to give us. So we had to wait some while when we were ready to go, and when he came back he's got a *bodhrán* for us."

"What's a bodhrán?" wondered Oswell.

"Aye, and that's just what we wanted to know. Riordan told us there were some other minstrels some years gone—not nearly so good as us—who left in an awful hurry, something about one of them getting too familiar with the wife of one of the townsmen. 'In their hurry, they left this thing,' he said, as he handed it to Mellán. Riordan said, 'They thumped on it, to keep the pace of the music steady, I think.'

"It was round as the moon at full, about four hands wide, like an embroidery hoop stretching out a piece of goat skin, so that when you tapped it with your hand, it made a dull bumping sound. Well, none of us knew what to do with it, and I was for giving it back, but Twedwr thanked him like it was a gift he was giving us instead of a man just trying to get rid of something he knew he'd never need.

"Then we were off. Riordan told us the next village large enough to have an alehouse, in the direction toward Baile Eoghain, was Baile Eoghain. He told us to tell Galvin, the owner of the Three Eels tavern there, that we come with his good wishes. The woman who'd brought us the stew and bread—Riordan's wife she was—gave us each a loaf, and we thanked them both again, and wished them a good farewell.

"Two days later, after a stop by a fast-running creek for a cold bath and a rest, and long after our loaves of bread were gone, we walked into Baile Eoghain, a small village that didn't look like much—we were surprised it was large enough to support an alehouse. Well, in truth the tavern there wasn't much, but it was a roof. We thought as we came into the town there wouldn't be much reason to stay, but the people were right gracious to us, and we stayed for two nights. The crowds coming to hear us weren't as big, and there wasn't as much money put into the bowl passed around, but the meals were better, and the room Galvin put us in was nice enough.

"We left there and came to a little settlement called Ros Mhic Treoin. There was no tavern there, so we were set to move on, but Mellán started talking to some of the children there, and told them we were musicians, and of course they wanted to hear a song or two. Just for the joy of making a song for children, we sang them 'The Butterfly's Blessing,' and wouldn't you know that a little crowd drew all around us before we finished. The head man of the settlement invited us to stay the night with himself and his wife and warned us all right sternly that we'd need to be staying well away from his daughters. They didn't have any silver there, but the people were generous and grateful, and gave us bread and a lump of cheese, along with some turnips and onions.

"That was the way of it for a time—we'd walk a league or two to the next village, town or settlement, and the people would gather around for the music. We would buy or trade for the supplies we needed, and usually we were given a place to stay for the night, and sometimes a coin or two, sometimes more.

"One stately older woman gave us a chicken, its poor wee feet tied together with a bit of cord. I wanted to set it free, but after it squawked and made such a pitiful noise, Twedwr finally twisted its neck, plucked its feathers and cut off its feet and all the parts we didn't want to eat, and boiled it in a pot we'd bought a few villages back. We ate it, but it wasn't much good, so at the next village we bought some salt and spices.

"We stayed for almost a week in an old harbor town called Menápia. The tavern there was called The Brave Sailors, the sign over the door was two men caught out in a storm in a little rowing skiff, one of them with his fist raised defiantly at the heavens. The tavern-man there also had daughters, four or five of them I believe, but he seemed more than willing for any of us to consider what possibilities they might be presenting. They were less fetching than some of the lasses we'd seen but seemed more willing—Twedwr told us they'd be glad to give us a kiss or something more, for the right amount of silver. I was still wondering about the something more he was suggesting when Mellán told him we'd be staying clear away."

"And did you?" Oswell asked.

"Did I what?"

"Did you stay clear of his daughters?"

"Oh, aye, I did—but I wondered about them and the something more. By and by, as the winter was starting to give way to spring, we arrived in Baile Átha Cliath, which made Dún Canann seem like a tiny village. It straddled the An Ruirthech, and where that river ran into the sea there made a grand harbor. There were three taverns there, and we visited each one: The Lobster's Tail, The Three Casks, and The Boar's Snout.

"Everywhere we went, Mellán asked about his family. An old grandmother told him his mother had died some years ago when her heart gave out, and somebody said he knew one of the cousins, but that he had left and gone up further north. It seems there weren't any kin of Mellán's left there, which was right sad.

"Well, we went to buy supper at The Lobster's Tail, and when I pulled the harp out of the satchel and started to play just a note or two, a crowd started to draw near. I played 'A Pony in Spring,' and each of us sang the verses we'd agreed we were to sing, and the crowd was right keen about it. Then we sang another song, and another after that, and Twedwr told a story, and Mellán sang one of the psalms—I knew the tunes for six or seven now—and the magic was so thick you could almost reach out and touch it.

"Then I put the harp back in its satchel and we made to look like we were about to leave, and the tavern keeper came over to Twedwr and told him we wouldn't have to pay for our supper if we'd play some more. So Twedwr did a little wrangling, and sure as the tide, the tavern-man was looking around at all the people buying his ale, and he told him he'd give us his best room if we would just keep playing.

"So of course we did; we went through all the songs we knew and then sang most of them again, and the common room of the tavern was so squashed up with people you could scarcely scratch your nose. Twedwr called the man over—Keegan was his name—and they had a little whispery chat, and presently Keegan stood up and called out that it was almost time for the musicians to stop, but if they'd drop a coin or two in the basket he was about to pass around, mayhaps we'd keep playing. So he did, and they did, and we did, too.

"Then Keegan stood up to announce they'd' run the place out of ale, and the crowd cheered their accomplishment until they saw that meant they'd have to leave. Then he told them we'd be back the next night, and he'd have much more ale for the glory of the gods, and they were cheering again as they left.

"The next morning, a man came to speak to Twedwr, and when he was gone, Twedwr came over to us to tell us what he said. This man, Eamon his name was, was the owner of The Boar's Snout, and he told Twedwr his place was bigger, and his ale was better, and the room he had for us was finer, and that we'd be gathering more coins in the basket—if we'd come and play there.'

"'And what did you tell him?' asked Mellán.

"'I told him I needed to talk with the two of you,' he said.

"'And what do you think we ought to do?' I asked.

"Then Twedwr said we ought to play one more night in The Lobster's Tail, and then we could move over to the Boar's Snout the day after that. So that's what we did, and then two days later, we moved along to the Three Casks. Two days after that, we were on a boat over to Angleland, our purses fair stuffed with silver."

Chapter XV

A Right Jolt It Was

Several days passed, and when Oswell returned to the ring of trees, he found the old man sitting with his back against his rowan tree, enjoying the sun on his face. When Pell heard the young man approaching, he opened his eyes and said, "Ah, well—you've come back. And here I was thinking you'd gotten tired of listening to an old man's story."

"Oh, no sir. I just needed to be seen around the monastery, or Father ... ah, well—I just had to be there for a few days."

"Hmm—well, mayhaps your Father Somebody is fretting about you coming to talk to a heretic. Have I got that about right?"

The young man hesitated, and the older man continued, "Never mind telling me about it, never mind it another heartbeat. This seems ever the way of it, some men in power just don't seem to be able to hold themselves from lording their power over those younger, or weaker. And when the younger or weaker come into power as their time comes, they're thinking somebody did this to me so I can do it to these other fellas, and so on and so it goes, sure as winter comes after fall."

Then the older man pinned the younger man with a gaze that Oswell could feel on his skin. "Remember that, if ever you have to be a bishop or some such."

"Me?" Oswell exclaimed. "Oh, no, they'd never make a bishop of someone like me!"

"Aye, well—there's a good start to it. Ah, now: have you broken your fast? I could ask Dáirine to bring us out a little bread and some good crumbly cheese if you'd like."

"No sir—I wouldn't want to be a bother."

"Nay, friend, it's no bother. I think she's a little keen to meet you, for some reason I can't imagine." Pell looked at his young, bewildered friend and continued, "I usually eat a little something after my morning song, so if you'll sing it with me, Dáirine will bring us a tray."

"Oh, well, I don't know if ..."

"Well, it will be a song you know. We can sing the one about singing a new song to God. Do you know that one?"

"Ah, well, I might do. Which number is that?"

"Number? I don't know the numbers of them; it's one about singing a new song to God. That's an idea people who hold authority in the Church seem willing to overlook." With that, the old heretic reached down into the leather satchel and produced his harp, tuned it up a little, and began to sing in Latin:

> "*Cantate Domino canticum novum*
> *quoniam mirabilia fecit salvavit*
> *sibi dextera eius*
> *et brachium sanctum eius ...*"

He nodded his encouragement to his young friend and realized that he was struggling, so he started again, this time in the tortured dialect of the Saxons and the Angles. Even if the student didn't join in, he would at least understand what was being sung:

> "Sing to the Lord a new song,
> because he has done grand things.
> His right hand has brought salvation,
> and his strong arm is holy.
> The Lord has shown us his salvation,
> he has revealed his justice to all the world.
> He remembers his mercy and truth to the house of Israel,
> and all the ends of the earth have seen his salvation.
> Sing with joy to God, all the earth,
> rejoice with gladsome songs.
> Sing praises to the Lord on your harp,
> in the voice of a psalm,

And with great trumpets,
> and the music of horns and pipes.

Make a joyful noise in the presence of the Lord of all.

Let the seas be moved and all that is in them,
> and so the world and all the creatures of God.

Let the rivers clap their hands now,
> and the mountains rejoice together at the presence of
> the Lord, who comes to judge the earth.

He will judge the world with justice,
> and all the peoples fair."

Then, as the last note faded, a young woman came out of the house carrying a tray with bread and cheese, two wooden cups and a jug. She put it down on the ground between them, and when she looked at Oswell with her beautiful eyes, he remembered Pell saying, 'I was afraid I might fall into those eyes and never find my way back out.' Pell noted Oswell's interest in his granddaughter but chose not to comment on it.

When she had gone back into the house, Oswell stammered, "Who is ... she's so ... is that your daughter?"

"My granddaughter, Áine's eldest. My daughter Áine Minor was named after my sister."

"But who is ... who is ... ah, who is Áine's mother?"

"Ah, well now—now you're wanting to get ahead of the story again. If you're willing to listen, I'll be happy to keep on with it."

"Yes, sir. You and Mellán and Twedwr were about to leave Éire on your way to Angleland."

"Aye, and a right jolt it was to be leaving Éire, where I had grown up, the only place I'd ever known, of a fact it was. Oh, it was a grand adventure, to be sure, but it was scary just the same, and my heart swelled up inside me to watch the sad sight of Éire shrinking away in the distance. But I didn't have but just a little time to dwell on it.

"Twedwr bought us passage on a little ferry boat that crossed over from Baile Átha Cliath to Segontium every other day, coming back the next. Twedwr and Mellán had never been out on the open sea, but I'd grown up on the water, or near it. I tried to tell Twedwr that a bigger boat might be better, but Twedwr said a smaller boat would be cheaper, and so—well, first Twedwr lost the bread he'd had for breakfast that morning, and then he lost the mutton he'd had for supper the night before, and then he lost his dignity and he was about to lose his will to live when we saw the first sight of Angleland up ahead of us, and we told him it wouldn't be much longer.

"He was moaning and praying to Manannán so pitifully that Mellán asked me about him, so I told him Manannán was one of the old gods, one of the Tuatha Dé Danann, the god of the sea. Mellán nodded and then I added, 'Also he's the god of the underworld, the place of the dead.'

"Mellán nodded again, and asked as serious as a buzzard, 'Is he praying to be delivered of the sea, or to be taken down to Hell then?'

"I answered. 'I think he'd tell you either one would be better than where he's finding himself just at the moment.'

"Well, by and by our little ferry boat finally bumped into the dock-pole and there was a lad there to tie up the ropes, and then we all made our way down the rampway onto land, although it was a land Twedwr and I had never stepped our feet on before. As land goes, it didn't seem much different from the dirt in Éire, but no sooner had Twedwr stepped off the planks than he dropped down to his knees and put his forehead on the ground. I heard him saying, and I think he was talking to the dirt itself: 'Never again, never again.'

"We started to ask people which way it was to Londinium, and I was surprised to find out it isn't Angleland we'd come to at all, but where the Cymru people are. The people there don't speak Gaeilge much at all and speak it poorly when they try. It was the language of the Cymru they were speaking, which uses parts of the back of your mouth and tongue that I suppose you have to grow up using to be much good at. Finally, we found somebody who spoke a passable Latin, and he told us it was to a town called Scrobbesbyrig we ought to go. He said he'd never been past that, but he believed Londinium was well past that, 'terrible far, days and weeks of walking,' he said.

"This was the first time we wondered if mayhaps we ought to buy some horses. I knew it was going to be a long walk down to Londinium, but I argued it would be just as long a ride on the back of a beast, and that I'd easier trust my feet. I fretted that I might be too large for a horse to carry, and if I'm to be honest with you, I was afraid I'd be tossed off its back.

"We walked all that afternoon and most of the next day, and by the time we came to Scrobbesbyrig, my feet were telling me mayhaps I ought to reconsider my attitude about horses and such.

"It was a pretty little town, nestled in the crook of the River Sæferne, and we were relieved to hear the people there speaking a form of this language we're speaking now, this stew of the speech of the Saxons and the Angles, with some words from Germania and Gaul on top and a fair bit of Latin underneath.

"We stopped when we came to an alehouse with a sign over the door that showed a pig swimming alongside a big fish—The Pig and Pike it was called. We took ourselves into the tavern and sat down, weary of foot and nearly starving, the dust of the road fairly strangling us. It was the middle of the afternoon, and there weren't many people there, just a few men having a quiet bit of ale, and then without a warning, here came the most beautiful woman ever I saw, before or since.

"Her long brown hair fell to her shoulders, framing her lovely face and her bright green eyes. This was no barmaid—here was a woman to be reckoned with, a woman with her own ideas and voice, a voice I wanted to hear. Sure, and my heart was lost before ever she said the first word.

"She asked what she could bring us, and Twedwr told her we'd be glad of two jars of ale and some water, and she left—far too soon!—to get it for us. But then in just a short little while she came back carrying our drinks and a loaf of dark bread, and as she put my jar in front of me, she smiled at me! I was completely swept away, like a leaf blown by a squall.

"My next conscious thought was to wonder what Mellán and Twedwr were laughing at, and why they couldn't leave a body alone. Then I dragged myself back to where we were and saw that they were laughing at me. I didn't find any humor in it, but I didn't mind them laughing; I just wanted her to come back. By and by she did, and she told us they had a good fish stew, and a fine pork roast. I asked her which was better, and she recommended the pork, so that's what I told her I'd like.

"Presently she came back with our meals, pork for Mellán and me, and fish stew for Twedwr. I gathered up enough courage to ask if she'd tell me her name, and she smiled a mystery at me and said, 'Nay,' before she was gone again.

"Mellán and Twedwr were half through their meal before Mellán had to remind me that I ought to be eating mine as well. When we were done, she came back for our bowls, and when she said, 'Brigid,' I could scarcely catch my next breath.

"Then, even as I was still rejoicing that I knew her name, Twedwr tapped my arm and said mayhaps it was time for us to offer up a tune or two. So, I took the harp out and tuned that one string that never seems to stay put and began plucking the strings. Just as always, the people in the tavern turned their heads toward us and moved a bit closer. Just as always, somebody went out to get somebody else, and the word spread, and by and by we were the center of a crowd.

"We played a few songs, and Twedwr told them the tale of 'The Fair Maiden's Regret,' the story of the beautiful young princess who seduced the dragon to steal his fire and then felt a great sorrow that she had tricked such a noble creature. Like any good story, it had grown some since the first time I heard it.

"After we sang another song or two, we made it look like we were about to be on our way, and sure as nightfall Feichín the tavern-man came over to Twedwr and they had a little whispering, and when Twedwr nodded to me, I started playing 'The Shepherd's Psalm' for Mellán to sing, and by the time he was done, there wasn't a soul in the place making a peep.

"Sometimes, when the magic was as thick as that, I'd stand up and tell them what Mellán had just sang in Latin, and it felt like this was one of those times.

"You know the psalm I'm talking about, I expect," Pell asked the young man.

"Yes, sir—the twenty-third Psalm."

"Aye—it's one of my favorites. To be truthful, I was hoping to impress Brigid, so I told the people this was a song written by King

David, an ancestor of the Christian god Jésu, and then I told them the words:

> "The Lord is my shepherd, I need naught more than that.
> He brings me to good pasture beside refreshing water.
> He restores my very soul.
> He leads me down paths of justice for his own Name's sake.
> Aye, even when I walk down paths in the shadow of death,
>   I will fear no evil, for you are with me
>   your rod and staff are a comfort to me.
> You set out a table for me right in the middle of my enemies.
> You have anointed my head with oil
>   and my cup is more than filled with good wine.
> Your mercy will go before me and follow me
>   all the days of my life
> And I will live in the house of the Lord forever.'"

"Well," Pell continued, "the people sitting there didn't know what to think about all of that, they're that chary about the religions of outsiders. Then I heard one person clapping, just one, and I looked to see it was Brigid. Then another person joined her clapping, and then another and another, until everybody there was clapping, and I sat back down and picked up the harp again. Twedwr leaned over to me and whispered, 'That was a close thing. Best you wait 'til you know how folks will tolerate talk about religion before you start with it. Some folks like it better if it's mysterious.' I nodded and he said, 'Let's do 'The Beltane Fire' just to get us closer to what they already know.

"So I struck up the first few notes of that song and everybody relaxed, and I looked over to Brigid and nodded her my thanks. She nodded back and smiled, and my heart soared like an eider duck flying away south at autumn.

"Then Feichín the tavern-man stood up to tell the people we were about done, but mayhaps if we could gather some coins in the basket he was about to pass around, we might be encouraged to play a few more. So, he passed the basket around and it came back with some coins, and we kept playing and Twedwr told another story or two. By and by, the tavern keeper had to tell the people he was run all out of ale. There was some general disgruntlement about that, 'til he went on to say he could get more ale, much more ale for the morrow night, if the people would all come back, and then he said he was hoping the musicians would come back as well.

"Now it may be I imagined this next part, but when the question of whether we were to play again the next night was in the air a bit, I thought I saw Brigid paying close mind, and that she looked pleased when Twedwr stood up and told them we'd be right glad to come back the next night, and there was a grand cheer.

"Then the people took their leave, some of them coming by to say something to one or another of us. An older man told Mellán he was sorry he didn't have a coin for the basket, but that three of his nanny goats had recently delivered three kids each—which was a great good fortune, of course, and he wasn't one to complain, but nine kids all at once were eating aught that wasn't moving and mayhaps some as were. He said his does couldn't make enough milk, and that he'd be honored to give us a kid or two as an appreciation for us coming to visit his little village. Mellán told him as much as we'd be grateful for his gift, travelling from one place to the next wouldn't be much of a life for a goat kid.

The man with nine baby goats left, and Mellán went up to the room we were to stay in. Twedwr was talking to Feichín the tavern-keeper, and I lingered there, just hoping to see Brigid, and mayhaps to thank her for her timely applause. I was just feeling fortunate to have aught to say to her at all.

"So after a while, when she came out through the doors to the kitchen, she saw me and smiled just a bit and then pretended hadn't seen me at all. So, all I could do was to keep standing there, which I did, and finally she came over close enough so I could almost hear her breathing, and I thought sure she could hear my heart beating loud enough to scare the birds into the night. She waited for me to say aught, and I said, 'I just wanted to thank you.'

"She smiled me that mysterious smile and said, 'Thank me for what?'

"I said, 'Well, for your clapping and all.' She just looked at me, and I felt like I needed to be saying aught, so I said, 'My friend Mellán is a Christian monk, and we are on our way to Londinium, or to Erith, which is the monastery he grew up in, which he says is close to Londinium, which I think is a long, long way.' She just kept looking at me, and I just kept talking, because I was afraid if I stopped talking, she'd go back into the kitchen, and I'd have to go up to the room. So, I kept on, making a fool of myself. 'We're going from town to village, me playing the harp and Mellán and our friend Twedwr who was a Druid—it's his harp—they sing, well I sing too, as you might have noticed, and trying to gather up enough silver to buy three horses, although I'm not sure about that part because I've never ridden on a horse before, so we can get there, to Londinium, or to Erith, which is near there. It's a long way.'

"So finally, I ran out of words, and she said, 'Tell me your name,' and I said, 'Pell.'

"'Is that your whole name?' she wanted to know, and I said, 'That's all the name ever I had, was just Pell.'

"'Could it be Pell son of somebody,' she asked, 'or Pell of somewhere?'

"'Nay,' said I, 'I don't think so. My Mam's name was Sadb, and her father was Eóghan ap Eóghan of Port Láirge in Éire. But my father was a Roman soldier who left when my sister Áine and I were young—I don't remember him. Nay, I'm just Pell.'

"'So, Just Pell, what is it that brings you to leave your Mam and your sister Áine, to travel all the way down to the monastery at Erith, which is near Londinium, which is a long way?'

"I looked to see if she was having a poke at me, but there was nothing mean in her eyes. I said, 'Well now there's a sad tale to tell, in truth it is.' And she said, 'If I give you a free jug of ale, will you tell it?'

"So, I told her I would, and she went back behind the bar and brought out two jars of ale, and we sat down right where I'd been sitting to play the harp."

Chapter XVI

You're a Right Arse, Just Pell

"In truth," the old man continued, "it is no easy thing to trust somebody, a terribly hard thing. I had no good reason to trust Brigid, who I'd only recently met and just barely talked to, and most of that no more than rambling nonsense. It's hard for me to explain it to you now, but I trusted her soon as I met her. Mayhaps sometimes that's just as it is, like when I met you, just a few days ago and here's me telling you my whole story, scars and all.

"We sat there and I talked for a long time. I told her about the death of my sister Áine and my grandfather's powerless uncaring gods, and about my great-uncle Eóchaidh teaching me to play the harp, and about Mellán and Father Cyneric coming to Port Láirge, and making boards and beams with Papa for the church building that was never built, and me carving the front-piece for the altar, and the meeting of the council under the Tree of Wisdom and me showing the elders the front-piece, and them putting the arrogant priest out to sea in a little rowing boat wrapped up in a sail, and me going home expecting Mam and Papa to be proud of me, but instead finding them having a fight, about me and that altar front-piece.

"She said she'd like to see the front-piece, and I told her I'd show it to her in the morning, that I wouldn't want to wake Mellán and Twedwr to fetch it. The truth of it was that I was afraid if I left, she'd get away. I didn't tell her that my grandfather killed my mother, because it was just too much for me to say out loud like that, but I told her that when my mam died, I didn't have any good reason to stay there, and my friend Mellán was talking about coming back to Angleland to the monastery where he grew up, and I told him I'd come along with him. Then I told her how we met Twedwr, and how it happened that he was coming along with us as well.

"Then, after all that talking, I asked her to tell me about herself, and she told me that her father owned the Pig and Pike, and that she was betrothed to marry Henry, the son of the town's mayor. So, all my hopes and fantasies came crashing down around my feet, and of a sudden as I was sitting there, it was as if I'd sprung a leak, and I felt like I was sinking away into bitter disappointment.

"I tried to school my face, but she knew—she was trying to save me from having these ideas about romance, but it was already too late. Then, just to talk about aught else, she told me that I play the harp beautifully, and that she herself loved to sing. So naturally I asked her to sing me a little something, and she sang a song her mother taught her:

'Hush now, baby mine, the wind is howling loud
Hear it blowing, hear it roaring
Your Papa's gone to catch some fish
But here we are, all warm and safe
    So you can go to sleep, lullay, lullay
    So you can go to sleep.'

"She stopped, but I thought there was likely a bit more to it, so I picked up the harp and played the first notes of the verse, and she was surprised that I knew the notes of it, but she sang it out." Pell picked up his harp and sang along to the tune he played:

"Hush now, baby mine, the rain is falling softly
Hear it tapping, hear it dripping
Your sister's up to tend the lambs
But here we are, all fed and drowsy
    So you can go to sleep, lullay, lullay
    So you can go to sleep.

Hush now, baby mine, the waves are coming home
Where have they been, and where did they go?
Your brother's out to find the wandering ram

But here we are, all bundled and cozy
    So you can go to sleep, lullay, lullay
    So you can go to sleep."

"Ah, and it was a sweet song as could make a turtle cry," he continued, "and I was already feeling weepy. When she saw that I was crying, she started crying along with me, so we could hardly finish the song. Her voice was at the same time sweet and strong, soft and powerful—it was, ah, what would a word be? It was of her own self, from her soul, and true, it was ..."

"Authentic?" suggested Oswell.

"Aye, that's the very word for it—authentic! Her voice was authentic to herself. Well, we talked a bit more and I helped her sweep up under the tables and such, and then I went up the stairs to our room where Mellán and Twedwr were already snoring in harmony.

"The next morning, I came down the stairs and she was already waked, making up the fire. So, I helped her as I could, or got in her way more likely, and she asked me if I'd like to eat a bite while I waited on my friends. I hesitated just a heartbeat, and she said with some flirt in her voice that made my heart soar, until I remembered she was betrothed, 'If you'll take a bite, I'll join you, if you wouldn't mind it.' Now I was thinking I don't owe this Henry fella aught, and if a lass wanted to break her fast with me, there was nary a thing wrong about that.

"Presently she brought out a platter of fried bread and cheese with a wide bowl of mushrooms, and a jug of goat's milk with two cups. It was all quite snug and I decided I enjoyed being in her company just because of herself, whether there was to be any romance in our future or not. We ate and talked and laughed, and I showed her some about strumming the harp. To be sure, it was a pleasant moment, and I thought I could be forgiven if I were a bit regretful, wishing aught could be different between us.

"By and by down came Mellán, and Brigid brought him some bread and cheese and a jar of milk, but I noted that there were no mushrooms for him. She put the food and drink down in front of him and was about to step away, but I asked her to sit back down, and asked her to sing the lullaby for Mellán. So she did, and he was taken by the magic of it same as I was, and as the last notes faded, we sat there for a time, just holding our silence. Then Mellán cleared his throat and thanked her for singing, and said he'd need to be leaving now, just to give us some space, but I said, 'Nay, there's no need of it. Brigid and I are friends—she's spoken for already, by the son of the mayor of this town.' I was sad to say it, but I tried to keep it cheery, like it was all just fine with me. My brother Mellán saw that it pained me hard, and that there was naught for it but that we move along, so he asked Brigid to sing the lullaby again, and this time he added some harmony that almost broke my heart, it was so sweet. Ah—the two of them singing together was sure to make the very angels of heaven wish they could sing so well.

"That night, we sang our songs and Twedwr told a few tales and we were all taken over by the magic of it all. The basket was passed around, and after another song or two, it was looking like Feichín the tavern-keeper was about to make the sad announcement that we were out of ale. But before he could, I stood up to say, 'We'll need a little help with this song, a little lullaby to send us to our dreams.' Then I looked around to find Brigid, who was shaking her head lively to tell me nay, that she didn't want to do it, and I said, 'Brigid, come up here and sing us a song.'

"The people looked around and when they saw her, they were startled it was her I was calling up to join us. She was not keen about it, but they were encouraging her, and a young man put his arm around her shoulders and guided us over to our corner of the common room. I thought, 'That must be the bastard, Henry.' She looked down at me and whispered, 'You're a right arse, Just Pell, do you know that?'

"I just looked up at her and smiled and started plucking out the first notes of the lullaby. She turned around and saw nearly the whole village looking at her, most of them a bit surprised to see her standing there, and then she started to sing. She was a bit wobbly through the first verse, but when Mellán joined in a harmony on the second, she sang it out sweet and strong.

"Well, you could've heard a spider blink in there, it was so quiet while they were singing. It was a song all the people there knew, a song their mams had sung them when they were just lads and lasses, but they didn't join in, nary a one of them, for fear of breaking the magic of it. And when it was done, they all just sat there, every one of them, not willing to make the first peep or cheep. So, I stood up and started a clap, and soon everybody was clapping for her, and I saw she was deeply touched by it.

"I reached over to pat her on the back or something, but I drew back before I touched her. I was thinking her Henry was sure to be watching, and I didn't want to give him any reason to be concerned, not wanting to cause her a trouble. So I just leaned over to her and said, 'Thank you, Brigid—that was well done.' And before she could say me aught back, Twedwr came up and put two silver coins in her hand, 'to pay you for your singing.'

"Now Feichín the tavern owner was telling everybody we were all out of ale again, and as everybody was leaving, they were telling one another to have a good night and asking us if we would be back the next. The truth of it was that we hadn't talked about it—I knew Mellán was eager to continue our journey down to Londinium, and I'm sure he knew I was hoping to stay there in Scrobbesbyrig for another night or two, hoping I might win Brigid over, but we hadn't spoken about it at all. So, as I was telling one of the older men of the town that I was hoping we'd stay for the next night, I looked over and saw Mellán talking to somebody, and I wondered what he was saying.

"The idea of moving on, of leaving Brigid there and going to the next town without her was a heavy load for me to carry, and it saddened me from my toes to my scalp. I was talking to some of the people there and taking a little extra time to show the harp to some of the lads there, when I noticed Brigid standing behind the bar, and from time to time looking over my way.

"I told the lads to be sure their dreams were stronger than their fears, and after they were gone, I sat down on my little bench to put the harp back in its satchel. I was thinking it would surely be terrible sad to leave, to tell Brigid to have a good life with the mayor's son, but what did I have to offer her? I could stay there and start a carpenter shop, and try to win her away from Henry, but even if I did, we'd starve before I had enough customers. Nay, it would be better for her if I were to just move on, mayhaps not even telling her a fare well.

"Now Twedwr came over and he leaned over to my ear and whispered, 'Mind yourself now, lad. Remember the Power of Eleven.' That was all he said, but the verse came back to me quickly: 'Eleven are the ways of a woman with a man, mysterious and strong.' Before I could even tell him I didn't have any idea what he was on about, and that I wouldn't be having any sort of love story with Brigid, he was gone up the stairs, and here she came, suddenly all weepy and forlorn.

"Well, she sat down right beside me on that little bench so I could feel the warmth of her shoulder touching mine, and when I saw the tears dripping down her face, I said, 'Here, now—what ails you, Brigid?'

"She looked right sad and said, 'I owe you an apology—I'm like the young woman who tricked the dragon.'

"Well, now I was already feeling lost in this conversation, and it was just getting started. So I ventured, 'In Twedwr's story?'

"'Aye,' she answered. 'And now I'm feeling the guilt and remorse that come from tricking such a noble creature.'

"Aye, well—I don't always see what's just in front of me right at first, and I had no idea what she was talking about. I was afraid mayhaps the mayor's son might have seen how I looked at her, or something similar. So, I was chary when I asked her, 'What noble creature did you trick?'

"She looked at me like the fool I am—not for the last time—and said, 'You! I'm talking about you, you daft man!' I suppose I must have looked as vexed as I felt, and she said, 'I lied to you, Pell. I'm not Feichín's daughter, and I'm not promised to anybody. Scrobbesbyrig doesn't even have a mayor—they tried it once before I was born, but they didn't like it.' She let her chin drop down, and I said, 'Well, I don't mind, Brigid—don't go getting yourself dreary for such as a thing that.'

"Her shoulders shook out a little sob, and I was thinking I'd make things worse for her with any word I tried, so I just sat quiet. In a short time, she said, 'I lied, Pell—I lied and you trusted me, and I let you believe the lies. And even when you were believing that I was promised to another man—a made-up man—you still treated me like I was somebody who means something, you treated me with respect. You told Mellán that we were friends, and I could see that was important to you, and that touched me, it touched my heart.'

"She stopped talking, and I tried to be gentle when I said, 'Why did you lie, Brigid? And why are you telling me the truth now?'

"Her face was heartbreaking gloomy, and I was wanting naught more than to soothe away her pain, but of course I didn't know how, so I just looked at her, feeling like a bonehead. She sobbed, 'I was afraid, Pell—I was just afraid of my feelings for you, and I knew you'd be leaving. I was trying to keep you at your distance, because I didn't want to be hurt when you left.' I didn't know what to say, and managed to say naught, and she went on, 'So I lied, Pell. I told you I couldn't be someone special to you, when that's all I really wanted!'

"Now it seemed like a good time for a kiss. I'd never kissed a lass before, and I was a little clumsy about it, but Brigid saw my bungling and helped me out."

Chapter XVII

The Witch Woman of Scrobbesbyrig

"Well, it all seemed to be going pretty well," Pell continued, "when there was a crashing whack, and I was thrown down on the floor, with a wee little man hitting me with his fists and trying to bite me!"

"What?" cried Oswell, alarmed. "Did you fight back?"

"Well, I stood myself up as best I could, with him hitting and trying to bite me the whole time, and Brigid stepped in to pull him away and shouted, 'Séamus, stop! You stop this right now!'

"The wee man stopped, but he was breathing murder and looking at me like I was a villainous brute. Now I saw that he was right small, but he made up for it by being right angry. She'd taken ahold of him, and now she leaned over to hug him, patting him on his chest, and I had a moment to take a good look at him, while he was calming down.

"He was short—the top of his head well below my shoulders, and his face was flat ... blunt somehow. His eyes were rounder than any I'd ever seen, and slanted differently, and his tongue was sticking out like there wasn't enough room in his mouth for all of it in there. His hands and fingers were also small, so I wondered if I'd met a lupracán, some wee creature full of mischief. But the stories I'd heard never mentioned a *lupracán* busting in on a fella trying to kiss a lass!

"They'd been talking the whole time I was looking, him saying in a different-sounding style of voice that he wouldn't let the bad man hurt her, that he's watching over her, like she watches over him, and her trying to soothe his anger away and telling him they watch over each other all the time, and that I was a good man.

"I dropped down to my knees and said, 'Halloo, friend. My name is Pell.' Straightaway he looked up at Brigid, who nodded to him before he turned back to me and said, 'My name is Shea.'

"Now Brigid straightened up and let him go, and I readied myself for another attack, but he stayed where he was. She said, 'This is my brother, Séamus. But I call him Shea.'

"Well, so I sat right down on the floor and held out my hand and said, 'It's a grand pleasure to meet you, friend Shea.' He looked at my hand a bit chary, but he took it with a great smile as my hand swallowed his like a cormorant taking up a wee sprat.

"Then Brigid sat on the floor facing me and said, 'Shea, Pell wasn't hurting me. We were … we were kissing. Do you know about kissing?' Shea nodded and said, 'Sure, I know all about that. I heard some of the men in the stable talking about kissing.'

"Brigid looked over at me to explain, 'Shea works here, here at the Pig and Pike, in the stable. He takes care of the horses that belong to travelers. He's right good at it, really.' He nodded, clearly proud of his work, and said, 'I feed the horses, and brush them and get the tanglies out of their manes, and tend to their hoofs and all, and make sure they always have lots of hay and water.'

"Now it seemed like it was my time to say something, so I said, 'That sounds a grand job. I've never even touched a horse. We don't have them where I'm from.'

"Shea was outraged to hear about such a place as had no horses and asked where I was from. I told him I was from Éire, and he said people must talk funny in Éire. I looked at Brigid, and she said, 'Well, you do have an accent, you know.'

"Then she said, 'Shea, you're usually hard asleep by this time of the night—is aught wrong?'

"He answered, 'Nay. I just wanted to bid you a good night. Are you and him about to kiss some more?' She laughed and said, 'I don't know, mayhaps. But it's something we won't be needing you to watch, so I'll tell you all about it in the morning. Is that a good idea?'

"He stood up and said, 'Aye, that's a good idea.' Then he turned to me and made a little bow, and said, 'Good night, friend Pell.' He turned again to hug his sister, and then he toddled away, back behind the bar, and he was gone.

"Brigid looked at me and said, 'I'm … sorry for the interruption. Shea is … well, Shea is just Shea.'

"And I said, 'I thought he was a lupracán!'

"'A … what?' she wondered. 'Oh, you mean a leprechaun? Nay, he was just … born that way.'

"I said, 'He's a fine young man, it seems to me. How old is he?'

"'Eleven, almost twelve,' she answered. 'He's … small for his age.'

"'Aye,' I said, 'what's—ah, is he sick or something?'

"She looked—oh, I don't know how to say how she looked: sad, defiant, loving, and angry, and all the time understanding what I was trying to ask her. She said, 'I don't know. He's never gotten any better, or worse. Shea is just Shea.'

"Then I said, 'As much as I'm hoping we'll find our way back to the kissing—just so you'll have something to tell brother Shea about in the morning—I'd like for you to tell me about yourself, the truth this time, and about my new friend Shea.'

"So, she told me. She was born in a little village upriver called Uiroconion. The Romans had long ago made a powerful fort there, but they were all gone now, so there wasn't much left. Her father was a good man, she said, but when little Shea was born, and was clearly different, the men of the village came around telling him the wee babe was an evil omen, that the gods were cursing them, and they should put the baby in the River Sæferne, to let him float away. They were right religious, these men. Well, it seemed her father was agreeable, but her mother refused to have her wee child treated so, no matter how different he was, and no matter what the elders of the village said.

"So, they kept the baby, and they all loved him dearly. But every time a calf died, or a storm raged, or if the rain hit the wheat crop at the wrong time, or aught happened that no one could explain, the men in the village would blame it on poor Shea.

"When he was just over five, in between one full moon and the next, the son of one of the elders had been washed over the side of his boat and lost in the river, and three lambs died at lambing. So,

she told me, the men of the village brought themselves together and
had a council, and there they decided it must all be little Shea's fault,
and that they needed his father to set him out in the river, in a little
coracle boat, to let the gods take him back.

"'But we heard what they were planning to do,' she said, 'and
I went down to the place where the men were and told them they
were just a clattering of old jackdaws. Da refused to put Shea out,
but a gang of four or five of them came and snatched him away. It
was a pitiful moment, my da trying to fight them off, my ma hitting
at them with her big boiling pot, and little Shea crying and reaching
out for his ma—oh, I dream about it still, it just breaks my heart.

"'But Shea lived through it,' I said, never one to let the obvious
go unspoken.

"'Aye, well,' she said, 'I sneaked down river to a place where I
knew I'd be well hid, and I waited. The moon was nearly full, so I
could see, and by and by here came that wee boat with my poor little
Shea in it—he was clutching onto the sides of it so he wouldn't fall
out, but he wasn't crying, he was just looking around. I waded out so
I could catch the boat, and then I got in it with him, and we floated
all night, until we came here, to Scrobbesbyrig.'

"I stopped her then, because that wasn't the way I was thinking
the story ought to have gone. 'You brought him here? I thought you'd
take him back to your parents.'

"'Aye,' she said, 'and mayhaps that was what I should have done.
But I reckoned if I had, the next time somebody's ram got lost or if
lightning hit a tree and started a fire, they'd all come blaming Shea
and putting him another boat down the river. Well, I hope I made
the right choice; we came here.

"'By the time we floated down to Scrobbesbyrig, the sun was
coming up, and Shea and I were right hungry, and mighty wet and
cold—poor Shea's lips were turning blue. Now, just as it happened,
there was a little bent over woman who was right then coming down
to the river to fetch up some water, and when she saw us, she pulled
us to the river's bank. She took us in—the holy Mother bless her—
or we would have died that very morning. She brought us into her

home and filled us full of hot porridge and wrapped us foot to head in blankets and set us by her fire to warm our bones.

"'That woman, Miss Astrid, was a healer and a midwife; she made cheese and wine, she baked bread and kept bees and goats and grew herbs and vegetables. It was Miss Astrid who taught me how to bake, and about plants that are good for healing different ills. And she taught Shea about caring for the living creatures, the goats and bees, and birds, and dogs, and every creature you could name. Oh, Shea loved all the animals, even then.'

"I said, 'Aye, well—did you ever tell your ma and da where you went? They must have been fretful, do you think?'

"'Aye, of course, you silly man. Two days after we came to her, Miss Astrid told us she knew a man going up that way, toward Uiro-conion, and she asked him to find our ma and da and tell them we're safe and well and living with the witch woman of Scrobbesbyrig. And before you ask, I'll tell you right now that Miss Astrid was no witch, and I'll knock the man down who says she was. But that was how the people thought of her, as a witch. She was just capable, and she never married or had any children until we floated into her life, and she spoke her mind freely, and she didn't do what the men around there thought a woman ought to do, so they reckoned she was a witch. They were right religious, as I said, and that was their problem.

"'A few days later, Ma and Da came to visit. Oh, and there was a great deal of hugging and crying and such. Ma said she didn't know whether to scold me for doing such a foolish thing as I did, wading out into the water and getting in the coracle boat with Shea, or to thank me. Then she hugged me again. After a time, Ma and Da talked with Miss Astrid, and they all agreed that it would be best for Shea and me to stay with Miss Astrid, at least for a while. Well, I didn't like it, but Miss Astrid helped me understand that with her, Shea would be accepted, accepted as the witch's foster, but accepted. She told me it would be better for Shea, and that it would be good for me, and for her as well. And she told me that my ma and da could come see us any time. She said we could just try it for a time, and if we weren't happy about it, we could go back.'

"I said, 'But couldn't your mother and father have moved down to Scrobbesbyrig, where the people weren't so religious about things like this?'

"'Nay,' she said, 'my Da was farming the land his father and grandfather had farmed there, growing barley and rye and keeping apple trees and all. Ma said it would break his heart to leave, so they stayed.'

"Then she took a deep breath and said, 'We'd been there with Miss Astrid for more than a year when Da came to tell us that Ma had died. She'd been kicked by a cow delivering her calf, and she was bleeding on the inside, he said. She died the next day and was buried before he could come tell us about it. I could see he was in an awful bad way.'

"I said, 'Oh, Brigid—I'm so sorry.' And she said, 'Aye, it was a right terrible thing, to be sure, a terrible thing when your mother dies.' I told her I knew that right well, and she took up my hand to her lips, and then sure I knew my heart was lost forever. A breath or two later, she went on with her story. 'And then some months after that, Miss Astrid's friend who had business up in Uiroconion told her that Da had started drinking right hard, and that the apples were withering on the trees. So, Miss Astrid and Shea and I went to Uiroconion, and it was as her friend had said—the land was sadly neglected. You could see that Da was suffering from a broken heart, and he had no help—all those religious fools didn't lift a finger.'

'We tried to do what we could, with Da either drunk or sleeping it away, and Miss Astrid too old and frail to be doing much, but then she had to go back and tend her own goats and all, and there was a lass about to have her babe and Miss Astrid was needed there for the birth, and I was right torn in half wanting to stay with Da and wanting to go with Miss Astrid both at the same time.'

"'So, I stayed with Da,' she said, 'and Shea went with Miss Astrid, which was the most sense we could make of it at the time, but everybody was completely miserable for a week or so.' I waited for her to tell the next part, not knowing what it was but thinking it was bound to be bad, and in a little while, she continued. 'Then one night, he came home from the tavern, out drinking with his so-called friends, and I told him I'd made up a stew and baked us a loaf. I was right proud of myself, and was hoping he would be, too. But instead, he told me that I sounded just like my ma, always screeching at him about one thing and another, and that I needed to leave him be.'

"Then she sat still and quiet for a while, and I sat quiet with her. When she did talk, it all came out in a rush, like something she's been holding back, something she'd been needing to let go. She said, 'All I said was, "It's right good," and it was like I'd taken a spark to knotty pine, like he just caught fire of a sudden. Well, he was so angry that it frighted me, and I backed away from him, and when he saw me backing away he came over in a rush, like he was angry that I was afraid, so I backed farther away and he was angry and he kept coming and I couldn't back away anymore and he took me by the shoulder and shook me to make stop crying, but I couldn't stop because I was so scared, and he …'

"'He hit you,' I said it for her. She nodded, and now I scooched over to right beside where she was sitting and pulled her into a hug, and we stayed like that for a time. She just cried for a while, and I was glad I was there to hold her. By and by she straightened up and said, 'After that, I went back to live with Shea and Miss Astrid. Some time later, Miss Astrid's friend came back from his business in Uiroconion and told her my da wasn't there anymore—nobody knew where he went, but he wasn't there.

"'Then Miss Astrid told us we were to be her children now, and I told Shea that would be the best thing for us. He wanted to know if he had to call her Ma, but she just smiled and said, "Nay, son—I'm still who I ever was, just Miss Astrid," so that seemed good to Shea.

"'We lived there for five more years,' she said, 'until Miss Astrid just up and died. One morning she just didn't wake up, and nobody knew why. Nobody knew how old she was, but there wasn't a soul who could remember a time when she wasn't out there in that little house, ready to set a broken arm or sew up a cut or make a potion to ease your pain or fight away an infection. There weren't many there as hadn't been born with her right there to hand them to their mothers, and that's just the truth of it.'

"She continued talking so softly I had to lean in a bit just to hear it, 'Well, she didn't have any family that anybody knew about, so the house and her land were ours. We tried to stay there in her house and keep up the bees and the goats and all, but it was just too much, and we were only children ourselves, and I was afraid we were going to starve. So, we walked into town and asked around for who might be willing to hire us, and somebody said ol' Feichín was always looking for people to hire at the tavern, so we went to talk to him. He said he'd be glad to hire me, but he didn't think he had a place for Shea, so I thanked him and started on my way. He called me back and asked me how Shea might be useful to him. I told him he loves all sorts of animals, and he asked me if he's ever had much truck with horses. Well, I thought about telling a lie, but I said, 'Well, nay—but he'll take to it quickly, you'll see.' And he did.

"I said, 'So Shea and you come here to work and live. How long have you been here? Do you like it? Did you ever see your da again?'

"She answered, 'Nay, we never saw Da again. I reckon he must be dead, but I don't know of a certain.' She was quiet for a time, and then she laughed, a right pleasant sound after all that dreary talk, and said, 'Aye, so—we came to live here nearly three years now, and we live in our little room in the back there. Shea works in the stable, he's just so good with the horses and the mule and all, and he loves it. And I pour out the ale and serve up the meals and ignore the men who've had too much and talk to me rude—it's just part of the job.'

"'Why would they be rude?' I wanted to know, and she said, 'Because they're men, and men are just men, so they grab at what they want, like I'm some poor fragile woman. But they're learning. And Feichín helps when a fella doesn't understand what I mean when I say no. He's thrown a fair few of them out on their ears.'

"So, we sat there for a time, and I didn't know what to say or do about all that, and she said, 'Now I think we ought to do some more kissing, just so I'll have something to tell Shea about in the morning.'"

"So, you kissed?" Oswell asked.

"Oh, aye, we kissed," grinned Pell, "well of course we did, and that'll be all I need to say about that."

Chapter XVIII

You Can Only Row
One Boat at a Time

Pell continued, "We stayed there in Scrobbesbyrig for two more nights, and the people coming to hear the music were starting to ask if we knew any other songs, so clearly it was time to go. That third night, Mellán, Twedwr and I agreed we'd leave in the morning, on our way to the next village and the next and make our way down on to Erith. My heart was about to break, but I had to go. I didn't think Mellán and Twedwr would be willing to take Brigid with us, and I was sure she wouldn't be willing to go without Shea. I didn't sleep that night, not a wink.

"The next morning, when I came down the stairs into the common room, I was surprised to see that Mellán and Twedwr were already up before me, and they were having a squabble. When I got close enough to hear, I heard they were arguing about taking Brigid with us, and my heart leaped up in hope. Mellán was saying he was in favor of adding to our little wandering herd, but Twedwr was chary about it. I heard the Druid say, 'Aye, it's powerful bad luck to go off travelling with a woman, everybody knows that!'

"When I went to stand with them, just to bid them a good morning, they stopped their talking and looked like two lads caught doing something they should not have been doing. I said, 'Well now, I'll just speak my mind and say no more about it. I don't know the first thing about women, so I don't know if aught will come from my feelings for Brigid, but I'd like to find out. Mellán, I promised you I'd go with you to Erith, and that I will do. If you two decide she'll not be going with us, I'll go down there with you and come back up here quick as I can, and hope she'll be waiting for me.'

"Then I took a deep breath and said, 'This is something for you two to decide, and I'll abide by whatever you say.' And then I added, 'You do need to know that if you decide to ask Brigid to come with us, she will be needing to ask her brother Shea to come as well. Have you met Shea? Little fella works in the stable—aye and well, he's … well he's just Shea, and there's no other way to explain or understand it. I'll just say you'll be needing to meet him before you invite her.' And then I walked away, to wait and hope I hadn't just done something terrible stupid.

"So, I sat outside, just watching the town wake up, and presently here came Brigid, all in a great bother. She said, 'I just talked to Mellán, and he said that he and Twedwr were talking to you about bringing Shea and me with you when you go! Is that the way of it?'

"Well, I was distressed that she seemed upset about that, and I said, 'Aye—I just heard about it this morning, too. How do you think of that?' Ignorant, I was. Just ignorant.

"She said, 'I'll tell you again: you're a right arse, Just Pell from Éire.'

"So, I said, 'What? What's got you so upset, Brigid?' Aye, and then she put in plain and forceful words what was in her mind, that she and Shea weren't something to be picked up and hauled off like a sack of onions, and that it wasn't our decision whether she and Shea would be leaving Scrobbesbyrig, and that they didn't need somebody like me to take care of them. And if I was wanting her and Shea to come with them, well then why hadn't I asked her about it?

"Well, I just sat there quiet as a trout, and by and by all her anger was out in the air. She was quiet for just a moment and I said, 'I'm sorry, Brigid. I was ….' I was looking for the right word, and she said, 'Selfish.' Just trying to be helpful, she was.

"Well,' I said, 'Aye, that's true, but I was trying to say I was ….'

"'Thoughtless,' is the word she suggested.

"'Aye,' I said, 'but that's not the word I'm looking for, I was …'

"She jumped in again and spat out, 'Blind to anybody but yourself.'

"I shook my head and said, 'Nay, well aye—I was that as well, and that's coming closer to it, and I thank you for all your help, but what I was trying to say is that I was ...' and this time she just looked at me, and I finished, 'I was just a man, Brigid, thinking like a man.'

"She looked at me and saw a daft fool, so I said, 'I was just born that way.' And when she said, 'Pah!' at me, I said, 'If I'm ever to be any better, I'm thinking I'll be needing you to help me.'

"Well, that tendered her up a bit, so I asked her if she wanted to go with us, which I saw right quick was a question she should have been asked much earlier, and she said she wasn't sure. She considered it a while and said, 'Tell me again where is it you're going.' I said, 'Well—I'm not real sure where it is or how far it is we need to go, but we're going down past Londinium, or near there, to a house of monks in Erith.'

"She said, 'A house of monks! I can't imagine such a thing. And you say you don't know how long it's to take you, or how far it is to go?'

"I answered, 'Aye, that's the truth of it.' Then, as she was looking at me like I'd misplaced my mind, I added, 'If you're not wanting to go, you don't have to. If you and Shea stay here, I'll come back for you, if you'll have me.'

"That seemed to touch her, and she knew I meant it. Now she was melting a bit, and I was right relieved. Then, as I was trying to tell her what a monk is, from only just knowing Mellán, and as we were trying to think what a house full of Melláns might be like, young Shea came busting out of the Pig and Pike and yelled, 'Brigid! Those two men asked us to go to Londinium! Can we go?' And now here came Mellán and Twedwr, looking pleased with themselves about their decision to bring Brigid and Shea with us.

"Well, I tried to warn them, but soon they were hearing words like 'selfish, thoughtless and blind,' as well as 'pig-headed, slow-witted and rude.' Before she was done, Mellán and Twedwr were looking so sheepish and dejected that she had to laugh, in spite of herself.

"Then she said to Shea, 'Aye, Shea—we can go, if only to keep these three silly lads out of trouble.' Then to Mellán and Twedwr she said, 'But we're not sheep that you can herd around, and we're not owned, not by any of you!' I thought that last bit was probably aimed at me, so I nodded as loud as I could. Then she said to Shea, 'Go get your things together, and I'll go talk to Feichín.'

"So young Shea started to trot off, but then he turned around and asked Brigid, 'Can Oscar come, too?' She made a compassionate face and said, 'Nay, dear Shea—Molly and Eleanor will be needing him to stay with them.' That seemed to satisfy Shea, who scurried away to gather his things. I didn't know who Oscar was, nor Molly and Eleanor, but I thought it had naught to do with us, so I didn't ask.

"Mellán, Twedwr and I got our things together, which wasn't much, but quite a bit more than it had been when we started, with our pots and pans and bags of grain and jars of spices and the bodhrán, which we still didn't know much about but were still hauling from one place to the next. And, of course, I still had the front-piece, which I'll tell you hadn't been a great deal of trouble, but it was a clunky bit of bother to be walking around with.

"In just a short time, here came Brigid with Feichín, and I was thinking he'd be trying to get us to stay another night or two, but instead he asked us if we'd be wanting to buy some horses, mayhaps a mule, and a wagon to pull behind it.

"Mellán, Twedwr and I didn't know what to say about any of that, until Shea said, 'The mule's name is Oscar. He's my friend, and a good lad.' It was plain on his face Shea loved this mule. Feichín said he never knew the mule had a name, and Shea replied, 'I named him Oscar, because every mule should have a name, and because he's a champion.' Apparently 'Oscar' means something to do with being a champion. I learned a lot from little Shea.'

"When I started to tell Feichín we weren't looking to buy any horses or mules, Mellán whispered, 'Well now, wait a breath or two. Mayhaps it would be nice to have a horse to ride, and mayhaps a wagon to carry our things.' Then Twedwr murmured, 'Were you thinking we'd be having Brigid and Shea walk from here to Londinium, hauling their belongings on their backs?'

"Aye, well—that put things in a different light. So, it was looking like we were to be riding instead of walking, which to be honest was a happy thought for my feet. But as I've said before, Mellán, Twedwr and I didn't know the first thing about horses, or mules, or wagons, starting with how much silver Feichín might be asking for all of that. They were all looking at me like it was my decision to make, so I asked Feichín, 'How much silver would you need to sell us a mule, a wagon and three horses? Sturdy, gentle, polite horses, mind.' Feichín did some reckoning and said, 'Well, it's a grand wagon, and fine horses. I couldn't let them go for aught less than two hundred pieces of silver.'

"Now we all looked at Twedwr, who'd been holding the money for us, and he said we had that much, but it had taken a great many songs and stories to gather it all up. But now Brigid said, 'Feichín, I'm staggered you'd be willing take advantage of us so! And here's me thinking you've been like a father to Shea and me and all. That wagon and donkey have been in your stable for how long, since Lughnasadh for sure, just eating your hay and taking up room you don't have. Now you have a chance to be shed of them, and you're wanting to swindle these poor wandering minstrels?'

"Well, now Feichín was looking all sheepish and forlorn, and I admit I was amused to see Brigid happen to somebody else. Presently he said, 'How about one hundred fifty?' and quick as a minnow she answered, 'How about one twenty-five?' When he nodded his reluctant agreement, Brigid gave me just the barest smile, and I looked at Mellán and Twedwr, who seemed keen about it, and I said, 'Master Feichín—we thank you kindly.'

"So we came into Scrobbesbyrig three footsore men, and we left three men, a woman, a wee little lad, a wagon, three horses, and a mule.

"We gathered up all our possessions, which still weren't much even after we added Brigid and Shea's things and put all of it in the back of the wagon, and then we were off to the next town.

"There will be naught good to come of me telling you about learning to ride a horse while we were at the same time riding it, except to say that Mellán seemed to take to it naturally, while Twedwr and I had to take a few falls before we could make much progress at all. They were good horses, and it wasn't that they were trying to buck us off—they just seemed slippery sometimes. After a mile or two, Shea told us the mares were wanting to follow the gelding, so we went in that order: first Mellán on his gelding, then me, then Twedwr, and then Brigid and Shea in the wagon behind the mule. So, in truth my feet might have been happier for the horses, but it took three or four days for the rest of me to join them in their joy.

"We'd surely have been lost if it hadn't been for Shea, who knew how to put on a saddle, take a rock out of a horse's hoof, and put the mule in its traces before the wagon. He thought it was right humorous every time Twedwr or I fell off a horse, but other than that, he was a good teacher.

"He'd named all our horses, saying horses should have names just the same as mules and people. The black gelding that Mellán rode was named Piran, the bay mare that Twedwr struggled with was called Molly, and the dapple-grey mare I was clinging to was named Eleanor. Shea told me it meant 'shining light'—I never did find out how he came to know things like that.

"By the time we came to a place to stop that night, I was bruised and sore and out of sorts, and generally not fit for polite company. It cheered me some to see that Twedwr was in the same sad state, but then to be honest it irked me to see that Mellán wasn't. Brigid was flummoxed to learn that we didn't have a tent and told us we'd have to get one next town we came to. Then she said we'd be needing to get two, saying she'd not be wanting to sleep in a tent with a herd of men.

"We'd stopped beside a little creek, and after she came back from what she called a private moment, she found our cooking pot and filled it about half full of water. Then I saw her unwrapping a joint of meat from a piece of cloth, saying Feichín had given it to her as a going gift. We settled the pot over the fire, and I peeled some praties, and Twedwr brought out our little store of spices. Then there was an onion cut and put in there, and we were on the path to having lamb stew for supper.

"It was a pleasant night in early spring, cool with a soft breeze and a moon almost full, and a circle of contented friends. After we ate, there was a great deal of sighing and thanking Brigid for the meal.

We only had three wood bowls, so we had to take turns, something else she said we'd have to get at the next village. Then Shea asked if I'd play something on the harp. Brigid said I might not want to, but I said I would, if he'd go and fetch the harp out of the wagon—I was so full of stew I thought I might pop open if I had to move right then.

"So, in a while here came Shea with the harp, and the bodhrán. I said, just to be making some talk, 'What have you there?' thinking he wouldn't know. But he said, 'It's a bodhrán. I saw them other fellas playing one, remember, Brigid?' She said, 'Aye, I remember those boyos, and their little drum.' She laughed and said, 'The more ale that tall one drank, the faster he'd thump on it, and the faster those other two had to sing along!' Then Shea said, 'He had a little stick he tapped on it.'

"Aye, well, we played and sang a song or two, and I saw Shea pick up the bodhrán and plunk at it with his thumb and noted that he kept the right time with the music. So, I said, 'Shea, if I make you a little stick, do you think you could tap it along when I play the harp?' He said he could, and then we played and sang some more, and he thumped away, and I have to say I was surprised at how much it added to the music, like a bit of level ground for everything else to stand on.

"Then he tried to sing, too, and that wasn't so pleasant for any of us, until finally Brigid had to tell him it would be better if he just played the bodhrán, how important it was that he put his mind on keeping us so we were all playing and singing together, instead of Mellán singing too slow or Pell playing the harp too fast. That was enough for him, and a relief to the rest of us.

"Then Twedwr said, 'There is a song you can sing part of, Shea. It's called "The Butterfly's Blessing," and the part for you to sing out, real loud now, is 'a blessing to you!' When we sang that song, Shea was so eager about singing his part that his keenness was catching, and a joyful song became that much more full of happy.

"We sang until Shea was asleep and Mellán was getting drowsy, and I wasn't far behind. Then everybody rolled up in whatever blanket or cloak we had and went to sleep on the ground. Well, I waited for Brigid to come over and give me a little kiss, but she never did, and

I was dead tired, so I just fell asleep. The next morning, she told me that she'd waited for me to come over where she was for a kiss, but I never did, so I laughed and told her I'd done the same thing, and I promised it would never happen again. It was years after that before I went to my sleep without her kiss on my lips.

"Later that morning, I saw an ash growing along the side of the little track we were following, and I stopped, grateful to unburden Eleanor of myself for a moment—and myself of her—and told Shea to come with me. I asked him to tell me about this little stick for the bodhrán and found a good hard limb that I hacked off the tree with my knife. Before we came to the alehouse in the next village, I'd whittled it down to about the length and width Shea was remembering, a little longer than two hands wide, and a bit thicker than my thumb, plumped out a bit on both ends.

"As Shea and Twedwr took the horses and the mule to the stable, Mellán, Brigid and I went into the tavern and sat ourselves down at a table. Presently a young woman came over and I told her we'd be grateful for three jars of ale, but Brigid said, 'Oh, nay—do you have wine?'

"Well, I'd heard of wine, but I'd never seen any before; when the lass brought it out I had a little taste of Brigid's, and I'd never had aught like it. But still I told her I'd rather have the ale. By and by, here came Twedwr and Shea, and we asked the young woman if we could get Twedwr a jar of water and Shea a little milk, and she told us what they were offering by way of a supper, mostly one style of mutton or another.

"After we ate, I brought out the harp and started playing a little tune, and then we sang 'The Beltane Fire' and just like always, the crowd gathered and grew, and we kept playing and singing until the common room was nearly full. By now we had the pattern of it worked out: while the people were still gathering, I would start to look like I was about to put the harp away, and the tavern keeper would hurry over, hoping we'd play another tune or two. Then Twedwr would haggle a bit, and if he didn't get what we wanted right off—our meals and rooms paid for—we'd play another song or tell another story and then start to pack up getting ready to leave, so the tavern owner would come back and give us what Twedwr had asked for. No innkeeper wanted to see a crowd of paying customers leaving.

"After that was all squared up, we sang our songs just as always, but now, Brigid's lovely voice was added, and Shea was keeping us steady thumping on the bodhrán, this time with his little stick. By and by he learned how to bring different-sounding thumps and such; it really was just remarkable to hear him on that thing.

"Note now, if you're still wanting to learn aught: Shea was the one with some style of tangle in his thinking, but he was the one who figured out about the bodhrán. Nobody could play that thing like Shea.

"That night, and for many nights to follow, we sang Brigid's lullaby last, usually just after the tavern-man told the people that he was all out of ale and wine, or whatever more the house had to offer. We stayed there that night and the next, and before we left, we'd bought two sturdy tents with all their poles and ropes and all, and more bowls and spoons and plates and such. We also bought a good knife for chopping the onions and turnips and praties we'd just bought, and salt and spices and such. And Brigid bought a razor blade she told us she was going to use to shave and shear us all. 'Springtime is upon us now,' she said, 'with summer soon to follow, and you'll be needing to shed some of your wool.'

"Well, we were chary about having her cutting our hair and such—Twedwr was the only of us with any sort of proper beard—but she could be right persuasive, could Brigid, and that night, after we'd solved the puzzle of putting up the tents, as the stew was just starting to steam, I sat down on a stone and she cut my hair back with this razor, and scraped away at my scrawny beard.

"It wasn't unpleasant, even with Mellán and Twedwr standing off at a distance, scoffing at me and telling me I was like a tamed horse now with a woman for a master, while they themselves were still wild and free. But the next day turned warm, and I didn't mind the heat nearly so much as my free, woolly friends, so that night, before we went into the next little village, they asked her to shear them as well. We went into the tavern in the next town considerably less shaggy than we'd been before.

"This was the way of things for some weeks then: we'd come into a town or village or settlement and sit down in the tavern or out in the open air, once or twice in a barn, and after a while, and usually after we'd eaten, I'd bring out the harp and start playing it, just to chum the water a bit. And a crowd would come together to hear the singing and buy some ale and wine and such. Then, after some bartering, we'd have free rooms or meals or drink, and usually a bowl or basket passed around, and we'd play until the tavern-man told them he was out of ale, or wine, or whatever he had.

"Then we'd decide whether to stay another night or move along to the next settlement. Sometimes we'd have to spend a night outside between villages, and most of those nights we'd have a fire and a stew, and we'd sing and tell stories all the same, just for the joy of it.

"Now and then we'd go into a village or town, and somebody would ask us to play a song we didn't know, and we'd try to cajole that person to teach it to us. That's how we learned 'The Jolly Man's Funeral,' which became a favorite of ours, and 'The Long Trip Home,' which would bring a tear to the eyes of a pratie.

"Will you sing them for me?" Oswell asked.

"Oh, aye, I'm sure I will if you're to be around for much longer. Other times as we sat around the fire, when we were just the five of us, Mellán would teach us another of the psalms, which I expect you already know. Nowadays I'll sing a psalm or two at the dawn, and one or two more at twilight."

"Why do you sing then, at dawn or twilight?" Oswell wondered.

"Aye, well. Those are the times between—between night and day, between day and night, both night and day, and neither. Twedwr said those were the times when your soul is most open to the voice of the divine Mother."

The student was scandalized. "But you are a Christian!"

"Aye, I am that. I believe following the teachings of the Lord Jésu bring us a grand wisdom. But I don't believe that the teachings of Jésu need be the only source of wisdom. God is not contained by the limits of our understanding, Oswell."

Pell saw that he was getting close to upsetting his young friend, so he tried to change his tone to be a little more pastoral, which had never been his specialty. "I have lived my life as a servant to the Truth of God as it is found in the teachings and example of Jésu the Christus, not as a servant to the Church, which always seems to be looking to narrow our Lord's ideas and shape them down to what they want them to be. I have pledged myself to the understanding of the teachings of Jésu as good news, as it was offered, good news for all the children of God.

"But full well you know there have been some as have tried to make following Jésu into just another way of telling people what they have to do, and what they can't do, saying they know the whole truth of it, and if a body thinks something else, they must be wrong, because some council voted it so!"

He stopped again, realizing that his passions were running too freely, and tried again. "God the Father, the Divine Goddess, Mithras or Dagda and the Morrigan of the Tuatha Dé Danann—ah, well—it's all too much for me. I do know you can only row one boat at a time, and following Jésu is the boat I'm rowing. I'm glad to be rowing it with you."

Chapter XIX

Ample to Think About

The next time Oswell came to see Pell, it was several days later, and this time he brought a friend. "Oswell! I'm happy to see you this morning, in truth I am. It's been a couple of days since you were here. And *salve* to your friend, whom I'm anxious to meet. Come and sing a song with me, and Dáirine will come out and bring us a little something to break our fast."

The old man took the harp out of its leather satchel and tightened or loosened a few strings, and the two younger men looked at each other. Oswell shrugged, and they sat down, each of them resting his back against a tree.

Then the older man said, "Ah, I think this harp and me are that much alike, both of us seem to need a little tuning from time to time." Then he looked at Oswell and said, "I let myself get blown off course last time I talked to you, and I'm afraid I stomped on your beliefs. I'm sorry I upset you. When you asked me why I sing at sunrise and sunset, mayhaps I should have told you it's because I'm a heretic, which you already knew." And then, with mischief shining in his eyes, he said to the other young man, "When you're a heretic, you can say whatever the hell you want to!

"Now, which of the psalms would you fellas want to start the day with?" When neither of them had a suggestion, he began to sing:

"O Lord, you have found me and you know me,
    you know my sitting down and my rising up,
    you know my thinking better than I do myself.
You walked with me in my travelling
    and stopped with me when I rested,
    full well you know my ways.

In truth, there's not a word I sing or say
    but you, Lord, hear it and know it.
You surround me, behind and before me,
    and I feel the touch of your hand.
Such a thing is too wonderful for me to reckon,
    so high it is I can't understand it clearly.
Where could I go to be away from your Spirit?
Where could I flee away from you being there with me?
If I fly up to heaven, you are there already,
If I lay down in my grave, you're there as well.
If I fly away into the dawn,
If I live in the deepest bits of the sea,
Even there your hand will be leading me;
Even there your hand will be holding me safe.
If I say, 'The dark will take me,
    and the light all around me turn to night,
Well, the dark isn't dark to you,
The night is as bright as the day;
The dark and the light is all the same to you.
It was you yourself who made me as I am,
You yourself who sewed me together in my mother's womb.
And so I thank you, as I am marvelous made,
The works of your hands are grand, and well I know it.
I was known to you while I was being made unseen
And woven together like the roots of a tree.
You saw me form before I was fully made in the womb
My limbs and guts were all written in your book
    when I was still being formed
    and there wasn't much to me.
How deep must be your thinking, Lord God!
How great is the number of your thoughts!
If I were to try to count them all,
    they would be more than the grains of sand
If I were to count them all,
    I'd be needing to live as long as you yourself."

Pell stopped and put the harp away, and as he saw his grand-daughter bringing out a tray, he said, "There's more verses to it, but they're all about hating your enemies and asking God to kill those as we hate and all—not the style of thing I'm wanting to sing as the day begins, and not the style of thing I think our Lord Jésu would be having much to do with, either."

After Dáirine settled the tray of warm dark bread, sharp goat cheese and three mugs of milk in their midst, the old man introduced her to his young friends, noting their interest as they watched every move she made. After she'd walked back into the house, the older man said, "Now, who are you, friend?"

The other student said, somewhat cautiously, "My name is Caillen, sir."

"Aye, and who are you, Caillen?"

"I'm … well, I'm studying up at the monastery, with Oswell. He said he was … enjoying his talks with you, so I asked him if I could come along."

The older man nodded, and looked at Oswell, saying, "Aye, and is that the way of it?"

Now Oswell and Caillen exchanged an anxious glance, and Oswell said, "Yes. Well, most of it. The fact is that I asked Caillen to come with me because I was nervy about coming back. Some of what you say is just so different from what we're being taught at the school, what the magisters say, and I … sometimes I don't know what to think."

"Aye and I'm sure that's so. Thank you for telling truth and thank you for the compliment. Caillen, you're more than welcome to come sit with me any time. You will have heard I'm a heretic, but you might find there are worse things a fella can be."

"Thank you, sir," said Caillen. Then, after a pause, he said, "But what compliment were you thanking him for?"

"For seeing that what I say isn't the same as what the magisters tell you. Now, I'm seeing in your eyes that you've got some questions that haven't made it to your mouth yet, Caillen. If you've of a mind to ask, I'll do what I can to put your mind to ease, if I can."

"Well, are you a heretic?" Caillen queried.

"Oh, aye, I suppose I am. It's just a word for somebody who disagrees with the men running the Church, is all it is."

"And if you don't mind, what did you and the … the men running the Church disagree about?"

The old man laughed and looking at Oswell, said, "Ha! I like this one, Oswell—right straight at the point, he is. Well, I'm telling Oswell here the story of my life, and that part comes later …"

"Oh, my apologies, sir, I …"

"Nay, you owe me no apology, friend. You can leave off some of the 'sirring' though; it'll be best if we're talking to each other as friends instead of you treating me like I'm a magister or some such, you talking up to me like I was better than you, me talking down to you like you've got no sense and no thoughts of your own. Now, I can get back to my story if you're wanting to hear it, but about all this disagreeing, I'll say this.

"I believe in God, that God made everything there is. I believe Jésu is the very son of God, come to live among us to show us the full nature of God and the full promise of humanity. I believe Jésu was born of a woman by the power of God. I believe he taught about love and mercy and forgiveness, and that he did miraculous things. I believe his teaching was so upsetting to some of the men in power in that place and at that time that they plotted to have him killed.

"Take note now—what he said challenged what they thought was good for them. It was better for some of them if their people needed to make sacrifices in the Temple, as that was their main source of influence, not to speak of income. It was better for others to keep the people of Judah quiet under the boot of the Roman army, to keep the *Pax Romana*. So, they killed him, because it was easier or better for them if Jésu was dead.

"I believe he let himself be nailed to that beam hoisted up on a pole on a hill between two thieves being crucified that day. I believe he died, and that just a few days later he was raised by the power of God to live again. I believe he went off into heaven and sent the Spirit of God to help those as would follow his teaching to share the good news of the love of God for all the children of God—all of us, now, hear me—Romans and Greeks, saints and sinners, bishops and heretics, men and women, slaves and free. I believe the followers of Jésu ought to be telling that good news in such a way as the people we're talking to can hear it, and understand it, and accept it. And I believe that we ought to be able to say what we think and believe without somebody else telling us we're wrong because we think or believe something different from the doctrine and dogma of the blesséd Church.

"I believe we need to have a real and genuine faith to believe in the love, mercy and forgiveness of God, as Jésu invites us to. But to believe in a god who's only laws and commandments, all you need is whatever it's all written down on. I'm not a Druid, but I think they were right about this: once you write something down, it's frozen forever, with no chance for our understanding to breathe or grow. I don't believe God should be written down; I don't think he could be. We're too quick to make graven images out of words written down. It's just something we do so we can pretend we're in control.

"Oswell, I can't unsay aught I said to you, and likely I wouldn't if I could. I might have said it a bit softer, though, and I'm sorry to have said aught that offended you."

"No sir," answered Oswell. "I … I'm not offended. Thank you for telling us what you believe—you've given us ample to think about."

"Aye, well then. Mayhaps 'ample to think about' will be worth your while."

Pell paused before he spoke again. "Now, Oswell here has been right patient to be listening to an old man's story, and you're welcome to hear it along with him, but I'm not keen about starting all over. I expect he's told you some of it, about growing up in a small village in Éire, and needing to leave there with my friend and brother Mellán the monk, and meeting Twedwr the Druid and playing his harp and singing our way up to Baile Átha Cliath, where Mellán were born, and crossing over the sea there to come to Angleland, and meeting Brigid and her brother Shea and coming along the Roman road on our way here, to Erith. Did he tell you all of that?"

"Yes, sir … I mean, yes, he did."

"Aye, good. But he didn't tell you this next part, because I haven't told him. We travelled down the spine of Angleland, following the stone road the Romans made, and stopping at taverns to play the harp and sing for our supper and a roof over our heads. Most places we'd be invited to stay a night or two in the rooms they offered, and almost everywhere they'd pass a bowl or a basket around for people to give us a coin for our singing.

"One afternoon we came into an old Roman fort town called Verulamium, and found it was a large enough town to have two alehouses—The Centurion's Gladius and The White Swan. The Gladius had a stable, so we went there—Brigid, Shea and me taking the horses and mule and wagon and setting them right, with Shea giving the stable boy detailed instructions about how to tend them and telling him he'd be coming to check that he was doing them right.

"By the time we got into the tavern, Mellán was at a complete loss, and Twedwr was flustered with the woman who was to bring us our ale. He said, 'She's saying she'll need to be seeing our silver before she can bring us aught, and I'm telling her you lot have all our silver, but she won't believe me! Well, and now I'm thinking mayhaps we ought to go over to the White Swan and see if they can trust us!'

"Well, it seemed like a powerful reaction to what ought to have been a small matter, and when I looked over to Brigid, she gave me a funny little smile, so I knew I must be missing something. Right about then, out came the woman that had Twedwr so twitchy. She was older, close to Twedwr's age, and quite attractive: tall and thin, but well-formed, with dark hair and dark eyes that told you there was something of a mystery there. There was something exotic about her, and when she spoke, you could hear that this was not the language she'd grown up talking. She said to Twedwr, 'This are your friends?'

"Twedwr answered, 'Aye, well of course they are—why do you think they'd be sitting here with me?'

"The woman asked, 'And who is holding this silver?'

"So I said, 'I am.' We had a heavy iron-bound box for our bags of silver by this time; I took one of the bags out and plunked it down on the table, then I took out a few pieces, more than were likely to need, just to show her. I was thinking that might improve her attitude a bit, as I'd seen before that people are nicer to people who have silver, but she said, 'And what will you want? We have ale, wine, beer and whisky, clean water or cow's milk for the lad.' We all told her what we wanted—ale for Mellán and me, water for Twedwr, wine for Brigid and milk for Shea—and she turned around and walked away without another word.

"Twedwr asked, 'What the hell is wrong with her, you think?' Mellán and I were just as mystified, but Brigid just gave a little giggle that left me wondering what she knew, and she said, 'Well, you were pretty rude right then.' Twedwr humphed, but didn't say anything.

"Presently the woman brought out our drinks, and by and by she brought out the food, which was delicious, but spicy. Then I pulled out the harp and a few people edged a bit closer, and after we sang a song or two, the common room was full to bursting and the tavern-man told us he'd be willing to pay for our drinks and food and give us a couple of rooms if we'd play and sing that night and the next, we agreed, and Twedwr told a story. We played until the tavern keeper told the people we'd drunk up all his ale, so I played Brigid's lullaby and Mellán and Brigid sang it so sweet and pure it was like heaven had come down around our ears.

"Eventually everybody left, until I thought it was just Brigid and me there, but then I saw Twedwr sitting at another table with his back to us. I was more interested in Brigid, of course, and we talked for a while and did a little kissing, and then we went off to our beds. It wasn't until I got to our room that I saw I'd left Twedwr in the common room, but in truth I didn't think much about it at the time. It just never occurred to me that ..."

Pell stopped, emotion stopping his voice before he said, "Aye, well—hmm. I ask your pardon."

"Why, what happened? Was he hurt?" asked Oswell.

"Did something happen to Twedwr?" wondered Caillen.

"Aye, of a fact something did," answered Pell, wiping the tears from his eyes.

Chapter XX

One Smooth Terrible Motion

Pell took a moment to find his composure, and the two young men waited as patiently as they could. Then he continued, "What happened was that, after all his lonely years, our friend Twedwr found love. Or mayhaps it would better to say it was love found him."

Pell continued, "This is the way of it. The next morning, Brigid, Shea and I wanted to explore the town. A man selling live chickens and ducks told us the whole town had been burned down to the ground by the warrior queen Boudica hundreds of years before, but then it had been rebuilt into a large town, with a bath and a forum, a public building and an amphitheater. The Romans had left some years before we got there, he said, but it was still much a Roman city.

"Shea was not much impressed by the history or architecture of the place, and pretty soon we were looking for a place we could get a little something to eat, when Brigid nudged me with her elbow, nodding over to her left to suggest I look over there, too. When I did, I saw Twedwr and the woman from the Gladius walking together, looking right familiar and all.

"I said to Brigid, 'What's all that about then?' and she let out that same little giggle as the night before. 'We'll see,' she said, 'we'll see.'

"After finding something to eat and looking around at what the town had to show us, we settled in for a supper at the Gladius that night. I was thinking the woman's attitude to us would have shifted some toward the positive, but she was just the same: not rude but just cool toward us. Right soon the room was as full as it could be, and Twedwr was telling the story of The Three Sons of King Cullen.

"He was past the part about telling us how the old king was looking to decide which of his three sons were to be king after him, and how the eldest was a selfish cold-hearted bastard who was lying and cheating to take the throne. He'd already told about the middling son trying to keep his older brother from winning, and he was just about to tell us how the youngest son, noble and pure of heart as the heroes are in these stories, was about to be the first to tie a rag on a limb of the tree by the Clootie Well and bring a goblet of that healing water back to his dying father so that none of them would need to take the throne. Just then I happened to notice her, the woman who brought out the ale and food. She was leaning on the bar, and you could see she was completely smitten, by the story and by Twedwr. I looked over to see if Brigid had noted it, and of course she already had. She looked at me and raised her eyebrows, to tell me this was significant.

"Now, as I've said before, I don't always see what's just in front of me right at first, and I wasn't sure of what was going on until the next morning, when we were getting ready to leave, and I became aware that now Twedwr and Brigid were having a squabble. It wasn't the first squabble they'd had, and it wouldn't be the last, but it was one that changed our life together. She wanted to ask the woman to come with us, and she was telling Twedwr that he wanted her to come as well. 'Nay,' he said, 'you're wrong about that now, lass. She's puzzling to me, I'll warrant, but to ask her to come with us—oh, I don't know about that. What if she doesn't get along with everybody, is what I'm wondering.' Then Brigid was about to say something and Twedwr went on, 'And what if she doesn't want to go anyway? I haven't talked to her about it, have you talked to her?'

"So, I came up, just to say good morning, and Brigid turned on me as if Twedwr was somehow my fault. 'All I'm asking is for Lily to come with us to Londinium, that's all. And this mule-headed old man is telling me I can't ask her!'

"Now Twedwr showed a little bit of a temper when he said, 'And who are you calling mule-headed, lass?'

"So, it seemed like it was time for me to step in and say something wise to restore the peace and harmony, but after I stepped in, I found I had naught wise to say. Instead, I said, 'So who's Lily then?'

"Brigid looked at me like I've taken leave of my mind and said, 'Who's Lily? That woman who's been bringing us ale and wine and our meals for the last two days, did you not think she had a name? Did you not think to wonder what her story might be? Clearly, she's not from Verulamium, or from any other place in Angleland; did you not wonder where she's from, and if she has some family somewhere?'

"I didn't know what to say, but Brigid wasn't saying aught more, and Twedwr was glowering at the both of us, so I said, 'She's just wanting to go to Londinium, is all?' Brigid nodded, and I asked Twedwr, 'It's not so far to Londinium, is it? Do you have a problem with Lily coming along with us?'

"Twedwr looked like he was afraid of something, and I said, 'She seems like a nice woman to me; if we can help her, I think that would be a grand thing.' Now I admit I glanced over to see if Brigid was thinking I'd said the right thing, and I was relieved to see that she was.

"But Twedwr just murmured the verse of the song, 'Eleven are the ways of a woman with a man, mysterious and strong.'"

Now Caillen looked at Oswell, wondering where that came from, and Oswell whispered, "It's from an old Druid song, 'The Power of One.' It's a memory song, using counting to teach. It's the first song Pell ever learned, and full of Druid wisdom."

Then Caillen hesitated and whispered, "Who's Pell?"

"He is," murmured Oswell, pointing at the heretic. "His name is Pell. I'm thinking 'Pelagius' must come later in the story."

The old man waited patiently, content to let them whisper, and when he had their attention again, he continued. "And so there we stood, undecided between the three of us, until Brigid said, 'Well, it seems she's desperate to make a change in her life. And it's just, it's just that I know what that's like.'

"Then I said, 'Aye, and I do as well.' Brigid and I both looked at Twedwr, who said, 'Aye, I know what that's like. Well then. But I'm not looking for any style of a romance, do you understand?'

"Well, I didn't know what I should say about that, but Brigid went and asked Lily if she wanted to go with us to Londinium, and

Lily said she'd be most happy to, and so now we were on our way—
six of us, and three horses and a mule pulling a wagon.

"It wasn't far from Verulamium to Londinium, and we could have
pushed harder to make it before the sun went down, but we found
a pretty spot by a little river and decided to enjoy the night out. We
were thinking that after Londinium, it would be on to Erith and a
house full of monks, and none of knew what might happen there.
So, we stopped beside the stream, set up our tents and made a fire.
Brigid and Lily wandered up the stream around the bend, leaving us
with stern warnings not to follow, as it was fully time for a bath, and
they wouldn't be needing any help from any of us.

"When they came back, all fresh and clean, they found me
peeling some praties and chopping them up for the pot, which was
over the fire, beginning to steam. I told Twedwr it was a good thing
for Brigid to have another woman around.

"Mellán was just about to put in a bit of salt pork into the pot,
but Lily said, 'Wait, please. Is this meat from pig?' Mellán told her
it was, and she said to Brigid, with some urgency, 'I do not eat pig.'

"Well and of course I'd heard that sometimes pork can turn bad,
so I tried to tell her that this pork was salt cured, but she said, 'I do
not eat pig. I'm sorry, but if pig is in stew, I do not eat.'

"So Mellán wrapped the salt pork back up in its cloth, and we had
a stew with no meat. Lily was a right fine cook, and she must have
dressed it up with something, because it was uncommonly good, and
we ate it until the pot was scraped dry.

"After we cleaned the pot and the bowls and put them away,
Shea brought out the harp and the bodhrán and we settled in for a
little music before we took our sleep. Brigid sat down next to me,
with Shea on her other side, and then Mellán by Twedwr. Lily had
to be invited to come and join us, and she sat between Twedwr and
Mellán, making our circle complete.

"We sang a few songs and worked on some harmonies for a while,
and then Shea, out of nowhere but his rich imagining, asked, 'I want
to know who the Pretty Lady is, and where she's from, and why she
talks all funny like that.' Ah, Shea was always a good one for getting
right at the point of things—like you, Caillen.

"Well and of course the rest of us all looked to Lily, thinking this would be the time for her to tell us about herself, but instead she hopped up like a swarm of bees was after her and hurried away, down toward the stream. Now Shea was afraid he'd said something wrong and was wanting to go after her, but Brigid gave me a meaningful look as she got up and followed Lily toward the creek.

"Well, I'd learned enough to know it was a meaningful look, but not enough to know what it might be meaning. I could see young Shea was upset, so I asked him to tell me how he made the bodhrán make different sounds, and that took up our time until by and by, Brigid and Lily came back.

"They sat down where they had been sitting, and Brigid nodded to Lily, who said, so quietly we all had to lean in, 'I am sorry I get up so. Shea, you do naught wrong to me. Only I have much I do not wish to talk about. I keep my thinking inside my head only.' Then, as we were all wondering what she meant by all that, she added, 'And Shea, thank you for calling me Pretty Lady.' And then she was done talking, and Brigid suggested we sing 'The Jolly Man's Funeral,' which is lively and light-hearted."

Oswell perked up. "Will you sing it for us?"

"Aye, mayhaps I will … but not just now. Right now, we're coming to a good part of the story. Well, an interesting part might be a better way to say it.

"We stayed there another night, just because we wanted to, and I noted that Twedwr and Lily were spending a lot of time together. I asked Brigid about it, and she said, 'For the very life of me I can't understand how one person can be so smart and so woolly-headed all at the same time,' but she wouldn't tell me how I was being woolly-headed. I was glad Twedwr had somebody he could talk to who was closer to his own age, though.

"The morning we were to leave, we folded up the tents and packed everything onto the wagon, saddled the horses and were just about to go when of a sudden here came four men, all looking right rough, all carrying swords and yelling that they would be taking our silver. One of them, the leader I suppose, said he knew we had silver in a box. He said they'd heard the stable boy at the Gladius talking about seeing it when we put it on the wagon.

"Aye, well now, up stood Twedwr to tell them we don't have any box of silver, and that the stable boy was lying. The ruffian close to him growled, 'Are you calling our Ced a liar?' and Twedwr puffed up and said, 'Aye, I'm calling him a liar and I'm calling you lot a pack of thieves!' When ruffian stepped closer to Twedwr, he yelled, 'You'll be needing to know that I am a Druid, and I can turn you all into …' but he never got to tell us what he was going to turn them into, because just right then the ruffian shifted his sword to his left hand and punched Twedwr in the jaw with his right, hit him so hard it knocked him right down, and Twedwr didn't move.

"In the next moment I was standing up, thinking I couldn't just sit there while a bully was killing my friend, and Brigid was telling me to sit back down. Well, I didn't sit down, and another of the men came over to me and said, 'What do you think you'll be doing, big lad?' So, I turned my right shoulder to him and punched through his belly with my left hand, and he fell down gasping for breath. Now another of the men came up behind me and snatched me up tight, and the other fella was coming for me, when Lily yelled out, loud and strong, 'Hey, boyos—here's something for you! Look here!'

"We all looked over to see, and what she had was she had her dress pulled down so that her breasts were bare and all. As I said, she was a well-formed woman, and now the men were much distracted. We all watched as the leader took ahold of her from behind, and as he was pawing at her breasts, she slipped the knife out of his belt and sliced a gash along the side of his throat in one smooth terrible motion, like she was slaughtering a lamb, without a second thought, like she'd done it before. All his blood just gushed out on the ground, quicker than I can say it out loud.

"Aye, and then, as all of us were looking on amazed, the fella who was holding me let loose to go help his friend, and Lily took up the fallen ruffian's sword and threw it to me, yelling 'Show no mercy, Gaius!' The sword fell by my feet, so I picked it up and tried to look like I was imposing and dangerous.

"The two ruffians considered how things were going, with their leader bleeding his life out, and their friend still trying to catch a breath, and they decided it was time to leave. But then one of them ran over to Lily, screaming 'You bitch—you kilt my brother!' and slashed at her with his knife, cutting her clear across her belly. She fell down in a pile, and Brigid rushed over to her, trying to stop the bleeding with her dress. When we looked back up, we saw the three ruffians had run away, into the woods, leaving us with their dead leader, and Lily bleeding from a fierce wound.

"Now a blur of things happened all in the same moment. Brigid was trying to help Lily, Mellán was checking on Twedwr, who was telling me to put some water in the pot to boil and to bring him the little box he kept under the wagon's bench, and now here came Shea out from where he'd been hiding behind the wagon. I told Shea to fetch Twedwr's little box and I went to the creek to fetch some water.

"When I got back, Mellán told me Twedwr had a sore jaw and a black eye, and that he would be fine in a day or two, but we couldn't get him to rest—there was nothing for it but that he was going to tend to Lily. We rekindled the fire we'd just put out, and put the water on to boil, and I went over to check on Lily and Twedwr, who was so terribly distressed I thought Lily must've died. Brigid hugged Shea, who was right upset, telling him it would all be right, that we were not going to let Lily die.

"Lily was still breathing, although every breath looked like an effort. Twedwr said, 'She'll need sewing, Pell, but I can't do it. She's about to die here, because I can't make my damn fingers sew her up!' Lily was moaning and sobbing and Twedwr was panicky, and I said, 'Then it's a lucky thing my Mam took in washing for some of the people of our village and taught me how to sew.'

"Twedwr had a needle and thread in his little box, and somehow I got the thread through the needle's eye. I was about to start sewing her up like it was a man's britches or something similar, when he said, 'Wait, Pell. We'll need Mellán, Brigid and Shea to come help hold her still, and I need to chew on some leaves for a little while.' Then he was up and gone to the wagon, calling the others to come help me with Lily, and leaving me to wonder why he needed to be chewing on some leaves just then.

"After a time, he came back with a strip of cloth he'd soaked in the steaming water and washed away some of the blood and such from Lily's wound, and then he spit out a wad of something greenish brown into his hand and smeared it into the cut. I asked, 'What does that do?' and he answered, 'I don't know, as a fact. It's something I saw the Druid healers do a time or two, before they sewed up a gash.' Then he added, 'Now sew her up, lad—just think of her skin like they were layers of cloth and join them up.'

"Then Mellán, Twedwr, Shea and Brigid all held Lily down as tight as they could, and I sewed the long jagged wound up with Lily screaming and hollering and praying in some language none of us knew. After a while, it was a mercy when she passed out, and then the sewing was easier. When I finished, it wasn't pretty, but the bleeding had stopped, and we started our long wait."

"Did Lily die?" asked Oswell anxiously.

"Do you want me to tell you now," came the answer, "or do you want to wait 'til the story gets there?"

"Could you tell us now?"

"Aye. She lived, and she … well, there's more to her story in this story I'm telling you. But she lived."

Chapter XXI

Content to Let the Days Pass Us By

Pell continued, "Mellán was for putting Lily in the back of the wagon and carrying her into Londinium as fast as we could, but Twedwr said he was afraid it would kill her, so we just stayed there. Mellán, Shea and I hauled the larger tent out of the back of the wagon and built it up around Lily, trying to make her as comfortable as we could.

"Brigid and Shea went into the tent with Lily, and Mellán, Twedwr and I were left to tend to the body of the leader of the ruffians, the one whose throat Lily had slit.

"Mellán suggested we bury him properly, but we had no spade, just the dead man's sword, and we quickly discovered the ground was full of too many roots and rocks for us to make a hole deep enough for us to cover him over. So Twedwr said we could float him down the stream, 'Let him be food for the turtles and scavenging birds,' he said, 'and the current can take him away to meet his gods, if aught will have him.'

"We had no better idea, so we dragged him out where the current was swift and let him float away. I thought Mellán would say a few words over him, but we just watched the murderous bastard drift down around the bend in the stream.

"Now Mellán was thinking we ought to toss the ruffian's sword in the stream after him, but I said mayhaps we'd be able to sell it when we came into Londinium, so we put it in the back of the wagon.

"With nothing much else to do, I cut up some little branches and wove a fish-trap and put it in the stream, as I'd noticed there were a good many bream and a few trout there. Before long, we'd caught three nice bream, and we made up a soup with them, adding to it from our stock of vegetables.

"There was no singing that long, fretful night.

"The next morning Twedwr and Mellán went to Londinium, to see if they could find a healer who'd come out to see if there was aught more we should do for Lily. I told Twedwr I'd go, that he ought to stay with Lily and all, but he said he couldn't just sit around doing nothing. We didn't know how long it would take to get to Londinium, but we didn't think it was far, so we were fretful when they didn't come back that night.

"But the next morning, here they came with an old straggly-looking woman riding Twedwr's mare. We went to meet them, and Mellán whispered to just Brigid and me, 'Well, she's not much, but she was the best we could find. Most of the rest of them just wanted to sell us amulets or magical potions, none were willing to come with us but old Maeve here. She's a dreary old crone, but she might know what she's about.' Impatiently, Twedwr asked, 'How's Lily?'

"'Still clinging on to life, breath by breath.' I answered. 'But the cut looks red and angry. She's weak, Twedwr, she's terrible weak. We got some water down her last night, but nothing so far today.'

"By this time Maeve had gone into the tent, carrying an old black leather bag, and presently she called for Twedwr. Mellán said, 'Well, I told her that Twedwr has some skill as a healer.' They were in there a scary long time; when they came out, the sun was almost down.

"We all gathered around, and Maeve said, 'Well, I must say, you've done a proper job of it so far. The stitching was a bit clumsy, but that and the poultice of primrose, valerian root, and chewed yarrow leaves likely saved this woman's life. She'll live, thanks to you lot, but she shouldn't be moved for a good long while.'

"I said, 'Thank you, Miss Maeve. It was grand of you come out here to see her, and it puts our minds to rest to hear all you've said. How long do you think it'll be before she can be moved?' And she answered, 'Mayhaps 'til Samhain, not much before then, before she should travel far. You could probably cart her into Londinium before then, in two or three weeks mayhaps, if she's strong enough. But if you take her even that far before she's ready, she could die.'

"We all said we'd gladly stay there for what time was needed, but staying out in the weather for two or three weeks would be tiresome.

"Then Maeve said, 'Well, as it happens, my great-grandson Aled is handy with the building of things. He made some style of tent frame for his father Meirion, so he could stay out of a night when he was hunting the boars. His hip was aching him terrible most all the time, and it helped him to have a place to sleep before the early morning hunts. Meiron said them framed up tents were almost as snug as his house, he did. When you take me back home, you can ask Aled to come help you, he's sure to be around somewhere.'

"As we were talking to Maeve, Twedwr came out of Lily's tent and said, 'She's calling your name, Pell. I think she has aught she wants to say to you.' I was chary about it, so he said, 'You might not have another chance, lad.'

"So, I went into the tent and sat on the ground beside her and said, 'Lily—it's me, Pell.'

"She stirred a little and held out her hand for me to take. I took it, and she said, 'I … I want somebody to know … who I am, my real name, before I … if I don't wake.'

"I said, 'Lily's not your real name?'

"'Nay,' she whispered, 'It's a secret since I … since we came here. It's not … safe for us … here.'

"Well, I was muddled by all of this, and all I could think to say was, 'Why are you telling me this? Wouldn't you rather tell Twedwr?'

"She answered, 'Nay, I … fear he will not understand. I see my father in you … a man of faith.'

"'Faith?' I said, 'I have no faith!'

"'Ah, nay,' she murmured, 'you do, you … just haven't found … found the words for it yet. But you will … you will.'

"Well, I didn't know what to say about any of that, and after a while, she said, 'My mother … called me Esther.' And then she waited, because she'd just told me her great secret, and now she was waiting for a response, but the name meant naught to me. I said, 'That's a beautiful name.' She smiled a little and said, 'Esther was a great … hero to … my people.'

"Now it seemed we were getting closer to where she wanted to go, so I said, 'Who are your people? Britons, Celts, the Cymru? Are you from Hispania? Or Gaul?'

"'Nay,' she murmured.

"'Romans?' I asked.

"'Nay,' she answered. 'Hush now ... let me say this.' So, I kept my quiet, and after she took up a deep breath, she said, 'Jews. We are ... Jews, Pell.'

"So, I sat there quiet for a time, not knowing what to say or if I ought to say aught at all. All I knew about the Jews was that my grandfather hated them, but I never knew why. Then as I was thinking Lily had gone to sleep, and wondering if mayhaps she'd died, she opened one eye and looked up at me and said, 'I'm a Jew, Pell. How do you ... think of that?'

"'I said, 'Well, if I'm to be honest with you, Esther, I don't care about any of that. Just get better, that's all that I care about. Just rest and get better. When you're feeling better, you can tell me all about the god of the Jews.'

"Well, she was holding my hand all this time, and now she gave it a faint squeeze and went off to sleep with a little smile on her face, which pleased me right well. I sat there with her for a while, and when I left, she was sleeping deeply, and her breathing was steady.

"Well, so I left her tent and told Twedwr she was resting peacefully, and then I went down to the stream where my fish-trap was, and I was glad to see three fat brown trout and just as many bream. As I was picking them out of the trap, and cutting off their heads and all, I wondered if mayhaps I ought to tell the others that Lily was Jewish. But then I thought this was Esther's story to tell, so I just put it away to the back of my head.

"That night, as I was preparing the trout to put in the stewpot, Maeve remarked that a fish like that could also be cooked by skewering them with a straight green branch, stuck in through their mouth and out through their tail. Well, to be honest, I'd never skewered anything before, but she was right persuasive, so I went to find some sticks so we could try it.

"When I got back with the sticks, Maeve was coming out of the woods. I assumed she was coming back from relieving herself, but she had picked a handful of green leaves which she put in one of our bowls. Then she asked to borrow my knife, but instead of using it to cut the leaves up, she used the butt end to grind them into something like a paste, and she added some oil and salt to it. Then, after she and I rammed the sticks through the trout, she slathered the fish with this paste, calling the leaves ramsons, which she said some people called bear's leeks.

"Well, I wasn't looking forward to having fish again, and I was doubtful about skewering, so we made a stew just the same, with the bream from the trap. But those ramsons made the trout into a treat, to be sure.

"That night, Lily was awake again for a short time, and Twedwr got her to drink some of the broth of the fish stew and a little water. After we ate, we sat around the fire, and presently Shea wanted to know if we'd be singing that night. We weren't keen on singing with Lily struggling as she was, but it caught Maeve's notice, so Shea got the harp and the bodhrán out of the wagon, and we sang a few songs. It had been a long day for everybody, and especially hard on Maeve, whose chin dropped down on her chest before we finished the second song. So, we sang her Brigid's lullaby real softly and thanked her over and over again. Brigid set her a pallet beside Lily, and she was off to her dreams.

"The next morning, after more thanking Maeve and giving her a generous handful of silver for her trouble, and after she showed Brigid and me where to find the ramson plants growing in the woods around there, we waved her farewell as Mellán and Twedwr took her back home. That same afternoon, here they came back again, with a little scrawny fella leading a mule pulling a little cart full of tools I recognized: saws and hammers and planes and such.

"Now Aled was not much on talking, but he did say he didn't need any help. After I showed him I knew what to do with an axe and a saw, he gave way and the work went right easily. By the next afternoon, our tents were stretched out over two sturdy frames, both of them supporting a center beam to pick the ceiling up higher and to make a slope so the rain could drain away. It wasn't like being inside a house, but it was considerably better than sleeping in a droopy tent. So, we thanked him and gave him some silver, too, and just by chance I asked him if he'd be willing to sell me his tools. Well, of course he wasn't keen about it, but I offered him twice what they were worth, so he agreed. That same afternoon he was gone, back to Londinium.

"Now some days went by, and every morning Lily seemed a bit stronger. After two weeks there was nothing for it but that she was determined to sit up. So, I told Mellán and Twedwr I needed some help, and we went into the woods and found some good solid trees to work with, and we chopped and sawed until we had what we needed to make a chair for Lily to sit up in. Well, it wasn't pretty, but the next day we were making another for Brigid, and then we just made one for each of us, with Shea's a little smaller than the others.

"With Londinium so close, if we needed aught, we just went in and bought it. So, it wasn't long before we had candles and more pans and plates and spices and such, and bags of vegetables and oats and barley for our livestock. Then one day, Twedwr brought me three bolts of fine wool cloth, some thread, and a pair of scissors, which I'd heard of but I'd never seen. Before long I was sewing up two new tunics for Lily and two more for Brigid, as theirs had been ruined when Lily was attacked. To be honest, I made five: the first one was a mess, but I got better at it as I went. In the evenings, Mellán and Twedwr would pick Lily up in her chair and bring her to sit out at the fire with us, and we'd sing until we got drowsy.

"So, we watched the stars spin in the heavens, and the moon went full and dark three or four times, and we were content to let the days pass us by.

"One morning Lily asked me what we'd done with the ruffian's sword, and I told her it was in the wagon. So, she wanted me to fetch it for her, and after she turned it this way and that, she declared it was a fine weapon, and that I ought to learn how to use it. I told her I would, just to put her mind at some ease, and she said her husband Gaius had been a soldier, and after he'd been injured, he'd been part of the training of recruits. That was how they came to Verulamium, she said, and that was where Gaius died, just dropped down dead one morning, leaving her to make her own way.

"She told me all that so she could tell me that she knew about swords, and about all the thrusting and parrying that goes with them, and she told me what I was supposed to do. She would sit there for hours while I practiced, telling me what I was doing right and what I was doing wrong. In truth, I was never much good with the sword, but after some time I managed to look like I might know what to do with it.

"By and by the days were getting shorter, and Twedwr told me Samhain would be soon upon us, when it would be time for us to leave. I said I wished we could stay, but remembering Mellán wanted to go to Erith, and Lily to Londinium, I knew it was a selfish thought. Twedwr had a thought about that, I could see that on his face, but he wasn't ready to share it, so I let it pass by.

"Mellán bought a leg of lamb in Londinium for us to cook one late summer night, with Lily in charge of the cooking, using something like a skewer to roast it over the fire, as Twedwr had set up some style of frame so he could turn the leg every so often and let it cook slowly. Mellán and I cut up some praties and onions and cooked them, and it was a right feast.

"That night, Lily came out of her tent leaning on a stick Twedwr had fashioned so that the fork of it fit snugly under her arm, helping her stand up straight. It was a right triumph, and we were all clapping for her and she was beaming a big smile at us. We ate the lamb, and it was delicious, and after a while, Shea went to get the harp and the bodhrán, and while I was tightening that one string that always goes loose, Twedwr said, 'It's almost Samhain now, and nearly time for us to go.'

"Shea said, 'Nay! We can just stay here, as long as we want!' But Brigid said, 'Aye, we've all loved it here, of a fact we have. But now, Mellán will be wanting to go to the monk house in Erith, and Lily is needing to get to Londinium. And after Samhain comes the winter, and I think we'll all be glad to be under a proper roof before the snows come.'

"So now Mellán was about to say something, but Lily spoke first. 'My friends, my heart is torn up in two and upset. You have all been so kind to me I don't have words to say how thankful I am. You saved my life, all of you did.'

"Shea said, 'You saved our lives, too—when you showed the bad men your …' but then he stopped, not knowing how to say what she showed politely.

"We all laughed and thanked Esther again for saving us, and she was embarrassed as she went on, 'My family I left behind, many years ago, when I marry Gaius, a Roman decurion. My family was upset that he was not, um, of our people, and when he was ordered to move, I went with him.

"'We moved to Verulamium,' she said, 'after he was wounded in terrible battle. After … he died, I was alone to look after myself, alone. But then you came along, and you took me into your family. I told you I want to go with you to Londinium because it was closer to home, but now …'

"'But now what?' said Shea. Ah, God love us, but he was direct to the point. But it was Twedwr who made an answer. 'Now you're thinking that this is your home, and we are your family.'

"'Aye,' she said softly, 'if you'll have me.'

'Well of course we will!' cried Shea, before looking up at Brigid and saying, 'We will, won't we?' And again, it was Twedwr who answered, 'Aye, of course we will.'

"Then Lily looked at me with a question in her eyes, and I nodded my encouragement to her. She asked me across the fire we were sitting around, 'You did not tell them?' and I said, 'Nay, Esther—it's your story to tell.' Now everybody else was wondering what we were talking about, and why I'd called Lily Esther. I nodded to her again, but she just nodded me right back, so I said, 'Our dear friend and sister is named Esther, who was a hero for her people. Lily is a name she took after her husband Gaius died. Gaius was a Roman, but Esther's family were Jews. She's fretting that you won't accept her when you find out she's Jewish.'

"Shea wondered, 'What's Jewish?' Nobody answered that question, but Twedwr stood up all fierce-like and said, 'I don't care if

you're Jewish, you silly woman. Don't you know I love you by now?'
Then he sat back down, embarrassed that he'd said that out loud.

"In that awkward moment, my brother Mellán the Christian
monk, recited, 'Hear, O Israel: The Lord our God is one Lord, and
you shall love the Lord your God with all your heart, and with all
your soul, and with all your might.' Esther covered her eyes with her
right hand as he was saying it, and when she uncovered them after he
was done, I saw she had tears flowing down her cheeks.

"So I asked Mellán, 'Was that something your Jésu said?'

"And Mellán smiled and said, 'Aye. But he was quoting a verse
from the Torah, the scripture of his people, the Jews.'

"I whispered to Mellán, 'Jésu was Jewish?' and he answered 'Aye,
that he was.' I thought about it before saying, 'The more I know Jésu,
the more confused I get.'

"It was Brigid who had the last word on the matter, as so often
happened. She said, 'Welcome, Esther—welcome to our family.'

Chapter XXII

An Argument I Lost, Several Times

Now the older man paused, aware that Caillen was unsettled. He waited until Caillen could restrain himself no longer, and started, "But the Jews ..." Now Oswell reached over to put his hand on his friend's arm, to warn him somehow, but Caillen blundered on, "The Jews killed our Lord!"

Oswell braced himself for what he thought was coming, but the old man winked at him instead, and said, "So I have heard. And where did you hear that, Caillen?"

Caillen looked blank but said nothing, so the old man went on. "From the magisters, from the bishops and such. Now, think about this. Did the Jewish leaders order the execution of Jésu from Nazareth in Galilee? Did the Jews take up a hammer and nail him to the beam? Was it the Jews who hoisted that beam up and fixed it to the post?"

"Well, no," answered Caillen, "but ..."

"Nay," said Pell with exaggerated patience. "You know it was the Romans. Are you thinking mayhaps the Roman governor was taking orders from the temple priests in Jerusalem? Nay, lad—the priests of the Temple have a good bit to answer for, but they were just like most men, trying to maintain the system that benefitted them. Of course the Church is looking to blame the Jews for the death of Jésu! Of course they're saying you have to be baptized, or you'll be sent to Hell after you die! Of course they're saying you have to receive the blessed Sacrament three times a year or you're liable to the fires of Hell! Of course they're saying that only the priests and the bishops and the blesséd Holy Father have aught to say about any of this! The institution protects the institution, the powerful defend their power, and the good news of Jésu be damned!"

Then it was as if he'd caught himself, and he stopped to take a deep breath. Then he looked at the two young men and said, "Is this not the way of it?"

They sat there in awkward silence for a minute or two, and then the tension left his body, and Pell said, "Ah, well. Oswell did warn you that I get riled up now and again, did he not?"

"Yes sir, he did."

"So, well. I am as you see me, and you see me as I am." Caillen looked at him questioningly, and Pell continued, "My friend Twedwr said that the day I met him, and it's just as true for me today as it was for him. You know who I am and what I believe, and that's who I'll be, and that's what I'll believe."

Caillen asked, "So, do you believe in baptism?"

"Aye," said Pell, "of course I do. I believe the Church can be wonderful, grand thing. It can be a right important tool for learning about Jésu, the love of God, the nature of reality, and the work we've been given to do together. I treasure the sacred writings, the canonical gospels, the sacraments. Important tools, all of them. But sometimes we become so fond of our tools—the vestments, the buildings, what's been written down—that we forget the job that needs doing.

"What vexes me is that we're trying to make our faith narrower and shallower, when what we ought to be doing is to be looking for ways to make it broader and deeper."

They sat quietly for a bit, and Pell went on, "And before you ask me—aye, I believe in original sin. I believe we're all born selfish and mean and lazy; that's part of who we are. But I also believe that we're all born in the image of God, and that we are in our nature generous and loving and compassionate, and that's part of who we are as well." He thought a moment, and added, "My main concern about the idea of original sin—without the idea of original grace to go with it—is that it teaches us that we begin lost, that we all start in a hole we ourselves have to dig out of, with a debt we all owe from before we're even born. But we can't earn the love of God, none of us can.

And none of us deserve it, any more than we deserve to be loved by our mothers. But the message of Jésu is that we are all loved, not lost but found by the grace and mercy of God, not because we deserve it or earn it but because God loves us, as He loves all creation.

"I know what you're being taught, and I know what I'm saying here goes up against it. I might be wrong, but I don't believe I am. But to have it told out across the whole Church that I am a heretic, to excommunicate me—to declare me anathema—for having a different way of seeing things, well, aye—mayhaps you'll forgive me when I get riled up now and again.

"I was telling Oswell my story, about my travels, aye—mostly so he'd know how I came to think and believe as I do. The Church is meant to bring people into the love of God through Jésu his son, to show the good news of God's love without limits and boundaries. But how arrogant are we when we claim God can reveal himself only through the Church? How conceited are we when we say God can offer his love and mercy only the way we say it's to be offered?

"Too many in the Church hold the Truth of God as its sacred trust—something to be guarded, to be kept as it has been received, something we should protect, sealed, closed. But if we do, if we keep the Truth of God just as it has ever been, then we give ourselves leave to stop listening for God's voice in our lives. We cannot stop God from speaking, but we can—and often have—stopped listening for Him.

"If the Church is ever only the theology of theologians, or the regulations of magisters and bishops, if ever it becomes naught more than the interpretation of words written long ago by men living in a world that's long gone, it will die. The Church will die, and it will be nobody's fault but our own for killing it."

He stopped then, weary—not just of speaking in that moment, but weary of the fight he'd been fighting—and losing—for most of his life. He put his face in his hands and leaned down, so his hands were touching his knees. The two students looked at each other, concerned about him. Then Oswell stood up, took the harp out of its satchel and handed it to Pell, saying, "Sing us a song, *cantor sapientiae*."

Pell looked up, cheered by the prospect of playing his harp, and wondering about the title Oswell had given him. "'Singer of wisdom,' well, hmm. That's a bit much. Mayhaps *veritas quaesitor* might come closer to the mark—'seeker of truth.' But a song, aye, mayhaps a song will lively us up a bit."

"How about 'The Jolly Man's Funeral,' O Truth Seeker?" prompted Caillen.

"Ha! Aye, that's a good one, to be sure, but better after the singer and the listeners have had a snootful of ale, mayhaps two. Nay, but how about 'The Joyful Psalm'? Surely you know this one."

The old man turned a peg or two until the harp was tuned to his satisfaction, and then he began:

"Be joyful in the Lord, all you peoples of the earth,
    serve the Lord with great gladness
    and bring yourself into his presence with cheery songs.
Hear now: it is he himself who is God and none other,
    he himself who made each of us, and not we ourselves,
    we are his people and the sheep of his pasture.
So bring yourself through his gates with songs giving thanks;
go into his courts singing praise;
    give thanks to him and call upon his holy Name.
For it is the Lord who is good, and his mercy will last forever
    and he will be faithful to us as ages begin and end."

Pell put the harp away and they sat in silence for a minute, each of them lost in his own thoughts. Then Caillen said, "Sir, I … I hope I didn't offend you, or make it seem as if I was judging you at all. I think maybe you're right about our education being limited and inclined to one point of view, and I'm grateful to hear another. Please accept my apologies if I was too … abrupt."

"Nay, Caillen, you have no need for an apology. You weren't abrupt at all. Much of my life has been taken up arguing this one point, and it's an argument I've lost, several times. But that's naught to do with you, you needn't give it another thought."

"You were telling us about Lily," Oswell prompted, "whose real name was Esther, and how you and your friends took her in, even though she was Jewish."

"Aye, that we did, that we did. I was telling you it was coming close to Samhain, which marked the end of summer and the coming of autumn. After Esther told us her secret, and after Twedwr spilt his about loving her, we stayed there for two more nights, knowing we would be needing to move on, but still hating to leave that happy, healing place.

"That same night, as we sat content around the fire, Esther asked if she could teach us a song of her people. We were all keen on the idea of it, and when she sang it, it was hauntingly beautiful. She didn't have a strong voice, partly because she was timid, but it was enough for us to feel the tune, even if we didn't understand the words. I usually pick up a tune right quickly, but this one was so different from any tune I'd ever heard that it took a long time to fix it in my head. It was ... ah, but it's hard to describe."

"Could you sing it for us?" asked Caillen.

"Aye," said Pell, "mayhaps that will be best." He lifted the harp from its satchel and played the beginning of a tune that seemed to the students simultaneously poignant and triumphant. Then he sang in Hebrew:

"Sh'ma Yisra'eil Adonai Eloheinu Adonai echad.

V'ahavta eit Adonai Elohekha.
b'khol l'vavkha uv'khol nafsh'kha
*   uv'khol m'odekha.*

V'hayu had'varim ha'eileh
asher anokhi m'tzavkha hayom al l'vavekha
V'shinantam l'vanekha
v'dibarta bam
b'shivto kha b'veitekha uv'lekhto kha vaderekh
uv'shakhb'kha uv'kumekha."

Oswell and Caillen were moved by the song, and they wanted to know what it meant, so Pell sang it again:

"Hear, O Israel, the Lord our God is One Lord.

You shall love the Lord your God
with all your heart and with all your soul
    and with all your might

Let these words
that I command you today shall be in your heart,
so that you shall teach them purposeful to your children
You shall speak of them
when you sit in your house and when you walk on your way,
at your lying down and at your rising up."

"It is a haunting beautiful tune, isn't it? It took me a whole night to learn it. That was the first Hebrew ever I learned, as well."

"You speak Hebrew?" asked Caillen incredulously.

"Yes," said Oswell. "And Latin, and Greek, and Gaulish, and probably three or four more. He says he just remembers things."

"It's a blessing, in the main part," said Pell. "But there are some things I'd like to forget, as well."

"Did Esther teach you Hebrew?" wondered Caillen.

"Nay, not much. She did teach us another song though, a prayer for the evening. It was also right difficult to learn, but it was worth it." Then Pell sang:

"Adonai, may it be Your will that I lie down and rise up in peace.
Let not my thoughts, my dreams or daydreams disturb me.
Watch over my family and those I love.
O Guardian of Israel, who neither slumbers nor sleeps,
    I trust my spirit to You."

Pell gave the song a moment to sink in, then put the harp away and continued his story. "As I was telling you, we stayed there for two more nights. Then the morning came for us to pack up our things—we left the chairs we'd made, hoping the next group who came wandering by could take a little rest.

"It wasn't long 'til we came rumbling into Londinium, a city too large and too dirty for me to want to live there. Aye, but even still, we thought it best to find a tavern where the people might appreciate a song and a story or two, just to refill our bags with silver. It wasn't long before we found the Lady's Slippers—the sign showed three elegant-looking sandals, which made you wonder what sort of a Lady she might be, to be needing three shoes, but there you are.

"We stayed there for three nights and found out that the monk house in Erith was still there doing whatever it was that monks should be doing, and that Mellán's Uncle Séamus was still there. And we found the best way out of the city, and which way was best to go to Erith.

"We reached the monk house one unusually warm day in early winter, and I was thinking this was the end of our travels. I suppose I thought Mellán's Uncle Séamus would come running out to greet us, like the father of the wasteful young man in the story that Jésu told, but nobody came out. We found the stable and settled our horses and Oscar the mule there, but it was clear the stable had been neglected for years; Shea was fussing over the state of things and went to find some water and hay.

"We had talked about this moment for months, and now it was here, we didn't know how to go about it. I was for all of us going up the monk house, but the idea of it made Twedwr itchy, and Esther said she wouldn't go in until she knew which way the wind might be blowing among the monks, about her being a Jew and all. So Mellán looked at me, and I looked back at him, and Brigid said, 'Let's go see Mellán's uncle, and see what we might see.'

"Then Mellán and I tried to make ourselves as presentable as possible, which was a challenge, and Brigid brushed her hair and washed her face and was much more presentable than either one of us. Mellán was especially nervy as we walked up to the doors of the main building, reluctant to tell his uncle they'd never built a church in Éire. He took hold of the big gargoyle knocker, and when he struck its feet on the door, it sounded like doom and desolation echoing all around.

"Nobody came to the door, and Mellán was about to take up the knocker and bang it again, when a young lad, younger than yourselves, opened it just enough for us to see one of his eyes. Mellán said, '*Pax vobiscum*,' the polite greeting he thought he was supposed to give, but the lad impatiently answered, 'Who are you to be coming here? And what do you want?'"

Chapter XXIII

Wouldn't It Be Grand, Though

Pell continued, "Brigid was not pleased to be treated so, and she was about to push the door open whether the lad was standing there or not, and Mellán looked at me for help. Well, I was thinking it wouldn't be worth the trouble of explaining myself, so I said, 'Halloo, friend. I am a monk of this house, back from long journey. My name is Mellán, and my uncle Séamus is here. We've come all the way from Éire to see brother Séamus. Will you tell him his nephew Mellán is come?'

"That seems to satisfy the young man, who told us to wait right there and shut the door on our noses. Mellán asked me, 'Why'd you do that?' I just shrugged and said, 'Well, I didn't think the lad would be much impressed if I gave him my name, so I gave him yours.' We waited there for a good long time, and presently the door opened again, and the man opening it was older, short of stature, with rounded shoulders, weak-looking eyes and about as bald as a mullet. He looked up at me like I was a ways off and said, 'Mellán?' Then Mellán found his voice and said, 'Uncle Séamus? Here, it's me: Mellán.' Now they embraced with great emotion, and after a while Séamus looked at Mellán and said, 'I remember you being much shorter.'

"And Mellán answered, 'Aye—I remember you being taller, and having more hair. It's been nearly four years since I left, uncle, and I suppose I've grown.' Then the old monk said, 'And I supposed I've shrunk a bit—I think my hair shrunk back into my head. And who are these two?'

"Mellán said, 'This is my friend and brother Pell, who grew up in Éire, in the village of Port Láirge, which is where Father Cyneric and

I went to bring the gospel of Jésu. And this is Brigid, our companion from Uiroconion in Angleland.' Then he said, 'Pell, Brigid, this is my uncle, Séamus.'

"The young lad who'd answered the door so rudely was standing behind Séamus, and now he stepped up and said, 'He's our abbot now, is Séamus.' The older monk smiled vaguely at Brigid and me, and said, 'So these are two you and Father Cyneric converted to the true faith, are they?'

"Mellán froze, not knowing what to say, but Brigid wasn't having any of that. She said, right respectfully, 'Nay, brother Séamus. Pell can speak for himself, but I'm not a Christian, nor aught else. The gods haven't done so much for me that I'd bind myself to any of them.'

"Then the older man nodded kindly and looked up at me, and I said, 'I'm not a follower of Jésu, but I admire some of what Mellán told me he said and did. And I'm glad of the notion that there is a god who's about love and mercy, and not just about power and punishing.'

"'And what of Father Cyneric?' asked Séamus. 'Is here still there in Éire?'

"Mellán answered, 'Well, nay. Nay, and there's a long unhappy tale.'

"'Aye, well, I can't say I'm surprised to hear it,' said the abbot. 'Then wait here while Derwin goes to find a drop of something to wash away the dust of the road while you tell it!' said Séamus. Then he added quietly, 'I regret that I can't invite you all to come inside, but as you might remember, women aren't allowed in the monastery.'

"Then Brigid said, 'I thank you for your consideration, but I can't stay. We have three more in our company who are waiting for us down by your stable.' Then she looked at Mellán and me and said, 'You go in. I'll be waiting with the others.'

"Well, I wasn't happy about going in without Brigid, but before I could say aught, the abbot said, 'Not a bit of it! I haven't had my daily walk yet, and it's been far too long since I've been to the stable—let's go meet your friends.' And just like that, he was off walking toward the stable, and all we could do was trot along to catch up.

"As we walked, we started telling him the story of Father Cyneric in Port Láirge, with him shaking his head the whole way. When we came closer to the stable, I saw they'd already put up the frames for both tents, and I was about to suggest that we continue the tale later when the older monk said, 'Hush now—what is that smell?'

"Well, I thought I should remind him that we were coming to a stable, and you ought to expect some smells, but then I smelled it as well: Twedwr and Esther had built a fire, and Esther was making a stew; I could smell some of her exotic spices reaching out to entice us, bringing the water to my mouth a full thirty paces away. Twedwr was trying to stretch the canvas tent over one of the frames, with limited success. I didn't see Shea.

"When they saw us coming, they came together to face us, Esther straightening her hair. I felt Brigid's hand in my back, pushing me to step forward and make the introductions. 'Abbot Séamus, may I present to you Twedwr of Dún Canann in Éire, and our dear friend Esther, whom we met in Verulamium, and who is, as you can doubt-less smell, a remarkable cook. Twedwr, Esther, this is Séamus, the abbot of this abbey, and Mellán's uncle.'

"Aye, so everybody told everybody how nice it was to meet every-body, and then the abbot said, 'And what is it that you're cooking there, Esther?' She looked embarrassed to be talking about what she had been thinking was a humble supper with such a high and lofty personage as the Abbot of Erith Abbey, but she said, 'It's a stew, m'lord—just mutton and taters'—Esther called praties taters—'with our last cabbage and some onion and fennel.'

"The abbot said, 'I am no one's lord—please call me Séamus. But what is that wonderful smell? Not mutton or taters, surely.'

"She said, 'Well nay, we've also found some ramson leaves and marjoram along the way, and I've tossed them in there, with some salt.'

"'Well, it smells delicious,' said the abbot, clearly fishing for an invitation to have a taste. But Esther was nervy about serving such ordinary fare to what she was thinking was a grand important man. She didn't see that he was all the same a hungry man, clearly snared by the spices she'd used in the stew. So, it was Brigid who said, 'We'd be honored to have you join us for our supper, Séamus.'

"Of course, he said he'd love to and told us that he got tired of being in the abbey every moment day and night. Then Brigid asked where Shea was, and Twedwr told us he was in the stable, tending the horses and the mule. Brigid called for him, and when he came, he was covered with what you might expect, so she tried to clean him up a bit before presenting him to the abbot. Then she said, 'Abbot Séamus, this is my brother, Shea.' The abbot wasn't finished saying how pleased he was to meet him when Shea said, 'Séamus is my name!' I'd forgotten that Shea's name was Séamus, none of us ever called him that, except a few times when Brigid used it when she needed to catch his notice.

"Surely the abbot saw that the other Séamus was different, but he didn't say aught about it but instead made a fuss about them having the same name and all, which made us all smile.

"Esther told us the stew wasn't quite ready, and Mellán, Séamus and I sat down to wait. Séamus wanted us to finish telling him what happened with Father Cyneric at Port Láirge, so we did. Then he said, 'Aye, I'm not surprised, but I do regret it. My predecessor Abbot Tómos was a good man, a kind-hearted man, but he was afraid of any manner of disagreement. Years before you went to Éire, nephew, he followed my advice and suspended Cyneric for a year, for the same manner of drunken immorality that you're telling me about. Then a few years later, there was another tawdry affair. I suggested that the bishop should strip Cyneric of his priestly duties and privileges, but Tómos listened to Cyneric instead, and sent him off to Éire to share the Good News of Jésu.'

"'Mellán said, 'Shifting the problem somewhere else, more like.'

"'Aye,' replied the abbot, sadly. 'And Tómos thought he would need a companion who spoke the language up there, and somebody who could keep him on a straight path and all, so he sent you, Mellán.'

"'He sent a very young man to shepherd a man he knew was willful and immoral!' I protested.

"'Aye,' said the abbot, 'that he did. It was against my objections, I told him to send me instead, but he refused, saying he needed me here. I don't think Tómos thought he'd ever see either one of you again, to be honest with you. I objected, but he was the abbot, and I was just a simple monk.' He paused for a moment, and then he said quietly, 'For me it was about my nephew going off with a man I despised. For Tómos, I think he was just that desperate to be rid of Cyneric. For Abbot Tómos, it was never about you, Mellán—it wasn't about you at all. He was just trying to send a problem away. I am sorry.'

"My friend Mellán just shook his head sadly and said, 'It was no fault of yours, uncle. We're all sworn to abide with the decisions of abbots and bishops and all. And in very truth, no harm has come to me. I come back a little older, and I hope a little wiser.'

"Then the abbot sat down on a little bench there by the stable, and asked Mellán to ask for a blessing of the food. Mellán thanked his god for food and friends and the end of the journey. Then Esther gave Séamus a bowl of mutton stew, and all our lives were changed. After we'd all eaten—and in truth it really was especially fine—he told us that the abbey's cook had recently fallen gravely ill, and they'd been searching for a new cook for weeks without finding one they could tolerate. He said there were eighteen brothers there, not counting himself, and every one of them was walking around all grumbly from hunger all the time. Then he said plainly that the tradition was that women weren't to come inside the abbey itself, but uncommon problems call out to us for uncommon fixes, he said, and he was thinking that if the other monks in the house could taste this stew, surely they'd find a way to make some way to step around that tradition so she could come into the kitchen and cook for them, if she were willing.

"Esther told him usually Brigid helped with the cooking, and the abbot nodded and said, 'If this works the way I'm hoping it will, we'll have a job for both of you.' Then Esther looked at the abbot and told him, 'I thank you, and I'd be interested to think about it, but you need to know that …' she took a deep breath, 'I'm Jewish.' Then she waited for some unhappy reaction from this Christian leader, but he just smiled and said, 'Well, with a name like Esther, I had assumed as much.' She didn't know what to say, and the abbot said, 'We'll pay you, of course, and find you a place to live and all.' Then Esther said, 'But what about Twedwr?'

"'Is Twedwr your husband?' the abbot asked.

"'Well, nay,' answered Esther, and then Twedwr added, 'But we've been giving it some talk.'

"Now the abbot looked distressed and said, 'Well, you can understand that we can't have an unmarried couple living together in the abbey. The brothers would never stand for that.'

"'Aye, Abbot,' said Twedwr. 'I understand that. But that's not the whole of it. Well, it's just that I don't know if you'd be so welcoming if you knew that …' Twedwr paused and looked to me for help, and I said, 'My dear friend and brother Twedwr here is a Druid.'

"And again, it was Séamus the Abbot surprising us: 'A Druid, you say? I don't think I've ever met a Druid! I'm fascinated at the idea of it. Are you a filidh?'

"None of the rest of us knew aught about being a filidh or even heard the word. Twedwr answered, 'Nay, I was training to be a bard, but … I had to leave the Druid settlement. Now, with this lot as you see here, I'm a wandering minstrel.' Bards we knew about from that verse from 'The Power of One,' 'The Power of Six is the six Sacred Bards who guard and sing the First Songs.'

"Then Shea spoke up, 'And I play the bodhrán!'

"'Well, now,' said the abbot, as if that settled things, 'there's something I'd dearly like to hear, young Séamus!'

"So Shea trotted off to fetch the harp and bodhrán, while Mellán and I pushed the wagon around so Twedwr and Esther could sit on the back of it. Mellán, Brigid and I sat on the ground, and Shea sat on the bench beside the abbot, and we started to play. It was like playing in a tavern, but for an audience of just one. We started with 'The Butterfly's Blessing' and I was right pleased to see the two Séamuses—or mayhaps that should be Séami—shouting out together 'a blessing to you!' at the end of each line to it.

"But a few songs later, when Mellán sang 'The Shepherd's Psalm' in Latin, with Brigid bringing the harmony, the old abbot was touched so deeply I could see the tears rolling down his cheeks. Then he stood up and said, 'Thank you, friends, thank you all. Thank you for the delicious supper and thank you for the music. You've given me much to think about, for a fact you have. Now I must take my leave of you to go back to the abbey, or they'll be out searching for me like I'm a lost sheep. Nephew, will you walk with me a bit?'

"As they left, we sang Brigid's lullaby, with me singing Mellán's harmony. I don't have Mellán's range or such a voice, but it worked— it was a right proper leave-taking. Well, now we didn't know what we were to think; Twedwr wondered if mayhaps we offended the Christian somehow, but Brigid said, 'Nay, let's wait 'til Mellán comes back and we'll see what is to be seen.'

"After a while, here came Mellán, his grin taking up most of his face. He said, 'Uncle Séamus says he wants to work something out so we can all stay here!'

"'All stay here?' muttered Twedwr. 'And what would I do here, I'm wondering.'

Brigid looked at me, wondering what Shea and I would do, just as I was. I shared my ignorance with a shrug, and she said, 'Well, it's not like any of us have any plans, other than Mellán, of course, but— oh, I don't know—wouldn't it be grand, though, if we could stay? If we could all stay together?'

"We spent the rest of the evening speculating about what might come and went off to our slumber still wondering."

Chapter XXIV

All the Family Any of Us Have

Pell continued, "It wasn't 'til the next evening that Abbot Séamus returned, although right before noon he sent the little fella who'd answered the door so rudely the day before, to tell us that the Abbot would like to come for supper again that night, with two other monks. So that put Esther and Brigid into a bustle, as we didn't have much to offer by way of a meal for guests. Finally, they sent Twedwr and Mellán into Londinium to buy a lamb's leg, some cabbages and praties and some spices and such.

"Not knowing what else to do, and just trying to stay out of the way, Shea and I did the best we could, finding some good long grass for our horses and Oscar the mule to eat, and gathering up some pine straw to make pallets for us to sleep on. The women sent us into the woods to see what manner of plants might be growing there that might be used for cooking or for healing, and I was right glad to find some ransom and marjoram, as well as primrose and yarrow. We didn't know how long we were to be there, and didn't know where we were to go if we were to leave, so we just acted like we were going to be there for a while.

"Mellán and Twedwr returned with our supplies and saw it was a time to stay out of the way of the two cooks, so they busied themselves stretching the tents over the frames again, tightening what was loose and loosening what was tight.

"There was a wide, lazy stream wandering past the stable, so we fetched up some water, and I saw some trout and bream and such. I was weaving a fish-trap with some willow branches I'd cut, when I heard Brigid calling out, 'He's coming! He's coming!'

"I looked up and saw the abbot coming, and there were three monks with him, arriving in different sizes and statures.

"The little thin one walking close as he could to the abbot without becoming attached was named Conal, as Mellán told me later. He would have had a full head of dark hair, but it was cut oddly, with the hair of his forehead shaved back halfway across his head. He was not much older than Mellán, and they'd been friendly before he left with Father Cyneric to come to Éire. I was glad to see that Mellán was glad to see him.

"The round one was Seán; nearly as wide as he was tall, huffing and gasping and sweating hard after the walk from the abbey to the stable. His hair was cut like Conal's, but he had a full reddish beard. My first thought at seeing him was that here was a man to find the joy in life, who knew his way around a dinner plate, and was no stranger to a jar of ale, either.

"The tall one was different, even though his hair was cut the same as the rest. He wasn't hostile, but he wasn't friendly, either. Mostly I think he was protective: of the abbot, of the abbey, of the traditions, of the faith. His eyes were sharp as a hawk's, his eyebrows grew wild on his face, he …"

"'Father Hywel!' interjected Caillen.

"Aye, Hywel." said Pell. "So, you know him then. I … haven't seen him since I came back. We were not … close."

"Alas" replied Caillen, "I'm sad to tell you that your friend died, nearly two years ago now."

"Well, I couldn't say he was my friend exactly, but we weren't enemies when I left. He was the monk to keep the money all straight back then. I thought he was too much about the business of it, and not enough about the faith."

"Yes," said Oswell. "So he was when he died. Even though he could hardly leave his cell toward the end, he was still managing our money."

Pell paused a moment before saying, "He thought I was an idealistic fool. And of course, he was right. Ah, well, the Lord bless him and keep him and make his face shine on him."

Both students said, "Amen."

After a respectful pause, Pell continued, "Just so. We saw these four monks coming to see us, and we scurried around a bit, doing naught really, but trying to tidy up around two tents beside a stable. As the monks came to a stop, Mellán stepped up and said, '*Pax vobiscum*' and this time he got the proper response, '*Et cum spíritu tuo*,' from all four. This time it was Mellán making the introductions, everybody sizing up everybody else, and the abbot said, 'I hope you don't mind that I brought some friends to join us for supper. They heard me bragging on the good cooking and the good singing and all, and they asked if they could come with me this evening.' And then he leaned a little toward Esther and whispered, 'It might go a long way toward us finding a way to step around our traditions if they could taste your cooking,' and then he looked around at the rest of us and added, 'and hear your music.'

"Then we hit a snag. After a bit of pleasant chatting, the stew was ready and clearly it was time for supper. Mellán asked the abbot to bless the food, but the abbot said he'd rather ask the host of the meal to offer a prayer of thanksgiving before a meal. We were trying to figure who the host of the meal might be, and Mellán and Brigid decided it was to be me! Well, I wasn't honestly religious back then, and I didn't want to be false about it, so I suggested it ought to be Mellán. But he was chary about praying with his uncle and those other monks hearing him. Brigid and Esther knew it couldn't be a woman praying, so we were just stuck for a time until Esther said, 'Twedwr is host of the feast. As our elder, he should pray.'

"Well, then it seemed we were either about to have a prayer from a Druid or starve beside a pot of lamb stew smelling tasty enough to tempt a stump to find a spoon, when Twedwr lifted up his right hand to the sky, rested his left hand on his head and sang,

'Blesséd be Mother Earth, for growing this food,
Blesséd be Father Sun, for shining warmth and light,
Blesséd be Brother wind, for spreading the seed,
Blesséd be Sister Rain, for quenching our thirst,
Blesséd the hands preparing the meal,
Blesséd our friends gathered here,
Blesséd our families, near and far.

By the mysteries of the Holy,
    by the grace of the Divine,
    blesséd be, blesséd be all.'

"Mellán and the abbot said 'Amen,' and then the other monks, and then all the rest of us said, 'Amen.' Even Hywel, Caillen. Shea was a bit late and a bit loud with his 'Amen,' which made us all smile.

"Then it was supper, and as a surprise Mellán and Twedwr had brought two skins of wine from Londinium, which impressed the monks and the women. I tasted a little, just to look agreeable, I suppose, but I wished it was a bit of ale; Shea's more honest, he took a sip and spit it right out.

"Then the abbot wondered if we might have a bit of music, so everybody found a place to sit, and we played 'The Butterfly's Blessing.' I was glad to see Conal and Seán joining in, and Hywel at least tapping his foot, just a bit.

"Then we sang 'All of Us Looking for Truth,' which seemed to be well received, and then Mellán sang 'The Joyful Psalm,' and he ..."

"That's Psalm One Hundred," Oswell explained to Caillen.

Pell said, "Mellán sang the psalm in Latin, with Brigid bringing a beautiful harmony. Aye, well and now the magic of it was so thick I wondered how we kept breathing. After a while, the abbot said, 'Here, now. My friends and I thank you most kindly for the delicious meal, and for the grand music—nourishment for our bodies and our souls. I can't begin to tell you how ... how grateful I am to you, all of you. Now we're about to leave and have a little discussion. Mellán, I'll ask you come with us for a while, and when we've come to a decision, Mellán will come back and tell you what we have in mind. How do you all think of that?'

"Nobody said aught, so I said, 'That suits us right well, Abbot Séamus, and we thank you. It was our privilege to have you join us this evening, all of you.' Then I added, 'I think I ought to tell you we all know Mellán will be staying here with you in the monk house. But for the rest of us, I think we'll all go or stay together. We've become all the family any of us have now.' I looked around to see if I was right in speaking for all of us that way, and they all nodded,

Twedwr and Esther in tears, Brigid's face shining her approval. Shea just looked relieved.

"The abbot nodded as well, and said, 'Aye, I understand.' Then he looked at his companions and said, 'Well, it's back to the abbey for us.' Then to us, he added, 'Mellán will be back in a little while.'

"Well, it felt like we waited half the night, trying to sit still and feeling like we were sitting on ice that might any moment crack underneath us, but by and by here came Mellán, and we could all see he was thinking he had good news for us. Of course, we all started pelting him with questions all at once, but he held up his hands and said, 'If you'll quiet yourselves, I can tell you what Uncle Séamus and the brothers had to say.'

"Then we were all quiet as turtles, and Mellán said, 'They all agreed with the abbot that they could relax the tradition about women in the abbey. I think it was Conal who said he'd never noticed many women trying to break into the place anyway. They were all keen on the idea of hiring Esther and Brigid to be their new cooks. They said they'd like to hire Shea to work in the stable, not only to care for our horses and mule, but also some of their own they've been stabling up in Londinium. And they'd like for Pell and Twedwr to stay and work around the place—there's a great deal of things to be repaired or restored. But before you do any of that, they want you to build a house here, for Twedwr and Pell and Shea, if he wants to stay with you.'

"Shea said, 'I want to stay with Brigid! Where will she be?'

"Mellán answered, 'Well, she and Esther can stay here, in one of our tents, or in the house we're going to build, or they can stay in the guest house on the other side of the abbey. And Shea, you can go with her or stay here with us, or you can go between the two places, if that's what you'd like.'

"Then Brigid said, 'I'm staying here, with Pell and Twedwr.' And then Shea and Esther both said at the same time, 'Me, too!' I thought that would be the end of it, but Mellán said, 'I'm staying here, too— with all of you. Pell, you had it right when you said we've become a family. I'll stay here, with my family.'

"We stood there just a moment, taking in the wonder of it, before Twedwr said, 'Now, about this house—could it mayhaps be a house and something more?'

"'What do you have in your mind, then?' I asked him.

"Twedwr ansered, 'Well, oh I don't know, it's likely to be the daft dream of a daft old man, but still … oh, never mind it, just let it slip away from you now.'

"'But it is your dream, beloved,' said Esther. It surprised me that she said 'beloved,' but Brigid stayed where the conversation ought to be. She said, 'You're thinking that as long as you're to build a house, you might just make it a house and something more than that.'

"'Aye,' said he, but he didn't say more, and Mellán gently asked, 'Could it be you're thinking we'll laugh at your dream, brother Twedwr?'

"Then Twedwr hung his head a bit and said, 'Nay. I'm just afraid it's a foolish dream, is all. And saying it out loud will mean it was a foolish dream that died.'

"Now I prompted, 'Well, tell us what it is, Twedwr, and have done. If it's foolish, we'll tell you kindly, but surely it won't be as foolish as letting a dream die because you were scared to say it out loud.'

"Esther whispered urgently, 'Tell them, Twedwr.'

"Twedwr took a deep breath and held his head up, and said, 'Aye, well—the nights we've spent in taverns across Éire and Angleland have been the happiest times of my life, and …'

"'You want to build a tavern!' I said. 'You want to build a tavern with a house at the back of it!'

"He looked at me like he was scared of what I was about to say next, but Brigid had the next word: 'That's a grand idea!' To be honest with you, I was thinking the same thing, and I said so, and then Esther and Mellán agreed. Shea said, 'Can we have ale there? Only wine tastes terrible.' Greatly relieved, like a fish thrown back into its watery home, Twedwr said, 'We can have the finest ale in all of Angleland!'

"Now we started talking about the building of a tavern house, and how big the common room should be, and how many rooms ought to be in the house, and I was asking if they remembered a tavern in Caer Lerion, or Ratae Corieltauvorum as the Romans called it, where the sound came bouncing back at us in such a lively way. I was thinking the sound did that because of the ceiling, which was made with some sort of lacquered wood, and suggested we ought to make a ceiling like that, when Mellán asked, 'So we'll be staying then? Only I told Uncle Séamus I'd come back and tell him when we decide.'

"Twedwr looked around at each of our faces and said, 'Aye, lad. We'll be staying. Tell your uncle we're grateful.' With a whoop, Mellán ran off to tell his uncle the grand news.

"Twedwr, Mellán and I went to see the abbot the next morning and told him about Twedwr's dream of building a house that would also be a tavern. We could tell he didn't really understand how that might work, but his nephew Mellán suggested mayhaps that was because he'd never been in as many taverns as we had. Most of the tavern-keepers we'd met lived in a room behind the tavern, or above it, we told him. Brother Hywel reckoned the abbey would be willing to pay for the building of a house, but not the building of a tavern. So, I thought that would be the end of it, but Twedwr pulled out a purse with the nine gold solidi his uncle had given him and said it ought to more than pay for the building of a tavern.

"But before the monks agreed to it, Twedwr—who had become a skilled haggler in taverns and inns from Éire to Erith—told them that while the house would belong to the abbey, the tavern and the land around it, should belong to us and our descendants. That seemed agreeable, and with that, the abbot gave us his blessing. Hywel wrote it out, and Abbot Séamus signed his name to it and sealed it with his ring.

"That same day we took our wagon into a sawmill outside of Londinium and began to haul a mountain of boards and beams to build our tavern house. Now the days were getting shorter, and the nights were getting colder, so we framed up two rooms pretty quick, with sturdy wooden floors and lots of wind-holes and shutters, walling the whole of it with good pine boards. These things I knew how to do from being Eóghan's apprentice, but I had to laugh remembering how he'd told the arrogant priest that none of us had wood for floors in our little village, that 'we all put our feet on the solid ground, inside our homes and out.' Well, we made a fine wood floor, and after that we put on a thatch roof, at a fairly steep pitch.

"For the winter fast approaching, the women would stay in the smaller room and the four men in the larger. After it was all built with living spaces in the back, the larger room would become the common room of the tavern, so that's where we put a large stone fireplace. Twedwr and a mason we hired from Londinium worked for nearly a week making sure the stone chimney would draw the smoke from the room. We'd been in so many smoky taverns, we wanted to be sure our chimney would pull the smoke out. The smaller room was more finished, with the inside walls chinked tight so no cold air could blow through. We had all spent too many nights shivering on our journey here.

"We also spent some time helping to get the stable in order again, repairing the part of the roof that had blown off, replacing some wood in the stalls, making troughs for feed and water. It wasn't too long before some of the horses owned by the monks came to stay, and Molly, Piran, Eleanor and Oscar seemed right glad of the company.

"On one of his trips into Londinium for more boards and beams, Twedwr brought back a plow. I'd never used one, being the grandson of a carpenter in a fishing village, but Brigid had and told us what we were to do with it, and how to do it. Before it got too cold, she had Mellán, Shea and me putting Oscar the mule in the harness, pulling and pushing the plow through rocks and roots, digging up a patch of ground for a garden, fifty cubits long and about half that wide. She told Shea to keep all the horse and mule manure in a pile somewhere downwind, and before the snows came, she was bringing scraps and such from the kitchen and the tables in the abbey, and we mixed the refuse in with the earth of the garden, shoveling and hoeing until our hands were raw. Brigid promised we'd be grateful for it next summer.

"Then the snows came. There was still much to be done, but we were glad to be able to move our work inside. Brigid and Esther worked in the kitchen, and the rest of us joined them for breakfast and supper. It took a ruined loaf or two, but Brigid figured out how their oven worked—she'd never seen such a large oven—and she was soon making beautiful breads and pies.

"One night, as we were eating supper in the monastery kitchen, Twedwr said we should make our own ale, rather than buying it from somebody else. He'd learned about making ale when he was working for Eithne's father, before he left the Druids, and he had some ideas about how he could set up a brewery that would serve our purposes. The truth of it was we'd done so much of the building ourselves, we hadn't spent even half of his gold, so we had more than enough to buy what we needed to make ale. Twedwr promised his ale would be the best we'd ever had, and he reminded us of his promise, and that he would be making it for others, and not for himself. Well and so, it just made sense for us to brew our own ale if we could.

"So Twedwr and I took Oscar the mule pulling our wagon into Londinium to get the big kettles and pots and pipes and all he needed to make the ale, and a few more saws and tools for me. I told Twedwr I wanted to build a little shop for all my tools, where I could fashion the wood into what was needed, and he said that was a grand idea.

"When it was about as cold as it could be, the monks celebrated the birth of Jésu, which they called the Christ's Mass. They had a grand feast; Twedwr and I stayed up all night roasting two turkeys and a fat goose, under the watchful eye of Esther who came out to baste them with some style of spiced butter. Brigid baked chewette pastries filled with pears and apples, and roasted walnuts, cloves, dates and honey. And for their Mass, Abbot Séamus invited all of us to come sing a psalm we all had to learn and then came to love. I don't know the number of it; we called it 'A Fresh Song.'"

Both young men said they would like to hear it, and Oswell stood up to hand Pell his harp. He tuned it for a bit, and then said, "The Latin of it is beautiful, but that part I expect you likely know. I'll sing it in this language we've been using. It's not an exact translation, but I think it holds fairly close to the point.

"Now let us sing to the Lord a fresh song
Sing to the Lord, all the whole earth
Sing to the Lord and bless his holy Name

Proclaim the good news of his saving grace day by day
Sing out his glory to all the nations
And his wonders among all the people.
For the Lord is grand and much to be praised,
He is more fearsome than all the other gods.
Now let the heavens sing and the earth be glad,
Now let the seas thunder and all that's in them sing!
Now let the fields be filled with joy
    and all that live and grow there
Now let all the trees of the wood shout their joy
    at the coming of the Lord to rule with justice."

He put the harp away and sat quietly for a moment, before saying, "I always liked the idea of singing a fresh song to the Lord. But it seems we're more likely to sing the same old songs, think the same old thoughts, say the same old words. Well, I suppose we're more comfortable that way.

"The psalm was right well received that night, and I was surprised that many of the brothers joined in the singing of it—in Latin, of course. After that, we were invited to come and sing a psalm or two whenever they had any manner of big worshipping. Sometimes Brigid and Esther couldn't come because they were busy in the kitchen, but Mellán, Twedwr, Shea and I made a fair job of it, with Shea playing the bodhrán softly, and the brothers seemed to be keen on us being there. I don't know whether the brothers knew Twedwr was a Druid, or that I was … whatever I was, or mayhaps they didn't care. They never asked, nor did I want to burden them with it.

"By and by, the winter cold was replaced by spring breezes. Well before it was warm enough to be comfortable working out of doors, Brigid had us out in her garden, plowing and digging, and then planting all manner of vegetables and herbs and such. In some weeks, the little sprouts came pushing through the crust of dirt, and we were growing onions, cabbages, turnips, carrots, and fennel and such, as well as mint, coriander, and caraway. There were other herbs and plants growing in the woods around us, all we had to do was to remember where they were.

"So it went, and so it went. We stayed there for eight years, eight good happy years. We built our house onto the tavern, big enough for all of us and two rooms for guests. Brigid brought in some beehives and goats, and baked and cooked with Esther, who was a natural manager and helped many a woman escape a life gone sour by hiring them and teaching them to cook and all. Mellán became the cantor, chief liturgist and musician of the abbey, Twedwr planted his sacred grove of trees—oak, rowan and ash—the trees we're leaning on right now, and made the best ale ever I had, just as he'd promised, even though he himself would drink none of it. People would come down from Londinium for the ale and the food, and for the music and the tales Twedwr would spin. We planted fruit trees—apples, plums, pears and figs. Little Shea became well known for his care for horses and mules, and people came from leagues around to have him tend to their animals; they said it was like the beasts talked to him somehow.

"I was right content with my life, content to stay here and love and be loved, content to spend my days in my little shop, making and repairing, content to play the harp and sing with my friends in the abbey chapel and in Twedwr's tavern. I painted the tavern sign, a man dancing wild and free, one knee up high, holding his harp over his chest with his left hand and his right hand—the one with the broken fingers—raised up in a fist. So, we called the tavern the Dancing Druid.

"We pegged lacquered boards up on the tavern ceiling, and the sound was lively and bright. It wasn't a place to tell secrets, as you could hear so well what was being said or sung. But it soon became a place for the brothers to come and relax, to sing a song, to drink a jar, and to talk with each other, with mayhaps more freedom than I think they might in the abbey.

"Many a night the abbot would come down to see us, and to join in the singing. It was the abbot, after a jar of ale or two, that taught us some of the bawdy songs they'd never sing in the chapel, like 'The Lady's Pleasures on Offer,' or 'Whose Breeches Am I Wearing?' and 'The Bishop's Wee Crooked Staff.'"

"Will you sing one of those for us?" asked Oswell with great enthusiasm. Then Caillen, to goad him, said, "No, surely he's forgotten them by now."

"Nay to the both of you," said the old man, laughing. "I will not sing you a bawdy song, nor have I forgotten them. I was saying that I was content, and so I was. Then several wonderful things happened all close together, and then something terrible."

Oswell guessed the cause for distress: "Father Cyneric."

Chapter XXV

A Wagon Trying to Pull a Mule

"Cyneric?" Caillen wondered. "The priest who went up to Port Láirge in Éire where Pell grew up? Was he wonderful or terrible?"

Pell nodded to Oswell, who said, "Terrible, I'd wager. But wait—I thought they'd put him out to sea!"

"And that's a bet you'd win," said the older man. "Aye, some of the boyos of the village put the arrogant priest in a rowing skiff and set him out to sea, but it was just to scare him. A sailing boat picked him up a few hours later and sent him back to Angleland the next day. Then, being Cyneric, he lied and cheated his way back into the Church.

"But before we come to that unhappy part of the story, there are some other things, right happy things I'm glad to tell you about.

"The first and best thing I'm thinking about is that Brigid had a baby girl, the sweetest little gift from God that anybody could have dreamt of. I'd been afraid that if we had a child, she'd be … oh, I suppose I was afraid she'd be cursed somehow, ill-made like my sister Áine, or … a bonehead like myself, but she was just perfect. It was Brigid's suggestion to name her Áine after my sister, and I was grateful and happy about that. Our life was already powerfully sweet, and then Áine Minor came and made it even sweeter.

"And I need to tell you about Bishop Felix, and the changes he worked in me and in our little group. It was Bishop Felix who baptized Brigid, Shea, little Áine and myself, the same day he … ah, well, if I'm to tell you the story properly, I need to wait a bit before we get there.

"Now, Caillen—I already told Oswell how I grew up as some manner of unbeliever, unmindful of the gods who seemed to hover around my little village like buzzards riding the winds. The start of my faith in Jésu was with a man who was a liar and a cheat. Then my friend and brother Mellán told me the story of Jésu and taught me to sing the psalms. Still, though, faith had always been something outside, something for other people, and not for me.

"But that first Christ's Mass we sang in the abbey chapel touched me right deeply. The worship was beautiful, and I was impressed by the faith of the brothers there. Then, toward the end of the service, as I was thinking surely it was about time for everybody to be leaving, two of the boyos serving at the altar went around real slow, snuffing out all the candles but the two beside the lectern. And then Abbot Séamus stood up and read a little bit from the gospel story as it was told by the Apostle Johannes.

"The words the abbot read snagged at something in my thoughts. To make sure I'd understood, the next day I asked Mellán to read it to me again. He told me they were some of his favorite verses:

> "'Before there was aught else, there was the Word, and the Word was with God, and the Word was God. It was in the beginning with God. All there is came to be through the Word of God, and without it was naught made. All that has come into being in God was life, and his life was light for all people. This same light shines in the dark, and the dark has never overcome it.'

"It took some time for me to know why that found a way to rest inside my heart, but it did. It was when Johannes wrote, 'This same light shines in the dark, and the dark has never overcome it' that chipped away at my shell of uncaring skepticism.'

"I thought I was familiar with the dark, with Áine's condition, and with my Mam being killed by her own father and all …"

"What?" Caillen was outraged. "I didn't hear that part of the story!"

"It was why he left Port Láirge with Mellán, when he was a young man," said Oswell. "I'll tell you about it later."

Pell nodded his appreciation, and said, "I thank you, Oswell. I'd not like to have to go back so far in the story to tell that terrible tale again.

"I thought I knew about darkness, but I'd never known what I could do about it, other than sit in it helpless. But this idea about the one true god being born as we are, to be a person come to shine a light into the dark, it was just so full of hope—even if I couldn't credit it, I couldn't let it go, either. I didn't want to let it go. This was the faith of my brother Mellán, and his uncle Séamus, and I didn't want to reject it completely. But it was also the faith of Father Cyneric, and that gave me the doubts.

"Well, as I said, the abbot came down to the Dancing Druid right often, and one dark winter night after we'd been there about four winters, he brought a friend: Bishop Felix.

"The bishop was needing a spiritual retreat, he told us, as he was thinking his life and work were getting stale somehow. He fretted that he might be losing the joy of it. So, he came down to the abbey at Erith to pray in the chapel and enjoy being away from his duties and chores in Londinium. Aye, he told us his plan was to pray and take some time in silence in the season of Lent, the days preparing for the celebration of Jésu rising up from the grave, but the truth of it was that he wound up spending quite a lot of his time in the Druid.

"Bishop Felix spent many an evening with us down in the tavern, enjoying Twedwr's good ale, singing along with us, even telling a tale or two. And right often he would stay after nearly everybody else had gone, just to talk to us: to Mellán, Twedwr and Esther, Brigid and Shea and me.

"Now, I'd heard the story of Jésu, and as I say I don't forget much, but it was good to hear it again in a different voice. My brother Mellán had told the story as it was written by Lucas the physician, but Felix also knew another telling of the story, as it was told by Johannes, one of Jésu's disciples. We'd heard the first part in the Christ's Mass service, the *prologus* as Felix called it. But what we didn't know was that Johannes had a different set of stories, and it brought me to look at the life and death of Jésu from a different point of view. Felix said Johannes' account was written much later, and was more solid, or mature, like an apple given time to ripen. So, as I was becoming more familiar with the story of Jésu, it was good to see it through different eyes.

"And there was something else. What Bishop Felix had that many another did not, was time and compassion, time to listen, to really try to understand what you were saying to him, without trying to think of what he would be wanting to say next. You never had the feeling that he was in a hurry to be somewhere else, or that there was somebody more important he could be talking to. We all liked and respected him, and we trusted him.

"You always felt like he put some value on what you were saying, especially if it was different from what he was thinking. He didn't try to step around it when one of us asked a question, but answered it, direct and honest. If he didn't know the answer, or if something made no sense to him, he'd tell you that, rather than trying to hide behind swank words so polished they'd gotten slippery, or some manner of scholar dodge.

"One night after the tavern was hushed and the mood seemed right, I asked him why my sister Áine had been born the way she was, with a wilted leg and her arm all drawn up and all. I told him my grandfather claimed the gods were punishing us, and that I could never bring myself to believe that. I told him I want to know why, if as the Christians say Jésu's god was so much about love and mercy, why Áine had been born so, and why she had to die so young.

"He said, 'Aye, there's a terrible thing, lad, a terrible thing. In very truth, anybody who's telling you they know the reason for such a dreadful thing is either a fool or a liar. The plain ugly fact is that we can't know everything there is to know, and some of what we most want to know is just too much for us. It's like sitting in a boat trying to see what's at the bottom of the sea—we know there must be a bottom, or all the water would just leak out. But the water's too deep. We can't see the bottom, but we know it must be down there. Aye, and we look up in the sky at night and see the stars in their dance, but what could be beyond the stars we see but more stars we can't see, and beyond them more, and beyond them still more after that, forever. We know God must be there, even if we can't see or understand.'

"Felix saw his answer wasn't enough for me, and he said, 'I don't know, Pell. I wish I did, for my sake and yours, but there's so much I just don't know. Why do babies die in the night, safe in their cribs? Why do storms come, bringing death and ruin? Why do some die so young, and some old people keep living after they're ready to die? The truth is that I don't know.'

"I thought he was done, and I was looking for something else to say, seeing it hurt him to tell me he didn't have an answer to my question, when he said, 'But I don't believe God is punishing you, or your sister, or your mother. I do not believe that, not for a heartbeat.'

"He was quiet again, and then he said, 'Can I tell you a story?'

"Of course we all told him he could, and that we'd gladly listen, so he said, 'It's a story from Hebrew scripture, a story I heard when I was a lad that seems to have gotten lodged in my mind somehow. Long and long ago, before blessèd Jésu, even before his ancestor King David, there was a man of God whose name was Ibrahim.'

"Esther gasped and whispered 'Avraham Avinu!' The bishop nodded and said, 'Aye, sister Esther—Father Ibrahim. God chose Ibrahim to be the father of his people and told him that his children and grandchildren were to be as many as the stars in the sky. And even though Ibrahim and his patient wife Sarah were childless, and he was nearly a hundred years old, he believed God, and soon after that, they had a son, whom they named Isak. Years later, Isak married Rebekah, and she birthed twins.

"'The first born was all red and hairy, so they named him Esau, which meant ... well, red and hairy. The second came close behind and seemed to be clutching at his heel. The first-born would be the heir when their father died, and it looked like the second was meaning to pull the first back in so he be first and get the birthright. So, they named him Yacob, which meant 'trickster' or 'cheater,' or 'one who'd take another's place,' or something along that path.'

"The bishop took a pull of his ale and said, 'You might like to know that the Angles made the name Yacob into Séamus, just like your good abbot. I'm not sure how you get from one to the other, but …'

"And now Shea, who'd been trying to stay awake, perked up and said, 'That's my name!'

"'And a fine name it is, Séamus,' chuckled the bishop. 'Or should we be calling you Yacob now?'

"Shea thought about it for a breath or two and said, 'Nay, I'm just Shea.'

"'Aye,' said the bishop, 'you're just Shea, and that's more than enough, just as you are. Now, when the twins were grown, Yacob did cheat his brother out of his birthright, not just once but twice—that's a good story, too, but not the one we're telling just now. After that, Yacob had to run away to another country, as Esau was so angry about it. Some years passed along, and Yacob had done right well, and had herds of sheep and eleven or twelve sons, two wives and two other women who'd borne his children. All was well with Yacob, and then the Lord God told him it was time to come home.

"'So, he gathered up all his sons and wives and sheep and such and they started the journey home, but the closer they got to where Esau was, the more Yacob fretted, as he was thinking his brother would still be angry at him. Esau was just a breath or two older than Yacob, but he was right tough, and Yacob was scared.'

"Well, about now I was wondering where all this was going to take us, and I looked around and saw everybody was just as lost as I was, save Esther. Felix continued, 'When they came to a stream called the Jabbok, Yacob sent his wives and sons and all he had across the stream, but he stayed behind, alone. And a man came and wrestled with him, and they wrestled all the night through, even after Yacob's hip bone slipped out of its joint. Then, when the sun was about to come up, the man said, 'Let me go now, for the day is breaking.' But Yacob said, 'I will not let you go, unless you give me your blessing.' Then the man said, 'What is your name?' so Yacob said, 'Yacob,' which as I've told you meant 'trickster' or 'cheater.' And the man said, 'Now your name is no longer to be Yacob, but Israel, because you have struggled with God and with man, and you have won out.' Israel means 'one who wrestles,' or 'one who struggles.'

"Well, to be honest with you, I was still wondering why he was telling us this story and how it was aught to do with Áine, but now I wanted to hear the end of it, so I nodded, and the bishop went on. 'Yacob asked the name of the man he'd been wrestling all night, but the man said, 'Why would you be asking my name?' And then the man blessed him, and Yacob named that place Peniel, which meant 'I have seen God's face, and yet my life was spared.'

"Now I looked around at the others hearing this story, and I saw they were just as vexed as I was, all except Esther, who'd heard it before. She nodded to the bishop, to let him know he'd told it right. I've always good with riddles and puzzles and such, but this one had me flummoxed. So, I said, 'Have you been telling us this tale to tell us that sometimes things just don't make any sense at all?'

"The bishop laughed, and asked, 'And why would you be saying that, Brother Pell? Did the story make no sense to you?'

"'Well, as a fact it brought up a good many questions, good bishop,' I answered. 'Who was it your man Yacob wrestled? Why would Yacob be staying on one side of the stream all alone by himself? Why was this mysterious secret man afraid for the sun to be rising? Why would Yacob ask him to bless him, and why did he say he'd seen the god's face? And why did Yacob think this man was someone to give him a blessing, or change his name?'

"Bishop Felix looked at me peculiar, like I'd said something smart, and Brigid said, 'Am I right in thinking this is a story from the followers of Jésu then?' And Esther said, 'It's a story from holy Torah, from the writings of my people.'

"The bishop said, 'It's an old story handed down from one generation to the next by the people of Israel, the Jews. Jésu and his first followers were Jews, and so these stories are sacred to us as well.' We sat quiet for a short time, tending to our own thoughts, and finally I said, 'Well, so why did you tell us this story, Felix?'

"The bishop took another swallow of his ale and looked down to see the sad sight of the empty bottom of his jar, but when Brigid offered to get him another, he said, 'Nay, lass—a little is enough, and too much is too much.' It was something I'd heard Mellán say before, we caught a glance between us and he nodded with a little smile. Twedwr nodded, too, but more sadly.

Then the bishop said, 'Yacob wrestling at the Jabbok is one of my favorite stories. It's from the Genesis, the first book of the Torah, and it's meant to be a powerful, puzzling, mysterious story. It's meant to raise up questions that have no answers. We're never told who the man was, or why he fretted about the sun rising, or who gave him leave to change Yacob's name. That's part of why I love the story, because there are so many questions that aren't answered in it, just like our lives, with so many mysteries we can never understand or explain.

'But mostly I like this story for this thought: Yacob is blessed because he *wrestles*, with God and with man.' said Bishop Felix. 'He becomes who he is, Yacob becomes Israel, because he doesn't give up, because he keeps wrestling.

"'In very truth, friend Pell, I don't know why your sister was born the way she was,' said the bishop. 'I don't know why she died so young. I don't know why your papa killed your mam.' I was surprised he knew about that, and Mellán whispered to me, 'I told him about your mam.' The bishop continued, 'I don't know why the God of love and mercy would let any of that happen. But it did happen, awful as it was. There's so much I don't know, will never know. But I'm wrestling, I'm still wrestling. It's just then, when I don't know, when the doctrines of the Church get thin and brittle, when it's too dark for me to see all the way to the bottom of the sea or all that's up above us in the heavens, that I need to hold on and keep wrestling, keep struggling and hoping and praying and trying to understand what can't be understood.'

"Now I saw that he was talking to himself as much as he was talking to us, and I saw that he was deeply touched by it, so much that he had tears rolling down his cheeks, and of course I did, too. Then, in a smaller, whispery voice, he said, 'I'm not faithful because I understand—I'm faithful so I can hold to the hope to understand some day. I'm faithful so I can keep wrestling, and I keep wrestling so I can be faithful. Following Jésu isn't easy or perfect, I know that. No religion will ever be perfect for long, because it's only just people like us are left to pass it along, and because our minds are limited, while God and his mysteries are not. I think following Jésu brings us closer to the truth than any other religion I know about or holding no religion at all. If you've got leagues of rocky ground ahead of you, a pair of boots that are a little tight on your toes or a bit loose around your heels is sure to be better than no boots at all. I can't imagine living without faith or facing the burdens and sorrows of life without hope.'"

Pell thought about what he'd just said and nodded to himself. "In very truth that touched me, fellas. For a man of such high regard, a bishop of the Christian Church, mind you, to be willing to say he didn't know, it was honest and real, it was …"

Pell looked at Oswell, who said, "Authentic."

"Aye, authentic," said Pell. "All my life, it had been easy for me to look past notions about religion when the one speaking them was false or uncaring, like my grandfather and his Tuatha Dé Danann, or my Roman soldier father who deserted us and left us with his god Mithras, or the arrogant priest Cyneric and his Jésu. My friend Mellán started me thinking mayhaps there might be something more to it, but here now, this man wasn't trying to convert us to his religion—he was clearly struggling with his own faith, inviting us to struggle along with him. I was deeply touched by it, and I could not look past it."

The old man sat quiet for a moment, and the two younger men respected his silence, and waited.

Pell nodded to himself and started again. "Another night, Twedwr asked, 'Good bishop, what I'm wanting to ask you about is how a word becomes a wee baby.' I was surprised that Twedwr had been listening to that part at the Christ's mass, but when I looked at him, he just shrugged.

"'Aye,' replied Bishop Felix, 'now you've hit on the very thing.' Then, handing his empty jar to Brigid, he said, 'Would you be so kind as to bring me about a half a jar more of Twedwr's good ale? I'll be glad to have it if I'm to be thinking such perplexing thoughts as that.'

"When she'd gone, the bishop leaned over the table and whispered, 'Pell, if you don't marry that lass, you're a damn fool.' Well, don't you know my ears turned hot and red, and Mellán and Twedwr had a big loud laugh about it, but I knew he was right. It wasn't my first time to be thinking it, but it was the first time to be hearing it said out loud.

"When Brigid came back with the bishop's jar filled and a pitcher to share with the rest of us, as she was standing over us pouring out the ale, she wanted to know what had us all laughing. Smooth as a lullaby, Twedwr said, 'Oh, Pell just said something funny, is all. Go on, Pell, tell her.' Well, I couldn't think of aught funny I might have said just then, and before I could stop it, my mouth just started talking before my mind had time to consider what might come out. I said, 'I told them I'm going to marry you someday.'

"Brigid set the pitcher down hard on the table, put her hands on her hips and said to Twedwr and Mellán, 'And what's so funny about that, I'd like to know.' And then she turned to me and said, 'And what day will that be, boyo, when you're thinking you'll marry me? And what gives you the idea I'd marry you? Did you ever think you might be needing to talk to me about it before you go announcing it to our friends?'

"Well, now of a fact I'd tossed myself into a deep dark hole. I couldn't go back and unsay what I'd said, and I couldn't tell her they were laughing because the bishop said I ought to marry her. This time I waited for my mind to line up something before I said it: 'Surely, it's long past the time I should have talked to you about it, and I'm very sorry. The truth is that I was afraid. I was afraid you'd tell me it was a daft idea. I was afraid you'd tell me nay. But I love you, Brigid, I always will, and I think I was just wanting our friends to know it. I shouldn't have said what I said; sometimes my mouth just gets ahead of my brain, like a wagon trying to pull a mule, I suppose.'

"Ah, well, sometimes you just stumble on the right thing to say. Then she leaned over and hugged me tight and whispered, 'You're a right arse, Just Pell from Éire. Have I ever told you that?' And I said, 'Aye, my love. You've mentioned it a time or two, and now I'm starting to think I ought to believe it myself.'"

Chapter XXVI

Until They Make a Cage Around You

The old man sat quietly for a minute, lost in the precious memory. Neither of the younger men wanted to intrude on the moment, and they sat there patiently, until Pell roused himself. "Then Brigid turned to the bishop and asked if he'd be willing to do us the honor of marrying us together. But he looked right sad and said, 'Aye, lass, sure I'd be willing, and the honor would be mine, but I can't. I'd be breaking the very rules I'm supposed to be making the priests keep. I can't marry two people who aren't Christians.'

"Now Esther spoke up and said, 'That sounds like one of the laws of my people, to marry only another Jew. That's why I left my family behind, to marry Gaius, who was a Roman. A body ought to be able to marry who they love.'

"'Well, you're the damn bishop,' declared Twedwr, who was all flustered by it. 'Can't you just change the damn rule?'

"But Felix said, 'Nay, friends, I wish I could. But then the other bishops and such exalted personages would come after me for breaking the rules and traditions, and …'

"'They'd come after you?' I asked. 'What does that mean, and why would they want to come after one of their own?'

"The bishop looked regretful, but he answered, 'Some of those fellas can be right full of spite and ambition.' Then he told us a long story about going down to a Council of bishops in Ariminum, in Italia. He was a younger man then, he said, all full of needing to be seen being right about everything."

"The Council of Ariminum?" Caillen asked Oswell, who responded, "Was that one of the Councils called to deal with the heresy of Arianism?"

"Aye," said Pell. "You know about Arianism, then?"

Caillen looked at Oswell, who nodded hesitantly, and then Caillen nodded, too. Pell said, "Arius taught that Jésu was the Son of God, but that he was made by God as part of creation, and so not coeternal with the Father. But that wasn't the teaching of the Church, as set in the creed written at the Council in Nicaea just twenty-five years earlier before the gathering of bishops in Ariminum. At that council, there was another creed proposed. It wasn't so different from the creed of Nicaea, but the emperor preferred the Homoean creed which favored the Arian position. The bishops approved the creed of Nicaea unanimously, but when the results were sent to the emperor, he overturned their decision. Ah, it was about power, who held the strongest sword.

"Felix said when they realized the council was becoming nothing more than keeping the emperor happy and had nothing to do with teaching the truth about Jésu, he and some of the other bishops left. When the council voted to accept the other creed, Liberius, the Bishop of Rome condemned the Council, and the Council condemned him right back. The emperor removed him and installed another fella to be the Holy Father instead, and it was a right hateful mess for years, all about nothing much, as far as Felix could make it out. He said, 'It was nothing more than politics, mostly—just men and their pride and ambition. I wanted nothing to do with any of it.'

"'So,' he said, 'two things came of that: one, I promised myself I'd never go to another council of the Church, and two, ever since then, some of my brother bishops have been watching and waiting for me to step off the path.'

"Then I asked, 'Why would they be watching and waiting? Why would they even care?'

"'So they can accuse me of teaching Arianism,' answered Felix, 'or some other foolery, so I'll have to step aside and they can get a friend or a relative to take my place. The Church is a grand idea, but it's all down to people to make it work, and people can be mean, selfish, and ambitious. Too many of us think the most important part is being right.'

"So, we all sat there wondering where that left us, until Brigid said, 'Aye, well, we'll be baptized then.' So, I was thinking we'd become Christians so I can marry Brigid. I'd seen some baptisms before when we went to sing at the chapel, and it didn't look like it was painful, so I was willing.

"You need to understand this: Brigid and I came along where most of us kept dozens of gods. We had so many gods you couldn't keep all their names in your head. Wells had gods, mountains had gods, rivers, seas, the winds and the moon and the sun and the stars all had gods. There were gods of Éire, Saxon gods, older gods, newer gods. If one seemed to favor you, you'd offer your sacrifices or prayers or do whatever that one asked of you, and after a time if that one seemed to draw away, you'd just go find some other god. So, when Bishop Felix said we'd have to become Christians for him to marry us, that wasn't of much concern to us.

"But then the bishop surprised us again. He said, 'Nay, friends, you can't be baptized.'"

"The bishop said you couldn't be baptized?" Caillen was indignant. "Why?"

"Well, of course that's the very thing we wanted to know. So, we asked him and he said, 'Well, that's a short question with an awful long answer. Over a hundred years ago now, there was a terrible struggle about who was to be the next Emperor of Rome. One of the generals was named Constantine, and he was fighting against ... oh, their names aren't in my head just now, but he was fighting against them, and he had a vision, or a dream, or mayhaps both, depending on who's telling the story. In this vision or dream, he saw two Greek letters—the Chi resting over the Rho—the first two letters in the word Christus. He was a soldier, and many a soldier have looked for signs and visions and such, hoping to curry the favor of the gods.

"'After he saw this sign,' said the bishop, 'he ordered all his soldiers to paint it on their flags and shields and such, this Chi Rho. And even though the other army had twice as many soldiers, Constantine won the battle and became the Emperor of the West. Soon after, he and Licinius, the Emperor of the East, ordered an end to the persecution of the Christians, which had started when the Emperor Nero blamed the Christians for the burning of Rome long and long before that. Well and good, but then I think it was that same Constantine who proclaimed it would be a good idea for people to be Christians if they wanted to do business in the Empire, and it wasn't much later that another Emperor made following Jésu the Empire's official religion, so that you have to be a Christian to be a citizen of the Empire.'

"I said, 'Surely the Christians back then were right pleased about everybody having to become Christians all just at once.' The bishop answered, 'Aye, mayhaps they were. But soon it became hard to tell who was a Christian because they wanted to follow Jésu, and who was a Christian because it was good for their purse. The persecution of Christians ended, which was a grand thing, and the Church had more members, and with the support of the Empire, there was more money. What we didn't have was people who really believed that Jésu was the Son of God, who came to bring the good news of God's love for all.

"'So,' he said, 'if you want to be baptized because you want to follow Jésu, I'll be honored to baptize you. But if you're just being baptized because you want me to marry you together, I want no part of it.'

"Now Brigid and I each looked at the other, and Brigid said we understood that, and asked what would be involved in following Jésu. He told us we'd have to believe that Jésu is the Son of the only God, who made all there is everywhere, and we'd need try to do what Jésu said we were supposed to be doing, which was to love God with our hearts and minds and souls, and to love and forgive everybody whether we like them or not, including loving and forgiving ourselves. I told him I thought we could try to do that, and he looked at me closely, and then it looked like he made a decision: "Talk to Brother Mellán about it, talk to Abbot Séamus about it, and when I come back for the ordination, if you still want to be baptized, I'll be proud to baptize you.'

"'And then you'll marry us?' asked Brigid. Now the bishop and Mellán caught the other's eye, and the bishop looked all sad and said, 'Nay, lass.' We were awful disappointed again, until he said with some merriment in his voice, 'Father Mellán will.'

"Well, now we've been tossed up and down so many times I was starting to feel like we were in a small boat on rough seas. I just stared at him, not knowing what to think or say, and Brigid, just as muddled as myself but never without a word, asked, '*Father* Mellán?'

"Now the bishop nodded to Mellán, who said, 'Aye well, mayhaps so. So now I suppose I need to tell you that while Bishop Felix's been here, he's been teaching me, making me ready to be ordained a priest. Next time he visits the abbey here, if the abbot approves, it'll be to ordain me a priest, and then I can do the marriage rites for you.'

"'If the abbot approves?' scoffed Twedwr. 'If your uncle Séamus approves, you mean. Are you thinking he might not?'

"'Nay,' said Felix. 'It's just another step on the path.'

"'Just wait for me to catch up here!' I said, 'Slow yourselves down! What is ordained?'

"It was Felix who answered, 'A man is ordained by a bishop to become a priest. A bishop lays his hands on the man's head, and we all pray, and God makes him a priest.'

"'Aye,' said Twedwr, 'and it's a man who becomes a priest, is it?' The bishop looked at him blankly, and Twedwr ventured, 'Never a woman?'

"Bishop Felix seemed surprised at the idea of it, like a woman becoming a priest was something he'd never thought of before, like a fish howling at the moon. 'Nay,' he said, but you could see he wasn't easy about it.

"'Only it's just the Druids train men and women alike,' said Twedwr, 'I suppose they just start with the idea that we're all just people and all.'

"Now Felix shook himself, like he was freeing himself from thinking what shouldn't be thought about, and he said, 'Well, God love us, but those fellas would be all over me like flies on a cowpat if I were to start talking about ordaining women!' Then, mostly to himself, he said real quietly, 'But why not, though, really?'

"He thought about it for a moment and said, 'Well, Brigid, you and Pell think about being baptized, and if you're serious about it,

I'll be most honored to baptize you.' He looked around the table at Twedwr, Esther and Shea, and added, 'I'll be honored to baptize any of you, all of you.'

"'Now then,' he went on. 'As we were talking about things I don't know or understand, I think I can add wondering why we don't bring women along to be priests to my growing list. I know some women as would be much better at it than some of the fellas I've ordained. But it's a rule, and part of what I'm supposed to do is to keep the rules. Now that I'm saying it out loud, though, that seems like some manner of awful weedy reasoning. It's a grand thing to have traditions and all, until they make a cage around you. At some point, you have to choose between what's your traditions and what's right.'

"I was about to say it was just the way the world works, except for the Druids, when Felix said, 'Now, Twedwr was asking about the Word of God becoming a baby, and I have a thought about it that might be of some interest to minstrels such as yourselves. In that passage from the story of Jésu as the Apostle Johannes tells it, he wrote 'In principio erat Verbum et Verbum erat apud Deum et Deus erat Verbum,' which is Latin, meaning 'In the beginning was the Word: and the Word was with God, and the Word was God.' That you already know, but that's not the interesting part.

"'Johannes never wrote a word in Latin,' said Felix, 'he wrote in Greek. I don't know why a Hebrew disciple of Jésu would be writing in Greek, but that's as it is. Well, I don't know much Greek, but I do know that those same words are different in Greek. In Latin the word for 'word' is 'Verbum,' but in Greek it's 'Logos.' And Logos means more than just 'word.' It's a word that was used by Greek thinkers from long before Jésu was born, some of them using the word Logos to mean 'the mind of creation,' or 'the music of the spheres.'

"'Music, do you say?' wondered Twedwr.

"'Aye,' said Felix, 'the idea of it was that those ancient Greek fellas were thinking something must be keeping all the stars and planets from knocking into the moon and all, and one of them wrote that all those heavenly spheres must be spinning around in a big huge dance, and the Logos was the music they were all dancing to. Now, as the Apostle Johannes was just starting to tell the story of Jésu, he wrote that it was the very mind of the universe being born, the music of the spheres. It was the music that all the universe was dancing to—the mind of God, the *Logos*—being born as a person when Jésu was born.'

"I said, 'Mayhaps that's why the bishops were so concerned about the Arians, because they were saying Jésu wasn't the *Logos* at all, as he was not eternal with God the Father.'

"The bishop looked at me like I'd said something odd, and I started to apologize, thinking I should say something about my wagon pulling the mule again, but he said, 'Nay, Pell. You just seem to think clearly about things that vex many of us.'

"Well, I didn't know it just then, but that was the moment my road started to take a very different fork than the one I thought I was on."

Chapter XXVII

Things Might Have Been Different

"Why?" asked Oswell. "What happened then? Did the bishop leave? Were you baptized?" Then Caillen prompted, "And how does Father Cyneric come back into the story?"

"Well, slow down a bit; we don't want to arrive before we get started. All will be brought into the light in its time, but you have to understand this before you can understand that. After Felix went back to Londinium, we had many and many a conversation with Mellán and the abbot and some of the other brothers, about following Jésu, and about the Jews and the Druids. There were different thoughts about and around it, some of which I carry with me still, and others I tossed away like stiff boots that didn't fit me.

"Still and all, I learned a lot in those conversations. It was in those talks late in the evenings that I started to find some answers about the nature of God and mankind. It was important for me to understand that all the monks didn't believe the same thing the same way, and that they were at peace with holding different thoughts about things. I was surprised to learn that there were things that Conal believed as round Seán did not, and on some points, their beliefs were slightly different from those held by Mellán, or Séamus. I reckoned that just as my friendship with Mellán was not the same as Brigid's friendship with him, so it was with the Lord God and his children: we don't all have to believe the same thing, or at least that's not the most important thing. The important part is that we all love and trust God with our lives and with the lives of those we love, and that we love each other, because we are all of us the children of God.

"That's the gospel, friends—that's the message of Jésu: love. Love God, love each other, love yourself. Love and let yourself be loved, forgive and accept forgiveness, and everything else will line up like wee baby ducks swimming after their mama."

Caillen repeated, "Like wee baby ducks ..."

"In that easy spirit," continued Pell, "I saw that Esther and the Jews had a voice in the harmony of faith, just as the Twedwr and the Druids and anybody holding their faith sincere had a voice. This harmony of faith became an idea that has been precious to me from that day to this—there can be no harmony if we're all forced to sing the same note. It is one of those ideas brother Hywel would have called idealism, and in truth, it was one of those ideas that landed me in considerable trouble later.

"Also, as I came to know the different brothers and priests, I saw that it was as Mellán had said about some Christians and church leaders, with 'some being better than others.' I saw that there were some as would put themselves before the work of the Church, even before the Lord Jésu himself.

"But I also saw some of the promise of the Church, that the followers of Jésu could do much good, shining a light of hope into the darkness of greed and despair. The Church can still shine the Light of Jésu into the darkness, and the darkness has not overcome it, because it reflects the very light of Jésu—when we allow ourselves to be guided by the Spirit of God."

Pell smiled, and held his hands up, palms facing his audience. "Well, now I'm preaching you a sermon, and I expect you're hearing more of those than you can stomach already. I'd best be getting along with this story, before I get too old to remember how it ends. Well, it wasn't long before Bishop Felix came back. He baptized us: Brigid, Áine Minor, Shea and me, and in that same worshipping, he ordained Mellán to the sacred order of priests, and the next day Mellán married Brigid to me, and Esther to Twedwr."

"But the bishop said it was against the rules to marry people who weren't Christians!" objected Oswell.

"Aye," said Pell. "He said he himself couldn't marry a Jew to a Druid, because he was the bishop, and he needed to abide by the rules. But he made sure that Father Mellán understood that he would find no objection to a freshly made priest doing it.

"Felix came back to Erith before we were expecting him because his superior, the Bishop of Londinium, was making him go to another council of the Church, and he was dreading it. He came down to the Dancing Druid to tell us he needed our help. He said he was getting old, and he needed somebody to travel with him, somebody who was easy on the road, somebody he could talk to about what all was going on at the Council, somebody he could trust. He was concerned that he couldn't trust most of the fellas he would be travelling with, and he wanted some eyes and ears to see and hear what the other bishops and clerics were saying and doing. So, he came to ask Mellán and me if we'd be willing to go down to Aquileia with him."

"Aquileia!" exclaimed Caillen in the same moment that Oswell asked, "Where's that?"

"Aye, Aquileia," replied Pell, "and an awful long way it was, to be sure, away down to north Italia, at the head of the *Mare Hadriaticum*. Well, and as I've said before, I've long known I had a great deal to learn about women, but by this time I'd at least worked it out that there were times when I was needing to be talking to Brigid about what I was thinking, and I knew this was one of those times.

"So, I told the bishop that I needed to talk to Brigid, and that's what I did. She straightaway told me I ought to go, and what a grand adventure it would be. Then, and mayhaps as a part of her trying to convince me to go, she said she wished she could go too, not thinking it was likely something that could ever happen. I told her it seemed like a fine idea for her and our young Áine to go, if the Bishop didn't object. In truth I fretted about taking a child of four years on a long trip, but Brigid said she would be fine, and it would be an education for her. So off I went to talk to Felix.

"Far from objecting, the bishop was right pleased about it. It seemed two of the other clerics in the delegation were bringing their wives as well, and he thought having a child along would remind us of the happy parts of life. So, I told Brigid, and we started planning our journey.

"I told Bishop Felix that I was fretting about the hardships of travelling all that way, not just on Brigid and Áine, but on all of us. But he said, 'Ah, nay, brother Pell. We'll be riding in carriages, not on a wagon or on the backs of horses, down the old Roman road to Dubris, where we'll take ship to Gallia.'

"When he saw Mellán and me trading a chary glance, he said, 'And we're to be escorted by a troop of Roman soldiers and various other officials of the church in Londinium. You'll find it an easy journey, and we'll have a lot of time to talk. And best of all for me, I'll have time to listen to my favorite minstrels play the harp and sing.'

"'But what about the carriages, and the horses and all?' asked Mellán. 'Surely when we come to cross over to Gallia, we'll have to leave them behind. Will we be walking the rest of the way?' The bishop said, 'Nay, my friends. We'll be taking the carriages and the horses and soldiers and cooks and servants on the ship with us!'

"It was more than I could imagine, a boat so grand as it could carry all those people and horses and wagons and all, and when I said that the bishop chuckled a little and said, 'Aye, a mighty grand boat indeed.'

"We talked about Shea coming with us, and Felix told us he'd be happy for him to come, but Shea said he'd rather stay there with his animals. Esther and Twedwr also chose to stay there in Erith, and said they'd look after Shea while we were gone.

"We started our journey around the beginning of summer, as the Council was to start in early autumn. We had a long way to go, and the bishop said he didn't want to have to push hard to get there on time.

"Felix told us we wouldn't need our pots and pans, or tents, as this would be a different style of travelling, but Brigid brought out the old sword Esther had tossed me the day we were set upon by thieves, and handed it to me, saying, 'Well—you never know.' When I started to object, she said, 'Better to have it and not need it than to need it and not have it.' I couldn't dispute that, so I wrapped it in some cloth and stuffed it down in my pack. Many's the time I've wondered how things might have been different if I'd just left the wretched thing behind."

"Different better?" prompted Oswell.

"Or different worse?" suggested Caillen.

"Aye, well. It could've been either one of those, but it would surely have been different, of a fact it would have been. Ah, well, we'll get there, but we're not there yet.

"We left Erith and started rolling down to Dubris' white cliffs, where we crossed over the Oceanus Brittanicus to Caletum in Gallia. And sure as the rising of the sun, that boat was grand enough to carry all of us, horses and carriages and all, with room enough to be walking around. The crossing of the Canalis Britannicus between Angleland and Gallia was not difficult, or unpleasant. Mellán and I had been fretting about being sick, remembering Twedwr coming over from Éire, but that boat was so big we hardly felt the rocking of the waves, and Caletum wasn't far. Áine Minor was rocked to sleep.

"The soldiers unloaded all the wagons and horses and such, and we continued our long travel down to Italia. It was as Felix had promised, easy travelling for the main part. We travelled in the day, not pushing too hard. If we came to a settlement we stopped and stayed in an inn or tavern, but many a night we slept in the tents or wagons, or under the whirling stars. The weather was mild, and with our escort of soldiers, we didn't need to fret about ruffians and bandits.

"Almost every night, whether we were in a tavern, or we'd made a camp by the side of the road, Mellán, Brigid and I would sing a song or two. We missed Esther and Twedwr's voices in the songs, and the stories he'd tell, and Shea's playing the bodhrán, but we did the best we knew how to do, and the rest of our travelling company seemed to appreciate it. Little Áine led the company in 'The Butterfly's Blessing': 'A blessing to you!'

"Most days we'd ride in the carriage: Felix, Mellán, Brigid, Áine and me, talking and singing and dozing when we felt drowsy. Sometimes someone else invited himself to join us, hoping to kiss the bishop's ring or something. We tried to be nice and all, but most of them didn't stay long. Mayhaps they just weren't easy with how familiar we were with the bishop, calling him by his name, disagreeing with him now and again, and singing songs that might have been a bit … more coarse than they were expecting."

"Songs like 'Whose Breeches Am I Wearing?'" asked Caillen.

"Or maybe 'The Lady's Pleasures on Offer'?" suggested Oswell.

"Aye," laughed Pell, "those and others, some we learned along the way from Bishop Felix. To tell you the truth, sometimes when he got weary of this person or that visiting in our carriage, he'd start singing one of those bawdy songs, and we'd join in, and they wouldn't stay with us for long after that. Felix said it wobbled their moral balance; Áine thought it was hilarious.

"The weather was mild, and the company was grand, and the leagues rolled along. The most bothersome distress fell to Brigid, who felt it was her duty to befriend the other two women in our company, Miriam and Orelia. She said Miriam would have been bearable without Orelia, but the two of them were almost never apart, and together she said they were like two scavenger birds bickering over scraps of gossip and whatever scornful opinions they could find for everyone they saw. 'Lord knows what they say about me when I'm not around!' she said.

"Orelia specially made a point of instructing Brigid how to care for Áine, which left her so angry she could hardly talk about it, which was right unusual. Finally, I convinced her she didn't need to fret about that, or to mix with those old besoms, and after that life was better all around.

"We did have a guest we welcomed into the carriage, a young man named Andreas. He was a servant to Valerian, the Bishop of Aquileia. It was Andreas who'd brought the invitation to the Council to the Bishop of Londinium, who claimed he couldn't come, as his health was failing. He said he needed somebody he could trust to represent the faith as he understood it, as it had been upheld in the creed of Nicaea, which was why he asked our Felix to go in his stead.

"It was Mellán who first met Andreas, and he introduced him to Felix and Brigid and me. Felix wanted to know about Aquileia and the state of the Church there, and as we were talking it became clear that Andreas' grip on Latin was fairly loose, and he was struggling to answer our questions. So, I asked him in Latin, 'What language is it your people speak?' and he said, 'It is many names. It is very old people, very large until the Romans. It is many forms of one language, Graeci.'

"Young Andreas had grown up in Kórinthos in Graecia, where the Apostle Paulus had visited, and where he had friends he wrote to. After we talked about that for a while, I asked him if there were many people in Aquileia who spoke the language of the Graecia, and he said there were. So, I decided it might be of some use to Felix if I were to learn Greek, and for the next three weeks Andreas and I often rode together, in a carriage or on horseback, or sometimes walking along, him teaching me Greek and me teaching him Latin. Both of these languages are awful complicated, and poor Andreas really struggled with it, but like Yacob at the ford of the Jabbok, he didn't give up, and by the time we got to Aquileia, he could understand most of what was being said in Latin and speak it well enough to say what he wanted to say."

"You learned Greek?" asked Caillen incredulously. "In three weeks?"

"Well, I learned the bones of it, anyway. It's terrible complicated, but we had hour after hour on the road, with naught much else to do. And it is, as my great-uncle told me, 'a grand thing to learn—a grand thing indeed.'

Chapter XXVIII

Killed by Words Written Down

Pell continued his tale. "But one visitor to our carriage was especially troublesome," said Pell. "The bishop of Londinium sent a slippery young priest named Eadgar to assist Felix. He seemed most keen to know the bishop's thoughts on every single thing. Aye, to know his thoughts and to shape them if he could. He was tall and thin, clean-shaven with short dark hair he kept cropped short as the Romans do, but with far too much perfumed oil to slick it back all the same. To tell you the truth, he reminded Mellán and me of Father Cyneric, younger, but that same sense of a wading bird waiting to snatch up a wee sprat.

"At first, I thought Eadgar was doting on his bishop, or that he admired him. He seemed keen to say whatever he thought the bishop wanted to hear, but as the leagues rolled by, I began to wonder. It was naught more than a look on his face when he thought nobody was looking, or the feeling I got from him now and again, naught I could prove or even point my finger to, but I thought it would be best to keep my eyes on him when I could.

"One afternoon as we bumped along, Eadgar was in our carriage talking on and on about what he said was a new creed, written to replace the creed from the Council of Nicaea about fifty years before. Eadgar said this new creed was to be discussed at the Council we were going to in Aquileia, and he seemed keen on persuading Felix to support it. But the bishop was right chary of it, as he was thinking the creed of Nicaea had put the whole issue with the Arians right, permanently. When Eadgar kept on yammering at him about it, the bishop said he hadn't seen it written out. After some time of Eadgar trying to convince Felix to agree to something before he saw it, at the next stop to water the horses and walk around a bit, he said he'd find a copy for Felix to study and stalked away.

"Mellán and I walked the other way, glad to listen to the world around us without Eadgar's voice in it, and as we were standing there enjoying the stretch in our legs, up walked the bishop and said, 'So, my trusted advisors, how do you think about young Eadgar?'

"I thought he was playing with us, so I said, 'Trusted advisors? I thank you for the honor, good bishop, but how did a fresh hatched Christian such as myself become an advisor to an exalted bishop so venerable as yourself?'

"But then of a sudden he was serious, and he said, 'It is your clarity of thought that I need, Pell. Your Latin is far better than mine; I've watched and listened, and I reckon you're thinking in Latin when it's Latin you're speaking. When I'm trying to speak Latin, I'm still thinking in the language of the Angles and the Saxons.'

"I told him it was just too hard to talk in one language and think in another. Whatever language I was hearing and talking was the language I was thinking. But before I could make that make sense, the bishop said, 'And you don't forget aught, do you? I've noted that as well, that you seem to remember everything. But it's the way you see things, the way you think about things that I really need. Aye, Pell, if you're willing, I would greatly benefit by having you as my advisor.'

"So, I answered, just as seriously, 'Aye, friend Felix, it would be my very grand honor to help you however I can.'

"'Thank you,' said the bishop. 'And Mellán, my trusted advisor, I've been touched by your gentle loyalty, and how you keep your calm. I'd treasure your help as well.'

"Mellán was quite pleased at the idea, and said, 'It will be my honor, lord bishop.'

"Just then Felix took us both up in a tight embrace, which caught us off our guard, and while we were still hugging, he whispered, 'It's hard to know who you can trust, when the people around you say what they think you want to hear, and nobody tells you the truth. That's what I want from both of you, the truth. Just tell me what you see and hear, and what you think.'

"So, we told him we would, and promised to be honest with him, whether he liked it or not. And he said, 'Thank you, friends. Now I'm run into a difficulty I need your help in solving.'

"'Aye, sir,' I said, 'we'll be glad to help you if we can.'

"'Well, it's touchy,' he said, 'and I need you to understand how things are before you see them for yourself.' Mellán and I just nodded, and he went on, 'You will be meeting a great many powerful men in the next weeks, men who think right highly of themselves, and have no respect for those a man who isn't pushing himself around in his own power.'

"Felix looked at me to see if I understood, and I nodded to tell him I did. Then he said, 'We need to get you some clothes as befit my wise counsellors—nay, hold yourself quiet, that's not the worst of it,' he said—'and we need to get you more of a name than just 'Pell' and 'Mellán.' He looked at me and saw I wasn't pleased about it, and he added, 'Something impressive.'

"'But I am just Pell,' I said. Then I ventured, 'Pell of Éire?'

"'Well, that's better,' he said, 'but it's still not enough for a bishop's advisor.'

"Then I said, 'That's far too much butter on that loaf, exalted bishop! Can't I just be myself?'

"'Oh, I'm not saying you need to be aught else,' he answered, smooth as a mother's kiss. 'You just need a more impressive name, to impress those as respect what's impressive. And some new clothes. Also impressive.' He saw I was a bit wavery, and he pressed on, 'It'll be just for the time we're here. And you'll always be just Pell and Mellán.'

"I nodded, and he said, 'Do you have a name you'd like to be called?' I told him I'd never thought about it, and he said, 'Well, now then, hmm. I propose we call you *Pelagius*, a bit of twisting your name Pell with a Gaeilge word for the sea, *pélagos*, mixed around so it sounds Roman. How do you think of that, Pelagius?'

"'Pelagius,' I said, trying it out on my tongue, 'Pelagius. Aye, that's as good as any other. Pelagius of Éire, then.'

"But the bishop said, 'Nay, there's no more than a handful of souls here who'd ever have heard of Éire. How do you think about

Pelagius of Brittania? Now there's a name to be reckoned with, I think.'

"I wondered whether I wanted to be someone to be reckoned with, but my pride got so tangled up in being Pelagius of Brittania of a sudden that I almost didn't hear the bishop tell Mellán he'd like to introduce him as Father Josephus Mellánius of Erith. Mellán agreed, and then the bishop said, 'Done. Now, tell me what you think about Eadgar.'

"I said, 'Well now, Eadgar. I think he's a right arse, to be honest. He's too oily, too perfumed, too ambitious by far. I don't know how or why a body becomes a bishop, but it seems Eadgar thinks he does, and that appears to be the course he's set for himself.'

"The bishop nodded, pondering what I'd said, and as he was still thinking, I added, 'And how is it that a bishop's assistant knows all about this new creed to be discussed at the Council when the bishop knows naught of it? Why is it so important to him that you agree with him? And why is any of this so terribly important anyway?'

"At that Felix looked a wee bit perplexed. He said, 'Well, the very future of Jésu's blesséd Church is weighing in the balance, between Arianism and Orthodoxy. You understand that, do you not?'

"'I understand what you're saying,' I answered, 'I just don't think it's true, or needs to be true.' He looks at me disappointed, like he was wondering whether he'd made a mistake in asking my opinion about aught, and I went on, 'It may be that I don't understand all of this, and if that's so, I'll be glad for you to school me, but as I understand it, some priest named Arius taught that only God the Father was eternal, and that His Son Jésu was created, which is to say Jésu came along later. Am I right up to there?'

"Felix said I was, and I kept on. 'What I want to know is, why do we care what some fella named Arius taught? If he's right, surely by and by we'll all accept it; if he's wrong, by and by he'll be forgotten.

"As he considered that, I added, 'Mayhaps this is like what Gamaliel was talking about, as the story is told in the *Actūs Apostolōrum*. After Jésu had died and rose up, the rabbi Gamaliel told the Jewish council of elders to stay away from Peter and the other followers of Jésu. He said, 'If this is the work of men, it will come to naught, but if it is of God, you cannot overthrow it, and mayhaps you'll find you've been fighting against God.'

"Felix was impressed I'd read the *Actūs*, and I told him I hadn't, but I'd heard it read a time or two. Then I ventured a little further out on ice that felt like it was getting right thin, and said, 'I suppose what I'm really wondering is, do we all have to think the same thing?'

"Now that I'm saying all this to you out loud, I'm thinking that right there is the very idea that sent my life down the path it took: Do we all have to think the same thing all at the same time? If the true message of Jésu is that we all love one another and love God, surely it can't be so fiercely important whether if Jésu was coeternal with the Father or if mayhaps he was the first of Creation. As for me, I believe Jésu was as the Apostle Johannes wrote it: 'In the beginning was the Word: and the Word was with God, and the Word was God.' But if one of you choose to believe that Jésu didn't exist until he was born of the Virgin Maria, is that something that ought to change the true message of love? Am I so arrogant as to say you must believe just as I say? Is it all that damn important that you should be declared you a heretic if you believe something I don't? What could that possibly have to do with loving each other, or loving God?"

Oswell and Caillen leaned forward, keenly interested, and Pell continued, "Well, this way of thinking might be tossing you both into a pit of trouble you won't be able to climb out of, but I think it's true all the same. No, if you take this path much farther, you might wind up a heretic, and there's not much good in that."

Pell was quiet for a moment, lost in his thoughts. Then he perked up and said, "But I was telling you about Bishop Felix, who thought about what I'd said, and answered me back, 'But sure and it's part of my duty as a bishop in the Church to defend Orthodoxy.'

"'Well, but what is Orthodoxy?' I asked.

"'Orthodoxy is keeping the faith as it's been set by the Church,' answered the bishop, 'as it's set forth in the creeds, the Old Roman creed first written by the Apostles, and the creed of Nicaea.'

"'So, if I'm thinking about this right,' I risked, 'God the Father made everything there is, and made a covenant with the people of Israel. Then after the leaders of the Jews let their vision get so narrowed they could only see God through the Laws of Moses, then the Music of the Spheres, which was the very Mind of God, became a person by the power of the Spirit of God to remind us that God was more interested in love and forgiveness than he was in punishing and the threat of everlasting Hell. Am I still on the Orthodoxy path?'

"Bishop Felix told me that I was, and I said, 'You've invited me to tell you the truth when I can, or just my thoughts whether they're true or not. So, here's my question: what about the Holy Ghost? Is the Spirit of God come and so soon gone? You know the Scripture much better than I do, but I believe Johannes told a long story about Jésu preparing his disciples for what was about to happen, and in all of that, Jésu said 'I have many and many a thing to say to you, but you can't bear them yet. But when the Holy Ghost comes, the Spirit of truth, he will guide you along into the truth, for he will speak not about himself but about what he's hearing, and he will show you what things are to come.'

"'So, good bishop,' I said, 'are we to think that the Holy Ghost has showed us everything we need to know, and now he's done with us? Are we following that same narrowing path of the Sadducees and the Pharisees, whittling God down so He looks like us, instead of us being made in His image? Are we thinking it's all written down in creed or scripture so we don't need to listen to somebody who holds a different thought?'

Bishop Felix had to think about that, and I added, 'The Druids taught in song and story and never wrote it out just for this reason: so truth could keep breathing, so it wasn't dead, killed by words written down. Are we so brittle, so fragile, so arrogant as to think we know everything there is to know about God, and after we write it all down, it's never to be pondered again?'"

Chapter XXIX

The Shifty Plots and Plans of Men

The two younger men looked at each other, each of them hoping the other would offer some answer or objection to the heretic. When none was forthcoming, they turned back to Pell, who said, "You don't have to agree with me. I'm not claiming to know anything I don't. And as I say, I don't want to be throwing you into a pit you can't get yourselves free of. But following Jésu can't be something you can just set in stone forever. Languages change, people change, the world around us is always changing. If we insist that the faith has to remain the same, the Church will become …" He stopped, searching for a word.

"Obsolete?" guessed Oswell.

"Irrelevant?" ventured Caillen.

Then the two of them said in rapid cacophony, "Outdated?" "Frozen?" "Worn out?" "Ineffective?" "Broken?" "Worthless." "Lost." "Dead."

"Aye," said Pell. "All of those. But hear me now, hear this with your ears and in your heart. Jésu told his friends, 'You are the salt of the earth. But if salt is no longer salty, how can it ever be salty again? It is good for naught but to be thrown out to be trodden under the feet of men.' He said, 'You are the light of the world, a city on a hill that can't be hid. Nobody lights a candle and then puts a bushel over it but puts the candle on a candlestick so it lights up the house. Let your light shine, so others can see your good works and give glory to God in heaven.'

"Now, you're welcome to agree with me, but I won't love you any less if you don't. You can be as orthodox or heretical as you choose, whatever that might mean. But love God and love other people as much as you love yourselves. Love, be salty, shine the Light of Jésu into the darkness, and all the rest of it will work itself out."

Pell looked at the two younger men and couldn't tell if they were inspired, offended or thoroughly confused. He reached down into the old leather satchel and retrieved the harp, saying, "Aye, well, mayhaps it's time for a song." He tuned a couple of the strings, and then sang:

"Aye—it's wonders and mysteries all our days,
    It's faith and doubt hand in hand.
Smart enough to ask but not able to know—
Such is the puzzle we are, my friends,
    Aye, such is the puzzle we are.

"Where does the sun go when it sinks in the sea?
    And how do the birds know how to sing?
Who taught the spiders the spinning of webs?
And what will the next new moon bring?
    Oh, what will the next new moon bring?

"How could my mother have loved me so well?
    What makes the tides ebb and flow?
What holds the water at the rim of the world?
And where do our freed souls go?
    When we die, where do our free souls go?

"What would we see beyond the stars
    if we took a ship into the skies?
And what mysteries are yet to be seen
deep in my dear lady's eyes,
    There in my dear lady's eyes?

"When we were children we asked these things,
    because we were wanting to grow.
But the wonder and mystery's been crushed away since,

Mayhaps we stopped wanting to grow.
    A shame we stopped wanting to know.

"Aye, let me away where the sun goes down,
    Let me sing with the birds in their songs.
Deliver me from the webs of men,
And forgive me all my wrongs—
    Lord, forgive me all my wrongs.

"Aye—it's wonders and mysteries all our days,
    It's faith and doubt hand in hand.
Smart enough to ask but ne'er able to know—
Such is the puzzle we are, my friends,
    Aye, such is the puzzle we are."

They sat in contented silence for a while, and Pell put the harp away. Then Oswell said, "That was beautiful, sir. Is that a song of the Druids?"

"Nay," answered Pell, "but it cheers me that you'd think so. Nay, I wrote that one, since I came back here." Another moment passed in silence, and Pell said, "I'm glad you liked it though, as it comes from a heretic and all.

"So, let's see … before I strayed from the story, I was telling you about the priest, Eadgar. Later that day, he came up to Felix and gave him a scrap of a scroll. He said nothing to me, but leaned in to whisper something to Felix, then he gave me a mistrustful look and slunk away.

"Later, when we were back in the carriage, I asked Felix what Eadgar had said, and what was on the scroll. So, he handed me the scroll to read, which of course I can't do, and he said, 'I'm thinking you should not be easy around Eadgar, Pell.'

"Before I was through wondering what he meant, the bishop said, 'Are you going to read the creed?' Then of course I had to tell the bishop that I can't read, and …"

"You can't read?" Caillen was aghast. "But you speak all those languages, Gaeilge and Latin and Greek and Frankish and all, how did you learn, how could you not be able to read?"

"Aye, well, I understand your consternation, my young friend; it's been a concern to me most of my life. As I told Oswell, I've tried many and many a time to make the letters make sense to me, but they just wriggle around all back and forth so the same word doesn't always look the same to me. It's like trying to follow one wee sprat in a school of thousands, all those letters and words just swimming and darting around. If I hear a word said, I understand and remember it, but if I see it written down, it's no use to me at all.

"So, I told the bishop that I can't read, and he had about the same reaction as both of you did, and after a while he asked Mellán if he would read what was written on the scroll. Then, as I was glad for us to leave off about me not being able to read, and trying to lighten the mood a shade or two, I said, 'What, Bishop Felix, you can't read, either?'

"I thought it was funny, but Felix said, 'Nay, I don't read much anymore. My eyes see what's far off well enough, but not what's right up next to me.' We bumped along for a short time, and then he said, 'I suppose I've just read too much. Mellán, I'm hoping you'll be willing to serve as my secretary on this trip. Will you do that?'

"So I asked, 'Not Eadgar?' and Felix answered, 'Nay, I need somebody I can trust.'

"My brother Mellán said he'd be glad to help however he can, and Felix said, 'Aye, we'll let Mellán do all the reading and writing, and we'll leave it to Pell to make it all clear.' Mellán accepted the parchment and said, 'What will you be doing, bishop?' Felix smiled and said, 'I'll be praying, lad—praying this council doesn't split the Church any further the west from the east, praying that we meet with no treachery, and praying that we all get home safe.'

'The so-called creed was in Latin, of course, and as Mellán read it out to us, I waited for it to take the form of the Old Roman creed or the creed of Nicaea, but it never did. To be honest with you, it never amounted to much at all, just a pile of squabbling and bickering, favoring the position of the Arians, and speaking against those who thought it was better to hold to the faith as it was set forth in the creed of Nicaea, is all it was.

"This creed Eadgar brought us was adopted at one of the councils of Sirmium, and part of it read: 'For it is clear that only the Father knows how he begot his Son, and the Son how he was begotten by the Father,' which was true, and if they'd left it there, we wouldn't have had aught to squabble about. But a principal idea of the creed of Nicaea was that God the Father and God the Son were *homoousia*, of one substance. This Sirmium creed claimed this: 'But as for the fact that some, or many, are concerned about substance'—I'm leaving some out here—'there should be no mention of it whatever, nor should anyone preach it. And this is the cause and reason: that it is not included in the divine Scriptures, and it is beyond man's knowledge, nor can anyone declare the birth of the Son, and it is written on this subject in Isaiah chapter fifty-three, verse eight.'

"This, I reckoned, was a right dangerous idea, that we should not be allowed to believe or preach about aught that isn't written down in Scripture, as if Scripture contained God himself, that what was written by men set the boundaries for God—nay, never! I told Bishop Felix that here was a treacherous path for the faithful to be following.

"In very truth the whole squabble wasn't worth a pile of flies, arguing about whether Jésu was made by the Father or was he coeternal with the Father. After Mellán read it out twice, I told the bishop it seemed to me something to take our minds and hearts away from what we're supposed to be doing, all so we could pretend to be understanding what we know full well we can't.

"And here's the truth of it: it had naught to do with loving God or loving each other, naught to do with following Jésu at all. It was all only just about the power of emperors, the ambitions of bishops, and the shifty plots and plans of men scheming to become bishops and emperors. So many of those grasping men were caught up in their hunger to win, to claim that they were right and somebody else is wrong that they didn't see or care what they were doing to Jésu's holy Church. They ..."

Here the old man caught himself before another sermon afflicted them all, scrubbed his face with his hands, and continued. "So, we went bumping along in our carriage, riding down the old Roman road, talking about the Church and what we should be looking and listening for at the Council, and singing and playing the harp and all.

"Oh, and it was a pleasant time, the road down to Aquileia, from Gesoriacum to Durocortorum, and then through Augusta Treverorum … well now, here's the problem with a memory such as mine: if you're too patient with me I'll be telling you what we had for dinner night after night, and week after week. Mayhaps it's enough for me to tell you we clopped down the *Via Claudia Augusta*, went up one side of the *Alpes* and down the other, and by and by we came into Aquileia, almost two full weeks before the Council was set to start.

"The journey was easy enough; all we had to fret about was Eadgar and the two shrews who were ever after Brigid to join them for one thing or another. But after we came to Aquileia, we didn't see much of any of them anymore—Brigid said they had bigger fish to catch there.

"Aquileia was right large, bigger even than Londinium, and filled with sights, sounds and smells we'd never before known. Most of the people there spoke some form of Latin, but it wasn't nearly so precise as the Latin I'd learned and was often used with much greater passion and volume, both in the number of words being used and the loudness they came at you with.

"The people of Aquileia were Romans, aye, but they were also Persians and Jews and Thracians, people from Germania and Anatolia and Noricum and more besides. It was a rich stew of peoples, languages and cultures, and a right spicy stew it was! When the other delegations started arriving, it was Babel all again, and our language was confounded—we couldn't understand one another's speech.

"It was there in Aquileia that I first saw bartering as an art. I'd seen it before, Twedwr haggling with tavern owners, but this was a bewildering game, and one I had to lose a time or two before I learned how to play. Brigid was seemingly born with a talent for it, and she soon became our chief haggler. She found us rooms at an inn called *Equus Nobilis*, the Noble Horse, which was right close to the Basilica of St. Marcus, where the council was to meet. The rooms were small but clean, and the food was exceedingly tasty. As the inn was soon swamped by the surge in customers, Brigid was hired to work in the kitchen there, mostly baking bread but learning some cookery tricks and styles we've enjoyed long after. Little Áine helped in the kitchen some, and Eirini, the daughter of the owner of the Horse, looked after her when she got bored with it.

"Aye, but none of that stopped Brigid from finding a man who made the sort of clothing Bishop Felix thought would be more suitable for his secretary and advisor. She took Mellán and me to buy new white linen tunics, and togas to go over them. I'd never worn a toga, and had never thought I'd need to, but Felix insisted. It was much longer and heavier than I thought it needed to be, and was a right nuisance start to end. But we were meant to be impressive, and so we were.

"Mellán and I waited for two nights, sitting bored in the common room of the Horse. On the third night, with Felix's encouragement, I brought out Twedwr's harp and we began to sing a little bit. We'd long since shifted from Gaeilge to the language of the Angles and Saxons, now we shifted again to sing it all in Latin. So, in 'The Butterfly's Blessing,' the words swam around from '*beannachd dhuito* to '*a blessing to you,*' and now to '*benedictio vobis.*' Oh, aye, it was right confusing for a time, of a fact it was.

"But still and all, we sang out the songs we'd known for years and a few others we'd learned along the way. And just as it always did, the music attracted a crowd like moths pulled to a candle. The psalms were right well received, but we quickly came to see it wasn't the right crowd for bawdy songs—there was naught they found pleasing about 'Whose Breeches Am I Wearing,' which had been a favorite since we'd learned it from the Abbot of Erith. Right then I should have known that people who didn't like a good bawdy song were not my people.

"A few nights after that, Mellán and I were singing and trying to draw Bishop Felix more into it, when I noticed my friend Andreas talking to a cleric whose vestments and regalia were of a right different fashion. When we stopped singing for a moment to let our breath catch up to us, Andreas brought the cleric over to me and said in Greek, 'Bishop Palladius, this is my friend Pelagius of Brittania. Pelagius, may I present to you Palladius, Bishop of Ratiaria, in Dacia.'

"Well, I'd never heard of Ratiaria or Dacia—the only word I understood after 'present to you' was epískopos, bishop. But when Palladius smiled to say something I didn't completely understand, I could see he was a man of character and nobility. His hair and beard were long and dark, and his eyes were intense and chary, but not cold. From the first, I liked him.

"Well mind you now, I was still learning Greek, and it's terribly complicated, so I had to line it all up carefully before I said, 'It is my great honor to be meeting you, bishop.' Or something near enough to that.

"Now I know I don't look like a body who ought to be speaking Greek, but there I was speaking it anyway, and Palladius looked right surprised. He said, more slowly this time, 'We shall see, my friend, whether it is your honor or not.' I thought mayhaps I'd confused the language, so I asked him what he meant, and he said, 'This Western Council is called for the correction of my haíresis.'

"Now, mind you: these weren't waters I thought I should be swimming in. I was twenty-seven years old, a Christian for just a few months, and there I was talking with a bishop from a place I'd never heard of, who was telling me it may not be an honor to meet him because of something called haíresis. Heresy wasn't yet a word I knew, in any language.

"So, I turned to Andreas and asked him what haíresis means, but he didn't know the Latin word for it. Then I turned to Palladius and told him I didn't know that word, and he said, 'Haíresis' is a teaching, or a belief declared to be contrary to the teaching of the Holy Church.' I was further vexed at the very thought of the Church declaring an idea contrary, and my face must have showed it, because he went on, 'I follow Jésu, of course, but my understanding of Jésu follows along the teachings of Arius.' Now I was trying to keep my disloyal face from showing aught more, and he whispered, scarcely daring to hope, 'You are not Arian, are you, Pelagius?'

"'Nay,' I answered, 'but I don't know why that would stop us from having a sip of wine together.' Then he gave up a smile that lit up his whole face, and just like that, we were friends. We were friends who disagreed, but we were friends just the same."

Caillen couldn't stay quiet any longer. "You took an Arian as a friend?"

Pell answered with more impatience than he intended. "Aye, and why would I not?" Then he took a deep breath and continued more calmly. "Palladius and I had different ideas about the nature of God the Father and God the Son. He was still a good man. In truth, he was fascinating to me, and I wanted to know how life was where he was from, and his reasoning for being an Arian. And—and hear this now—I found out what he thought and believed made sense to me. I was never an Arian—I had my own *hairesis*, I suppose—but Arianism made sense to me. I think it wasn't outrageous, except to those looking to use outrage for their own purposes.

"That night and the next, Mellán and I sang in the common room there at the Noble Horse, and we ate and shared wine with Palladius and Andreas. They tried to teach us some songs in Greek, but their music was strange to us, even harder than learning the songs of Esther's people, and we soon gave it up."

Chapter XXX

By Unspoken Understanding

Pell continued, "The night after that, Bishop Flavius Cynericus Valentius made his grand entrance into the Noble Horse with his entourage."

"Cyneric?" Oswell was incredulous. "A bishop?"

"No," said Caillen. "He said 'Cynericus,' not 'Cyneric'."

"Aye, so I did. As Cyneric and his toadies came into the common room, one of his group clapped to catch our notice, and then presented him to the people there as 'Flavius Cynericus Valentius, bishop of Vinovium,' but Mellán leaned over to me and whispered, 'Well, look who the devil himself dragged in!' So I looked, and there he was, Father Cyneric, the bastard priest of Port Láirge."

Oswell repeated his incredulity: "A bishop?"

"Aye," said Pell. "Mellán and I knew him straightaway, although the look of him was quite different in several ways. He was older, of course, but he still had the sharp eyes and beaked nose of a kestrel hawk and movements and manner of a redshank wader. His dark hair was oiled and long enough to be slicked back into a bunch, and his beard was long and cut square across the bottom. His tunic was longer than any I'd seen, hiding his long skinny legs nearly down to the ankle, and it was made of bright white linen. Over it, he wore another garment with sleeves past his elbows, made of some material that made it look right stiff and uncomfortable. It was adorned with strips of purple cloth, very fine and ornate, as befitting his exalted rank. Days later as we were sitting in the Council, we saw several other bishops wearing the same style of thing, and Bishop Felix told me it was a tunicle, made to fit over the tunic, and sewed of very fine wool. I told Felix the tunicles looked heavy and hot; he told me they were costly and showy. None of them were so gaudy as the one Cyneric wore."

Now Caillen protested, "But here: you said he was introduced as Cynericus."

"Aye, that he was, but he was Cyneric all the same. I suppose he wanted a more impressive name as well. My first thought was to sneak away so Cyneric wouldn't see us, but as Mellán and I had just told the people gathered around us we were about to sing a song I'd written called 'The Nature of Man,' we couldn't just slink away. So, we sang the song, the whole time fearing that the Cyneric would look up and see us for who we were and make some manner of ugly moment of it, but there wasn't any reason to be concerned: Cyneric paid us no mind whatsoever.

"By and by Brigid came in with little Áine, saw Mellán and me all flustered, and wanted to know what was going on. With my wee girl on my lap, I nodded over at Cyneric and told her who he was. Well, she'd heard Mellán and me talk about him from time to time, but now that she was seeing him, she wasn't impressed. She shrugged and said, 'So?' and I whispered that we didn't want him to see us. 'Why?' she asked. 'What do you think might happen? That proud rooster might throw some words at you?' She said, 'You've naught to fear, neither of you. He's come for the Council, same as you, you're bound to bump into him late or soon.' And then she said, 'It's him as should be afraid of you.' I looked my question at her, and she said, 'You know the truth about him, who he is and what he did. You know things he won't be wanting these other fellas to hear.'

"Then I thought, 'Well then, we'll let the son of a bitch see it's us,' so I told Mellán we should sing 'The Beltane Fire,' in the Gaeilge as we'd learned it from Twedwr. I explained to the people that Mellán and I were from a part of Brittania called Éire, but the bastard didn't even look up. Then I said I'm from a little village called Port Láirge, and that we'd be singing this song in the language I grew up speaking, but Bishop Cyneric wasn't listening, he was just looking around the room to see who it might benefit himself to meet, which of course he assumed left us out.

"Then Brigid told Mellán and me we ought to be just as mindful of him as he was of us, which was not at all, so we just kept singing and playing the harp, and Cyneric just kept scanning the room for something he could snap up like the wading bird he was. After a while I got lost in the music, and the next time I looked over, Cyneric and his delegation had left. The very air in the common room seemed fresher to me.

"The next morning Mellán and I told Bishop Felix that our old adversary Cyneric had come into the Noble Horse common room, and now he was a bishop! We'd told him about Cyneric, of course, and Felix was right curious to learn how such a man had become a bishop, and why he was there. Later that afternoon, he found us again and told us what he'd learned.

"He found four of the bishops who'd come down from Angleland with us, drinking wine in the shade of a flowering acacia tree, and they invited him to join them. As they exchanged the pleasantries of the day, remarking on the number and variety of bishops and their entourages, Felix had casually asked if any of them happened to know a bishop named Flavius Cynericus Valentius, or where the Diocese of Lindum Colonia might be. As it happened, one of the bishops there was the bishop of Gaer Weir, which was quite near Lindum Colonia, and he knew Cyneric, well enough to despise him. He'd had enough wine to give himself permission to speak more freely than bishops usually do, and Felix said he confirmed our description of Cyneric as arrogant and ambitious.

"This bishop said that one of the older priests in his diocese had known of Cyneric when he was growing up in Vinovium. He said this man's grandfather had been the bishop there long and long before, and that his grandfather had gone to the Council of Arles. So of course, they had to talk about the Council of Arles for a while, but then the bishop of Gaer Weir told them the old priest had told him that young Cyneric had been beaten severely by a young woman's father, who'd accused him of mistreating his daughter, and that Cyneric had then stolen some money from his father and run away.

Then he'd heard that some time later, Cyneric had made a big show of repenting, and became a monk south of Londinium, and that later he'd pestered the bishop there until he ordained him a priest. Well then, it was no surprise to hear he'd soon found some more trouble to get into, and the abbot suspended him for drunkenness and an improper relationship with a young woman. But after that, he said, he hadn't known what happened to Cyneric.

"So, our bishop Felix told them that he'd been sent to Éire, where he made the same style of mess, and the people of the village there had set him in a little boat and out to sea. Then another bishop said he'd met him a few years ago at some synod or another. He was introducing himself as the assistant to one of the bishops, and then the next thing he knew he was a bishop himself, somewhere up north. They all agreed that he was no good, and that they needed more wine so they could ponder how such a man could become a bishop.

"Some days passed after that, pleasant days of exploring the city of Aquileia, eating supper with Brigid and Áine, and Mellán and Felix, singing with the people in the Noble Horse in the evenings. Each day more delegations arrived, and each night the Horse's common room became more crowded. The innkeeper's name was Petrus, and a very rock he was, nearly as wide as he was tall and every bit of it muscle and sinew. He'd been a smith until he'd lost an eye to a wandering spark, he told us; now he was enjoying running the Noble Horse. He offered to pay us for bringing people in for the music, but we told him nay, and he told us he'd give us our rooms for free, which pleased us right well.

"Three nights before the Council was to start, Bishop Palladius came into the tavern, but now his manner was drastically changed. I walked over to the table where he and another man were eating, and they both looked nervy, hunted. Palladius didn't know many words in Latin other than those in the mass, so we spoke Greek, which was slow for me, as I was still learning it.

"He said, 'Pelagius my friend, this is my friend and *synsynomótis*: Secundianus, bishop of Singidunum.' Then to this fella he said, 'Secundianus, this is my friend Pelagius of Brittania, advisor to Bishop Felix Hortensius Terentius of Londinium in Angleland.'

"I told Secundianus it was an honor to meet him, and then I told Palladius I didn't know the word *synsynomótis*. '*Synsynomótis* is,' he paused for a moment to search for the words, '*Synomótis* is a person who's plots or schemes, *synsynomótis* is a person you plot or scheme with.' He wrote it all down with his finger on the table to try to help me see it, and I watched his finger busy making out the letters like it made some sense, but it was all muddlesome to me. I didn't feel the need to tell these two fellas I couldn't read or write Greek, or any other language, so I asked as respectfully as I could, 'What is it you're plotting and scheming?'

"Aye, you're bold when you're too young to know better, and bold again when you've nothing much to lose. Palladius told his friend I was somebody he could trust, and Bishop Secundius said, 'We plot or scheme nothing. It is the self-styled Orthodox who plot to control us for speaking the truth, who scheme to silence us.' I could hear the hurt and anger in his voice."

Now Pell looked at the two younger men and said, "Well, as I've told you, my Greek was not so good that we could make our way through all this talking without me stopping them and asking them to tell me the words for Orthodox, control and silence, and many and another more. It took a great deal more time there in the Horse than it did here telling the two of you about it. But they were patient, and my store of Greek words was growing.

"As we talked, I saw that bishops Palladius and Secundium believed they were defending the faith as they had received it, the same as Bishop Felix and most of the other fellas there believed they were defending the faith they'd received. And there I was thinking that it was a simple difference in what they had been taught about Jésu, with those who called themselves Orthodox having learned most of it the same as the Arians, but for that one difference. But I don't think it ever mattered as much as they made it out to. All of them would have told you they believed Jésu was the Son of God, and that he was born by the power of the Spirit of God, and surely that was what mattered. All the rest of it was just bickering for people who enjoy bickering, or those who think they can be more powerful or more highly regarded by winning an argument, something for them to fight about.

"I tell you the very truth of it, if you put all those bishops in the same room with no doctrine or creeds to fuss about, before the sun sets they'd be arguing about whether it's to set in the West or the East. Two or three of them would likely tell you it would set in the North, and one would be trying to convince you it wouldn't be setting at all!"

Pell took a deep breath; Oswell and Caillen watched and waited as he calmed himself. "Nay, my friends. If it were only about what they believed, it would be easily settled. The spice that fouled the stew was the politics of it, the pride and ambitions of men. But then other men joined in, just trying to do the right thing, and they got caught up in it and took one side of it or the other, until it threatened to rip Jésu's holy Church into quarrelsome factions. And for what? So one side can imagine they've got answers about things they can't know? And why is it so important for us to pretend to know? I think it's so we can pretend we are in control. That is the original sin: we want to know, to pretend we are the masters, not the servants.

He thought for a moment before asking, "Can I tell you a story?" They nodded, and he said, "It's a story you already know, but it's a good story all the same. Just after God made everything, he planted a garden and made a man to care for it, breathing his own spirit into the dust and calling him Adam. God told the man he could eat from any of the plants in the garden except for the tree of the knowledge of good and evil, or they would die. Adam had everything he needed, except for a helper. So, God took one of Adam's ribs and made a woman, Eve."

The two students nodded their familiarity with the story, and Pell continued. "God had also made the serpent, who was right sneaky, and put it there in the garden with them. This serpent said to the woman, 'Did God tell you that you couldn't eat all the plants here in the garden?' And the woman said, 'We can eat all from of the plants except for the tree in the middle of it—if we eat the fruit of that tree, we will die.' And the serpent said, 'Nay, lass, you'll not die. God knows when you eat the fruit of that tree, your eyes will be fully open, and you will be like Him, knowing good and evil.' So, she ate the fruit, and gave some to Adam, who also ate it. Then they knew they were naked, and they hid from God. Do I have that right so far?"

"Yes, sir," said Oswell.

"Good. The serpent told her 'You will be like God.' That's the original sin: like Mother Eve, we want to be in control of everything, knowing what's not for us to know. We all want to be God. I think it's because we don't really believe what we say we believe. If we believe that God is the Maker and Sustainer of the world, and if we trust God as we say we do, we wouldn't have to pretend to know, that we're in control. We wouldn't have to insist that we're right, and that whoever disagrees with us is wrong."

"But surely it matters," ventured Oswell, "whether Jésu is coeternal with the Father, or made by the Father as part of creation."

"Does it matter? Aye, it matters as to how we understand how Jésu is both God and man at the same time. It matters how we understand. My question is whether understanding is more important than believing. If you think you're needing to understand so that you can believe, I'm thinking you may never believe."

Pell watched the two young men as they wrestled with these thoughts and then continued. "Aye, well, I was meaning to tell you a little about the Council of Aquileia, starting with the two Arian bishops, Palladius of Ratiaria and Secundianus of Singidunum."

"They were heretics, weren't they?" asked Caillen.

"Oh, aye," answered Pell. "But they were good men who believed what they said they believed. The night before the Council proper was to start, I saw Palladius and Secundianus sitting all gloomy at a table across the common room. So, I told Mellán to come with me, and we walked over to see what's gotten our Greek-speaking friends so dreary. They were bitterly sad that some of the other bishops they knew, other Arian bishops, weren't coming to the Council. So, they knew before the Council was to start that it wouldn't be going well for them. On a whim, I stepped across the room to ask Bishop Felix if he'd like to meet two Arian bishops, and he said he would. He picked up the pitcher of wine he'd just started drinking and said, 'I was hoping to get some help with this wine.'

"We walked over to their table, and it felt like all the eyes in the room were pushing and pulling at us. I made the introductions in Latin and in Greek, and Palladius graciously asked us if we'd sit. So, we did, and Felix put his pitcher of wine on the table and said in Latin, 'Well met, brothers in Jésu. We could be talking about the many things we agree on, instead of the few things we don't, but it seems it's the disagreeing that we're here to discuss.' I repeated all that in Greek, or something close to it, and the two other bishops nodded their woeful agreement. Then Bishop Felix said, 'And I'm thinking that you and the other Arians aren't likely to change your minds.'

"'Nay,' said Secundianus, 'no more than you are to change yours.' I told Felix what he'd said, and he nodded his understanding. So, we sat for a time in the melancholy of that moment, and Secundianus caught the eye of our friend Petrus and whispered a word in his ear. By and by the innkeeper came bustling back, carrying something wrapped up in a cloth. He put his bundle on the table and pulled back the cloth, proudly presenting us a steaming loaf of dark bread, and saying 'This is good bread, made by the Lady Brigid.'

"Then, by unspoken understanding, Bishop Felix poured us each a goblet of wine, Bishop Secundianus lifted the bread, offering thanks to the god we all serve and put it on the table, and then Bishop Palladius took it and broke it, offering it to Secundianus, Felix, Mellán and me, and we ate. Then each of us took up our wine, lifted it up to give thanks, and drank it dry. And I know as sure as I'm able to know aught else, that Jésu himself was with us in that moment." Pell looked at the two young men and saw that they were considering what he'd said, and concluded, "Sometimes I think all our words just get in the way.

"'And he was known to them in the breaking of the bread,'" said Caillen.

Chapter XXXI

Bright Shining Hatred

"Good morning to you!" Pell was sitting with his back against his rowan tree. "I haven't seen you for many a day now."

"Good morning, exalted teacher," said Caillen, but it didn't sound like he meant it.

"Aye, well—exalted is just exactly what I'm not," laughed Pell. "But here now, what's vexing you? I've seen happier faces at funerals than the pair of you are bringing me this morning!"

Caillen looked over at Oswell who said, "Father Aelfred says we're to stop talking with you." Pell just smiled and waited, and Caillen said, "He says your heresy is a plague in the Church, and that we are in danger of becoming tainted by it."

"But here you are," said Pell.

"Well," said Oswell, "we just wanted to thank you for telling us your story, and for the songs, and for your hospitality."

"And Father Aelfred has gone to Londinium for the day," added Caillen.

"I was hoping to hear the end of your story, though," said Oswell.

"Aye, well," said Pell. "As to that, my story's not over yet; as you see, I'm still breathing. And when my body takes its last breath, my story will go on, and I hope I'll still be learning fresh songs to sing to the Lord."

"But what happened at the Council of Aquileia?" asked Caillen. "And what were you and Bishop Augustine arguing about? Why were you declared a heretic? And what happened to Mellán, and Twedwr and Esther? What happened to Brigid?" Somewhat sheepishly, Oswell asked, "And who is Dáirine?"

"Well," answered Pell, "if you can sit with me a time, just while Father Aelfred's away, I can tell you all of that right quickly, so you're not digging the hole you're in with Father Aelfred any deeper. I'll try not to splash any of my heresy on you."

They sat, and Pell continued. "I can tell you the rest of the story if you're wanting to hear it, but I'm thinking you've already learned what Father Joseph sent you to learn. But first, we need to have a song and a bite to eat to start the day."

Without waiting for an answer from the two students, Pell pulled Twedwr's old harp from its satchel and felt the two students relax in contented anticipation as he tuned it just a bit. Then he sang:

"I lift up my eyes to the hills around me,
    from where is our help to come?
Our help comes from the Lord,
    who made all the heavens and the earth.
He will not let our feet be moved;
    he who watches over us will not slumber.
He who keeps Israel safe
    will neither slumber nor sleep.
It is the Lord himself who is our keeper;
    the Lord is in the shady tree at our right hand.
The sun will not harm us by day,
    nor will the moon frighten us by night.
It is the Lord himself who will guard us from all evil;
    and he will keep us safe all our lives.
The Lord will watch over our going out and our coming in,
    from this time day forth and forevermore."

On cue, Pell's granddaughter Dáirine brought to out a tray of milk, bread and cheese, with a bowl of honeyed figs for the men to share. Both of the young men thanked her, and Pell took her hand and kissed it before she left them.

Caillen saw that Oswell was distracted by Dáirine, so he said, "What happened at the Council of Aquileia?"

"Ah, well—as to that, mayhaps we can break our fast as the story rolls by. After we listened to bishops prattle on and on for several days, Felix leaned over to Mellán and me and said, 'There's naught to say that hasn't already been said, now everybody just wants to have their chance to say it.' Palladius did make a grand speech about how he had hoped to be coming to a council that brought bishops from the East and the West together, but after he and Secundianus arrived, they realized it was just them with a herd of bishops from the West who weren't interested in learning aught they didn't already know. He said it wasn't fair, which to my thinking was true, but it didn't change aught.

"Bishop Valerian of Aquileia was steering the meeting, but it was Ambrose of Milan setting the sails. I never met either of them, but Bishop Felix held Ambrose in high regard, and he seemed like a good man. I believe the unity of the Church was his foremost purpose, but it had become twisted around to mean we all had to think and say and do everything the same way. Valerian seemed most interested in the opinions of the two emperors, Theodosius in the East and Gratian in the West. When Palladius was speaking, I was watching Valerian, but he wasn't listening. So, I told Felix and Mellán that Palladius' boat was already leaking bad before ever he and Secundianus got it pushed away from the dock.

"By and by Bishop Cynericus stood up and talked until everybody was more than sick of his voice, and then he talked some more. The more he talked the angrier I got, and I was already having trouble sitting in one spot when Cynericus demanded that the Council declare Palladius and Secundianus be declared anathema, which Felix told us meant they were to be denounced and excommunicated. Well, it was just as soon as Cyneric stopped his blathering that I found myself marching up to the podium to speak to that grand chattering of bishops and priests and all, and don't you know they were all right curious to see what a sprout of a boyo such as myself was about."

Horrified, Oswell asked, "What did you say?"

"Well, God love us, at first I was as surprised as they were to find myself standing there. But then I gathered myself together and said in fluent Latin, 'Exalted elders of Jésu's holy Church, I am Pelagius of Brittania, advisor to Bishop Felix Hortensius Terentius of Londinium.

Well and well I know that I have no rank or title that gives me the right to address such an assembly of learned and reverent men such as yourselves. So please excuse my youthful boldness, but I mean to speak to you in the Name of Jésu the Christus, Lord of us all.'

"Then in far less fluent Greek, I said 'I stand before you to make an appeal for brotherhood among those who are the children of the One God, our Father in heaven.' Mostly I was talking to Secundianus and Palladius, but I could read in their faces there were some other bishops there as spoke Greek, some quite likely much more than I did. But even though many of the bishops there must have known Palladius and Secundianus spoke very little Latin, and even though there were bishops whose Greek was better than mine, every word spoken in that Council 'til I stood up had been spoken in Latin. It was like Father Cyneric coming to Port Láirge and not even trying to speak our language until it was too late, just another way of bullying, to insist somebody speak your language or be left out. It's naught but saying I'm smarter than you are, and the proof of it is that you don't even know what I'm talking about.

"But now I'm off my path again, getting myself riled and all. Out of the side of my eye I see that Cyneric was looking at me and whispering to the men he'd brought with him, wondering who I was, whether and where he'd seen me before.

"I put him out of my thinking and said again, this time in Latin, 'I stand before you to make an appeal for brotherhood among us, as children of the One God, our Father in heaven, and so brothers in Jésu the Christus. We are here not because we disagree, but because we want to agree. We want to look for what is good and true, so we can share the Good News of the love of God the Father we have been showed in His Son Jésu. I put before you that this is what ought to be important to us, to find the truth, to look for what is good, and trust the Lord God to bring us together in love.

"Then I felt the rightness of what I'd said, and I was boldened to keep on with it. 'This quarrel we're allowing to split brother from brother is about whether Jésu was without beginning, eternally begotten as we have it in the creed of Nicaea, or was Jésu first made before all else, but still made and not eternal as God the Father was eternal. I understand this is important, important enough to be talked about and debated. It seems to me that it's important enough for the leaders of Jésu's Church not just to talk about, but also to listen about, and especially to listen to those as disagree with you, unless ...' and now I paused to raise up the drama and also to take a long breath, 'unless you're willing to tell us and all of God's Church that you already know everything there is to know about God.'

"Well, there was some murmuring and muttering about that, but as I looked around, I could see that there were many of them listening right hard, and I was feeling the magic of the moment, like the magic of Mellán and Brigid singing her lullaby to a crowded tavern common room. I said, 'I think the important decision you need to make here is whether it is more important to you to love as Jésu has taught us, or to be correct in your doctrine. I am surely the least learned among us, but I do not believe Jésu told us we were to be correct. He did tell us to love God and love each other, and that everything else will come along.'

"Then I thought it was about time for me to sit down, but before I did, some words my brother Mellán read to me once started wriggling around in my head, so I said them, in Latin and then in Greek.

"I said, 'Mayhaps it would be well to remind us of what the Apostle Paulus wrote in his letter to the followers of Jésu in Corinth, as they were squabbling, like we're squabbling still: 'Love is patient and kind; love is not envious or prideful or rude. It does not insist on being right but rejoices in the truth. Love suffers all things, believes all things, hopes all things, endures all things.' And then I ended by repeating, 'I stand before you to make an appeal for brotherhood.'"

They sat there in silence for a minute, and then Oswell asked, "Then what happened?"

"Then I stepped down from the podium and went back to where Felix and Mellán were sitting, and a handful of the bishops began to clap, which warmed my heart right well. But it wasn't all of them clapping, not even half. Powerful men don't like being scolded, even if it's truth. And then up stood Bishop Flavius Cynericus Valentius, who called out across the room, 'Wood boy!'"

"Oh Jésu, Joseph and blesséd Mother Maria!" exclaimed Caillen. "What did you do then?"

Pell sat in silence for a moment, and the two students waited. Then he said, "I looked around to see the confusion of all those bishops wondering what Cyneric was talking about and looking at me for answers. The room was as quiet as the bottom of the sea. And then I remembered something my great-uncle Eóchaidh told me when I was young."

"His great-uncle was a Druid." whispered Oswell to Caillen.

"Another Druid?" asked Caillen. "I thought they were all dead."

"Well, it's what we were taught," whispered Oswell. "But now I think that was … an exaggeration."

"Aye, an exaggeration," said Pell. "My great-uncle Eóchaidh was a Druid, I believe, and my dear friend Twedwr surely was, unless you're telling me he was lying the whole time I knew him."

The students looked at each other, considering, and Pell continued, "Hear me now: there is more to the world than you're being taught. More to the faith, more to God, more than we know, more! The teaching of the bishops and magisters wants to reduce everything down to where it's written down and understandable, to narrow the faith, to make things all white or black with no gray between, not leaving any space for mystery or eternity or aught we can't understand. That leaves no room for God, the Maker of Mysteries.

"But understanding, knowing, cannot be the work of the Church, not only because there's so much that can't be understood or known, but because the work of the Church is faith—faith and love."

The two younger men looked down, and Pell said, "'And the serpent said, 'Nay, you will not die. God knows when you eat the fruit of that tree, your eyes will be fully open, and you shall be like God himself, knowing good and evil.' We want to be in control—that's what all that knowing and understanding is about—so we try to reduce God and his world down into terms we can control. And then we will be like God himself. The original sin."

They sat for a moment, and Caillen said, "Master Pell, you were going to tell us what your great-uncle, Eóchaidh the Druid, taught you."

"Caillen, Oswell already knows this, and now you need to know it as well. I grew up in a little fishing village away up in Éire, where the River Suir joins the River Barrow to form the Celtic Sea. There are many and many different kinds of fish there, and I grew up catching and eating most of them. Now the pointy-nosed pike is a right bastard among the fishes of those waters, more like a shark than a fish, bony and hard to clean, and will eat aught it can get in its mouth. Bream and trout are more pleasant fish, and you think of them as friendlier, more neighborly I suppose, as fish go. What my great-uncle said was, 'Pell, the world is run by the pikes of men, and you and I were born to be trout. Stand up to the bullies when you can, but sometimes you can't win a fight with a pike unless you become a pike yourself. And that, nephew, that you do not want to do. Better to swim away a trout than to become a pike.'"

"So you swam away?" asked Oswell, disbelieving. "I thought you'd stand up to the bully! You just ran away and hid?"

"Nay," answered Pell. "If I'd swum away, likely you'd never have heard of me, and I'd never have been a heretic at all. Nay, I tried to stand up to the bully, and I paid the price for it. I didn't swim away when I ought to have swum, and I didn't become a pike, either. I just got eaten.

"Oh, lads, I was young and simple-headed. I was all full of what I was thinking was righteousness but turned out to be nothing more than everyday daft pride. It was just arrogance, is all, just trying to be bigger than I was.

"Nay, fellas, when Cyneric called out 'Wood boy!' I was hearing the clapping of some bishops there but not seeing the scowls of those as weren't clapping. Simple as I was, I was thinking they wanted to solve the problem of Arianism, not realizing there were some who just wanted to use the problem to their advantage, or as a way to have their way, to win."

"So, what did you do?" asked Caillen.

"I called back, with a smile and respect I wasn't feeling at all, 'Pax vobiscum, episcope.' Then he made his way through the bishops who were parting to make him a path, and when he was standing about a pace away, he said, 'Wood boy? From Port Láirge in Éire? Is that truly you? The last time I saw you, you were just a carpenter's apprentice in some little miserable backwash village, full of unwashed heathens and savages.'

'Aye,' I answered, 'my home, my family and friends. And the last time I saw you, you were being tossed into a little rowing boat for the tide to take you out to sea.' Now everybody was looking at him, wondering what I was on about, and I added, 'I see the experience completely failed to teach you any humility.'

"Then he stood up as tall as he could and said loudly, 'How dare you speak to me in such a way? What authority do you have to be making such accusations against a bishop in Jésu's holy Church?'

"'Authority?' I answered just as loudly, 'I have no authority at all, Father Cyneric, except the truth. I speak only as a child of God and a servant of Jésu.' Then he leaned in close and said so only I could hear him, 'You should not be here, wood boy! You don't belong here. You're naught but a savage dressed up in better clothing.'

Pell paused, but Caillen was impatient. "So, what happened then?"

"That next moment was a flock of thoughts struggling to catch my notice all at once. It wasn't much time that passed, but there were too many thoughts clanging around in my head. In that dreadful moment, my mind took me back to that terrible night with the village council under the Tree of Wisdom. I remembered poor timid Niamh the potter's wife coming up to speak, and how scared she was. I remembered her telling us the bastard had told her how he was to be a bishop one day, and how she would live an easy life with him, how they'd be treated like a king and queen. And I remembered how heart-breaking it was when she told us that he just threw her away— like a worn-out shoe, she'd said—when he met the fair Saoirse, my cousin's wife.

"Then I remembered the elder Danu saying that Cyneric was to pay me twenty-five pieces of silver for the front-piece I'd carved for an altar in the church he never built. At the same time what I wanted most just then was to slap the sneer off his arrogant face. Ah, but then I was reminded of the life of our Lord Jésu I carved out on that front-piece, and I tried to remember what I'd just said to the

Council, about Jésu telling us to love one another, and me making an appeal for brotherhood. I tried to hold on to that thought, but it was weak and dim compared to the bright shining hatred I felt for Cyneric.

"Then I thought about what Brigid said, about how I knew things about him that he wouldn't want his brother bishops to know about. And then, I'm ashamed to say it, but all my fine words about brotherhood just melted away like dew in late summer. I leaned in toward him and whispered into his ear, 'Would you like for me to tell your grand friends about your time in Port Láirge, Cyneric? Do you think they'd want to know about Niamh the potter's wife? Or mayhaps about my cousin's wife Saoirse, or how you cheated Eóghan, my grandfather? Do you not think they should know who you really are, Cyneric?'

"It was just at that moment that my dear friend Mellán stepped in between us. I think he was afraid that I was about to hit the bastard, as in truth it had been a pleasure to consider. Mellán growled, 'We'll not be backing away, arrogant bishop.'

"Now Mellán was never a large man, and no kind of imposing at all, but he was taller and younger than Cyneric, who looked up at him like he'd never seen him before. Then something lined up in his weaselly mind and he said, 'Mellán? The little Gaeilge monk boy?' Mellán just looked at him, and repeated, 'We will not back down.'

"Now Cyneric looked at me and whispered, 'Tell them if you've a mind to, and we'll see who they believe, a brother bishop, or a wood boy from Port Láirge in Éire and his pet monk.'

"So I started to make my way back up to the podium, and the bishops were starting to make a path for me, when Cyneric snatched the sleeve of my tunic and said, 'What do you want, wood boy? What will it take for you to keep your silence?' And I answered, 'You owe an apology to Mellán, who suffered much in your service.' Cyneric snarled, 'Is that all?' and I said, 'And you owe me twenty-five pieces of silver for that front-piece I carved for the altar of your church.'

"Cyneric took a step back like I'd slapped him in the face. Just in that moment I saw one of Cyneric's people whisper something in his ear, and he straightened up, and took a deep breath before saying out loud enough for everyone there to hear: 'This young man is an Arian!'

Chapter XXXII

How Should We Be Afraid

"An Arian?" Oswell was incredulous. "He accused you of Arianism?" Then Caillen blurted out, "But I thought your heresy was ..."

Pell was amused, and he prompted Caillen, "Aye? And just what was my great heresy, Caillen?"

To his credit, Caillen was reluctant to say it, but he said it anyway: "I thought your heresy was, well, Pelagianism."

The older man thought this was quite funny, and he chuckled his way through this next: "Pelagianism? Well, you've got to be careful about having an original thought, or they'll up and name it after you, and then beat you down with it. It'll be the heresy of Caillenism mayhaps, or Oswellianism. How would you think about that?

"Nay, all that came later. For now, Cyneric was just trying to throw me into a pool of disgrace and dishonor, so the bishops wouldn't likely credit aught I had to say. He went on to tell the Council that I'd been seen drinking with Arians, that I was friendly with them, and that I was trying to corrupt Bishop Felix Hortensius Terentius of Londinium to Arianism as well."

"But that was all just lies!" protested Oswell.

"Aye," chuckled Pell, both touched and amused by the young man's naïveté. "But a man like Cyneric doesn't feel he ought to be limited to the truth. There are some, you'll find, who will say or do anything that serves them in the moment.

"Now in truth, most of the bishops there were right tired of Bishop Cyneric, as he had talked a great deal more than most of the rest of them, and if you've ever been around a clattering of bishops, you'll know that took some effort. But the idea of a young man trusted to serve one of their fellow bishops now being accused of sowing the seeds of dreaded Arianism was something that snatched at their minds.

"In very truth, I was completely flustered by the moment. There haven't been many times that I haven't known what to say or do, but this was one of them. Later I learned that Felix had gone to the podium to speak on my behalf, but it didn't pierce through the knot of thoughts and feelings I was trying to untangle. By and by, Mellán came up behind me and whispered, 'Go on now, Pell—Bishop Valerian is calling you up to speak. Go defend yourself, Pell—go now!'

"As I've said, I don't forget much, but if I'm to be honest with you, I don't remember much about what happened then. I was fully flustered by how quickly the tide had turned around, so that rather than me hauling in the net, now I was finding myself trapped in it.

"I remember thinking it was like I was watching myself walk up to the podium, and I remember my mouth being as dry as a bucket of dust when I got up there. I remember telling the bishops that I wasn't an Arian, and I remember deciding it wasn't the right time to be bringing up Cyneric's several sins back in Éire.

"I do remember trying to tell the bishops that Palladius and Secundianus were good men, and that they were our brothers in Jésu who'd just been taught differently than the rest of us. I remember trying to tell them it was naught more than simple arrogance for us to think we know everything there is to know about God, and that we don't all really have to agree about whether Jésu was eternal or created right at that moment. I remember thinking clearly that I shouldn't say 'appeal for brotherhood' again, as a phrase quickly wears thin. I remember seeing and hearing Cyneric and some of the other bishops shouting back at me and then when I woke up, I remember Brigid holding a cool cloth on my forehead and saying what a fright I had given her."

"What? Wait—what happened?" asked Oswell.

"Did you faint?" wondered Caillen.

"Did somebody hit you, knock you down?" demanded Oswell.

"Or were you ill?" pressed Caillen.

"Aye, well quiet yourselves and let me tell you the truth of it: I don't know. Mellán and Felix said I just collapsed there at the podium, just crumpled down right where I was standing, and they had to come and pick me up and haul me off like a sack of barley.

"When I woke up, I tried to stand, thinking I'd go back up to the podium and say something, but I was as weak as a lamb newborn and cold as a tench, and I sat right back down. The room seemed like it was spinning, and I was sweating hard. There was a loud buzzy humming in my right ear. It was night when I woke, but I don't know how long I had been asleep. After quite a long time, along came Felix and Mellán to see me, and Felix told me that Bishop Valerian had decided we were to go down to Rome, where we would all be questioned by a group of priests whose job it was to nose out heretics and sorcerers and such."

"Sorcerers?" asked Oswell. "They thought you might be sorcerers?"

"Aye, I suppose," said Pell. "Mellán thought mayhaps my fall had disturbed them. And right then I had a disturbing thought: Jésu's holy Church was afraid. Why should the followers of Jésu be afraid of somebody like myself? Or as to that, why be afraid of Arius and his teaching? Or any other heretic, or sorcerer, or anybody anywhere? If we are the followers of Jésu, and if Jésu is the very Son of Almighty God, how should we be afraid? But why else would we have priests looking for heretics and sorcerers, unless we were afraid of them? It made no sense that the Church should be afraid of me, but there it was, and now we were being sent to Rome.

"Still and all, when Felix suggested it might be best to make no mention of my friend Twedwr the Druid or Esther his Jewish wife to this group of nosing priests, I was rankled by my own cowardice, but I agreed it was probably best not to complicate things any further.

"We had to leave the Council before it was over, but we knew how the wind was blowing. Several of the other more level-headed bishops had taken their leave, and Secundianus left for home just after we did, leaving our friend Palladius to hear the Council declare both of them heretics and anathema. Since Bishop Felix was on his way to Rome with me, and some of the more sensible bishops were gone, Palladius was the only one who voted nay. Later we learned that Valerian gave Palladius a chance to renounce what he believed, but he told them he could no more do that than they could renounce what they believed. Oh, it was a sad, miserable business, start to end.

"So, we gathered ourselves up and started our trip down to Rome. It was a much smaller group travelling with us now, and not so happy as the group we'd travelled with down from Erith. It felt like we were prisoners, and the thought of it was vinegar in my blood. I felt I was to blame for us having to leave and getting Felix and Mellán in trouble with the Church. I felt like Brigid ought to be angry and disappointed with me. And the more they told me none of that was true, the harder it gnawed at me. Oh aye, I was brooding, angry that I couldn't go as I wanted. I was angry at Cyneric for claiming I was a heretic, and at myself for not being able to defend myself. In truth, it was a dark, gloomy time.

"We clomped along past Venetia where the people went from place to place in flat little boats, the port city of Classe, and through Ariminum, Interamna, on our way down to Rome. In other people's eyes, or if things had been different, it might have been a pleasant journey, but my eyes were poisoned and nothing I saw was beautiful.

"The commander of the Roman guards assigned to us was a grizzled veteran of the legions named Silvas. He made some effort to be sure we all knew he was tough and heartless, and how bothered he was at having to hold the soft hands of a bunch of church people as we travelled down to Rome. Silvas and his men were there to make sure we arrived in Rome to face the priests looking for heretics and all. Felix and Mellán tried to talk to him, but he clearly wanted naught to do with any of us.

"Well, except for Brigid, who has her own magic that very few are able to resist. Silvas went out of his way to make sure she and Áine were as comfortable as possible. She told us he wasn't a bad man, he was just a soldier.

"Not far from Rome, we came to a town called Hortanum and stopped at an inn whose sign was a painting of two swords crossed. Silvas knew the language they spoke there, so he arranged rooms for us.

"Now my sweet Brigid was trying to break me out of the melancholy I'd been bogged in, and after we ate our supper, she brought out Twedwr's harp and laid it on the table before me. Sure as the setting of the sun, the people in the common room started looking hopefully at Mellán and me, and Mellán said, 'This may be our last chance to sing for a while, brother.' So, we sang, and Brigid and Áine joined us, and even though we were on our way to judgement, the music was a very tonic for my soul.

"We sang all our songs, some of them twice, and it didn't seem to matter that most of the people in the common room couldn't understand much of what we were saying, as it was the music and the voices in harmony that was the magic of it. After a time, the owner of the inn came to give us what looked like some manner of sack. Mellán tried to tell him that we didn't want it, as we didn't need the coins he'd gathered nearly so much as the people who'd parted with them. But it was too late to refuse without it seeming rude, so he thanked him kindly as he could. Brigid gave the man a little kiss, and he turned bright red as a ripe plum.

"It was a nice moment, and it set me thinking about happier times, when it was just Mellán and me, and then Twedwr came along, and then we were joined by Brigid and Shea, and then Esther, travelling town to town, playing Twedwr's harp and singing our songs. It was a right pleasant evening, and to be honest I wasn't paying much attention when we were going to our rooms. Mayhaps things would have turned out different if I'd been more mindful.

"The inn was an old Roman villa, shaped like a big square with a little garden in the middle, the common room and kitchens on one side and rooms all around. As we were walking to our rooms, I was fumbling with my pack, trying to stuff the sack of coins down into it, two men stepped out of the shadows, urgently demanding something in their harsh language. Brigid picked Áine up, and Felix and Mellán looked at me, thinking I could understand what they were saying, but I couldn't tell up from down, they were talking so fast. But clearly, they'd seen the innkeeper give us that money, and now they meant to relieve us of it.

"Both of the men had knives, dreadful long sharp knives, and I'm not ashamed to tell you I was just as terrified as anybody. My first thought was to give them the money in my pack, but before I could tell them that, one of the men grabbed up Bishop Felix by his wrist and held it behind him so that he was standing behind him and put his knife across his throat. Felix was trying not to show it, but I could see it was hurting him. If I'd had more time to think I might've done something different, but in the blur of that moment, with Felix being hurt and my wife and daughter in danger, I dropped my pack, pulling out the sword in the same motion. The thug pulled Felix tighter, causing him even more pain, and I could see now the knife drawing a little blood as it bit into his neck.

"I stepped forward and rammed that sword through the other man's belly, all the way through him so my fist knocked him down. The sword slid out when he fell, and then I held out the bloody blade at the man holding Felix. He glanced at his friend screaming in the moonlight, looked at me hard, and then pushed Felix at the rest of us and ran into the night like a scared rabbit.

"It was another moment when I had too many noisy thoughts trying to edge each other out to get my attention, like seagulls squawking for scraps. I was relieved we'd survived the attack, and glad that Felix and none of us were hurt or dead. I was fretting that the screaming of the man I'd stabbed would wake up the people in their rooms, and I thought I ought to chase after the other thug. As I stood there completely flustered and muddled, the man soon stopped screaming, and I knew he was dead.

Then it hit me square that I had killed a man. That was the thought that was the most grievously worrisome, and when Brigid and Mellán rushed over to tend to Felix, I turned aside and my belly heaved out bile and ale and ... well I suppose everything it could find to heave out. Then, sure as winter storms, after I vomited everything I could, I felt the dizziness take me over, and I fell down, right in my own sick.

"Now they were all fussing over me, and I hated being so weak and such a bother. But poor Brigid was trying to clean me up, and as Mellán and Felix helped me to my feet and we were walking to our room, Mellán asked what happened to me, and was I hurt. I told him I'd killed that man, and then we had to stop so I could take a breath, trying to keep my head from spinning."

"Then what happened?" asked Caillen.

"Well, the innkeeper came around and was regretful that we'd been attacked, and he told us he had to call the local authorities, who came the next morning and asked us all a great many questions about who we were and where we were going and how did it happen that I killed one of their local ruffians. Silvas told us what they were asking and gave them our answers. The locals seemed to know about the fella I'd killed, and it was no great surprise to them that he died at the point of a sword; they were just perplexed that it happened at the hand of somebody such as myself, in the company of a bishop and a priest.

"Now the gloom that had been chewing on me since I'd tried to tell the Council that I wasn't an Arian, since I'd tried to stand up to the bully Cyneric, now that dark, dark melancholy was just about to swallow me whole. I had killed a man. There was nothing I wanted to eat or drink, there was nothing I wanted to see or say or hear. It was more than it was worth to get myself out of the bed; I just wanted to bury myself in the blankets and let the world keep finding its way without me. I had killed a man, and that was all I could think about. It near took me over.

"Finally, Brigid and my brother Mellán came into our room with a bucket of water she'd borrowed from the stable, and threatened to throw it on me if I didn't get up. I knew she would have, so I got up and got dressed and pretended to be myself, but I knew it was a lie: I had killed a man, and I would never be myself again."

"How did you ever get back to being who you are?" asked Oswell. "I mean, how can somebody ever move past something like that?"

"Nay, lad," answered Pell with great sadness. "You can't ever move past something like that, and you can never be who you were before it."

"But he had a knife at the bishop's throat!" protested Caillen.

"And you had to make a decision in that instant, or Bishop Felix could have been killed!" added Oswell. "Or Brigid or Áine!"

"Aye," said Pell, sadly. "I know that. I knew it then. They could have killed all of us. The ruffians could have taken Brigid and raped her. They could have hurt Áine, killed us all. A great many things could have happened, but the one thing that did happen was that I killed a man. Whatever else might have happened, that's the thing that did. But I'll tell you what could not happen, and that was for that awful moment to loosen its grip on my mind. All those things that might have happened were just shadows and mist against what did. I knew I did what I had to do, but … ah, well—there's a great distance between knowing something in your head and feeling it in your heart. It took a long, long time for me to know that in my heart.

"I never even knew the man's name, the man I killed. I still see him sometimes, lying there with his blood gushing out; sometimes I wake up from my sleep hearing him scream. I reckon there are some things as never let you go.

"I wallowed in that darkness for more than a day, with my wife and friends helplessly worrying about me. Finally, it was the soldier Silvas who helped me. He sat down on a little bench as I lay on the bed. I was expecting him to tell me we had to be on our way to Rome, but I was surprised how kind he was as he told me about the first time he'd killed a man.

"It was in his first battle as a new recruit, he said, when the Western Roman army was fighting the tribes of the Alemanni away up north in Durocortōrum. They were trying to attack the enemy with whelming force, but the day was dreary and foggy, and some of the enemy sneaked around behind them and killed many and many Romans before the legions in the front knew what was happening in the back. Then the army turned around and came pounding back to defend its rear.

"Silvas was among the Romans in the rear, and they were taking the worst of it. They formed a turtle shell of their shields, he said, and the Alemanni soldiers came wave after wave trying to break the shell, but they couldn't. Then the lines were pushing at each other shield to shield, he told me, trying to stab at the other fella's legs and feet if they could. The mud was soaked with blood, Alemanni and Roman, some of it his own, as he was wounded just below his left knee, but he didn't know that until it was all over.

"Then he had an opening, he said, when the fella just before him lowered his shield for just a moment, and Silvas reached out with his

gladius and stabbed him through the eye. He said, 'I thought I'd feel
… oh, I don't know, victorious or heroic or some such, but instead, I
puked my guts up, all over the poor sod I'd just kilt and all over my
own feet.' So, I asked him what happened next, and he said, 'Well,
hell—there were men stabbing and killing, and men being stabbed
and kilt all around me, most all of us bleeding and sweating and
cussing front and back, right and left. I didn't have time to ponder
about it, I was just trying to stay upright.'

"He said he just kept fighting, and he must've killed four or five
other men that day. He said the truth was that he didn't know how
many others he killed nor even how many other battles he was in
after that. He said he just went where the officers told him to go, and
killed who they told him to kill. 'And that's always a part of me,' he
said, 'but it isn't all of me. You just can't let it be all of you, lad. You
can't let it take you to your grave. You did what you had to do, so
now you need to put it away in some little room in your mind and
close the door on it.'"

"Did you?" asked Oswell. "Did you close the door on it?"

"Well, aye, but it took a great long time, and that damn door
keeps getting loose, even still. But it was a great help to know somebody else who'd killed a man and knew the consternation of it.
And—and I've always thought this was strange and wonderful—
Silvas and I became friends. He was still gruff and grizzly, and I was
still right innocent and full of the way things ought to be, but … that
afternoon as he told me about the first time he'd ever killed a man,
I saw him as a man, and not just a soldier. And I suppose he began
to see me as a person as well, respecting how I defended my wife,
daughter and friends. He growled, 'If I'd been with you, we would've
skewered both the bastards!'

"He was mystified by how we could look at the world through
our faith, and he said he could tell we truly believed what we said.
The way he talked about Church people in Rome with all their
schemes and plots to gain advantage over each other reminded me
of the wiggleful worm from 'The Butterfly's Blessing,' 'crawling and
climbing and gnawing all day.'

"We talked all that afternoon until the sun set, and he told me to get up, as now it was time for supper. So, I did, and as he helped me stand, he took my forearm in his right hand so I could take his in mine. He leaned in close and said intensely, 'You can't go back and change aught now. You had to kill the bastard, and you did. Put it away now. Your wife and little girl and your friends are waiting on you.' Tears filled up my eyes and I wiped them away. Then the old soldier said, 'You're a good man, Pelagius of Brittania.'

"Then I said, 'You sound right surprised by that, Silvas.'

"'Aye,' he replied, 'I suppose I am. Mayhaps I ought to say you're a good man, for a priest.'

"I told him I wasn't a priest, and that seemed to be some relief to him, like scratching an itch he hadn't been able to reach. Then he said, 'Well then, what are you?'

"Well, I had to do some little thinking about that. I washed my face in the wee bowl we had in our room before saying, 'I don't think I have a good answer as to who I am just now, Silvas. I was a carpenter's apprentice, and then I was a travelling minstrel of sorts. After we got where we were going, I became a builder and a man to put right what had been broken. Then I became a father, and then a Christian and a husband, and then somehow I became an advisor to Bishop Felix going to Aquileia for the Council. Now it seems we're going to Rome to find out if I've become a heretic or a sorcerer as well.'

"He asked me what a heretic was, and I told him, so he had to chew on that a bit. Before he was done considering, I said, 'I think you're a good man as well.'

"Silvus looked at me playfully and asked, 'A soldier who's a good man?'

"Now I know he was trying to make light of what we were saying, but I answered, 'Nay. I think you're a good man who's a soldier, which is more likely than being a soldier who's a good man. You're a good man first, and then a soldier.'

"Now he got a bit teary and was a bit awkward about it. He growled, 'Shut your yap now, before I run you through myself.'

Chapter XXXIII

You Won't Even See Them

Pell continue, "We stayed there for two more nights, and the second night we sang and played in the inn's common room after getting Silvas to tell the tavern-man that we didn't want any more money, but my heart wasn't in it and it was more a chore than a joy. The innkeeper agreed not to give us any more money, after we told him that we'd be glad to let him give us our rooms and meals and drinks for free.

"So, you'll know—the money in that sack—the money that man died for—wasn't any great treasure. It really wasn't all that much, just scores of small coins made of copper they called *assis*. Even though that sack was full, it wasn't of much value—we would gladly have given those thugs all of it, but … well, that's not what happened. We used those coins when we … ah, but now I'm jumping ahead of the story.

"We stayed there until clearly it was time for us to be on our way, and then we rode on and came to Rome in all her gilded, shameless, vulgar glory."

"You didn't like Rome?" asked Caillen.

"Nay, lad, I confess I did not. Have you ever been there, either of you?"

Both of the students said they hadn't, and Pell nodded. "Well, I don't want to sway your thinking, in case you ever have to go. And mayhaps my feelings about it were darkened by being broody and all. But still, well … nay, I'm not going to say that.

Oswell thought for a moment and said, "Tell us what you thought about Rome."

Pell laughed and answered, "Well, I suppose the two of you deserve my honesty, after you've sat and listened to me honking on and on like a goose in the moonlight. So I'll tell you what I thought about Rome this way: the problem with my cousin Aodhan's wife Saoirse wasn't that she was pretty—her problem was that she knew it. By and by, being pretty became such a part of her that it was all she was, and after some time, she knew that her beauty would fail and leave her with naught. Being pretty on the outside is a tide that comes in but once, and when it's gone back out, it'll never come back in. Now Brigid's a beauty inside and out …

"Ah well, God love us, I'm meant to be telling you about Rome. I thought Rome was like a woman whose beauty had been failing for some time, but she refused to let it go. The whole time I was there, she seemed to be looking for more perfume, more ribbons for her hair, more and more attention to her appearance, more and more neglect of her people.

"But in truth it wasn't the city that was troublesome to me, it was the Church. Nay, that's not quite right, either—it was the clergy of the Church, strutting around in their fancy costly plumage like roosters, each of them trying to outshine all the others by having the most flatterers or the tallest hat. And all the while they just walked right past the poor of the city—flocks and schools of them, men and women and children—as if they didn't even see them. They were too busy trying to impress each other with who they'd had supper with or what paper they'd read about high and lofty points of theology that nobody with any sense would give a frog's croak about.

"When we came to Rome, Silvas and his men delivered us to a strutting little fella who looked us all toe to head, taking note of the wear and dirt on our clothing. He declared himself to be Father Flavinus Sergius Lucianus, archdeacon to Damasus, bishop of Rome, and then he waited for us to tell him what an honor it was to meet him. Judging by how the man introduced himself, it was clear he thought he was a very important personage; his vestments and trimmings and trappings would make the grandest of roosters hang his head in shame.

"I stepped forward and presented Felix Hortensius Terentius, Bishop of Londinium, and Father Mellán of Baile Átha Cliath in Éire, the bishop's secretary and advisor. Then I presented Brigid of Uiroconion in Brittania and our daughter Áine, before introducing myself, Pelagius of Brittania, advisor to Bishop Felix. I suppose I was hoping to impress little Flavinus, but I needn't have bothered. It was clear from the first moment I saw him that the only people he was ever to be impressed by was himself and whoever might be useful to him.

"Left to himself, he'd have ignored us as being beneath his notice, but his duty was to show us to our rooms at the monastery. If it had been just me, or only Brigid and Áine and me, I expect we'd have stayed in something simpler, but as we were with a bishop and a priest, we were given three rooms: a nice large room for Felix and Mellán, another for my little family, not as nice or large, and a third room set between for the five of us to sit together."

"How long were you there?" asked Oswell.

"Well, there's a question simple in the asking and complicated in the answering. Altogether, I was there near eighteen years. Bishop Felix was quickly found to be blameless and orthodox, and after about a week he blessed us and sained us against the powers of the world and the evil one, and then Silvas and his men escorted him back to Londinium. They let Brigid go to take Áine back to Erith some years later, when Alaric and his hordes were approaching Rome, and I finally convinced Mellán he should follow. When I left Rome, I had to go to Carthage, and then to Jerusalem.

"But all of that is way ahead in the story. After we came to Rome, we waited all the next day to be summoned to meet with the priests whose job it was to look for heretics and all, but we got no word about it. So, we waited again the next day, and the next, and for many a day it seemed waiting was all we could do. The wait stretched out into weeks, then months, and finally years.

"We waited for somebody to come back from the Council they were having in Constantinople, which took an exceeding long time. The Holy Father, Damasus the exalted Bishop of Rome, was constantly having to deal with all manner of plotting and scheming against him.

One of the women who lived around there told Brigid there had been a grand squabble when Damasus became the Holy Father, as they were choosing somebody to follow Liberius. Apparently, there had been another fella named Ursinus, who was Liberius' man, and there were some who wanted Ursinius and others wanted Damasus to be the next pope. There was various trickery and treachery and hundreds were killed, one way and another. I'll tell you it was hard for me to credit that the followers of Jésu could act like that, but Brigid said the woman swore it was true.

"Then they had a grand gathering there in Rome to limit what writings ought to be in the canon of Scripture—and that took weeks and months, head to toe. Somewhere in all of that, I reckon they all just forgot about us, and after some time, we stopped trying to remind them. There wasn't any good reason for us to stay, but we couldn't leave without somebody signing some scrap of paper, and before long nobody knew who ought to sign it, or what it was that somebody ought to sign.

"So, Bishop Felix went back to Londinium just after Samhain, shortly after we came to Rome. Then before the spring equinox, here came Silvas knocking on our door to tell us that he'd delivered Felix safely home. He wanted to see whether there aught he could be doing for us. Brigid asked him about his duty to the army, and he said the army had been his life and his family for many a year, but now he was thinking he was getting too old to march and fight. He told us he'd resigned from the army, and if we'd have him, he wanted to be helping us for a while, that he was looking for something more to his life before it ended.

"Mellán said of course we'd be most grateful for him to join our company, and suggested he could come and stay with us, now that Felix was gone and all. So that same afternoon he brought his scant few possessions and stayed with us, our guide and guard and trusted friend.

"It was Silvas who showed us around what he called the Eternal City. I have to admit I was right impressed with the Colosseum, where they had grand spectacles, where gladiators did their fighting, where Christians had been shamed and killed centuries before. He took us to see the Hippodrome and the Circus Maximus, and we could scarcely credit so many people coming to see a race or a hunt. We saw the mausoleum the Emperor Hadrian had built for his own burying place and the bridge he built over the Tiberis River to get to it. There's many and many emperors and their families and all buried there now. Silvas took us to the Thermae Agrippae, the bathhouse built by the Emperor Agrippa before bless'éd Jésu was born. But what impressed me most was the Pantheum.

"The history of the place was interesting, built by Agrippa centuries gone, and built up again by Hadrian after it was burnt down. And the planning of it, everything built just right, so the whole thing doesn't just fall down, that was amazing to me as well. But there was a feeling there, a sense of spiritual fullness—whether there were people there or not, that huge dome above and all the ground beneath was always crowded."

"Crowded? How do you mean?" asked Oswell.

"Aye, it's always been hard for me to understand, and even harder to explain. I went there many and many a time when we were in Rome, and many a time I was there from morning until the sun had set. It was crowded even when I was the only person there: crowded with God.

"It's an old temple—built for some god or goddess, but then there were other gods and goddesses invited there, I suppose, or their statues were there. That's why it was called the Pantheum—*pan theum*: all the gods. It's a place not just for the narrow concepts of God that all the religions seem determined to fit God into—it's a place to bathe in the full mystery and glory of our unknowable God, the Maker of heaven and earth, of all things visible and invisible. It just felt full of the one true God.

"Well, we waited a little and we waited a lot, and the seasons rolled along. We could go anywhere in the city with Silvas as our guard, but we were given to understand that if we tried to leave the city, we'd be hunted down and brought back at the point of a sword. I thought there must have been some manner of muddle in the Church or in the Empire, but Silvas told us it was just the way the Empire usually worked, and he said the Church was just another arm of the

Empire, so it was the same there. I didn't want to believe that, but I couldn't convince even myself that it wasn't true.

"One morning as we were walking near the Roman Forum, we saw scores of poor and homeless people begging, and scores of men and women from the wealthy families walking by, without seeming to have seen the beggars at all. It was right disturbing to us, but the worst of it was that Silvas didn't seem to be vexed by it at all. 'They've always been there,' he said. 'You get used to it—after some time you won't even see them.'

"Well, I don't mind telling you that chewed on us right hard the rest of that day, and that same afternoon Brigid and I went down to the monastery kitchen to ask if we could use one of their ovens. The kitchen-master—Cornelius was his name—was right protective of his patch, but he had no defense against Brigid. He asked her what she wanted to do, and she told him she wanted to bake some bread. I think when he agreed to it, he assumed she'd be cooking two or three loaves, mayhaps once or twice.

"He asked us what manner of bread we were thinking of baking, and I answered, 'Barley bread.' But Brigid shook her head and said, 'Nay, love, that's the poor bread. We'll be baking the bread for God's children from wheat flour.' I told her we could likely make more bread from barley, and that I'd grown up eating barley bread, but she was fixed on it, and as I've said before, when Brigid was fixed on something, usually the best thing for me was to agree with her, so that's what I did.

"Then Cornelius gave her a lump of sour dough to start her own batch. She tried to tell me about the yeasties and why it was a very special gift, but it didn't look like anything special to me. She very carefully saved some of it back, so we'd have some for the next day, and every day after that we saved some back. I imagine some of those same yeasties were still hard to work in every loaf ever we baked, doing their mysterious work.

"The next morning, Brigid sent Mellán and Silvas to find a market to buy some wheat flour using that sack of copper assis we'd got at the inn in Hortanum, the same coins that man had been trying to take from us with his knife at Bishop Felix's throat. She told them to spend it all, thinking it wasn't likely enough to buy much, but it would be grand to put that blood-stained money to good use. We were surprised when Mellán and Silvas came back with a cart full, three large sacks of wheat flour. Silvas just grinned at us and said he got us a good price.

"When I asked what we would ever be able to do with so much flour, Brigid said, 'Well, we can make a great many loaves—there's a great many as need it.' And she straightway began to teach Mellán, Silvas, Áine and me about the baking of bread, about the magic of the yeasties, about working and kneading the dough, the patience of letting things rise and rest, and shaping and proofing and baking. It quickly twisted around into some style of contest between the three men, but it was good-hearted enough, and we were all pleasantly surprised to find that Mellán had what Brigid called 'a natural talent for baking.' Silvas and I were not surprised to find that we did not.

"So, we laughed some and fussed some and burnt our fingers more than once, until Brigid declared that our real talent was making a mess of a kitchen."

Chapter XXXIV

A Son of the King of Heaven

Pell continued his story. "Well, that first morning, we baked four loaves to give to those as were hungry. Áine helped Brigid, and their loaves were perfect, Mellán's were good but a little burnt on one side. Mine had at least risen up some; poor Silvas' were flat as a platter. We walked back to where we'd seen so many poor people the day before, and I was thinking we would call out that we had bread to give, but Silvas warned that our position would likely be overrun before we could retreat if I did. So, he and Brigid approached a ragged woman and quietly gave her Brigid's loaf and then found another woman and gave her Mellán's loaf. By this time, some of the people around were starting to see what they were doing, and they started to press in close. They were even glad to get Silvas' loaf and mine, pitiful as they were. Then Silvas bellowed out in his soldier's commanding voice that we had no more, but we would come back the next day, and we retreated as quickly as we could.

"The next morning Brigid, Áine, Mellán and I went back to the monastery kitchen, wondering where Silvas was. We made up the fire under the ovens and started making some of the dough and all, and by and by here came Silvas, who'd brought a handcart and three friends, gray-haired men retired from the army, same as himself. We soon found out his friends weren't interested in learning to bake; Silvas said they were to keep the crowds from pressing in too close. He said, 'It's military training, is all—just making yourself ready for what might happen.'

"Mellán, Silvas and I each cooked three loaves—I was especially proud of my third one, and even Silvas' were better than the day before. Brigid and Áine made four loaves with ripe olives in them, three for the poor and a smaller one for us to share. When I started to object, thinking it was for the poor that we were baking the bread, Mellán said, 'But you know how blesséd Jésu said, 'The laborer deserves to be paid,' and even I couldn't be arguing with Jésu, especially about something that smelled so good it brought the water to my mouth.

"We shared that loaf among ourselves and the three soldiers, and then we put the other twelve loaves we'd baked into the little hand-cart Silvas had brought. When we came to the place where we'd given out bread the morning before, there were hundreds of people waiting for us. The three soldiers and Silvas took up their posts in a square around us, making sure to show their swords, shields and spears and all, so the crowd knew to keep some distance.

"The twelve loaves were gone as quick as a blink, and we were right glad twelve families had a meal, but we couldn't help but see the disappointment in the faces of dozens more, sad for the families who'd be needing to look elsewhere for their daily bread. One of the soldiers was surprised, saying he'd never known there were that many hungry people in the Empire's capital, in the very shadow of the center of the Church of Rome. Another one, Scipio, said he thought his wife might want to help, and then his friend Tatius wondered if his sister could join us.

"Well, don't you know the next morning when we came to the monastery kitchen, there were six retired soldiers, Scipio's wife and her sister, Tatius' sister and two aunts and two other women who were somebody's cousins or neighbors, all waiting to help us bake bread for the poor. Two of the soldiers brought handcarts as well, so we had three.

"Now we had more help than we needed, and I was for sending some of them home, but Brigid said, 'Nay, my love—let them stay, let them help. They've all seen the wretched poor, and now they have a chance to help.' I agreed, of course—but then Silvas came up to say, 'It's a grand thing to have so much help and all, but we'll need more flour to make up enough dough for each of them to make even one loaf.'

"Now I was wondering where this path might be taking us—thinking if we made a hundred loaves that day and two hundred the next, still the day after that there would be hundreds and hundreds more with their hands out, begging us for bread. Brigid saw me thinking and knew what I was fretting about, and she took my arm in hers and whispered, 'All we can do is all we can do.' And of course, that's just one of those things you can't argue with: 'All we can do is all we can do.'

"Mellán, Brigid and I stepped aside to talk about it, and decided we could use some of the money we'd gotten from singing our way down to Erith from Éire. It seems odd to say it, but we hadn't spent much of that money, and we didn't think Twedwr or Esther would mind, as it was part theirs. Silvas and Scipio went with Mellán to fetch some money from our rooms and then to the market with the three carts, and when they came back, they had sacks and sacks of flour, with some salt and olives and dates and onions and all.

"Now we all turned to Brigid, who told us all how grateful she was that we were there and then asked Mellán to say us a blessing. He said, 'Lord bless us all today. Bless those who are hungry, those who are afraid, those who grieve, those who have no homes. Bless those who are more fortunate, those who try to help, those who lend a hand. Keep us all safe, Lord, and give us your peace. Amen.'

"Brigid had learned from Esther about organizing women in the monastery kitchen in Erith, and she quickly set us all to working at mixing and setting, keeping the fires right and putting loaves in the ovens and taking them out. We were eleven bakers, Mellán, Silvas and me and eight women, and Silvas and I were still the worst. We all made three loaves except for Brigid and Áine who made four, each of theirs with dates chopped up and mixed in the dough. After we wrapped the loaves and stacked them in the carts, we all shared out one of their date loaves, just a bite for each of us. It was a grand communion.

"When we went back to the Forum, there were many starving families there, more than we'd seen before. The soldiers took their positions and we cut each loaf in half, so we handed out sixty-six loaves, and still it wasn't anywhere near enough.

"Now Mellán and Brigid saw me sulking about it, and they came over to cheer me. Mellán said, 'Mind now, blesséd Jésu said, 'You'll always have the poor with you,' which helped me not at all, and Brigid said, 'I wish we could help them all, love. But I'm grateful to be able to help the ones we can,' and that helped me right well.

"We put the cloths we used to wrap the loaves back in the carts and started rolling them back to the monastery, when a lady from a wealthy family called out to Silvas. We were thinking he must know her, so we waited around, and presently he came with the woman, meaning to introduce us.

"He said, 'Lady Aurelia, may I present to you the Lady Brigid of Uiroconion in Brittania and her daughter Áine, who's here with Father Mellán of Baile Átha Cliath in Éire and Pelagius of Brittania, advisors to Bishop Felix Felix Hortensius Terentius of Londinium. Friends, it pleases me right well to introduce Lady Aurelia Vipsanius of the Palatine Hill, a very old family of Rome. She called me aside to say that she wants to help, thinking I was in command, but I told her the one she needs to talk to is the Lady Brigid here.'

"Now to my surprise, Brigid curtsied. We'd seen some fine ladies do that, but I didn't know she knew how. I don't think it was something she'd ever done before, but she was always naturally graceful. She said, 'Lady Aurelia, it's a grand honor to meet you. Would you like to join us in the morning to bake the bread?'

"Well, the Lady Aurelia seemed genuinely surprised at the idea of herself working, and I realized she's likely never had to lift a finger in her whole long life. She said, 'Good heavens, no!' But Silvas said she wanted to help, so I said, 'What can we do for you, Lady?'

"Then she took a ring from her finger and handed it to Brigid, closing her hand tight around Brigid's hand as she gave it to her. She said, 'Take this to Cadmus the baker on the Via Sacra at the foot of the Palatine Hill. Tell him I sent you and show him this signet, then tell him I said he is to give you whatever you need at his cost, and that I will pay him generously for it. Tell him that you are about an important work. I'll be sending a messenger to him straightaway, and he'll be expecting you. Whatever you need, do you understand?'

"We thanked her for her grand generosity, and she said, "I've lived right here in Rome every day of my life, and every day I've seen poor families without a scrap of bread to eat. I was taught to not see them, do you understand? But you lot, you came in from wherever Brittania and Éire might be, and you saw them. And more than that, you taught me I should be seeing them as well, so now I can't unsee them. I know I'd just be in the way in your kitchen, but this I can do. My late husband was the Senator Caius Crispianus Vipsanius Aemilius, I expect you've heard of him. He left me with a son with who'd argue the beard off a buck goat, and more money than we could spend in two lifetimes. I'll be glad to think some of that money is going where it is needful.'

"Then she added, 'Whatever you need, Cadmus will have it or get it, and he'll know he's to sell it to you for a good price. I'll settle up with him, you won't need to fret about that. I'll send my son Caelestius to fetch the ring back on the morrow. Just keep making the bread and feeding the people here.'

"So that's what we did. Soon we had all the flour we needed, and Cadmus even brought it to the monastery kitchen for us. After we'd taken over his kitchen for week after week, when Cornelius the monastery's kitchen master told us we would be needing to find another place to bake the bread, Cadmus helped us find a suitable place nearby, and the Lady Aurelia paid for the workers who came in and built us three large brick ovens, each with a place for a fire below.

"Soon we had so many bakers and soldiers wanting to help that Silvas drew up a *rota* of who was to be working and when. Each morning there were twelve bakers, each one with a helper, and each charged with cooking three loaves, twice the size of those as we started with. The fires were blazing and the ovens heated before the sun rose, and when the workers came, we started with a prayer, usually brought by Mellán. Then it was mixing, kneading, waiting, rising, shaping and proofing, and then the first batch went in the ovens, then the second, then the third. When all the loaves were out and wrapped, we shared one loaf among us all. There were no words said, no ritual was needed, but we all knew it was a holy moment."

Pell stopped and looked at his two friends. "Now I'm thinking you're wondering what any of this is to do with being a heretic and all of that. Well, one morning I noticed another fella there in the kitchen. He wasn't a baker, and he wasn't a soldier, he was just there. He wasn't in the way, but he wasn't helping, and when Brigid walked by, I asked who he was. She said, 'That's Caelestius—the Lady Aurelia's son. He's been here for the last few days.'

"'What's he doing here?' I asked, and she said 'I don't know. I don't think I've ever seen him do aught at all.' But then I needed to get somebody something, and the next time I looked, Caelestius was gone.

"Scipio and another fella took up the organizing of who would be getting the bread each day, making little marks on a scrap of parchment and hearing the pleas and grumbling of those as wouldn't be getting any that day. The loaves were considerably bigger now, and we cut each one in half, each larger than the loaves we made at first, but still it was never enough.

"I was grateful to let go of my place among the bakers, in part to make room for our eager helpers, but more to save myself the shame of steadily cooking the sorriest loaves. So, most days it was Silvas and I who started and tended the fires, and then we just wandered around making sure everybody had what they needed. Sometimes if Mellán wasn't there, Brigid would ask me to say the prayer. I was glad to do it, but I never thought it was as smooth or natural as it was when Mellán prayed for us.

"One morning after I'd offered up the prayer, the old soldier who'd been helping Scipio keep track of who was to get bread each day, came up to me all sheepish and said, 'Do you really believe all that, what you just said?' Then as I was trying to remember what I'd said, he said, 'Do you really believe that the god Jésu loves us, all of us?'

"And just then, like a lamp being lit in a dark room, I understood there was some hurt deeply buried in him, something he was fretting about, something he was afraid would keep him from the love of God. Of course I was curious to know what that was, but then I thought it didn't really matter. This man is God's child, and

God loves him, not because he's lived a moral and virtuous life, but because God is God.

"So I said, 'Aye, friend. I believe God loves all of His children, every one of us.' And he hung his head down so I could scarcely hear him and whispered, 'But Father, you don't know what I've done.'

"Well, I wanted to tell him I wasn't a priest, but it wasn't the most important thing right then. Instead, I said, 'Nay, I don't. I reckon you've got some things as weigh you down hard, all those years in the army, terrible things you've seen and done. I don't know aught about that, but I don't need to. What you need to know is that you are a son of the King of Heaven, and that He loves you, just as He loves all his children. Nothing you've ever done can change that.'

"Now he looked at me like I was trying to sell him a crippled mule, and when I added, 'That's what I believe, and what I hope,' he muttered, 'But that's not what the bishop said.'

"So of course I asked him, 'What did the bishop say?' and he answered, 'He said you have to be drownded in the waters of Babatismus, or some such, or his god won't love you and then when you die, you'll burn forever in the fires of Hades. Father, I don't want to live burning in fire forever, but I don't want to be drownded. I don't even know where Babatismus is!'

"It was one of those rare moments when I found myself talking before I knew what I was going to say. 'Nay, friend,' I said. 'If Jésu's father is our father, as Jésu taught when He told His disciples to pray 'Our Father in heaven,' and if Jésu's father is the one God who made all the heavens and the earth we're living on, do you really think aught we do will decide whether He's willing to love us or not?'

"'It's a grand thing to be baptized,' I said, 'there's no drowning to it. I was baptized not so long ago. It just means you 've accepted the teachings of Jésu about God and you've committed yourself to follow Him best you can. It's not meant to say you'll never be doing aught wrong again—as you surely will—but that when you do, you'll have a way to be forgiven, and a way to forgive yourself.'

"Then, remembering that Bishop Felix said he wouldn't baptize Brigid or me just so we could be married, I said, 'But you can't go getting baptized just to save yourself from the fires of Hades. It's not something you do to protect yourself from evil, like an amulet or a charm; it's something to make real that you mean to live your life following the teachings of Jésu, the Son of God.'

"I could tell he wasn't completely sure about all that, and right at the moment one of the bakers was loudly complaining her oven wasn't hot enough, so I said, 'Tell me your name, friend.'

'Marcello,' he told me, and I said, 'Well, Marcello, mayhaps it would be well to have some time to think about all this. Can you come back on the morrow?' He said he would, and I told him we would talk more. Then I was off to stoke up the woman's oven before she caught herself afire.

"After all the loaves were brought out from the ovens, as we were passing out a bite of one of the loaves Brigid made—this was one with honey and chopped figs, my favorite—I noticed Marcello looking over at me, whispering to Caelestius. I decided I'd go over and introduce myself to our benefactor's son, but after we'd eaten the common loaf, he was gone again.

"The next day, after the first batch of loaves went in, here came Marcello, and this time he brought two others with him, another of the retired soldiers, and Caelestius. Marcello made no introductions, but said, 'Tell them what you told me, Father.'

"Well, this time I'd had time to consider what I wanted to say, and I said it. 'First, I'm not a priest. You need to know that I'm fully aware I may not know what I'm talking about. But to be honest, the priest and the bishop and the Holy Father himself may not know what they're talking about, either. It's never about what we know, but what we believe.'

"It was the first of many and many a conversation we had in the kitchen as we waited for the dough to rise, or for the bread to bake. At first it was retired soldiers and Caelestius and me, but soon others came, a few more soldiers, but mostly people brought by Caelestius, others like himself who were displeased or angry."

"What were they angry about?" asked Caillen.

"Well," replied Pell, "mostly about the Church."

Oswell was indignant. "The Church?"

"Aye," answered Pell sadly. "Not the faith, understand, but the Church. They were much concerned with what they called the excess of the Church, the grand vestments and gaudy huge cathedrals and such. They said that the work of the Church ought to be feeding and clothing the poor and sharing the Gospel to all the people. I agreed and shared some of my ideas about orthodoxy and such, which seemed to fill their sails. Aye, they were a lively bunch, and no mistake—all full of vinegar and ready to change the world around them. I didn't know Caelestius was writing down what was said, what I was saying, until it was already copied and shared. If I'd known he was putting my words to parchment, I would have stopped him."

"Because writing it down would be proof that you were critical of the Church?" asked Oswell.

"Because writing it down takes the life out of it, and traps the one who spoke an idea into defending what was said," answered Pell.

Chapter XXXV

Woe Is Me, For I am Lost!

"So," said Oswell, "these people gathered around to hear you in the kitchen while the bread was baking—you told them what you believed."

"Aye," said Pell, "that is the way of it."

Then Caillen said, "I'd be happy to hear that."

"So, this was like your statement of faith, your creed," said Oswell.

"Aye, I suppose that's true," replied Pell. "I told them what I believed then, and I believe it still."

Oswell started, "What did you say about …"

"Oswell—hush!" interjected Caillen. "Let him tell us what he told them. I need to hear this."

"Nay, Caillen, you're looking at this the exact wrong way around. You don't need to be hearing what I say about this, or aught else, not from me or anybody else. You need to listen to what you believe to be true in your own heart and mind. You don't need more teaching, you just need to trust what you say you believe. Too many of the followers of Jésu don't truly believe what they say or haven't thought about it.

"Surely by now I've told you everything you need to know about me, the rest of it's just bishops and councils, boring as watching moss growing on a rock. We can leave that to the scholars, and they're welcome to it. Nay, the exciting part is what happens next, about the two of you, and what you'll be making of Jésu's blesséd Church.

"When the teaching of the Church, all that doctrine and creeds and all, when you believe it to be true—praise God, that's grand. But if the teachings and traditions come between the truth and your-selves, then you've got a dreadful decision to make.

"When Bishop Felix told me the good news about Jésu as it had been written by the Apostle Johannes, he said Jésu told his followers, 'If you continue to follow me, if you're true disciples, you'll know what is true, and it's the truth that will set you free.'

"The truth, the truth—the truth is that it was God who made everything there is. God made people, and all of us—Romans and Greeks, Christians and Jews, men and women, poor and rich, slave and free, Orthodox and Arian, west and east—every one of us is a child of God. Every one of us is loved and treasured by God our Father, and that, my friends, is the truth as sets us free. If there's something as comes between you and that truth, if the bishops or magisters or anybody tells you something as would bring you to forget or ignore that, if they say this person's evil or that person's no longer loved by God, this is what you need to hold on to: the truth that the Lord God loves us all, even those you don't agree with, or don't particular like."

Caillen asked, "But what if they're wrong?"

Pell laughed and answered, "Then they're wrong. There are worse things than being wrong. But could we possibly think that God no longer loves us when we're wrong? If that were true, God wouldn't love any of us!"

Pell watched the two students as they considered this, and then said, "Mayhaps I can say something about truth that would be of some help to you. So: take the finger you point with and point up." He joined them in pointing up, and said, "So we all agree about up, that's good. It's good to have friends to agree with. God love us, I've known some as would disagree even with that. Now point down."

They all pointed down, and he nodded and said, "Now point to your left."

They all pointed to their lefts, and Pell observed, "Your left is that way, but my left goes over there. What's true for you may be different from what's true for me. Now let's see if we can all point north."

Caillen waited to see which way the others would point, Oswell hesitantly pointed off one way, and Pell confidently pointed another. Then Caillen pointed the direction Pell was pointing, and Oswell changed his mind and pointed with them. "Aye," said Pell. "Now that we agree about which way north is, you can point toward the place you were born."

Pell and Oswell pointed in different directions, and after a brief and careful calculation, Caillen pointed another. Then Pell asked Oswell, "You think Caillen's telling us the truth, that he was born somewhere off that way?"

Oswell was surprised by the question, but said, "Well, I suppose so."

"He didn't seem to be very sure about it, though, did he?"

Oswell said, "Well, he told me he was from Calleva Atrebatum, and I believe it's that way."

"Aye, but have you ever been there?"

"Well, no," Oswell admitted. "But why would he lie to us?"

"Nay, I'm not saying he was lying. I'm saying he's wrong."

Now Caillen said, "No, I'm from Calleva Atrebatum. That's west, right?

Pell smiled and said, "Aye, Calleva Atrebatum is off to the west, nearly fifty leagues. Now, where do you reckon the sun'll go down today?"

Oswell, glad to be on firmer ground, said, "The sun goes down in the West. Every day."

"Every day?" asked Pell, his eyes twinkling. Then he said, "Now point to which way is west."

They both took in the realization they'd been tricked somehow and pointed slightly ahead and to their left.

Pell nodded and said "Here's what I want to say about all that. First, you believed me when I pointed mostly south—you thought I was pointing north because I'm older or because you think I'm wise. You believed me because it was easier to believe me than it was to think for yourselves. And because you believed me that south was north, then you didn't even know which way was home." The younger men thought about this for a moment before nodding.

"And second," Pell said firmly, "just because we all agree about something doesn't mean we're right, and it doesn't make it true."

The two younger men nodded again, and Pell said, "Now, point to the moon."

Both students looked into the midday sky and then looked back at Pell. Caillen, cautious about being tricked again, said, "The moon's not up yet."

"Aye," said Pell. "Not up, so we can't see it just now. But it's still somewhere, don't you think? Just because we can't see something doesn't mean it's not there. So, where do you think it is?"

There was a long pause, and after he realized Pell was not going to help them, Caillen said, "I don't know."

"Now that's an important thing to know," Pell said, "sometimes we just don't know. We're smart enough to know the moon's bound to be somewhere, but not smart enough to know where it is. Some things we know because we just know: up, down. Some things we can learn: north, south. Some things you we figure out, if that's north there, then home is that way. And some things we just don't know." Then he picked up his harp and sang:

"Aye—it's wonders and mysteries all our days,
      It's faith and doubt hand in hand.
Smart enough to ask but not able to know—
Such is the puzzle we are, my friends,
      Aye, such is the puzzle we are."

He put the harp down and continued, "It's awfully easy to become muddled, to forget who you are, to lose your way home. At night, when you can see the moon, you can use the north star to find your way home, or which way you're needing to go. The north star shows us all the directions, do you understand?"

The students nodded, and Pell said, "The north star of our faith is Love. God loves all of His children. That sets all our directions and shows us the way home. Then, after we know where we are and where we're going, we can be about the work of the followers of Jésu, which is the work His Church ought to be about: to love God as fully as we can, and to love His children as we love ourselves. That's our north star, that's our chart. It's naught to do with Arianism, or Manichae-anism, or Pelagianism, or Oswellianism or Caillenism. Love God, love God's children, if that's not the foundation we're building on, the whole damn house will fall in."

"You make it sound so easy," said Oswell.

"Oh, aye—it's easy enough to say, easy to understand—it's just damn hard to do. Ah, well—you'll always need to be learning, but if you know where your northstar is, if you're willing to love and let yourself be loved, you know everything you need to know."

They sat there for a minute, each of them lost in his own thoughts, until they heard the door closing, and saw Dáirine coming toward them. This time her hands were empty, but she clearly had something to say.

"Ah, Dáirine, my heart!" exclaimed Pell. "You've come at just the right moment. Even I am starting to find my voice wearisome now!"

Both of the young men laughed, and Dáirine with them, and Pell noted that Oswell seemed especially enamored by the sound of it.

"Well, you've been remarkably patient," she said, her voice ringing with love and pride. "Papa says you're not here to sway him into Orthodoxy, and I'm grateful for that. Many and many have tried before, and I reckon he's just as much a heretic as ever he was."

"Woe is me, for I am lost!" wailed Pell, putting on a forlorn face.

Then Dáirine became serious. "Papa, there's a priest to see you. He came knocking at the door, asking for the heretic Pelagius."

Oswell and Caillen looked at each other nervously, but Pell was calm as he asked, "Could you tell him to come around here and sit with us?"

"Aye, that I did. He said he'll not sit on the ground like an unwashed savage. He said I was to tell you he would sit at our table to speak with you."

Pell replied with the appearance of civility that he was not feeling, "So the priest comes to my home and tells me where I should sit? No, granddaughter. If he's come to talk to me, he can come to where I am." He turned to the two young men, saying, "Is this not what I have been telling you—if you want to talk to somebody, go where they are, and talk how they talk."

Oswell said, his panic rising, "It's Father Aelfred, back from Londinium. If he catches us here ..."

"What?" asked Caillen. "What will he do?"

Oswell stared at his friend blankly. "What? He could kick us out, send us back home. He could …" Then Oswell stopped, thought for a moment, and declared, "No, you're right. You can't live your whole life afraid of what the bullies might do."

Then Oswell turned back to Dáirine and said, "Would you tell him he's invited to come sit with us, and that we have plenty of trees to lean against here. But he can't tell a man what he's to do in his own home."

Pell thought Dáirine looked at Oswell like she was seeing him for the first time again, and he caught something in her glance that reminded him of a beautiful tavern barmaid from long ago. He said, "You can offer to bring out a blanket for him to sit on, if he wants it."

Dáirine nodded and went back into the house. A few minutes later she returned, leading a sullen priest and carrying an old woolen blanket, which she set on the ground in front of a hazel tree.

Pell offered his most disarming smile and said, "Welcome, Father!"

Oswell and Caillen mumbled their greetings, feeling somewhat abashed, but the priest, older and sterner, simply nodded. He was wearing a black cassock under a white rochet which was in turn under a scarlet red mozzetta, a short cape. Ignoring the cleric's obvious discourtesy, Pell said, "I wish you a good morning, Father. I hope the new day has found you well."

"*Pax vobiscum*," was the priest's answer, to which Pell replied, "*Et cum spíritu tuo.*"

If the priest was surprised that Pell answered in perfect Latin, he didn't show it. He'd come on a mission to protect his students from the heretic and would not be fooled by any diabolical courtesy.

Pell looked completely at ease, hosting a gathering of friends. "Will you sit with us, Father? I believe my granddaughter has brought a blanket so your fine vestments won't be getting dirty."

The priest sat on the blanket but leaned forward, not resting against the tree. Pell smiled, noting the man's caution. He knew he had nothing to lose in this or any encounter with any representative of the abbey, or of the Church. He smiled to himself as he remembered what he'd told Oswell earlier: "When you're a heretic, you can say whatever the Hell you want to!" But he'd been enjoying his time with the two students, and he didn't want to cause them any further trouble.

"So," said the priest with just a hint of a sneer, in the language of Angleland, "you are the famous Pelagius, the heretic. You have caused a great deal of trouble to the Holy Church of Jésu the Christus."

"I am as you see me," said Pell, "and you see me as I am."

The priest stared at him, not sure what to make of that, and Pell took advantage of the moment to say to his three guests, "Sing with me in gratitude for the new day, and then we'll talk about whatever it is you think needs to be talked about. And mayhaps my sweet granddaughter might be so good as to bring us out a little something, would you, dear heart?" As Dáirine nodded and took her leave, Pell picked up the harp and tuned two of the strings, and then without a word, ignoring the nimbus of tension crackling all around him, he began to play the harp and sing the Psalm he called "I lift my eyes" in Latin.

Oswell sang along somewhat cautiously, partly because he was still struggling with Latin, and partly because his superior wasn't singing at all; Caillen mumbled the words he knew while looking at his feet. The magister sang not at all. Before the last note faded, Dáirine came out of the house, carrying a tray with four mugs of goats' milk, four round loaves of freshly baked bread and a round of sharp yellow cheese.

Pell said, "Thank you, dear heart. You already know Oswell and Caillen here; I'd be happy to introduce you to this fine fella, but I haven't heard his name yet." They all looked at the priest, who reluctantly said, "Aelfred. Father Aelfred."

Pell said, "And this is my granddaughter, Dáirine." They all looked at Aelfred, who chose to say nothing to the beautiful young woman who'd brought him breakfast, and Dáirine said, "It's a pleasure to meet you, Father Aelfred." Again, he said nothing, and Pell kissed her hand and thanked her again before she went back into the house.

Oswell and Caillen both reached for a loaf but stopped when Aelfred began, "Almighty and beneficent God, eternal in majesty and infinite in power, you have given us this day as you give us our lives; help us to spend our time profitably in the study of your blesséd Scriptures and the doctrine of your Holy Church, so that we can proclaim the One True Faith you have entrusted to us in your precious Son Jésu Christus."

Both Oswell and Caillen said "Amen," and picked up their loaves, but the priest was not yet finished. "Give us strength and courage as we renounce the evil powers of this world and fight against the deceits and seductions of Satan. Guide and shield us as we shine the light of truth into the gloom of heresy and the shadows of false teaching."

The students thought he might be finished, but they waited just in case, and sure enough, he wasn't. "Give us confidence to meet the challenges of the Devil and the ruses of his agents among us who beguile with eloquent deception. Preserve the faith of your holy and blesséd Church, O Lord, defend it from all evil, without and within. For unto you shall be given all glory and praise, this day and evermore, as we join our voices with the saints and martyrs in heavenly chorus and say … Amen."

Pell and the two students said "Amen," and Pell took a loaf of bread and broke it in half, saying, "Aye, and we thank you for the day and this bread and cheese and friends and family—for all good gifts. Amen." Oswell said 'Amen' again; Caillen looked at Father Aelfred, who said nothing.

The two students and Pell ate their bread and cheese and sipped at the goats' milk, but Father Aelfred abstained, stiff as a post, still as a stone. When they had finished, all of them sat waiting for Aelfred to say what he was there to say. When he did, the frost was evident in his voice.

"*Pelagius haereticus*, you are not welcome here."

Oswell and Caillen were horrified at his rudeness, but Pell smiled, unflustered. "Aye, and mayhaps it's I as ought to be saying the same to you."

"We don't want you here," the priest continued.

"Aye, friend, I understand. But as I expect you already know, I own this land and this house. It was deeded to me some years ago, by Séamus, the abbot of this monastery, and bishop Felix Hortensius

Terentius. So, I will live here until I die, and some fine day, Brigid and my dear brother Mellán and I will be buried just next to Twedwr here in his holy grove. And over your objections, and likely over the objections of the holy Church, Father Aelfred, I believe I shall be welcomed into the glorious company of the saints in light ..."

"I do object, impenitent heretic! You are *excommunicatus*, you have no claim to ..."

"Into the glorious company of the saints in light," Pell continued over Aelfred's interruption, "not because I was always right, but because I am a child of God. You may disagree with me, and I have certainly disagreed with no end of magisters and bishops, but I was always faithful. Well, mostly always. And mostly always honest. And mostly always looking to find what was true, instead of what was easy, acceptable to those in power, or useful to me."

Then, in perfect Latin, Pell said, "Are you heavily burdened by the idea that some words written on parchment declaring that the Church is to refuse me the Sacraments because I am an impenitent heretic will prevent me from entering into the heavenly Kingdom of love? Do you have the power by virtue of your priesthood to decide who is loved by God? Then you have eaten the forbidden fruit, Lady Eve, and now you believe you have the knowledge of good and evil. You must think you are even more powerful than the Lord God."

The students hadn't caught all of that, but Father Aelfred had, or at least enough of it to be righteously offended. Responding, he gasped, "How dare you?"

Pell responded in the language he preferred. "I dare as a follower of Jésu," he snapped. "I dare naught more than the truth. And the truth is that you have come to my house uninvited, rudely greeted me and ignored my granddaughter completely, took my place in praying over the food you were offered, a prayer that wasn't directed to God but at me, refused the food you were given, and then you tell me that I'm not welcome or wanted here in my own home! No, the question needing to be asked is how dare *you*?"

Pell paused and looked at Father Aelfred like something he hadn't wanted to find on his dinner plate. But then his face and his tone softened. "No matter how hard you try to see it otherwise, boyo, it's not easy to follow Jésu; it wasn't ever supposed to be. It's not about dressing up and playing a part. It's not about doing what you're told or following the rules. The blessed faith should not reduced to doctrine and dogma—it is the love God has for us, and the love we have for God. If you're to follow Jésu, friend, you'll be needing to pay some mind to what he said we are to do—you'll be needing to love."

Then before the priest could respond, Pell quoted the words of Jesus from the Gospel of Matthew, "All who exalts his own self will be made humble, but the one who humbles himself will be exalted. But woe to you, scribes and Pharisees, false teachers—for you lock people out of the kingdom of heaven. You don't go in yourselves, and when others try to enter, you stop them!"

Now the priest tried to stage a rally, "How dare—who do you think ..." but it failed.

"Keep your quiet, priest," Pell ordered so sternly the two students were alarmed. "Keep your quiet so you can hear what you need to hear. Do you not know the Gospel is about love? How do you think you can follow Jésu when you're not willing to love?"

"You dare to lecture me?" Aelfred sputtered.

"Well, nay," answered Pell. "I expect we've all had more than enough lecturing, to be honest with you. Nay, I'm not about to be lecturing, and I don't think you'd listen if I were. But you never know, mayhaps if you were to listen, you'd find I might have something to say that you need to hear."

The priest seemed surprised by all of that, and they sat in uncomfortable silence for a long moment.

Caillen, hoping to build a bridge, began "Father Aelfred, I want you to know ..."

"You will be silent," interrupted the priest. "You and Oswell have put yourselves in a very serious predicament, young man, and I'm afraid I'm going to have to report your disobedience to your superiors."

Oswell started to say something but stopped, and the priest nodded once, as if the matter of the students' insolent defiance was settled. Then he turned back to Pell and said, "In the name of the Holy Church of Jésu Christus, I forbid you from speaking to these two young men, or any other students reading theology at the monastery. Do you understand?"

"Oh, aye," said Pell, and he waited for the priest to nod again before continuing with a smile, "I understand full well what you're saying, and I understand better than you that it means naught more than a frog's fart on a windy day."

The priest started to object, but Pell spoke over him. "You've come to my home. You're sitting in a sacred grove planted by my friend. You have no power here, arrogant priest. How could you claim to speak in the name of Jésu Christus and say such hateful things, to keep these fellas from even wondering about what they're being taught, about what they believe? Have you got such a big-headed understanding of yourself that you think you and your friends have the Lord God all squared away in the little box you've made of his Church?"

The priest was indignant and clenched his fists as if he were ready to strike Pell. "This is why you are forbidden, foul heretic! This blasphemy is why you were declared anathema! I am forced to …"

"Stop. Stop this right now," commanded Oswell, so forcefully that even Pell was taken aback. Father Aelfred stared at him in disbelief. Oswell's eyes filled with tears, and he seemed to be having difficulty catching his next breath, but he sat up straight and continued: "We have learned well what you taught us Johannes the Apostle wrote about our Lord Jésu, after he washed his disciples' feet, when he said, 'I give you a new commandment, that you love one another. Just as I have loved you, you also should love one another.'" Then Oswell had to pause to choke back his emotion, and Caillen picked it up, "By this everyone will know that you are my disciples, if you have love for one another.'"

"Just so, brother Oswell, brother Caillen," whispered Pell gratefully, "right well so."

The priest sat fidgeting, clearly looking for an argument which would reestablish himself as the authority in this conversation, and just as clearly failing. Oswell said, "Blesséd Jésu told the scribe, 'Hear, O Israel: The Lord our God is one Lord, and you shall love the Lord your God with all your heart, and with all your soul, and with all your strength. And the second is like it, You shall love your neighbor as yourself.'" Then Caillen added with a sparkle in his eye, "'And everything else will line up like wee baby ducks swimming after their mama.'"

Chapter XXXVI

One Wee Bawdy Song

Pell was deeply touched by what Oswell and Caillen had said, and was enjoying the silence that came after, until it looked like Father Aelfred was about to say something, so he picked up the harp and began to sing a lively tune:

"Oh, the night was dark and fearsome cold
    and the frothy ale was flowing
When the Lady Bea tied up to dock
And the tavern hussies were knowing,
    Aye, the strumpets were all a-knowing.

"There was ale, then wine, then Irish whisky
    'til they were all of them right well groggy
And even the strumpets let go of thought and sense
'Til it was all tremendously foggy
    Oh, aye, it was all exceedingly foggy.

"The morning disturbed them out all too soon
    Sailors and harlots waked in tangly pile
Saying who was who, and who did what
But the strumpets only smiled
    Oh aye, the hussies only smiled

"Well, you wouldn't want your sister or your mother dear
    to e'er become a prostie (no, she'd never be a prostie)
But all these strumpets were somebody's daughter once
And rented love is costly, boys, aye—rented love is costly."

At this, Father Aelfred stood with as much dignity as he could find and said, "I … I'll be taking my leave now. But I am … I will not …" And he left. Pell nodded to his friends and finished the song:

"Then Captain Mick of fearful tales
        came roaring through the doors
And said 'Soon's the time to catch the tide
Now leave off from your whores, boys
        Aye, so leave off from your whores.'

"So up they jump, and it's scrambling about
        all grabbing and snatching and swearing
'Til ol' Fintan cries out 'Well now, hold up here –
Who's breeches am I wearing?
        He said, 'Hold up now, whose breeches am I wearing?

"Well, you wouldn't want your sister or your mother dear
        to e'er become a prostie, no, she'd never be a prostie
But all these strumpets were somebody's daughter once
And rented love is costly, boys—even rented love is costly."

As he put the harp away, Pell chuckled, "It works every time, friends. You just sing one wee bawdy song about something happy and the self-righteous scatter away quick as sprats." They all laughed, and Caillen asked Pell to sing another bawdy song; Pell said mayhaps he would, but not just then. "I want to thank you, my friends, for what you said to Aelfred. It was brave of you, and I'm hoping it won't cost you."

Oswell answered, "You have to stand up against the bully; your fear is the bully's food and drink."

And Caillen added, "We're trying to make our faith narrower and shallower, when what we ought to be doing is to make it broader and deeper."

Pell was startled and flattered to hear himself quoted. He was quiet for a moment, and then said to no one in particular, "Well, God love us. Now I reckon you've learned everything you were sent to learn."

Now Oswell had a question he'd been saving for the right moment. "Teacher, does it bother you that people say you're a heretic?"

Pell understood that it was a serious question, and he thought about it for a long moment before answering. "Aye, well, it did fluster me at the time, when the Holy Father Zosimus excommunicated me. I was simmering mad for year on year after that, feeling like it wasn't right to punish a man so, just for saying what he believed and then being too stubborn to say he was wrong."

Caillen sat up in alarm, "You think you were wrong?"

"Nay, that was the problem all along, I suppose. I didn't think I was wrong. I still don't. I could have said I was wrong, though, and saved myself a big pile of trouble. It just wouldn't have been honest; it wouldn't be the truth. And the truth is important.

"But here's the thing, though, what I've never been able to fix my thinking around: how could any of us think we could say that some other person can no longer come to the altar and receive the blessed bread and wine? How can we say everybody has to think or believe the same thing, and if you don't believe what I believe, you must be wrong? The naked arrogance of it just makes my head spin around.

"Just stop from time to time and think about what you're being taught, and about what you're saying. Do you really think the Lord God would create all those people, his own children mind you, and then send a great many of them to Hell because they haven't been baptized? Do you think He is likely to stop loving you because some council or Holy Father declared you a heretic? Do we really think so highly of ourselves that we are the only way people can be invited to live in the love of Almighty Eternal God?

"The truth, my friends—we ought to be looking for the truth, using the love of God and the teachings of Jésu as our guiding star. If the followers of Jésu only care about following the doctrines and dictates of men the Church has raised up to be powerful and important and stop looking for the truth, if all we care about is what's written down in Scripture or scholarly works and stop loving God's children—our Father's children—then we are no longer following Jésu, and no longer serving God."

Pell took a deep breath to say more, but stopped before it could turn into a full rant. They were quiet for a while, and Pell added, "Aye, well—mayhaps I am a heretic."

And Oswell said, "But you're a faithful heretic."

The tears welled up in Pell's eyes, and for a while he couldn't say anything. "But here," he finally said. "What I think or believe isn't nearly as important as what the two of you think. Pelagius from Brittania and all those bishops and scholars I've argued with are soon forgotten, leaving naught behind but stacks of words written on paper. But the work of the Church goes on, and it will be guided by such as yourselves now. Now it's about what you think, what you believe. So, Oswell, without using too many words, tell me about Jésu."

Both students were surprised by this sudden and severe change of course. Oswell began, "Jesus is the Son of God, born of his mother the blesséd Virgin Mary by the power of the Spirit of God. He healed the sick and gave sight to the blind, and preached love for all people. He was a threat to the powerful Jews and Romans, and they plotted to kill him. And on the third day, Jesus rose up out of the tomb and spoke to His friends before He ascended up into heaven to sit at the right hand of God."

Pell said, "Thank you."

Caillen said, "Well, was he right?"

"Right?" answered Pell. "Oh, now, I don't know about right. What you said was most likely orthodox, if I take your meaning. But was it right? I'll you ask this: Is it what you believe? Is it true? Is it honest?"

They sat for a moment, and Pell continued, "What you say you believe needs to be what you yourself believe, not just something you heard or read and now you're trying to parrot it back." He looked at his friends, who nodded, and Pell continued. "So: Caillen, tell me about the Church."

"Oh," said Caillen. He'd assumed Pell would ask him to tell him about Jesus and had been lining up his words and sentences. "Well, I'm not really very good about putting things into words."

"Aye," said Pell. "Putting things into words limits our thinking, like boiling down a stew to thick it up. But as weak as our words are, they're the best tool we have if we're wanting to invite God's children to live in His love. So, Caillen: tell me about the Church."

"Well," started Caillen, "I'm not sure if I can remember it right, but one of our magisters said …"

"Nay, Caillen," Pell interrupted. "I don't care what one of your magisters said. I don't care what you can tell me some scholar said about this or that or aught else. How do *you* think of the Church? Tell me about God the Father. Tell me about the scriptures. Tell me about the sacraments. Tell me about the priest, and the bishop. You need to know what you think about these things—not what the magister said, or the scholars wrote, and not what I've been blathering on about. You need to know what *you* think, and you need to be able to put what you think into words the people you're talking to can understand."

Several heartbeats later, Pell said very quietly, "I reckon that was my heresy, that I believed what I believed because I believed it, not because it was what the Church had taught me. I thought what I thought was true, and honest, even when others said it was heresy. And I wasn't willing to be so dishonest as to say I was mistaken about it."

They sat for a moment in a silence more awkward than comfortable, and Pell was just considering singing "The Jolly Man's Funeral" to lighten the mood when Dáirine came back to the grove. "Nanna says it's time for you to be coming in, as you'll remember we're having dinner out tonight, and you need to look presentable."

"I didn't forget. But I'm nearly done telling these two boyos my story, about how I came to be a heretic and all. That bonehead priest Aelfred up at the school may not let them talk to me after this, so I need to finish my tale. I was just about to tell them about the gathering of soldiers and clergy in the bread kitchen, about Bishop Johannes and Caelestius and all."

Dáirine folded her arms across her chest to send the signal that she was impatient with him, but Pell continued. "Every morning as the bread was baking, here come these fellas into the kitchen, every one of them useless as boots on a dragonfly, and …"

"Papa," said Dáirine so firmly that Oswell and Caillen sat up a little straighter. "Nanna said I was to tell you: you'll be needing to come in *now*."

The expression on Pell's face was the one we've all worn when we're trapped into doing something we don't want to do, even though it's the right thing. "Could you go tell her I'm needing a time or two, and then I'll be coming in?"

"Nay, Papa," answered Dáirine firmly, "that I will not do." Then she turned to the young men and asked, "So what has Papa been telling you? Where is he in the telling of the story?"

Oswell was dumbstruck and awkward, but Caillen said, "He's been telling us about his travels, and his time in Rome with … your grandmother Brigid and young Áine, and Mellán and Silvas the soldier."

"Has he told you about leaving Rome yet?"

"No," said Oswell, eager to be part of the conversation. "He said he stayed there for eighteen years. Did he come back here?"

"Well, as you see, he's here now. But no, first he went to Jerusalem. Has he told you about his friend Johannes the bishop of Jerusalem?"

"Nay, child," Pell sulked. "I haven't come to that part yet."

"Or Bishop Augustine, or pompous Jerome, or his lapdog Paulus Orosius? Has he told you about Caelestius the Pest?"

"Hush now, child," said Pell. "I was just about to tell them about Caelestius, but …"

"Why do you call him a pest?" asked Caillen, realizing there was a different side of the story.

"Ah, well," she said, "it's not my place to speak ill of him, really. But you ought to know Papa will not likely tell you the full story. Even now, Papa won't say a word against any of them, even Caelestius."

"But I haven't finished my story," said Pell, "Mayhaps I could just …"

"No, Papa," said Dáirine, holding her hand down to help her grandfather stand. "You're needing to go now. But if you'll trust me, I'll tell them the rest of it, the good Lord knows I've heard it often enough. I'll tell them what they'll be needing to hear, not in such painful detail as you would, mayhaps, but I'll tell them."

Pell looked like he was thinking about it for a moment, then he started the long painful process of standing up. Oswell stood and reached down for Pell's hand to help him, realizing for the first time that Pell was a large man, well over six feet tall. He said, "Thank you, *Veritas Quaesitor*. Thank you for your time, and for sharing your story. We may not be able to come again, but I'm glad Father Joseph sent me to learn something from you."

As Dáirine took her grandfather's hand, she smiled up at Oswell, saying, "Father Joseph? Josephus Mellánius?"

"Aye," answered Pell. "Though I suppose we ought to be calling him Abbot Josephus Mellánius now, if we still have to be impressive."

"Father Josephus Mellánius," Oswell muttered, putting the pieces together, "Father Joseph is Mellán from your story?"

"Aye, he's one in the same, the same Mellán as came to Port Láirge all those years ago now, the same as sang with me in taverns from Dún Canann to …"

"Papa," Dáirine interrupted again, "Nanna was quite firm about this—it's time for you to be coming in the house now. You know how she is when her mind is set."

With that, the old man turned first to Caillen and then to Oswell, hugging them both and kissing them on both cheeks. Then, without another word, he walked slowly into his house.

Chapter XXXVII

Two Hairs on a Dog's Tail

Dáirine looked at the two young men and said, "Well, I'm no story-teller, not like Papa. So mayhaps we'll all be relieved if you'd ask your questions and I'll try to answer them. How do you think about that?"

Caillen said, "We have a great many questions, I'm afraid."

She laughed and said, "Surely having questions isn't something you ought to be afraid about, is it?" They both shook their heads, and Caillen sat down with his back against his tree. Dáirine said, "Aye, well, we've got some talking ahead of us, but I'm not about to sit on the ground with my back against a tree, wearing my best dress and all. Let's go into the tavern where we can sit in some of Twedwr's chairs."

The young men were surprised. Caillen said, "Tavern?" and Oswell said, "Twedwr's chairs?"

She said, "Well, we call them Twedwr's chairs—he drew them up, but Papa made them." Then Dáirine laughed, and her laughter filled the two students' imaginations and lifted their spirits. "Didn't you know our house was built onto a tavern? Didn't he tell you about the Dancing Druid?"

"Well, yes he did," stammered Oswell, "but I guess I just didn't think it was still here."

"And where did you think it might have gone?" She picked up the old leather satchel and turned to walk to the house, leaving the two students behind to wonder if they were to follow, until she turned around and said, sounding very much like her grandfather, "Come with me, silly boyos."

Oswell had never been in a tavern before, but he imagined it would be dark and dirty, with sticky floors and the smell of smoke and grease in the air. The Druid was nothing like that, with the floors recently and regularly swept and mopped, and a large fireplace that efficiently drew the smoke out. The lamps hanging from the rafters were unlit at midday, but the windows let enough light in so that it was quite pleasant.

Dáirine went to the far corner, where there was a raised platform with three stools and a bench, where she carefully set the satchel and took out Twedwr's harp. On the bench there was a round, shallow drum, about fourteen inches across, with a small stick whittled so that it had a subtle bulb on both ends.

"Look," Oswell pointed it out to Caillen. "Shea's bodhrán."

Dáirine spent a minute or two to tune the harp and then played a lively tune to check her tuning. Satisfied, she put the harp down on the satchel, and Oswell said, "What's that tune you're playing?"

"Oh, it's just a little ditty I wrote, thinking I could be like Papa. But he's right easy with folks listening to him singing and playing the harp and all. I'm not so sure of myself as he is."

Oswell said, "Will you play your little ditty for us?"

Dáirine was surprisingly shy, and said, "Well, surely your friend Caillen doesn't want to waste his time listening to me singing aught."

Caillen said, "But I do. I'd love to hear it."

Dáirine took up the harp again, saying, "It's the story of Jonah and the whale, looking at it through the whale's eyes. Papa calls it 'The Tale of the Whale.'" Then she sang:

"Oh, the life of a whale is all just the same
        you're not likely to see aught new
So every day's completely the same.
        Just swimming and singing the day through
        Singing and swimming life through.

But different the day when I felt a wee pull
        to swim where I'd never before wandered
And I found a man floating, tossed out from a boat
By sailors who feared their lives squandered,
        The sailors were seeing their lives squandered.

So I swam myself up and I swallowed him whole
    thinking there's the end of his tale
But the hand of his god was laid on him right firm
And he was kept all healthy and hale
    Aye, he was kept all hearty and hale.

I'd never talked to a such a creature before
    Mama warned me stay clear of a man
But I heard him praying out to his god
Saying 'My freedom is in your hand!'
    He said 'My days are full in your hand.'

So I said, 'How do you come to be in me, friend?
    And how do you think you'll get free?'
He said 'I was trying to run away from my god
Who was trying to make a prophet of me
    He was trying to make a prophet of me.

So I said, 'Would it have been so terribly bad
    to say what he wants you to tell 'em?'
But he said, 'If I do, they'll all turn from their wicked
His mercy is dreadful compelling
    Aye, you know his mercy's compelling.

He said 'That's why I was fleeing away
    for the Lord is most gracious and kind.
He's slow to anger, he'll just pull back his hand
For sinful Ninevah, plenty his mercy'll be
    For all their sins, plenty his mercy'll be.

'But friend,' say I, 'it was that same mercy
    when the Lord called up a great fish such as me
To swim up and save you from drowning!
Surely you'd never long last in the salty sea,
    No, you'd not last long in the sea.'

But he didn't hear me, he was starting a fire
    and I knew in my bones I'd not like that
When I heard the voice of his merciful god,

saying swim closer to land and spit the man out
    So I swam to the shore and I spat him out.

Well, I hope he went on to Ninevah
    I hope he spoke out the god's plan
I hope they turned from their wickedness to live
And I hope I never eat another man,
    Nay, I'll not be eating another man."

Oswell and Caillen applauded, complimenting her playing, her singing, and the song itself, and she thanked them, still self-conscious. Then she gestured to a table with four rough chairs and said, "Take your seats and I'll get us a little something to sip on," before going behind the bar. Oswell and Caillen sat, and Dáirine returned with a plate of bread and butter, and a pitcher with three cups.

"It's a bit early for ale, so I brought mulsum and a figgy loaf," she said, cutting the bread with a small knife and handing them both a piece. She took the knife and spread some butter on her slice, and the young men followed her lead.

She poured some of the drink into their cups and held hers up, saying "Slántu," before taking a sip. Oswell and Caillen responded in kind, and she said, "Now then, I know Papa's left the story so you're wondering about a thing or two. What questions are you wanting to ask?"

There was an awkward pause, and Caillen said, "What does 'Slántu' mean?"

She laughed again, and answered, "'Slántu' is a family tradition. It's an old word from Papa's beloved land of Éire, meaning 'health to you,' or something similar."

Oswell said, "And what is mulsum?"

"And a figgy loaf," added Caillen.

"Oh!" said Dáirine, "and here I was thinking the two of you knew something about something." Oswell started to apologize, but Dáirine put her hand on his arm and said, "Hush now, I was just playing with you. You can ask me whatever you'd like. Mulsum is a sort of weak wine with honey in it. Do you like it?"

"Yes," said Caillen.

"Very much," said Oswell.

"And a figgy loaf is bread with honey and figs. Nanna baked it, it's Papa's favorite."

"Mine, too!" said Oswell, his mouth full of figgy bread.

Caillen said, "Tell us about this place, the Dancing Druid."

"When Papa and Nanna first came here, they built a house. Their friend Twedwr was a Druid, and his wife Esther—well, she wasn't his wife yet, but she was a Jew. They didn't feel easy about going into the monastery, so Papa and Twedwr built a house for all of them. It was Twedwr's idea to build a tavern on it, and that's what they did. He and Papa made these chairs following after some chairs they made when Esther got hurt. Do you already know about Twedwr and Esther?"

"Yes," said Caillen. "Your Papa told us how he and Mellán left Éire and met Twedwr, who was a Druid."

"And then they met the Lady Brigid and her brother Shea," added Oswell, "and then they met Esther, who was a Jew, and she was almost killed when some robbers tried to steal their money."

"So you were listening," smiled Dáirine. "They went all the way up to northeast Éire, across the sea to Angleland, all the way down to Londinium, and here to Erith, playing Twedwr's harp, singing songs, and telling stories. Papa used to say by the time they came here, they were 'a monk, a Druid, a barmaid, a wee little man, a Jew, two horses, a mule and myself.'"

"When did you come along?" asked Oswell. "Where were you born?"

"My mother is Áine. Papa calls her Áine Minor, as she's named after Áine Major, his sister who died in Port Láirge when he was a lad. She was born here, in this house, before Papa and Nanna went to Rome. She met and married my father Atticus Bernardo Opelicus, an officer in the Roman army and the son of a wealthy Roman family. I was born there in Rome, before Nanna came back here and Papa went to Jerusalem."

"Are your parents still there?" asked Oswell. "In Rome?"

"Aye," said Dáirine. "My father's a senator now, trying to keep the Empire together. I'm afraid it's an effort doomed to fail, but he's faithful to the Boy Emperor Honorius and his man Stilicho, who seems to be making most of the decisions. My mother enjoys being part of the upper crust of Roman society. Too fancy, too much pretending for me, I'm afraid."

Oswell asked, "So Nanna is your grandmother, the Lady Brigid?"

"Aye, though I don't know where you're getting the idea she's some style of lady—she'd laugh if she heard you say that."

"What happened to Twedwr and Esther?" asked Caillen.

"I was just a wee girl when Papa and Nanna heard that Twedwr was bad sick, something about his heart, I believe. That's when Nanna and I came back here, and by the time we got here, he had died. He left a piece of paper, an agreement with the abbot and the bishop saying the house and the tavern and all now belong to Papa, to be used to help Aunt Esther and Nanna. He's buried out there in that circle of trees Papa likes to sit in, where you've been talking to him. A few years later, one of the old soldiers brought Uncle Mellán here, saying that Papa was having to go to Jerusalem, as some Holy Father or another ordered it. Uncle Mellán said he'd had more than his fill of bishops and councils and such. When the old soldier said he was going to Jerusalem to look after Papa, Aunt Esther decided she'd go with him, back to the land of her people. I don't know aught more about her after that."

Oswell wondered, "How did Mellán become Father Joseph?"

"Well, to be truthful, I'm not actually sure about all that. Josephus was always part of his name, but I think he wanted to use a more impressive name, something that sounded less Gaeilge, something more familiar to those who've read the Scriptures. But I wonder if mayhaps he wanted to get completely away all that heresy foolishness, and being called Joseph was part of him making a new start. He's a good man, is Father Joseph. Papa says he knows his own heart."

"That's just what he told me," said Oswell.

"Who was Caelestius," asked Caillen, "and what was his part in this?"

"And why do you call him a pest?" added Oswell.

"I don't think I ever met Caelestius, or if I did, I was pretty young. So whatever I know I heard from Nanna, and some little from Papa.

Nanna calls him a pest, and it riles Papa, so I call him a pest just to poke at him a bit. But I don't think Nanna's playing when she says it."

"So, how was he a pest?"

"Well, I don't know if he's told you, and I don't think many people know this, but Papa can't … he doesn't … well, surely it's not my place to be telling you that."

"He told us he can't read or write," said Caillen cautiously.

"He told you that? I didn't think he told anybody about that. Nanna says it frets him sore, thinking other people will think he's not smart if they knew he couldn't read. But I've watched him try to read, and it looks like it pains him.

"They met Caelestius in Rome. His mother gave them money so they could bake bread for the poor. He was right clever, too smart for his own good, Nanna says. After they started baking bread, some people started gathering in the kitchen, just to talk and all, soldiers at first, and then priests. Well, when the priests took the talking over, the soldiers stopped coming, and soon it became a gathering of church people who were upset about something in the Church. Nanna said Caelestius was taken with some of what Papa said—you know how he gets riled sometimes, and especially when it's to do with bullies, such as bishops using their vows to serve themselves instead of God's people. Caelestius got it in his head that he ought to write some of it down.

"Well, some of what he wrote was right direct about some of the faults and failings of the Church. Papa was troubled by priests and bishops he said lived lives of vulgar immorality, spending fortunes of the Church's money on themselves, the houses they lived in, the lavish clothes they wore, the food and drink they indulged in, all the while paying no mind to those who were starving and homeless. He questioned the notion that people did good or bad because they were born to be sinful, and not because they themselves chose it. Papa said some of the clergy were saying that their depravity wasn't their own fault, but God's. After he heard Papa get all vexed about that, Caelestius wrote some of it out, and then he sent it to some of his friends, who sent it to some other people, and before long it seemed like the whole Church all over Rome was buzzing like a hive full of angry bees about what Pelagius of Brittania had said.

"After that, there were some letters and papers going back and forth between a bishop in Africa named Augustine and his student Orosius and a fella named Jerome, all of them twisting what Papa thought and said, 'til they got it all tangled around and around so much that Papa said even he didn't agree with what they wrote Pelagius had said.

"Now, Papa would tell you Caelestius wasn't trying to harm him, and that he really believed what Papa believed, and mayhaps that's true. But Nanna would tell you he was just trying to make a name for himself, and that he didn't give a fig about aught but winning the argument, and mayhaps that's true as well. But sure as the rising of the sun, it was because of that pest Caelestius that Papa had to defend himself against some of the leaders of the Church.

"Well, mayhaps I need to slow down a bit and say this: Papa did not agree with some of what Augustine wrote. I don't know if I've got all this right, but from what I've heard, Augustine taught that everybody since Mother Eve and Father Adam has been stained with sin, not because of what they choose but because it's our nature, being born of lust and all. Papa says we all sin, of course, but it's not because we have no choice, but because of the choices we make. And Papa says as we're all born in the image of God, we're born with original grace, and we can choose to do the right thing. Augustine says if we do aught good at all, it's because of God's grace in us. It's no than two hairs on a dog's tail to me, but I think that's what had them all so upset, or part of it."

They sat in silence for a minute, until Oswell asked, "Why did you all leave Rome?"

"Well, as I've said, Nanna brought me here when I was about three or four, when we heard Twedwr was terribly sick. Uncle Mellán, or Father Joseph as you know him, came when I was about five, I think. Papa and Caelestius left Rome when it was looking like the Goths were about to take Rome by force. He wanted to come home then, but they couldn't go north because of the Goth armies. So they went south to Carthage, I think, and by and by they were summoned to Jerusalem for a council. He said he thought they'd be safe there, as his friend Johannes was bishop there. But he was wrong about that, he said. They had a council meeting there and declared them heretics and excommunicated them."

"What happened to Silvas and the old soldiers?" asked Caillen.

"I think most of them stayed to defend Rome. Silvas went with Papa, of course, to Carthage, to Jerusalem and all the way back here. He's buried there in Twedwr's grove as well."

Then Oswell quietly asked, "What about Shea?"

"Ah, my great-uncle Shea, the sweetest man ever I met. He lived a long life with his family and a barn full of horses and mules and dogs and cats and an old crow he taught how to talk. He used to say that crow was smarter than most people he knew. Shea died a few years ago; I think his big heart just finally gave up. I miss him still. I miss him right hard."

The three of them sat quietly for a moment, and Dáirine asked, "Do you have any more questions?"

Oswell shook his head and Caillen said, "No. Thank you for telling us all of this." But then he said, "Wait! What happened to the life of Christ?"

Dáirine just looked at him, not knowing what he was talking about, until Oswell said, "The front-piece your Papa carved when he was a boy in Port Láirge, the one Father Cyneric didn't want."

"Oh, aye—I know the one—he brought it home with him, clunking it all the home back from Jerusalem. It's really quite beautiful. But don't you want to know about the councils that named him a heretic, and others as found him orthodox?"

Oswell said, "No. Father Aelfred told us he was declared a heretic at the Council of Carthage by Holy Father Zosimus. But Father Joseph said he'd been declared orthodox at another council somewhere, when he finally said that some of what had been written in his name wasn't what he thought at all. It sounds like there was some politics, with ambitious men working to further their own goals, those who agreed with Pell, and those who didn't. I don't think we care about that anymore."

"If we ever did," said Caillen. "It sounds to me like they were just splitting fine hairs to find something to argue about."

"Aye," said Dáirine. "It sounds like you've been listening right well. Now I'm about to have to go, but before I do, let me tell you two things. First, Papa would never want you to think he claimed to be right about everything. But he would say he, and all of us, have the right to believe what we believe without some bullies trying to force you believe as they do. He would say we ought to always to be looking, listening, asking questions, trying to find the truth, the truth as sets us free."

"It sounds like you've been listening, too," said Oswell.

"Aye, for a fact I have."

"What's the second thing you wanted to say?" asked Caillen.

"Well, I don't think Papa would mind me saying that he and Nanna and I will be having supper with Uncle Mellán up at the monastery tonight, welcoming the new bishop of Londinium, and then after that, I'd be surprised if they didn't come here to the Dancing Druid to have a bit of ale and a song or two."

The two young men looked at each other and Oswell asked, "Could we come, do you think?"

"Well, as you see, you're here already," said Dáirine.

Chapter XXXVIII

A Bit to Drink and A Song to Sing

The bishop looked at the people gathered there in the monastery chapel: church people, people from the town, highborn and low, many of whom he knew and a good many he didn't. Some were listening to his homily intently; some who expected to be bored were not disappointed. He'd been preaching for a few minutes, and he realized he was boring himself. He decided to abandon his manuscript and speak from his heart.

"I am glad that you are here, that we are here together. There will be some as may be surprised that the Church is hosting the funeral of a heretic. Life surprises us, don't you find—perhaps it is because we underestimate the generosity of the Giver of Gifts. You might be surprised to see my old friend Aelfred sitting with you, who once forbad my brother Caillen and myself from ever speaking to Pell again. You could be surprised to see that selfsame Caillen, who struggled mightily alongside me through endless battles with the mind-numbing declensions and conjugations of Latin, now serving the finest ale in all of Angleland in the Druid's Dance, a gift to us all. I myself am surprised to see me arrayed in a cope and miter, not something I ever sought, or desired. In truth, I thought the Church had better sense than to make me a bishop. But here we are—all of us surprised, all of us surprising.

"In truth, Father Aelfred and Pell disagreed more than they agreed about many a thing. But each came to respect the other, each teaching of them, each learning. It is the way we ought to be.

"Caillen found his path was not leading him to the priesthood and made his peace with it. Luckily for us, his path led him to a tavern—a path I hope we'll all be taking this evening. And I have cherished truths I learned from Pelagius the Heretic, that we give ourselves to the love of God in all things, even if it means you have to be a bishop. Ah, Lord."

Bishop Oswell looked lost in his memories for a moment before he continued, "The night I fell in love was the first time I ever sneaked out of the monastery. It was the first time I'd ever sneaked out of anywhere, really. As it turned out, it was not the last; apparently my friend Caillen had been sneaking out quite regularly, and he knew which window we could jump out of without anyone noticing, low enough to the ground so we could climb ourselves back in. But that night, my first night at the Dancing Druid was quite memorable.

"When we came into the tavern's common room that night, the crowd was gathering, but it was not yet full. Pell's granddaughter Dáirine led us to a table off to the right of the platform where she said her Papa and Uncle Mellán would be shortly. I asked her what options were available for drinks, and she said, 'Ale and wine. You'll be having ale.' She has been, ah … guiding me ever since.

"Then she walked away, gracefully navigating her way through the crowd, and in just a few minutes she came back with a jar of ale, two cups and a plate of sausages and olives. It was the first time I'd ever had ale, so that took some getting used to, but the sausages and olives were quite good from the first morsel.

"When Pell, Abbot Josephus Mellánius and the Lady Brigid came into the tavern, everyone stood and applauded. They made their way slowly through the crowded tables, stopping to greet old friends, sharing hugs and laughs with people who were obviously delighted to see them. They stepped up on the platform, Pell getting a little help from his wife and granddaughter, and then I saw Dáirine lean in to tell him something. He nodded to her and looked straight at Caillen and me and nodded to us as well.

"Dáirine brought them drinks, ale for Pell and Mellán, wine for the Lady Brigid, and Pell tuned the harp before saying, '*Pax vobis, amicis!*' to which we all replied, '*Et cum spíritu tuo!*' Then, assuming a solemn demeanor, he said, 'As you know, it can be an awful serious world we live in, filled with pain and woe.' He paused, showman that he was, before continuing, 'So I propose,' and here he struck a chord on the harp, 'that for tonight,' and another chord, 'we call on whatever faith we have,' a third chord, 'to put all that away to one side,' another chord, 'and let the world toddle along without us!' We all cheered, and he continued, 'For tonight we're come together for a bit to drink and a song to sing!'

"I remember wondering how many times they'd sung it as they started singing 'The Butterfly's Blessing' and marveled at how they could still find such joy in the rest of us singing 'A blessing to you!' with such unbridled enthusiasm. I cried without shame when they sang 'The Nature of Man':

'How could my mother have loved me so well?
    What makes the tides ebb and flow?
What holds the water at the rim of the world?
And where do our freed souls go?
    When we die, where do our free souls go?'

"I laughed with everybody else when they sang 'The Jolly Man's Funeral' and 'Whose Breeches Am I Wearing?', neither of which are appropriate for this moment today. It was impossible to sit still when they sang 'The Beltane Fire', and I cried again when Father Joseph and the Lady Brigid sang the lullaby 'Hush Now, Baby Mine'. I was afraid it would be their last song, but then Pell called my future wife up, and after a little coaxing from her grandparents and a crowded common room, she played the harp and sang 'The Tale of the Whale'. It's the story of Jonah from the whale's point of view, a song she wrote. It seems appropriate to quote a bit of it, talking about a prophet at the funeral of her dear Papa, faithful heretic:

So I said, 'Would it have been so terribly bad
    to say what he wants you to tell 'em?'
But he said, 'If I do, they'll all turn from their wicked
His mercy is dreadful compelling
    Aye, you know his mercy's compelling.

"I remember that night, the first of many celebrations of life and love at the Dancing Druid. I remember hours of conversations with Pell and Father Joseph, questioning and speculating, and being reminded that the true work of the Church is to love and be loved, not to insist that we all think and speak and believe the same. Very often I marveled at Pell's insistent pursuit of the truth above all else, and I can't tell you how many times I've asked the whale's question: 'Would it have been so terribly bad to say what he wants you to tell 'em?'"

"Now the years have passed, and Pell has gone to the Communion of Saints, reunited with his dear friends Mellán, Twedwr and Silvas, and with his sweet strong wife the Lady Brigid, and with many and many friends who've gone before. Some will have known him as Pell, 'Just Pell' from Port Láirge in Éire, or as advisor and adversary of priests and bishops, as a friend to lowborn and highborn, a minstrel, a bread baker, or a Seeker of Truth. Some who never knew him will call him Pelagius the Heretic, but it is the great privilege of those who have known him to call him a mentor, and a beloved friend.

"I have been honored beyond my worth to be ordained a priest in Christ's holy Church, and now to serve as bishop. Pell thought it was hilarious that I 'had to be a bishop,' another honor I don't deserve. The greatest honor of my life, of course, is to have married my lady Dáirine, whose Papa we remember today. And it is my great honor to dedicate this beautiful front-piece to the glory of God and in loving memory of Pell, a servant of God. My thanks, and the gratitude of the family, to my old magister Abbot Aelfred, for inviting our son Pell Minor to restore the front-piece, and for suggesting that it find its home here."

Here Oswell stepped down from the pulpit to pull away the cloth frontal, revealing Pell's front-piece which had been affixed to the front of the altar in the chapel at the monastery in Erith. It had been thoroughly cleaned and re-stained, and several pieces had been glued back where they belonged; Oswell and Dáirine's son Pell was beaming with pride, and so were his parents.

Bishop Oswell waited a moment as the congregation admired it, shifting around to see it more clearly. Then he took the incense boat from the acolyte whose job it was to present it and placed three spoonsful of aromatic resin into the thurible, and took it from the thurifer and walked around the altar in a small circular procession, rocking the incense pot side to side to fan the charcoal and make more smoke. Then he stopped at the north end of the altar and declaimed "*In nomine Patris et Filii et Spiritus Sancti, Amen.*"

Just before the blessing which would end the service, Oswell said, "Now, the congregation is invited to go to the Dancing Druid to continue this celebration of life and love, likely and appropriately a more ... energetic celebration, where my friend Caillen the tavern master will welcome you warmly, and I expect you'll find 'a bit to drink and a song to sing.' The family and I will go to the service of Committal, in what I think of as the unconsecrated but still sacred grounds in a nearby circle of trees, where we will lay Pell's body between his friend Joseph Mellán on one side and his beloved Lady Brigid on the other, between Twedwr the Druid to the west and Silvas the Soldier to the east, to trust in the mercy of God, which I know is 'dreadful compelling.'

"And then, though I've conclusively and repeatedly proven my lack of musical ability through the years, I will likely take up the bodhrán and thump along with Caillen and Dáirine as they sing the love of God, and I will tell of a certainty that I will be bitterly disappointed if we don't hear 'The Power of One,' which ends:

"'The Divine Mother, the Star in the Twilight,
    sings to me in her own voice:
'O my child, my beloved wayward child—what will you ask?'
'Fairest of Heaven,' sing I, 'teach me a song!
    Sing me a song of the Power of the unknown and uncounted,
        until my heart knows it full.'
'The unknown!' she sings in her own true voice,
'The Power of the unknown is the Truth we cannot Know—
    the Infinite stars in the Heavens,
    the limitless ambitions of greedy men,
    and the Mind of the Highest Holy, whole and full,
        Who is and ever was—One!'"

Then Bishop Oswell concluded the heretic's funeral by asking God's blessing on the congregation.

"And now, children of God: Go forth into the world in peace, be strong and of good courage.

Hold fast to that which is good; sing to the Lord a new song.

Render to no one evil for evil, make no peace with oppression.

Weep with those who weep, laugh with those who laugh, wonder with those who wonder—trusting and hoping in the grace of God.

And the blessing of God Almighty: Father, Son and Holy Spirit, be among us, and remain with us, always. Amen."

www.ingramcontent.com/pod-product-compliance
Lightning Source LLC
Chambersburg PA
CBHW051329020726
47501CB00007B/1988